I0551812

Photograph by Justin DeWitt

Boakyewaa Glover is the author of three novels: *Circles* (2009), *The Justice* (2013), and *Tendai* (2013). She also regularly maintains a blog displaying her short stories, poems, articles, and movie reviews. A self-professed entertainment addict, Boakyewaa considers life to be the ultimate muse.

She is currently the regional change management manager for Newmont Ghana Gold Limited; as well as the Group Director for Minds on Fire Group, a publishing, entertainment and creative lounge company.

Circles

Circles

Boakyewaa Glover

MINDS ON FIRE

GHANA

CIRCLES

Copyright © Boakyewaa Glover 2013

All Rights Reserved

No part of this book may be reproduced in any form
by photocopying or by any electronic or mechanical means,
including information storage or retrieval systems,
without permission in writing from both the copyright
owner and the publisher of this book.

ISBN: 0989225216

ISBN 13: 978-0989225212

This book is a work of fiction. Names, characters, places and
incidents are either the product of the author's imagination or
they are used fictitiously. Any resemblance to actual events or
locations or persons, living or dead, is entirely coincidental.

First published 2009 by
Athena Press

2013 re-print by
Minds on Fire Group
No. 1a Gowa Close,
Roman Ridge,
P.O. Box 9008, Accra
Ghana

Printed for Minds on Fire

To my mother; thank you for my life and your unconditional love.

To my brothers, Nana Kofi and Nana Akuoko, and my extended family, I couldn't have asked to be born into a better group of people.

To my father; thank you for the gift of words.

My deepest gratitude to Jonathan Hutchful, Seton Nicholas,
Estella Anku-Kidd and Tikki Gyedu-Adomako for their
dedication, encouragement and support as I wrote *Circles*.
With warm thanks to all my friends and family who supported the
publication, launch and marketing of *Circles*.

Epiphany

The weather was so humid and tepid I felt stuffed and boxed in. My two-bedroom, 1,100-square-foot apartment had suddenly become strangely constricting. I wasn't feeling like myself and it wasn't just about the weather. I paced up and down, almost as if I was on a manhunt and, any second now, I would find excitement hidden somewhere. There was nothing interesting on TV and, as a TV addict, that was a major setback. There was actually never anything interesting on TV on Fridays. I had always wondered if there was some mysterious industry logic behind it. In any case, it left me completely bored senseless. My next addiction, the cinema, wasn't any help either. I had been to the cinema a couple of hours before, so that option was done. I desperately needed to do something. My phone rang as I lay on my bed going mental with boredom. I looked at the number and answered excitedly.

"Hey you," I said.

"Hey, what's up with you? You haven't called me in like for-ever," he said.

I closed my eyes at the sound of his voice. I loved his voice. It wasn't necessarily sexy, but it was his voice.

"I know. I've been so swamped with work, it's insane. On some nights I go to bed at 2 A.M.," I said.

"So what are you doing right now? It's Friday night."

"Nothing much; I'm really bored, and it's driving me crazy. There's nothing on TV, and I've already been to the cinema and I don't have anyone to go clubbing with. Truth is, I'm not even interested in clubbing."

"So come visit me," he said.

"Hmmm, I have gym at 9 A.M. tomorrow so I'll see if I can set off after that. I don't know though. I mean, just driving there for one day?"

As much as I was bored, I was skeptical about driving almost six hours to visit him. I had a lot of stuff to do the next day. There was gym, and then laundry and grocery shopping and a bunch of other important, life-altering chores.

"I mean come and visit me now, right now," he said.

I raised an eyebrow. What? It was past midnight. Florida was at least six hours away from Atlanta. I wasn't sure I was in the mood to drive that far at this hour.

"I don't know, it's really late," I said doubtfully.

"Come on, be spontaneous. We'll just lie in bed and cuddle, and talk."

That sounded good, and tempting. I thought about it for a brief minute and then decided to go for it. I hadn't done anything that crazy and spontaneous in a very long time. Why not? I was bored. And I had kind of missed him too.

"Okay, I'll leave in twenty."

"Cool, call me when you set off, yeah. Drive safe."

I hung up and rushed around throwing clothes into a small bag. It was going to be for just two nights and two days. As I packed, I was getting more excited. This was going to be fun!

As soon as I walked through the door, we were kissing intensely. I had missed kissing him. He had the sweetest lips. I started to feel heady as his hands slipped underneath my T-shirt. I let his hands unclasp my bra and roam my chest freely. Then he lifted my T-shirt and dipped his head. I exhaled as he took a nipple in his mouth and his hand caressed the other breast. By the time we got up to his room, I couldn't stand it. It was so intense and beautiful being with him again. I didn't want it to end. I hadn't made love with anyone in close to eight months.

"That was just awesome," I said, sighing.

He laughed. "You're so silly."

"Seriously, that was really good. I still have goosebumps."

He chuckled and lay next to me.

I turned and looked at him. He was looking different from the last time I saw him. He was bigger now, in a nice-built way. I preferred this look. I loved the feel of his new muscles, his chest, back and arms. We chatted for a little bit and then I fell asleep. It was past 5 A.M. and I was tired from the drive and the sex.

The next morning, he left for work and was gone almost the whole day. He was a doctor and they probably had the worst work hours. I slept in for a while, thinking about what had happened the night before. I was feeling tingly all over. I needed him again. I couldn't believe I'd been off sex for that long. This celibacy pact of mine was just frustrating. At a point, I thought it was important, and maybe it still was, but I was beginning to realize I was a very sexual person. This was really why I had decided to try celibacy. It was because I wanted to be by myself and put an end to the complications that had plagued my life. But after last night, I knew caging up my feelings and needs was useless. I needed him again so badly I couldn't stand it.

Later that night, I went to hang out with his room-mate for a while, chatting, and waiting for him to come home. When he eventually did, it just wasn't what I expected.

We all spent hours in his room-mate's room, talking about nothing and everything. I kept looking at him. I wanted to reach out and kiss him and hold him. I started dropping hints about what I wanted. I was going crazy. I needed him again so much. Eventually, I decided to call it a night and went to his room. I lay in bed waiting for him to join me. When he finally did, he changed, got into bed and fell asleep. I lay there for a while, stunned. What the heck?

"So, I need to ask you something."

We were sitting in his living room. The morning had gone by pretty fast and I needed to head out soon. But we hadn't had sex again since Friday night and I didn't get it.

He looked up from his computer when I spoke, a questioning look on his face.

"I just don't understand last night or this morning. You asked me to come over, in the middle of the night, and we had sex just once? That's not what I was expecting," I said, the disappointment evident in my tone. I folded my arms across my chest and stared at him.

He shrugged his typical nonchalant shrug. It irritated me.

"Well?" I needed an answer.

"I actually didn't mean for Friday to happen," he said.

"What? You asked me to come here," I said, perplexed.

"To chat and cuddle."

"Listen, you started kissing me, within ten minutes. You initiated this."

"I know. You and I are such good friends, and it's really good the way it is now. And I think that sex would complicate the way we are. And lately, those arguments we've had, it's because we sleep together. I think you and I would be better friends if we don't sleep together at all."

I stared at him for what felt like a lifetime. I couldn't speak. The bastard. The ignorant, insensitive bastard!

"Those arguments, it's because you did something wrong to me. Actually, scratch that, it's because you keep doing really crappy things. It has nothing to do with whether or not we're having sex. You messed up. You shouldn't have done the stuff you did. Even if we weren't still physically involved, it'd still be wrong. I don't get how you don't understand this very simple thing. You messed up, that's just the bottom line."

"I don't want to argue, I really don't. I think you and I are really good as friends. It just works better that way."

So why hadn't he thought of that Friday night? I wondered. "You should have thought of that on Friday, seriously."

I took a deep breath and stared at him. There was no use saying more. He wouldn't understand. He'd never been able to understand me. Never! I ran my hands through my hair, trying to calm my nerves. My heart was beating fast. I could feel tears well up in my eyes. I didn't even know why they were there. I was upset and disappointed in myself and the situation I was in. I was bitter and angry.

I was twenty-nine years old and nothing had changed since I was fifteen. Nothing was any different. I was in a job I loved more than anything, but I was still involved with people I really should have cut loose years ago. I was a writer on CNN's International Desk, and I was really good at my job. But everything else was falling apart around me.

I tried desperately to maintain control. And then I had it, an epiphany. That's what Oprah calls it, that sudden OMG moment, that realization that hits you, and feels like it's been there all along: epiphany.

I have had so many epiphanies. I don't even know if they were really truly epiphanies. But I realized I was having one more right now. I knew I had to start living my life, my dreams, right now.

Not tomorrow. Not next week or worse, next year. It had to be right now. Is that really an epiphany? Doesn't everyone know you have to live your life?

Every life coach, guru, parent, teacher, everyone harps on about it, right? You have to live your life. Easier said than done, my friends, easier said than done.

I didn't want to be thirty-five and bitter; bitter about where I was and what I was doing and whom I was with. I needed to be in control. I needed to live for me, be me, do me. In some ways, I should feel lucky right? I am not yet thirty, I am single and I have no children. Isn't that the best way to wipe the slate clean? Not necessarily. I wasn't thirty yet, but I had packed so much into twenty-nine that made me feel like forty. I had baggage on my shoulders that was dragging me down, history that I just can't seem to shake.

This was my life. Why couldn't I just start over? Why won't these haunting thoughts go away? I am tied so strongly to the past and I am not even sure why. Didn't Jesus Christ die so we could all have a clean slate? But I am still haunted, still swimming in a pool of murky memories. Living in the past had brought me to this point, sitting in his living room, listening to the same nonsense he'd been spewing all these years. How had I gotten to this point?

I realized it was time to re-evaluate my life and the choices I had made. Why was I still in this damn awful ridiculous situation? What was wrong with me? Wise people say you need to learn from the past; you need to learn from experience. A friend also recently told me, "Assess yourself and your life first, and then move on." I hadn't done that. I had been bumbling through life, just going through the motions without stopping to take stock of what I was doing and why.

I really didn't want to remember my past though. I wanted to move on. I wanted to let it all go, but I really couldn't. I couldn't will myself to move on. Emotionally, physically, mentally and whatever else—all tied to the past. I went to his room and lay on the bed. I decided to attempt the pseudo psychology stuff, take that trip down memory lane I had been avoiding. I had to tackle the painful task of evaluating my disastrous past. I closed my eyes. Bring it on. Let's get this done. I need to move on.

The Beginning

How far back do I want to go? That's the thing about the past. It's hard to determine when my downfall really began. At what point did I start to go wrong? I can think of different points, different events. But to be honest, I know exactly when and where it all began—1995, sweet sixteen.

Truth or Dare

"Okay, so what's it going to be, Rabbie, a truth or a dare?"

I looked up at Lynn and gave her a lopsided smile. This was amusing. Truth or dare really has one goal: to get two people who wouldn't normally get together to do something naughty. Or at least to get the thought in someone's mind. Which was why I was wondering why Lynn had brought up this game with this crowd. There were four of us. Lynn and Selassie had been dating for almost two weeks now. They didn't need a game to do what they wanted to do. Selorm and I... We were like the sidekicks. Selorm was Selassie's best friend and I was Lynn's best friend. Selorm and I knew each other from school but we weren't close. I really couldn't understand why Lynn wanted to play truth or dare so badly. Lynn was a sexy girl, even at sixteen. She had a certain air of confidence and appeal. Her looks weren't striking, but she had a good body, lithe and athletic, which added to her sexuality. And though Selassie wasn't built or lean, he was fairly good looking with a welcoming face. The two of them definitely didn't need any games to get attention. But they wanted to play truth or dare so I decided to go along with it.

"Dare," I said lamely. I really couldn't be bothered. She could throw any dare at me at this point.

I turned to look at Selorm. He looked distracted as well. Selorm and I were lying stretched out on Lynn's bedroom floor. She had the softest carpeting ever. It was cream colored, thick and lush, and felt like butter against your skin. She had lots of pillows strewn over the floor, giving the carpet an even more luxurious look. Her bedding, light brown and silky, also had a grown-up look and feel. I think she stole it from her parents or something. It looked too good all the time. That room was the ultimate den of iniquity. At least that's what I thought at the time. I liked visiting Lynn primarily because I liked being in that room. Things just happened there—for her mainly, but I had a good fun view from the sidelines.

I heard giggles from the bed and Selorm and I both shook our heads. It was the second time that week Selorm and I had met at Lynn's, and I think we were both beginning to feel like we were at a peep show. Why did we bother tagging along? Selorm sighed, which made me laugh, and then he looked at me and laughed.

Selassie leaned over the bed and looked down at us.

"You two look cozy down there," he said and winked.

I shook my head. Gosh, how obvious could he and Lynn be?

"So do you know your dare? You should kiss Selorm for, like, five minutes," Selassie said.

I laughed. It was a nervous laugh. Kissing Selorm wasn't a bad thought, but I didn't want to act all excited and interested. And in all honesty, I wasn't exactly interested or excited. It just wasn't a bad thought. Lynn leaned over the bed as well. So now I had the two kissy trigger-happy love-struck teenagers staring at me. If I was white I'd be turning red as a beetroot.

From the corner of my eye I could see Selorm turn onto his side and look down at me. I felt him staring at me. I had to turn. The kiss was a little awkward, on my part more than his. When his lips touched mine, I really wasn't sure what to do. This wasn't my first kiss. It was just my first in about a year, and with someone I had never really thought of kissing, and we had two observers, who at any minute, I felt were going to clap or something. Of course it would be awkward. He pried my lips apart and I felt his tongue. I sucked in my breath and then I kissed him back.

"That's what I am talking about!"

Selassie's exclamation completely threw me off. I pulled away a little and Selorm lay on his back. The situation seriously couldn't get any more embarrassing than it already was. Selassie and Lynn lay back on the bed, talking and laughing, while Selorm and I lay on the lush carpeting silently. I couldn't even turn to look at him, but I am a seconds type of person. If I do something once, I have to do it again, to cement the memory. I turned slightly, and realized he was staring at me. He smiled, and I grinned, and then we started kissing again.

Selorm was a pretty good kisser, although I didn't have that much experience to know any better. But I knew he was way better than my last kiss. Essien had been downright awful. He had been the first tongue kiss, and it had been the sloppiest kiss ever. There had been one more kiss with Essien after that initial fiasco, just for me to be sure it was that bad. And it was definitely that bad. Selorm didn't rush it at all. It felt like he was just as uncertain as I was.

There were a lot of things that made that afternoon's kissing session an awesome one. Selorm was really good looking, in the sweetest way. He was fair, tall, and rather lanky. He had sweet safe eyes that made you feel he was laying it all out there. He didn't seem pretentious, or full of it. He had such soft lips and soft hands. And here we were, two people who barely knew each other in junior secondary school, lip-locked just days after meeting again. I liked that part. The absurdness of it all, the randomness of what we were doing.

Our little kiss fest was cut short when we heard moans from the bed. We froze, pulled apart and then we waited, just to be sure we had actually heard what we thought we heard. When Lynn moaned again, louder, we both burst out laughing. Those two were ridiculous!

"Do you want to go for a walk?" he whispered softly in my ear.

Darn it! That's what they meant in the books—"he whispered softly in her ear." It felt like cool air on my neck. I tingled.

"Yeah, sure," I said.

We stood up slowly, and I really tried not to glance at the bed. But I didn't see much even when I did. They were under the light-brown silky spread, covered from head to toe. Someone was half on top of the other, but I wasn't even going to try and figure out whom. Selorm held my hand and we walked out of the den of shame, through the kids' TV room, out the back door and to the front gate. It was only then that we really started laughing.

"Did they really have to start with us right there?" I asked.

Selorm shrugged. He wrapped his long arms around my shoulders and we started walking.

The next few days were like carbon copies of that day. I woke up each day knowing I was going to have another kiss-a-thon with Selorm at Lynn's place. We camped out in her living room now. On rare occasions, we subjected ourselves to a few moans from the bedroom carpet. I am not sure if what Selorm and I were doing constituted dating. At times it felt like it, when we were together, kissing, talking, walking and holding each other. Then there were times that he and Selassie would be gone for ages. I was a little anxious, but I was also completely giddy. I really couldn't wait to see him each day. It was bliss. But that's the thing about bliss, right? It has to tumble down eventually.

It was Saturday. The event was called Recognize. It was *the* summer event. What we had all been waiting for, the Ghanaian teenager's version of a networking event. Shows at the National Theatre over the summer really had nothing to do with the actual show. This one, I think, was a variety/rap show. It was more of an opportunity to show off everything. To show off your boyfriend, to show off your hair, your clothes, your friends and the car your parents just bought and have no idea is gone from the garage. Anything that could be displayed was going to be displayed.

I was going through an Aaliyah phase at the time. If I had an iPod back then "Back and Forth" would have been at the top of my favorite list. I loved her style to bits. She reminded me of my inner self. I say inner me because I was definitely not her size. I was 5'7" on a thick frame. But she had a tomboy flair, a casual "couldn't be bothered with beauty, make up and clothes" attitude. And that was me, to a T. So I put together my best Aaliyah outfit; black Dr Martens boots and black heavy jeans, sagged low. Yes, I let my jeans hang low, with my older brother's CK boxers just peeping over the belt. I topped it off with a cropped bustier and threw over a light see-through top. I rocked that look. I nailed it from top to bottom and I felt good. Selassie, Selorm and Lynn picked me up. Selorm and I sat in the back and kissed. I was glad I was with him. He said I looked good.

The guys dropped us off and said they had to go get some more friends. Lynn and I went in to mingle. An hour later, I couldn't find Selorm anywhere. Selassie was back, and he said Selorm was with some friends somewhere in the building.

The National Theatre was huge, full of screaming excited kids. Looking for a tall lanky boy was tougher than I expected. After half an hour or so, I found him on the second floor. He was with a bunch of girls. Three of the girls were in my school. We were not friends, but we knew each other. I was not happy. He came toward me and hugged me.

"Hey, sorry, I was looking for you," he said.

Liar.

"Where is Lynn? Where are you guys sitting?" he asked.

"We're downstairs. Are you coming?"

"Yeah. I'll be down in a second, okay?"

Liar.

I took a deep breath, glanced over his shoulder, gave the girls my best dirtiest look and then mumbled "fine." I went back down to the main auditorium. I found Lynn, and someone else was in my seat—just perfect. She probably hadn't even noticed. She was busy chewing Selassie's face off. Our seats were on one side of the main auditorium towards the wall, and there were some other familiar faces standing around in that corner. I noticed one of them, a friend from primary school called Jon. I hadn't seen him in like a year. I smiled and he waved me over. We hugged.

"Hey, how are you? It's good to see you," he said.

He sounded genuinely happy to see me. My girls and I from primary school had a best friend, Nick. Nick and Jon were best friends. So I knew him pretty well. I even used to have a crush on his older brother, Seph. I think every girl I knew had a crush on Seph.

"It's really crowded, huh?" I asked.

"Yeah, but I am cool standing. So where's Selorm?"

Jon knew about Selorm and me, because, like Selorm, he was part of Selassie's group.

"He's upstairs with some girls," I said casually.

Jon smiled sympathetically and I shrugged. He put his arms around me and I leaned into him. He adjusted himself and I fit right into his arms with my back to him.

I am not sure how many minutes it was before I felt it, a light breeze on my neck. I didn't move. I thought I had imagined it. Then he kissed my neck again and I turned my head slightly to look up at him. Then he kissed me.

For the life of me, I can never say why it happened. There was absolutely no precedent. Nothing had ever been insinuated or implied or suggested, ever, between us—nothing that I knew of.

That kiss, that kiss knocked me off my feet and I never recovered. It was the sweetest, most beautiful thing ever. We just kissed. It wasn't a light lip touch, a peck or a lip swipe. It was a full-blown, deep, knock-your-socks-off kiss. I turned around completely and I kissed him. We just kissed. I didn't care where we were or who was watching. I couldn't let go.

I can't say how long the kiss was. It felt like a lifetime. We drew apart briefly, he held me, we smiled and kissed some more. And that's the way it was for the rest of the show.

At one point, I caught Lynn's astonished look. Selassie didn't look excited either. But I couldn't give a damn. Where was Selorm, huh? Just then I heard Lynn's voice in my ear.

"Rabbie, Selorm is here."

I turned and saw her and Selassie head off to the entrance and then I saw Selorm staring at me from the lit doorway. And I knew I had crossed a very serious line. Jon's shoulders stiffened and he turned my face away from Selorm, towards him.

"It's okay. It's okay."

I don't know why he was saying that. It wasn't okay. Was he for real?

"Excuse me," I muttered.

I started walking fast towards the entrance. Selorm, Selassie and Lynn disappeared through the light. They were walking so fast. I could hear Selorm screaming, but I couldn't catch what. Oh my God, what did I just do?

"Rabbie!"

I heard Jon scream my name from behind me. I should have

run after Selorm, but I didn't. I stopped and turned to Jon. He didn't look fazed. What the heck was happening?

"Hey, we didn't do anything wrong. Calm down. Let him lose some steam, but remember we didn't do anything wrong."

He kissed me again, right there, in the lit foyer. He held me and kissed me, just seconds after I was trying to catch up to my supposed boyfriend who had caught me kissing his close friend! Wonderful! And I let Jon kiss me, his lips on mine and his arms around me. I really didn't want to be anywhere else, or with anyone else. We broke apart after a while. I was calmer now.

"Let's go to the parking lot. See what's going on. But we did nothing wrong. Okay?" he said.

I nodded.

"I swear I am going to kill him! What the heck was that? What was that? No, don't tell me to calm down! No one should tell me to calm down. What the heck was that?"

I could hear Selorm's voice from a mile away. Jon and I were holding hands as we walked toward the parking lot. I immediately dropped his hand. This was not a good idea.

Selorm and Selassie were standing near Selassie's car. There were two other guys. I knew one of them, Edem, a family friend, also went to the same primary school. But I couldn't see Lynn. Selorm had a bottle in his hand. He smashed it against the car when he saw us, and the tirade continued. I realized there were a few more bottles on the ground. He was flailing his long arms, and Edem and Selassie, who were both a lot shorter than him, were trying to restrain him.

"What the heck was that? What did I do? What did I do?" Selorm screamed.

Selassie came towards me. He ignored Jon.

"Rabbie, Selorm's been drinking, he's not himself. He's just upset. I am going to take him home. Wait here for me," Selassie instructed.

"I am so sorry. Is he going to be okay? Where is Lynn?"

"Back in there somewhere."

Selorm was still walking towards us, but Edem and the other guy held him back. Selassie went back to him.

"Hey, let's just get you home, okay?" Selassie said to Selorm.

"Damn you both!" Selorm screamed, glaring at Jon and me.

I turned my back and started walking away. Jon followed. He was subdued now. We sat on a ledge in the parking lot and watched Selassie and the boys bundle Selorm into the car. He was still screaming and cussing. This was surreal. Jon put his arms around me and I held him. That night, and how it was handled, I would chalk down as regret number one in a long upcoming string of regrets.

What is hard even to wrap my brain around is why Jon and I even kissed. How did that happen? And why did it feel so perfect? He kissed my cheek with such tenderness and sincerity. I turned my face to him and he kissed me. We kissed for so long, so deeply. My heart was beating so fast. Where had all this come from?

"I love you," he murmured.

I felt my heart skip a beat. Why did this feel so real, so honest and so true? When it was all so random, one night, one act of spontaneity? And yet I knew; I knew I was exactly where I wanted to be.

"I love you too."

Teenage love; nothing serious, right? Not possible to fall in love like that, just hormones talking, maybe? I am twenty-nine years old now, and that was one of the most perfect and sincere moments I have ever felt. It's hard to describe teenage love with serious words. No one takes you seriously. For over ten years after that kiss in the National Theatre auditorium, my heart remained his. I was sixteen years old and I felt undeniable love for the first time, love that haunted me and eclipsed every other event in my life for what felt like a lifetime. What was the recipe? Was it a full moon that night? I can't remember.

I had something good then. I had something perfect. I was so in love, and he was so in love with me. It's not easy to know if a guy truly loves you. That love that is written all over his face, spewing from deep within his heart, his soul. That love that holds no questions; you don't think about it, you don't analyze it. You just know this guy right here loves you.

But I had begun something, hadn't I? I had started myself on a path of pain and hurt. And I didn't know how to stop.

Jon

My relationship with Jon... goodness, I could describe it in so many ways. After that first night of sweet kisses and bottles breaking, we didn't miss a beat. There were no questions. No questions like: Is this the right thing? Should we end it? What about Selorm? I let it all go. I didn't care and neither did Jon.

After Selassie dropped Selorm off, he came back for us. I have no idea where Lynn went that night. Jon and I sat in the back of Selassie's car and we kissed all the way to my end. We didn't care that Selassie and Edem and another guy were in the car. We didn't care that Selorm had just freaked out because of us. We didn't care.

The rest of the summer was mainly like that. And ironically, a lot of our kissing and hooking up was in Lynn's house. Like I said, the den of iniquity.

We were so in love, you couldn't pry us apart. It was a weird transition, I will admit. The circle now became Selassie, Lynn, Jon and I. Selorm did recover. It was the alcohol that had caused all that drama. Yes, I had hurt him, yes I had been wrong. I wouldn't even excuse my part in it. But what Selorm and I had was a brief thing. He had other interests. He wasn't in love. It was hurtful how I did it, yes, but he got over it. We ran into Selorm once or twice after that Saturday night at the theatre. Of course, he didn't hug and kiss us, but neither did he break our necks. That was fine by me. I felt sorry and remorseful, but it wasn't enough to derail my happiness.

Jon was now my baby. We got on so well. We were so tight. We spent each waking moment together. And at night, we would talk on the phone for hours, talking about everything and nothing. Most of our time was spent at Lynn's place or my place.

Jon, physically, was similar to Selorm. That's when I noticed I had a trend, a preference. I hadn't realized it before. Jon was good looking, fair and tall. Those three characteristics, and that's it, I am done for. I couldn't be blamed though. At 5'7" I was taller than the average sixteen-year-old. On a physical level, I couldn't picture dealing with short guys. That must sound shallow, but I simply can't bend to kiss someone. I started to think about my preferences a lot more when Jon came into my life. My ex, Essien, the sloppy kisser, was fair and tall. And his cousin Stephen whom I had a secret crush on was good looking, tall and fair. And there was Patrick, from primary school, also fair and tall enough for sixteen. He's currently stagnated at 5'11". Jon was like the epitome of that description. He wasn't just fair, he was mixed race. His mother was white, from Italy, and his dad was Ghanaian. He was at least six feet back then. And that face... oh my goodness. He was so beautiful, his cheekbones, his eyes, his skin and his lips. I was smitten, bitten and sucked dry by the love bug.

The angel face didn't hide the fact that Jon had a couple of demons. I actually never saw it during that time. I heard about his temper and the baseball bat he carried. I remember getting a call from Lynn to come to her end. Jon and Selassie were there when I arrived. Both guys looked dejected and Lynn looked terrible too. Lynn was usually well put together, even if she had nothing to do. This afternoon, she looked like she had slept in her top and pants. They were creased, and a little stained. She lay curled up on her bed, her eyes looked so tired. Selassie, who usually looked cheerful and energized, looked drained. He lay next to her, his arms around her shoulders. And Jon stood near the window, his face expressionless. Something was definitely wrong.

"What's going on?" I asked.

Lynn lay back on her bed and sighed.

"Your boyfriend and my stupid boyfriend got into a fight last night. Jon hit a bus driver with a baseball bat. So they were thrown in jail. I've been at the jail all night, trying to get them out."

My mouth fell open.

"I didn't hit him. I smashed his windows. There's a difference."

Selassie laughed at Jon's comment. Lynn smacked him and I glared at them all.

"And no one thought it was necessary to call me?"

Jon moved away from the wall, and did that thing he always did to me—tried to calm me down. He put his arms around me and kissed me. But I wasn't going to let it go that easy.

"Lynn, you should have called me."

"Your boyfriend didn't want you to worry." She sounded slightly nonchalant.

I shrugged Jon's arms off my shoulder and walked out of Lynn's room. I had heard stories of his temper, his fights and that baseball bat he kept in his car, but this? Attacking someone?

"Rabbie, wait, I didn't want you to be worried. Please, listen."

I knew he didn't want me to see that side of him, but getting thrown in jail? Why was I finding out now? It was 4 P.M. and now they decide it's okay to tell me? I was upset Lynn was in the loop and I wasn't. I was upset Lynn was there for my boyfriend and I wasn't.

He managed to catch up to me and we sat in the living room and talked. Looking at his face, I tried to picture where this temper came from. I never saw it. There were glimmers here and there, but nothing really. He looked so sweet and innocent.

"Someone should have called me. And why would you do that, seriously? What if he had had something on him? Like a knife or a machete?"

"Then I would have beaten the crap out of him and decorated the pavement with his scalp."

My breath froze in my throat.

"That's what you can say?"

"He cut me! He crossed right in front of me. I almost had an accident. I went off the road. I could have hit and killed someone."

"So you thought it was best to smash his windows? Great judgment."

"You weren't there. I was angry, he did a stupid thing."

"You did a stupid thing too."

He leaned back and closed his eyes, and I realized this was our first argument. It sucked. I leaned back into him and held him tightly.

"I love you, Jon. Something worse could have happened."

"I can take care of myself. Nothing can hurt me."

He held me close as he said that, and I decided to let it go. There was no way he was going to believe he had done anything wrong. I had my first glimpse of his famous temper. I didn't like it, but I wasn't going to fight it. I would only lose. We kissed. It was what we did best.

Kissing is a beautiful thing. I love kissing. Realizing that I love kissing was probably my first epiphany. Jon's lips on my mouth, his breath on my face, his hands on my waist, holding me tight... really, what could be better?

The Second Truth or Dare

It was another Saturday, another night of mistakes and regrets. This day, just as the night I kissed Jon, I will never forget it. It was the night I truly sealed the deal as the worst messed-up girl that ever lived.

My older brother, Josh, met a girl. Sorry, that doesn't say much. Josh meeting a girl back then was like Josh breathing. It was his life. This girl was different though. Actually, sorry, another mistake, almost all the girls he met or was involved with were special. Josh had this pull over women. He had a swagger, a look that just won them over. It was really sad to watch each girl go down one after the other. This one was called Adesua. At the time she reminded me of Sharon Stone's movie characters. Adesua was a typical femme fatale. She was the type of girl guys couldn't get over. She had a great body. She wasn't Ghanaian, she was slightly mixed. I don't even remember what the combination was. And she had an accent. Accents and mixed races. Irresistible, perfect for Josh.

Adesua was a guest at our neighbor Junior's house. Junior and I were close friends. I used to hang out at his house all the time. I set him and Lynn up. They dated for about a year. Junior and Josh were good friends too.

So one Saturday, Josh set up a date with Adesua, but she didn't want them to be alone, so Josh dragged me along to Junior's house. I was supposed to be the chaperone for my older brother. Go figure.

It was pretty late when we got there, almost 10 P.M. Junior was out, and his parents weren't home either, which, I guess, was why Adesua wanted someone else to be there. She insisted I hang out with them. The poor girl seemed so nervous and terrified of being alone with Josh. So we all sat in the living room, watched TV and talked. It was tedious and boring. I got up and went in search of some other entertainment.

I found the study. I am drawn to books. Although this time, I just wanted a phone. I found one, curled up in a large cozy armchair and called my baby. Jon and I talked for a long while. I just loved hearing his voice. He didn't need to say much. It was just good enough having him on the other line, breathing, talking. After several hours, past midnight, I decided to hang up and go drag my brother home. But he and Adesua had moved to the bedroom, and the door was locked. Perfect! How did that happen? I thought she was scared? Oh my brother, did he put a spell on her or something? I really thought Adesua would resist. Now there was no way I could go home alone. I knocked, but no one responded. I tried again. Still nothing and I couldn't even hear anything.

"Hey."

I swung around from the door. It was Junior. I didn't even hear anyone come in.

"You startled me," I said.

"What are you doing here?"

"Josh dragged me here. He wanted to see Adesua, and she didn't want to be alone with him, and now they are in there, alone."

Junior laughed. "Josh is the man. Seriously, I need to start taking lessons."

I rolled my eyes and walked past him. "I need to go home."

"Ah, give him some time. Let's hang. I haven't seen you in a while."

I shrugged. "That's because you've been busy with Sandra."

He laughed. "Yep. She's great. Maybe, just maybe, I can love again after Lynn."

I smiled. I thought Junior and Lynn would last for a long time. But things don't always happen just because you think it. Junior cheated, Lynn moved on. Simple.

I sat on the sofa and he sat beside me. We talked for a while, about his relationship, Lynn and Jon. It was good to talk. He was amused at how in love I was.

After an hour, I had had it. I walked to the bedroom door and knocked again, louder. No answer. How long does it take? I went to the bathroom, stressed and feeling cornered. It was late. I wanted to be home, sleeping.

"You cool?"

I swung around. Junior stood directly behind me in the bathroom.

"Stop startling me."

"Is that all I'm doing, startling you?"

He moved a little closer, forcing my back against the wall.

"Cut it out, Junior. I am tired," I said.

"What am I doing?"

"You know what you're doing. Just cut it out."

I shoved him a little and he grabbed my hands.

"Let's play truth or dare," he said.

I laughed. "What? Are you serious? Junior, I am tired and I want to go home, and I want to talk to my boyfriend."

He leaned closer and I started getting agitated.

"Seriously, Junior, cut it out."

He brought his face close to mine.

"Kiss me, and I'll stop. One kiss. That's all," he said.

What was I, the kiss fairy for the summer? Was this some joke? God needs to have a laugh so he sends these random events into my life?

"No," I said.

"It's a dare, you have to do it."

"Seriously, stop it, just stop it."

He was fast. The next minute his lips were on mine. I should have shoved him again. I say those words over and over again in my head. I should have shoved him again. I should have pushed him. I should have done something!

But I honestly didn't.

I suffer from a disease. I didn't know what it was back then. Neither did I have a word for it till years down the line. It's called curiosity. Yes, it killed the cat, and has just about ruined my life.

I am like an adrenaline junkie, except mine is curiosity. Anything that has a red flag, anything that comes across as forbidden, I must try. Sometimes I am not the initiator of the action, but once the ball starts to roll, I take control. I didn't have control that night. But I know I allowed that kiss to happen because I was curious, and that's downright lame.

I've always wondered, if I could go back in time to change something, what it would be? It would be that unfortunate kiss in Junior's bathroom. Every other deed and action pales in comparison to that moment.

Others could argue that there must be other deeds a lot worse. I am sure at my current age it must sound funny regarding a kiss I had at sixteen as cheating. It was like a peck, less than five seconds! It wasn't even sex! No, but I was in love with Jon, completely and wholly, and he loved me too. He was my world. Nothing else compared to doing that to him, to me, to us. Nothing! When you cheat, if the relationship means anything to you, you hurt yourself as well. You tear your own heart apart. I messed up so bad, there was no recovering. I am anchored in that moment in that bathroom. I am partially stuck there, reliving it, willing myself to shove the fool. But it's happened. And I never pushed him away.

I think I started to cry and Junior stepped back. I walked past him to the living room and just sat there, numb. I stretched out on the sofa and covered my face with my hands. This was the end of me. What was happening? What was wrong with me? Had I no heart? As I think about it now, thirteen years later, I can't excuse it or explain it.

Eventually Josh and I went home. I didn't look at him. I blamed him. I was angry at him as much as I was angry at myself. I was so devastated, but it was about to get worse.

My younger brother told my mom we were out all night and Josh and I got grounded. Josh and I didn't take my younger brother along on stuff we did. We left him alone so many times. And my mother traveled a lot, so he was even more alone than normal. I didn't blame him for telling on us. I would have done it ages ago. I wasn't upset with him. I was just stuck in that bathroom, reliving that awful moment when Junior's mouth touched mine. Being grounded was nothing.

The worst part about being grounded, though, is the boredom and the thinking. I was home, couldn't go out, couldn't get visitors and I couldn't even tell Jon why I had been grounded. I was going insane. I called Junior.

"I am going to tell Lynn, and Jon."

He shrieked. "What? Are you insane? It was just a kiss. What's wrong with you?"

"I can't stop thinking about it. They need to know."

"Oh come on, Rabbie, tell me you're joking. We didn't do anything. Forget about it. I am sorry."

I closed my eyes. He was right. What was wrong with me? But I really couldn't deal with it. My head felt full. I felt like I couldn't breathe. I couldn't deal with the guilt.

I hung up and called Lynn, and I didn't think twice. I told her what happened. I don't remember that conversation word for word. She wasn't immediately pissed; her main concern was Jon. She told me not to tell him. I said I had to. I could hear Selassie's voice in the background. Damn it. Now what would Selassie think?

I hung up on Lynn and called Jon. Oh mistake, mistake, mistake, mistake!

I don't remember how I told him, but the words somehow spewed out of my mouth. I cried, called it a mistake, begged, said I loved him and poured my heart out. What was I thinking? Wrong question—*do* I even think?

I broke Jon that day. Someone might say it was karma. He kissed me in the theatre, when he knew I was with Selorm. So he had it coming. But he didn't deserve it. I loved him, and he loved me. Karma is supposed to hurt wicked people, not him. He started to cry on the phone, then he hung up.

I knew I shouldn't have called. There was no going back. I had started a chain reaction now. I was in deep shock. What had I just done? What was I doing?

Jon and I didn't talk for the rest of the day. The summer was about to end. I was going back to boarding school in a week or two. I needed some closure. I let him be for a few days and then I called and said I needed to see him. He came to my place and we sat in his car and talked. We really talked. As I looked at him, listened to him, I knew I would regret what I had done for the rest of my life.

"I love you," I mumbled. "I really love you."

He looked at me. There was so much pain in his eyes.

"I love you too. I love you."

My heart broke at his words. What sort of person was I? He still loved me.

"It meant nothing. I swear."

He nodded. "I am willing to put this behind me, but I don't want you to ever see him again, ever."

I hadn't expected forgiveness. I was stunned a little.

"Yes, yes, anything you say. I won't."

He held my face and we kissed. We were back.

"It's going to be okay," he whispered.

We would be okay. We would be okay!

Wesley Girls High School—First Year, Third Semester

Going back to school was hard. I was a changed person. The thirteen summer weeks had changed me drastically. I was not the same person. I would never be the same person. The best part was that Jon and I was still together. I was still giddy in love.

My three years at Wesley Girls High School were some of the best moments of my life. That's undeniable. I had fun. I formed relationships and friendships that I would keep for life.

But I also had terrible moments there. Incidents that I thought I would never recover from. I encountered bitches who later became friends and friends who later became bitches. Girls! I tip my hat off to girls. We know drama. TNT stole that slogan from us, trust me. Girls are the strangest, messed-up insane creatures ever. Girls can kill you, I joke not.

I hated boarding school. I hated being left there each semester. I hated the endless rules and regulations. I don't do very well with restrictions. I hated sleeping in a huge room with over fifty girls, with no privacy. I hated the horrible bathrooms and dining areas. I hated the chores, cleaning the toilets and scrubbing the gutters and fetching water on my head. What I hated most? The damn bells! The bells were rung, like, every half an hour. Our lives were dictated by bells. Bells were rung for breakfast, lunch, supper, walks, cleaning, study time, phone calls, breaks, bedtime. You could not take a step until a bell had rung. I could not stand it. I had bells ringing in my ears years after I left. The second worst thing after the annoying bells was the love/hate relationship with the girls.

Girls are in constant competition with themselves and each other. I could never understand that. Prior to Wesley Girls, the only thing I bothered competing with other people on was academic achievement. In Ridge Church School, at the end of each semester, all the students in a class would be ranked and then all the students within a grade would be awarded prizes at the end of the year. Those were my goals. I would be ticked off each time my rank fell below third out of fifty or so students. Thankfully, I think I fell to fifth just once in my entire three years at junior secondary school. I was so motivated by achievement; it was my all. I won a prize each year for academic excellence. Lynn usually beat me, and sometimes Portia and William. William was insanely competitive and each time I beat him, it gave me such pleasure.

I remember when the BECE results came out, and my results said eleven ones, I broke down and cried like I had lost a parent. I sobbed and wailed with so much angst and so much passion. It was the end of my life. How could I get eleven ones? The highest anyone could get was twelve ones and I wanted twelve ones. How could this happen? I was no longer extraordinary. I truly felt my life was over. And then weeks later, it turned out the results were wrong and I got twelve ones. Of course I got twelve ones. What idiot thought I didn't?

Those were my motivations: academic achievement, excelling, standing out and being smart. Then Wesley Girls and all its drama happened to me. I didn't lose my edge or my drive to excel. I just encountered other motivations, almost as strong and almost as devastating.

I understand parents who worry about their teenagers dating. It is distracting. I would never deny that. It is possible to be studious, smart and still be into the guy thing. But trust me, it is darn hard to balance.

There are really two types of smart people. There are those who are naturally smart. It's part of their DNA, at their fingertips. It's almost effortless. Then there are those who study day and night, and push hard to get that prize. I was somewhat lucky enough to fall into the DNA category. The thing about those of us in the DNA category is that our potential could be limitless if we made the effort. Our downfall is our minds are too open, so open it's easy to be distracted. Students in the other category, the hard workers, cannot afford to be distracted.

I would say my friend Nana is also in the DNA category. I never knew anyone who could have fun and still get such good grades. It was annoying sometimes. But then again, I am sure friends I have clubbed with who have seen me still ace exams get annoyed too. I would put Bella in the hardworking category. I never knew anyone who worked harder than Bella, and she got the grades she worked hard for.

So Nana and Bella were my competitors; academic competitors. I liked to be around people like that. They gave me focus, they gave me drive. They reminded me of why I was in school and where I wanted to be.

I liked hanging out with Nana too. She was fun. She could do the work/play balance with such finesse—sometimes a little too well. Bella and Nana were my core group, for those reasons.

And there was Jo. Jo was one of my best friends from Ridge Church, one of the original five chicks. We were the only two from our group who ended up in Wesley Girls. I was grateful for that. I loved Jo. She had this wisdom and sensibility that was beyond her age. She had a soul that was sincere and genuine. I could never figure out why she was like that. She had her own family drama, but in the midst of it all, she had principles.

There was also Esi. Esi was a senior who "adopted" me as her girl. Seniors had "girls." I thought it was ridiculous when I started school. Nana loved it. It meant attention and friends and fun, and that wasn't my deal at all. Nana had several "girls" and a lot of the seniors wanted to be her friend. I couldn't be bothered. But unfortunately the seniors didn't leave me alone, because of my brother.

Josh, my brother, had a colorful past, especially with women. He loved a girl once, really loved her. I don't know why or how, but she broke up with him and that killed his big teenage heart. He swore, literally, that he would never love again and he would become a heartbreaker. He got this big chalkboard and wrote "Crash and Burn" on it, and listed his plans for women domination. It was sad then, but I laugh as I think about it now. Josh went through a lot of women and he left a lot of debris along the way. He was a popular boy. Everyone knew him. It was fun being his sister, till I got to Wesley Girls High.

"Oh, so you're Josh Daniels's sister, eh."

"Where is Josh Daniels's sister? I want to see her."

"Is that Josh Daniels's sister? Come here."

My cousin Maso and Josh's friend Emefa saved me from most of that. But I was still punished without reason, harassed incessantly, all because my brother got his heart broken and lashed out at all women. I think most of those girls really just wanted him. They definitely weren't going to get a mile close just by punishing me!

Esi came in during that time. She didn't know my brother. I liked her for that. She was very sweet and she took me in as her girl. That part I initially thought would be tedious. Students made such efforts for their "girls." There were all these notes, cards, exchanging food at dinner and little acts that I really couldn't be bothered with in the beginning. But I was grateful I had an ally up high.

I really started to like Esi later. She was smart, honest, cool, funky and beautiful. I could deal with that. And she was a good listener.

I also bonded with a girl in my house, Afua. She was just like me in so many ways, it was unbelievable. She was Triple A—her first, middle and last names all started with A. Afua was such a tomboy, she took the title from me, or maybe we shared it, I don't know. We both always, always wore pants. You wouldn't catch us dead in skirts. We both loved to perform. There was so much we had in common and so much we loved about each other. She had a spirit similar to my own. I really liked hanging out with her. And she was smart too. That is always a good thing.

Then there was Ajua and her sidekick Maame; or was it Maame and her sidekick Ajua? Those two were like twins, seriously. They had the same skin color, fair. They were about the same height, short. They were also about the same size, too skinny. Although I think Ajua took the cake on that one. Ajua and I were in the same social clubs, and I thought she was a pretty cool girl. They were both also Nana's friends, so naturally I got to spend time with them too. Sometimes, I thought they were a little too attached at the hip but I admire friendships like that. When I looked at them, I saw loyalty. I hoped it would be there forever.

My life at Wesley Girls would have been so simple and so different had I stuck to my core group: Nana, Bella, Jo, Maso, Emefa, Esi, Afua and the Siamese twins Ajua and Maame. The list may sound long, but they were genuinely good people. Things would have been so simple. But my circle got bigger and with it came ultimate drama.

Selassie's group of guy friends also had a group of girl friends in Wesley Girls High. Naturally there was friction between me and the girls. They were there the night that Selorm freaked. They were the girls he was with on the second floor. Selorm had been pursuing one of them for a while, Sammi. Sammi was probably the love of Selorm's life. I was just a pit stop, I believe. Sammi wouldn't give Selorm the time of day, but she still kept him around. Girls are such sadists.

Sammi and her friends, Abena, Cami and a bunch of others, didn't really like me. Initially I think it was because of Selorm, which was stupid. Girls could never direct their attention at the real culprits. If they wanted to be pissed, shouldn't Selorm be the one? I really couldn't care. Back then, such things never troubled me. I thought girls had too much time on their hands. I didn't have a minute to dwell on whether Sammi, Cami and Abena were gossiping about me. I had other things to think about, like how Bella beat me in Science so now I had to get her back in English.

But honestly, you can only stay focused for a while. Somehow, someway, you really can't ignore the BS.

"Hey, Jon is here, with Selorm and the rest."

I looked at Jo and sighed.

"Seriously, I wish Jon would stop rolling with Selassie and his crew. It means I have to deal with those girls every Saturday. I don't get what their problem is. I mean, look at Selorm and Jon, they're friends again. Why can't we be like guys? And it's not like Sammi and I are friends—I didn't even know about her."

Jo laughed. "Saturdays are a pain for you, huh."

"Oh, you have no idea. It's ridiculous how petty they can be. But I miss Jon!"

"You better get out there now. Your boy is too hot to leave him waiting around for you. Girls are desperate!"

I smiled and got up from my bed.

Visitors' days were bitter sweet. It was sweet seeing Jon, but hard because we couldn't kiss. I missed kissing him. Jo went with me. She had a visitor as well, plus she knew Selassie and his boys. I said hi to

Selassie, nodded at Selorm and then hugged Jon. He looked so good!

"Hey, I missed you!" I sounded like a ten-year-old.

He smiled. "I missed you too. Seven whole days—it's so stupid that we have to wait that long."

I nodded. "Boarding school is stupid. I really can't stand it. I am just surrounded by too many stupid people, it's overwhelming."

Jon laughed. I liked his laugh. I just loved the boy.

We sat on a bench and held hands and talked. He said he was going home for a while, for family stuff. He asked if I would be going home soon. I said we had a break in November, but that was close to two months away. He said he would try and take a break then too. Until then, we would have to deal with holding hands.

"I wish I could kiss you now," he said softly, staring at me.

Our visitors' space stretched from the car park, main auditorium, down to the kitchens. It was an expansive area but it was also not private. There were seniors, teachers and parents everywhere. Kissing would get me expelled. I could do stupid, risky things, but not that. Getting thrown out of school would derail my lifelong plans. I squeezed his hand tighter.

"I know. I wish I could kiss you too; in due time, my dear."

I put my head on his shoulder. That was doable. "I love you," I added.

"I love you."

Bitches Become Friends

Hours later, I was sitting on a bench in the auditorium, waiting for entertainment night to begin. Esi sat next to me. I smiled at her.

"I saw you with your beau today," she said. I laughed.

"He's really cute," she said.

I couldn't stop grinning. "Isn't he?"

"How's it going in class?"

"Bella beat me in Science. She got ninety-seven, I got ninety-four. That girl is just insane. I am sure she doesn't eat or sleep. She probably doesn't take a break to piss."

Esi laughed. "Why do you let it bother you so much?"

"Oh, it doesn't bother me much anymore. I get her in English all the time. I have that nailed. I am the Michael Jordan of English."

Esi laughed again. "Hey, let's step outside. This show isn't going to start anytime soon."

We went outside, and Esi dragged me to her friends, Yvonne and Angela. I didn't really like fraternizing with seniors but these girls were cool.

"Rabbie, I was actually looking for you earlier today. We're having a sixth form variety show next weekend and I want you to perform. I figured it could be you, Sammi, and two others. We want you to do Boyz II Men."

I froze and stared at Yvonne. I loved performing. Performing is one of the best things I remember from Wesley Girls. I had a reputation for that. I could perform; dancing, writing and acting. That wasn't the problem. But perform with Sammi? I wasn't sure how I felt about that.

"Uh, can I just put my own group together?"

"Sammi wants to do Boyz II Men, so you should do it with her." That was Angela. I think Sammi was her girl.

I could have argued, but decided not to. Sixth formers were

gods. They could punish anyone for just about anything. Forget LA gangs shooting each other up for an inane reason like some kid wearing the wrong hat; sixth formers could destroy your entire life for just a glance.

"Sure, should be fun."

"Pick a good song and it better be a good show!"

I talked with Esi a bit and then I went to find Jo.

"So, Yvonne wants me to perform Boyz II Men next weekend."

"Oh cool! You love them! Which song?" she asked.

"I'm thinking 'On Bended Knee.' "

"Great! Can I join?"

I smiled. "Of course, but guess what? We have to do this with Sammi."

Jo laughed. "This should be interesting. I guess that's what Angela wanted, huh?"

I nodded. Honestly, I was freaking out about performing with Sammi. She was a cool girl. Before the summer, we had spoken a few times. We had even performed before. It was just the crowd she rolled with. Abena irked me, and Cami just seemed off.

The next day I went looking for Sammi. I went with Jo. She was like a neutral buffer. They had no beef with her, so they would have to be a little cordial. Jo didn't resonate confrontation. It was hard to just pick on her. You had to have a really good reason.

We found Sammi and she was actually alone, which was a blessing. I really tried to avoid dealing with bitches as much as I could. It can be tedious.

"Hey Sammi, how are you?"

She smiled at us. She was lounging on one of the campus garden benches, writing a letter. Writing letters was such a Wesley Girls thing. We wrote notes and letters to friends, seniors, families, boyfriends, anyone. Some people even wrote notes for girls who slept in the same dorm as they did. I liked writing notes too, but not to that many people. I had a very short and selective list: Esi, Jon and my family. Once or twice, I would drop Nana a note. I couldn't deal with a lot at a time. I couldn't multitask my relationships. It takes a lot of effort to maintain friendships and relationships.

"I'm good. How are you guys? What's up?"

I sat next to her and Jo stood, my sweet guardian angel. If it came down to a fist fight, she couldn't do squat, but at least she was there.

"So Angela and Yvonne want you and I to do Boyz II Men this coming weekend."

"I know, Angela told me. I told her I liked your 'Water Runs Dry' performance last semester. You're the Boyz II Men chick around here."

I laughed. I *was* the Boyz II Men chick. I was addicted to those guys. Every song of theirs just had a story. I was flattered Sammi had liked my performance. When I first got to Wesley Girls, I did "Water Runs Dry" with the seniors. That was fun, especially considering I was the only newbie and they were all sixth formers. This might not be tough after all. Performance supersedes boy fight.

"Cool. So it's going to be me, you, Jo and maybe Bella. I need to get that girl to quit studying for a minute."

Sammi laughed.

"Oh yeah, she is in my dorm. I know what you mean," she said.

"Okay, so I'm thinking 'On Bended Knee.' What do you think?"

"Yeah, I love that one! That should be great. Do you have it?"

"Oh yeah, I was singing that song in front of the mirror all summer. I have a tape and the lyrics. And we only have a week. So we should start tonight or something."

"Angela has a cassette player. I can get that and should we meet in the auditorium after supper?"

"That works. I am going to write down the lyrics, and get Bella on board. So see you later, then."

"Yeah, okay, bye then. See you later."

As Jo and I walked away, I was stunned at how well that conversation had gone.

Working with Sammi was a breeze. She was such a laid-back girl. I just couldn't believe it. There was no antagonism, no arguments and no tension. She couldn't perform though, not even if her life depended on it. But she was a great person. We didn't talk much about the boys. Once or twice, we would find a bench, just the two of us, and talk about school, and how much we hated it. A few rare times, she asked how Jon was, and I realized she was dating one of Selassie's best friends, called Elvis. I thought that was interesting. What kind of clique was Selorm in? He just couldn't get his friends out of his way.

Through Sammi, I became better friends with Abena and Cami. Abena still irked me. She had this high irritating voice that just reeked of insincerity. I felt I could not turn my back on that girl. Cami I couldn't quite figure out. She came across as though she'd kiss the ground Abena walked on. The merger of groups wasn't so smooth. But soon we all started to hang out, Sammi, Nana, Abena, Cami, Ajua, Maame, Jo, and I.

There was also Nkrumah, who was Nana's friend. Nkrumah was pretty cool, but she never quite fit in completely with the rest of us. But then again, we all never fit in completely. We called ourselves the "Nine," but there were definitely little pockets of loyalty. Sammi, Cami and Abena had history and a bond. Jo and I always had each other's backs, Ajua and Maame had their thing, and Nana was tight with everyone basically. Having such a large girl group is like managing a boy band—it just doesn't work! It never really did. Somewhere along the line, there was also Anna, whose father was the Vice President of Ghana. I definitely liked her. She had sincerity in her eyes.

I mention sincerity a lot because it's key for me. If you don't like me, don't pretend you do. I can never pretend. I wear my emotions on my sleeve. It's rare for a girl not to be slightly two-faced. A girl can laugh with you, talk with you, compliment you and as soon as you turn your back she is digging your grave. I don't know at what point all girls are taken through that training. I missed it somehow. For the life of me, I cannot stand that crap. You piss me off, you will know I am pissed off. I cannot smile at you, when I want to slap you. It's beyond me. But it is a skill, believe me. And some girls have nailed that skill to the max.

So my circle became bigger. The bitches (Sammie, Cami and Abena) became my "friends." But I use the word "friends" cautiously. Any minute now, they could drag me down in the mud and bury me there. Friends—yeah, right.

The Beginning of the End

"Jon hasn't written to me in two weeks."

It was prep, our mandatory study time. I was sitting next to Nana. She had a bunch of letters in her hand. Nana was pretty popular. I was popular too. I think I have been popular most of my life. But popularity doesn't give you anything. It makes your life and your issues that much more known. You can't do anything without having someone in your face, in your business. And honestly, I never sought out popularity. Everyone just knew who I was. It made me come across as egotistical. People would remember my name and say hi, and I wouldn't know who they were, neither would I care. But I am not egotistical. It just takes a lot of effort to keep up with acquaintances and friends and random meetings, and all that. I just really couldn't be bothered. And I still can't be bothered.

"Have you written to him? Have you called?" Nana asked.

I stared down at the two letters I had. One was from Lynn and the other from my mother. Then there was a note from Esi. That was it. Of course I had written, and I had tried to call.

"Yeah, I've tried. I think there is something going on with him."

"Give it some time. I know they're coming to our mid-semester variety show."

We had this big mid-semester performance coming up. And of course I was performing. I think it was TLC, and I was doing Left Eye's rap. I also had a second performance, as Diddy. There really couldn't be a show without me. And my Diddy performance was the opener. I was looking forward to that. But I couldn't shake the feeling that something was wrong. Jon wrote every week! And he hadn't been to see me in three weeks.

"Yeah, he said ages ago he would come. I just really hope everything is good with us."

"Hey, he loves you, you know that."

He loves me. Love is flimsy, just as it is strong. I knew he just hadn't been the same since the Junior debacle. I would die if I lost him. My teenage life wouldn't be worth living. But I just needed to do my Diddy gig first. Life could fall apart after that.

And life did.

Jon didn't write for a while and I started to hear rumors. Rumors of another girl, some mixed-race girl back in Accra. I don't make rash decisions based on rumors. I didn't even ask him about it. Like I would get an answer anyways; he wasn't even writing. He came to visit, a week before our variety show. It had been a month since I last saw him, and five weeks since he last wrote. He acted aloof and cocky; said he was busy with school, home stuff and just had a lot on his mind. I pestered him about not writing, told him how much I had missed him. I was a sorry-ass girl. I was whiny, and he was cold. My heart was breaking.

"What is this? Do you still love me?" I asked.

"I don't know."

I was stunned. Bloody hell! What did I miss? Had I been in a coma? Did something happen? What?

"Huh?"

"I don't know. I am just not in the right frame of mind. I mean, you did that thing with Junior…" His voice trailed off.

Junior? Junior? I thought we had moved past that. And it had been two months, if not more, since Junior. We never talked about it. Apparently we should have.

"Junior? Why are you bringing that up?"

"I don't know. I have been thinking about it."

"What do you want me to say? I am really sorry about that. It was nothing. It was really nothing."

"I know. I have just been thinking about it."

I couldn't speak. What do I say? I couldn't think. I couldn't think!

"You said you let it go. I love you."

He looked at me. I looked into his eyes. There was something there. I couldn't figure out what. It was like he was trying. Trying to be a tough guy? Trying not to love me? Were the guys giving him a tough time about the Junior thing? Did he feel like a wimp for forgiving me? Was that what this was all about?

"Baby—" I started to say.

"I have to go," he cut me off.

I was stunned. I watched him get up and walk towards the boys, Selorm, Selassie and Edem. It was about the boys, wasn't it? That damn group of boys. I called his name but he didn't turn around. Selorm looked at me. He looked a little sympathetic. The same sympathetic look Jon had when I told him Selorm was with some chicks. They were idiots, all of them.

I was in pain that night. But through my pain came anger. I couldn't deal with crap. You could bathe it, clothe it, wrap it, but once it's crap, it's crap and I can't deal with that. He would get his in due time.

Two days later, I got a letter from Jon. He said he was coming to the show, to see me, and he had missed me. I crumpled the letter and threw it in the waste basket. I was done.

Third Biggest Regret

The day of the highly anticipated variety show came. I was psyched. This was the best part of boarding school. This was where I felt like me. Performing just made me high. We were doing the performance in front of the chapel, completely inappropriate but the best location possible. There was a long walkway from the visitors' entrance to the stage, and we had seats lined up on all sides. I stood on the second floor with Sammi, Jo, Nana and the rest of the expanded crew, staring down at people milling in. That's when I saw the guys come in.

As they strolled down the walkway, we leaned over the balcony and peered down at them. We felt so good. The guys looked so put together, and had this entourage vibe. A bunch of good-looking cats; and everyone knew whom they were there for. For the first time in a while, I allowed myself to be a stupid, mindless, boy-crazy teenager. I felt good about the attention. The boys looked up, saw us and waved. Jon gave me a big smile. I tried to smile back. He was about to get toasted. Crash and burn, my love, crash and burn!

My performance was awesome! I could see Jon was getting a few taps and some attention from it all. It irked me a little. To me, he no longer had a right to my glory.

After the show, we had the chance to socialize with our

visitors and I went looking for him. They were grouped around someone's car. I couldn't figure out which one of them would have a car at boarding school.

"Hey, you were great!" Jon said.

"We need to talk."

That phrase, huh, we need to talk. Girls have been using it since they could say "mama."

His smile disappeared. Damn right, Skippy!

I sat in the back of the car. The door was open and my feet hung out. He sat on a ledge in front of me.

"This isn't working for me. Your attitude the last couple of months… I don't think I deserve that," I said.

"I had things to sort through."

"You've completely ignored me and treated me like crap practically since we've been back in school. I said I was sorry. Don't tell me you forgive me and then act like you don't care about me. If you can't forgive me, then say so. Let me know where I stand."

"I do care. I've just been…" He couldn't finish.

"Well, I can't do it anymore. So if you want to be angry, you can just go be angry. I cannot keep begging you, or trying so hard. That is not me."

"I have been distracted, but it's not going to be like that anymore. I just needed time."

"So now you can have some more time." I was so upset and so done.

"I am sorry, I am sorry. Please, listen to me. I know I have been a jackass. But I am sorry, don't do this."

I looked into his eyes and I saw his pain, saw how much he meant what he was saying.

There is a very fine line between standing up for yourself and being stone cold. For as long as I can remember, I have stood up for myself. I am such a big advocate of believing in yourself, not taking crap and disrespect from guys; if he messes up, he should step. All my friends know this. If a friend's boyfriend cheats, I'd be the last to know, because my reaction would be, are you kidding? Kick him to the curb! I am Ms. Independent. If you disrespect me, you're through. Whether you're fair, tall and good-looking, you are gone.

But—and there is a but—people do deserve second chances. I

have been given a few in my life. Jon gave me one. I kissed another boy and he said it was okay. He tried to make it okay. He didn't walk.

The heart, it's a funny thing, isn't it? It can be full of love one minute and then pumping with pure bile the next minute. I didn't hate him though. I could never hate him. But I did not have the patience or understanding to deal with ambiguity.

And so I made my biggest, worst decision ever. I crossed the line from standing up for myself to stone-cold brutality.

"I can't do it. I am sorry. I am just sick and tired of this," I said.

"What do you want me to say? I am sorry. I am trying."

"You haven't tried."

"Don't do this. Don't do this," he said.

I don't know what world I was in. I don't know how I did what I did. I am thinking about it so hard now. I see that moment in my head all the time. He was sitting or kneeling in front of me. He was holding my hand. He was sorry. He was sorry! And I let go of his hand, and walked away. I heard him stand up, heard him call my name. He added a little force to it. I could hear the anguish in his voice. And I still walked away. I was such a heartless fool.

I heard Jo behind me, calling my name. I disappeared into one of the classrooms. Minutes later, Jo and Nana found me. Then I bawled my eyes out. I didn't even know why I was crying. Wasn't I the one who had walked away? Walking away from him was hard, but then the fool I was at the time felt I was justified. What the heck?

Jon wrote once. I didn't reply and then that was it. He didn't write back. That's the thing about guys, right? They give it one shot. If the girl won't budge, they move on. Life goes on. He moved on. And unfortunately as soon as the guy moves on, that's when the girl realizes she's been a fool. What is new?

It was then I wrote *Basic Reality*. *Basic Reality* was a book about Jon and me, about me loving him. I tried to hide the characters as best as I could. And I really thought I had. Then I sent the book to Nick, Jon's best friend. He was like my editor, my proof reader. He always read all my stuff. Then somehow, Jon, Selassie,

Selorm and everyone else read the book. I don't know why it became scandalous. But all of a sudden, there was this fuss; even my new-found girl crew started to make a fuss. Yes, I threw one or two of them in there, but big deal. I don't think that book helped my situation at all.

I was sorry I walked away from him. I was sorry I didn't try. I was so sorry. I was still in love with him, and I regretted my brief insanity. Nothing was helping. And I kept making it worse. So I decided to do a big gesture of love. I could write a book on big bold stupid gestures of love. Oh yes, I definitely could. And I know Jon and all his friends remember my gestures of love. I was the originator of that idiocy. Let me think. I have done the love songs tape gift; recorded a bunch of songs on a tape and sent it. I have also recorded myself on a tape, just talking, and sent that. I did all that before it became cool. Way before Larenz Tate did it in "Love Jones." I have done the poetry thing too, way before Janet Jackson did her poetry thing in Poetic Justice. I have done the regular corny stuff—the cards and the letters. Oh my goodness, the letters. My first over-the-top letter I wrote to Jon was from Boyz II Men, "On Bended Knee." Each line in that song, each word, each sentiment, touched me to my core. And I wanted him to be touched.

I just wanted to say I was sorry. That's all. But it didn't move him. That letter, just like all my other big bold gestures to Jon, got blown out of proportion. Boys! They just have to share, don't they? So my letter got passed around. I know Nick saw the letter, and Selassie, and probably Selorm and their entire school. I felt violated. People I didn't know brought up the letter. All I was trying to say was I was sorry. I missed him so much. I needed him back so badly.

But there was no going back, and November sealed the deal. In November, most of the Cape Coast schools had a break from school. I called him that first weekend we got home. I told him flat out I was sorry and I loved him.

"I think we should really just move on."

As he said those words, I closed my eyes. I knew this was it. He was stubborn. I was not going to get another chance. This was really it. I couldn't fight it, I couldn't force it.

"I love you. I will always love you," I cried one last time.

He didn't respond for a while.

"I just think we should end it."

I was so stunned, I couldn't say anything. This was my fault. I was losing the one person I loved most in the world.

We hung up and then that was the end. He was gone. I wrote the date down. Saturday, November 12. We started on a Saturday. We ended six months later on a Saturday. My world and my life were changed forever.

I am not sure how I survived the next few days and weeks. I tried not to cry, until I heard a song that broke me down completely: Whitney Houston's "Where do broken hearts go?"

> And if somebody loves you
> Won't they always love you?

The words just hit me hard—if somebody loves you, won't they always love you? Maybe, and maybe not. What was next? How could I possibly make it? I could barely breathe. That was such a devastating period for me. My grades took a soft hit. School and boys, oil and water. It can work for some, but it's pretty hard. I tried to lean on friends: Esi, Nana, Emefa and Jo. I crawled back to my core group. I needed some reassuring. But I really didn't. I just wanted to be a mess. I never went out to see Selassie and his friends when they came. When we ended, Jon stopped coming over anyways.

I was thankful he didn't hook up with some other girl from my school. That would have been hard. In the three years I was in Wesley Girls, he never dated anyone from there. The guys were sympathetic, which surprised me. But then again, they knew I was smitten. It was embarrassing. Everyone knew I had it bad. I was so gone, it was laughable. I buried myself in writing. I wrote poems for just about anyone. I became more active with school clubs and friends and I started studying again. I suspected I would never forget him, or stop loving him, but I also knew it was really over. And I just had to move on. I just had to. But it wasn't working. He was the love of my life. I can't describe fully how I felt. I was sixteen, and I was insanely in love. What hurt most was that I tore the relationship apart. I messed up. I kissed Junior, and I turned my back on him. I messed up a truly good thing.

I can't count how many nights I prayed to God to take me back in time, to give me a chance to make it right. I promised God I would never mess up again. I asked God to let him love me again. That's all I wanted. I hated myself so much.

I sunk so low that I couldn't see beyond my misery. I couldn't remember what was going on in anyone else's life. I was self-absorbed for so long. I had no clue what was going on with the other girls. I didn't care really. I was just so heartbroken. Girls and boys break up all the time, and then move on. Weren't boys all the same? They weren't. I couldn't do that. I wanted my baby back so badly. I hated Junior. I hated him for a long time. And then I hated myself. Each song on the radio was about heartbreak. It was pathetic. And I wallowed in it. I let the misery wash over me. I just hated myself for being stupid.

But little did I know that being stupid and reckless was going to take up permanent residence in my life.

Edem

Bad things happen in threes, right? Mistakes happen in threes too. One group, three guys. Perfect. Could I truly be any worse?

Edem and I started to talk and write to each other some months after Jon and I chose the blue pill that sent us to our doom. It really started as something just platonic. I knew Edem from primary school, and even way before then. Our parents were friends. I knew him when he was walking around in semi-diapers. Edem was the life of the party, the joker of the group. He was really fun to be with and he got on with everyone.

Edem wasn't my type per se. His fairness barely passed my "fairness" threshold. And he was just my height. And good looking? Close to that threshold too, but not quite there. He definitely wasn't Jon. But he had something about him. He had this "don't take life too seriously" attitude that was quite attractive to me. I am over-the-top serious. I take everything seriously. I am not the perpetual smiley happy-go-lucky person in the room. Everything has to be dissected and torn apart. I could go into depression if I realized some particular top I had planned on wearing had a stain on it just minutes before I had to leave. I am intense.

So Edem was very different from me. Nothing appeared to faze him. I was so tightly wound and stretched, I could have snapped at any time. And Edem just unwound me. Others started to notice the connection between Edem and me. No one really had anything better to do than to notice guys and girls hooking up, or appearing to hook up.

I really liked talking to him. With Selorm and then with Jon, it all started with kissing, random and unplanned. Edem and I started from the basics, talking. And we talked all the time. I needed the humor. He made everything so light and insignificant.

Bonding with Edem brought drama. It was to be expected; you would say first Selorm, then Jon and now Edem? Of course there would be drama.

Edem and I really started talking because Jo started talking to Selorm. Friends tend to gravitate to where their friends go. It always happens. Guys, and girls, can roll in packs, but there are always closer-knit groups within a pack. For Selassie's group, it was Edem and Selorm; they went way back. And Jon's buddy was Nick. Once Selorm and Jo started talking, Edem and I naturally became friends. I was with Jo all the time.

I never felt awkward about Selorm and Jo. Selorm and I never got to the point where I was emotionally invested in what we had. I was totally fine with them being together. They were such a cute couple. I am not sure if Selorm was okay with Edem and me but he never let on. He was probably at the point where he figured, "This is who she is." It's a terrible thing to think about someone, but I was a terrible person.

I don't think I had any strong beliefs then. I had a tunnel vision on fulfillment. A part of me thrived, flourished, by doing things I really shouldn't have done. It was innate, but it was there. I wanted to be bad. I wanted to push the limits; it excited me. It was a sort of validation for me. Unconsciously, perhaps, I was trying to prove I was wanted. I had a pull factor, or something. I hit a mental block each time I try to psychoanalyze my actions. All I know is I was a twisted, unscrupulous person. Ah, it feels liberating to say that—twisted and unscrupulous. If I had a shrink, he or she would be proud of me.

Another Summer

Here's the thing about summer, and why so much happens over summer. When you're in boarding school, you are completely and totally deprived of everything. You get three vacations in a year. There's a brief one-week respite after the first semester, then there are the thirteen weeks of summer and then ten days or so for Christmas. Throw that into the mix of being in an all-girls or all-boys' boarding school. When would you let loose and go crazy? Summer, summer, summer!

Edem and I built up this momentum of communication during the first two semesters. There were the letters, the notes, some cards here and there and phone calls. In my own self-absorbed way, I was excited about the summer. I had already started thinking of kissing him. Would I? Could I? You might be asking right now, did I think of Selorm or Jon? Yes, yes, yes, I am not that bad. I just didn't care *enough*. I cared to a degree, but there was this rush I felt. I felt heady just thinking of doing something with Edem. And people sit and wonder why others do bad things. It is such a rush. I would throw my head back thinking about it and grin from ear to ear like a Cheshire cat.

Edem started coming by my place as soon as we got home. I really liked talking to him. He was so much fun. And you would think funny guys can't be romantic, but he was. He was so attentive. He would call without fail. He would visit all the time and he would always be game for spending time together. He made me feel good. There was no pretense, no trying to figure things out—does he like me, does he not. We were just comfortable with each other. Jo and Selorm were pretty serious by that time. They had been together for a few months, and that made it easier for Edem and me to meet up. The four of us did stuff together all the time. Kissing Edem also came naturally. He was pretty good. I was beginning to think maybe all guys were good, except for Essien. Maybe Essien was an anomaly.

I spent that summer balancing my "friendship" with Edem, family and Lynn. Selassie and Lynn had broken up ages ago. Lynn had moved on, and so had he.

I couldn't take what Edem and I had to the next level. He wanted to make this serious, I didn't. Yeah, sure, people knew we were spending time together, but a foolish part of me thought if he wasn't my boyfriend, maybe what I was doing wasn't so bad. I felt if we made this serious, that would be three boyfriends from the same group. In a completely immature way, my reasoning was I wanted Jon to remain the most important person in my life out of that group. I didn't want to give Edem the same status Jon had. I felt it would disrespect my relationship with Jon even more. I wanted it to be: I didn't love three guys from the same group, I loved only one. I wanted it always to remain clear whom my heart was for. It didn't matter who had come before him, or who came after. I wanted it to be crystal clear how much Jon had meant to me and how much he would always mean to me. If anyone was going to look back and remember that time, I wanted there to be no illusions; Jon was the man. Officially dating Edem would only muddy the waters.

So I stretched Edem out for almost a year, through out my second year at boarding school. All we did was talk, write, kiss, walk and spend time together. I made it crystal clear we weren't in a relationship. Remember, I said girls are sadists. We just want it our way, all the time. And usually it just comes back to bite us, hard.

My Evil Phase

Christmas 1996, Edem decided to ask me out again. He said he loved me and he wanted to be with me. He just didn't understand my hesitation. And I actually realized what I was doing to him wasn't fair. It was Friday, and we were walking around my neighborhood kissing. Yes, yes, I know, I kiss all the time.

Edem sounded so serious. "I just want to be with you. Think about it," he said.

"Okay, okay, I will. I know, I know. But I am traveling tonight, for Christmas. I'll be back on Sunday. We can talk then, okay?"

He kissed me, so softly. Oh, they knew how to do that so well! I kissed him back, made it deeper.

"I'll miss you," he said.

I held him tighter, kissed him again. "I'll miss you too. See you Sunday."

Sunday rolled up. I had thought all weekend about Edem, but I still wasn't sure. I liked him a lot. I liked being with him. But there was something so strong holding me back. Did I feel Jon and I could be together again? Did I feel going out with Edem would jeopardize that for good? Something was just missing. I called Edem that Sunday night. He didn't answer. I called Selorm. He was with Jo; they said they were in my neighborhood and they were going to drop by.

"Hey, how was Christmas in the mountains?" Jo hugged me.

I shrugged. "Same as it has been for the last seventeen years of my life."

She smiled; a sad look crossed her face. I looked at Selorm; he had a strange look too. Oh, I knew that look.

"Where is Edem? What's going on?" I asked.

"Rabbie, Edem asked Abena out over the weekend, and she said yes," Jo said.

We were in my kitchen. I was boiling water for hot chocolate. My hand stilled on the pot. I didn't even feel the heat.

I laughed. "Nice one, very funny."

Selorm spoke this time. "Listen, he told me you guys talked on Friday. He knows you won't go out with him. He and Abena talk every now and then. She likes him and she wants him. He wants to be wanted," he said.

"Are you guys serious? I told him to give me up until Sunday! Abena? Are you kidding? Since when? How come I never knew? He never mentioned her name!"

Jo took the pot from me. I looked at my palms. They were badly scalded. I had burnt my hands over the fool. I leaned against the wall and closed my eyes.

"Tell me this is a joke, please?"

Jo was silent. Selorm sighed.

"We both know you didn't like him enough," he said.

"You don't know that. You can't say that," I countered.

"Rabbie, is there anyone you really like? Edem didn't mean anything to you and I didn't mean anything to you," Selorm added.

Jo glared at him and I just lowered my head. This was unbelievable. Edem flipped the script. I never saw this coming. And Abena of all people! Since when had they been talking? Jo hugged me and I saw Selorm walk out the door. I was glad he left, because I started to cry right then. I cried so hard.

Edem's actions hurt me very badly. I was sad for a full day and then I knew I was going to make both he and Abena regret it. I was going to prove he had made a mistake. Prove he still wanted me and always would. Who was he to do this to me?

Two days later, he called and I asked him to come by. He did. This was going to be easier than I thought.

"You made a mistake, you know."

I didn't waste time.

He held my hand. "Listen, we all know how you feel about Jon. I just know you wouldn't take this, us, anywhere."

"You don't know that. I said give me up until Sunday. You didn't wait."

He touched my hand. I stared down at it. I looked him

directly in the eyes. I gave him my best pained look. I looked away, closed my eyes and made him think I was holding back a tear. He touched my face. I walked away from him.

We were standing in front of my apartment building. It was late, past 11 P.M., and the street was dark. He was rumbling on about something and I ignored him.

"You need to go. I am tired. You made a mistake. That's all I wanted to say to you."

I walked him down the road to where the cab drivers lounged waiting for passengers. Then I stopped walking, bent over and shook my head. That killed him.

He pulled me towards him. "I love you. I am crazy about you. I just don't understand you. I didn't think you even cared or felt the same way."

He kissed me, and I let him. It took two days, two short days after he asked Abena out for him to say those words to me, to me. As he held me, I stared out into space. This was really just the beginning.

"I will leave her today."

God forbid, like I wanted him.

"I don't want to be with you. You made a choice. You couldn't be patient. You couldn't wait. How? I can't let that go. You need to go home."

"Rabbie…"

He kissed me again and I didn't stop him. The more he kissed me, the more he would know he had messed up. She couldn't possibly be a better kisser. I knew that.

Eventually I managed to say bye, and I left him at the junction, looking confused. Confusion was good. Confusion was only the beginning.

During the last week before we left to school, Edem was around all the time. I continued to tangle the possibility of us together, but I made it clear it was never going to happen. I would kiss him and I would let him kiss me. I let him hold me, call me and be around. Yet I managed to remain aloof. I wanted to hurt him so badly. And I had the time and the patience for it all.

Friends Become Bitches Again

Edem dating Abena split our group up. At first it was subtle and not full blown. There was camp Rabbie, with Jo, Nana, Ajua and Maame; and camp Abena, with Cami and Sammi. I think throughout our previous two years, we had really just been trying to be friends. There was always a "them" and "us" mentality. Sammi acted neutral most of the time, but I always knew where her allegiances were. The group's bond was thin to begin with, so it was perfectly natural it wouldn't be strong enough to withstand the consequences of Edem and Abena.

I ignored Abena completely for a long while. I was pissed. And I didn't care who it affected. But beyond being pissed I was a woman on a mission. I was going to have him so smitten and obsessed, she would have nothing significant left.

I'd look at Abena and be amused. What did she really think she had?

Knowing he was cheating on her with me gave me enormous pleasure. I would smile each time she got a letter from him and got all excited. In my hands, I held my own letter.

The goal was simple. I wanted his heart and then I wanted to crush it. She might have the title, but a title was nothing without true love. What use was it if he called you his girlfriend, yet he said "I love you" to another? What use was it, if he kissed and touched another girl the same way, if not with more intensity than he kissed you? Really, what use was it if he woke up thinking of me, while she woke up thinking of him? What use was it, if everyone knew, except her? She'd just be a fool. And I was determined to make both of them fools.

He messed with the wrong girl. And Abena deserved retribution just as he did. She knew Edem and I had been talking all year. She knew we were involved. She knew. This was completely territorial on her part. She probably wanted to prove a point. But that's the thing about starting fights. You have to be really certain whom to pick fights with. Girls are never strategic about how they attack others. It's all based on vindictiveness and emotions. But there's a vindictiveness scale; you might think you're at the top, but you have no clue which queen bee out there is off that chart. Abena actually erroneously thought she had something. Girls. Such mindless fools.

The game was on.

Oh, the Tangled Web We Weave

In a terrible twist, which I sincerely hope had nothing to do with my actions, Selorm started to cheat on Jo with Sammi. That's the thing about love that so many girls fail to understand. Selorm was, and always had been, in love and obsessed with Sammi. He could date another girl, but his heart was always with Sammi. And if you date a guy like that, you really can't win.

Sammi and I bonded over our indiscretions. It was so twisted, I can't understand how it happened. Sammi's best friend Abena was dating Edem, and Edem was cheating on her with me. And Sammi knew this. She knew and kept quiet because she was doing the same, with my best friend's boyfriend. How do we do these things? It's mind boggling. Was it boredom? I think we all just have wickedness in us. That's what it was.

Sammi and I found out about each other because it was inevitable. It was a very uncomfortable situation. This web I was in just didn't make sense. Selorm was with me, then with my best friend Jo, and now he was messing around with my new partner in crime, Sammi. And I was first with Selorm, then his friend Jon and now his best friend Edem. You just can't make this stuff up.

It was hard watching Jo go through her issues with Selorm, when I knew fully well why he was distracted.

It was hard to hear her say something like, "I haven't received a letter from Selorm in two weeks," when I knew Sammi had just gotten one. Another freaky part was Sammi and Jo lived in the same neighborhood. You could walk from Sammi's house to Jo's house in five minutes.

I don't know what Sammi's motivations were. I can only speak for myself. I suspected she wasn't in love with Selorm, but he was smitten with her. There is something primal and satisfying to have a guy kiss the ground you walk on, when he is supposed to be with someone else. Cheating is a terrible thing. There is no excusing it on so many grounds. But there is something about being the other woman that gives you a certain level of power and control that can be addictive. Here is a guy, who to the world, is supposed to be with this girl, yet his mind, body and soul is nowhere near her. And you know exactly whom he thinks about and how much he craves you but can't have you. Being the other woman only becomes problematic when you stupidly fall in love. Then there really is no difference between you and the girlfriend. Then he now has two whiny attention-seeking girls breathing down his neck. Being the other woman is only worth it if you are completely secure in your role and you want no more, and perhaps no less. Being the other woman only works if he is the lapdog and you are the vixen. At seventeen, I learnt that a little too early. And some lessons are hard to forget or change.

I did not want to be Edem's girlfriend. If I did, I would have said yes to him. My goal was to prove it didn't matter whom he was with; that just wasn't where he wanted to be. How does a seventeen-year-old come up with such a devious plan? I swear women are just born with an evil gene, and it can be triggered anytime.

All that was one of the most deliberate acts of malice I ever did. And it felt bloody darn good at the time.

Sammi and I usually met up to talk after visitors' day. We found a bench, and discussed everything. We would even read each other's letters from the boys who weren't ours. Benches are a good place to talk when you have a lot to hide. You can see everything around you, spanning 360 degrees. In a class, anyone could be behind a window or wall. In a dorm, anyone could be listening in the next bed. Benches in open spaces just worked, because we had a lot to hide.

When the boys came to visit, Sammi and I would look at each other. We didn't smile knowingly and we were never too obvious. We were pros.

Edem wrote all the time. And on Valentine's Day, it was a little too close for comfort. It was one of those few times I felt some pain. He bought Abena a huge teddy bear and flowers and chocolate. The first time I saw her teddy, I wanted to rip it apart. But then I got my little box. And there were two cards and a chain. In one of the cards was a long letter. He poured his heart out, said all the stuff he'd been saying for months. He loved me, he loved me, he loved me. I didn't reply. It was also one of the rare times I felt guilty. Teddy bear to one, and words of love to another, that was wrong. I was cold-hearted then, but for a second on that day, I felt sorry for her.

Jo unfortunately was in more pain than Abena was. Abena probably suspected Edem was cheating. But she had an oblivious attitude to it all that is disturbingly similar to that of a forty-five-year-old woman who discovers her husband is cheating but who really has no options so decides to turn a blind eye. I found it disturbing not because I wanted her to leave him. I honestly found it troubling because she was a woman, and I wanted her to have some damn dignity.

The Last Summer

The last summer of school eclipsed all the other summers. I had turned eighteen some months earlier; and turning eighteen was one of the biggest events of my teenage life. All my young life my mother's favorite words were, "You can't drive till you're eighteen, you can't go clubbing till you're eighteen, you can't have a boyfriend till you're eighteen, you can't stay over at friends till you're eighteen, you can't visit boys in their homes till you're eighteen, you can't… till you're eighteen."

Did she think I would never turn eighteen? I made a list of everything she forbade me to do, just waiting for when I turned eighteen. I was pretty obedient up until then. I did nothing (except kissing) right up until that summer. Then I started checking off each forbidden item, one after the other. I let loose.

First was the clubbing! We had twelve weekends during that summer, and I went clubbing every single Friday, Saturday and Sunday of those twelve weekends. Every single one, so that makes thirty-six club nights in one summer. And I didn't just club, I *really* clubbed. I was crawling home around 4 A.M. each night, tired and drained, but always ready to start it all over again. My clubbing life happened mainly because Abena had strict parents. She couldn't go anywhere. And Sammi had an overprotective mother as well. She could go out if she was with Abena, and Abena couldn't go out. Jo was usually at home too; she was her mother's only child. Ajua and I hardly saw each other over the summers. I saw Nana a few times, but not much. So with most of the girls unavailable, that left me to party with my undercover boy, Edem. Cami, very early on, joined the club bandwagon. That made things a tad bit complicated, but I didn't mind. In the weirdest way possible, Cami and I started to bond. It's interesting that flashing neon lights and loud music could turn bitch-turned-friend-turned-bitch back to friend. We actually became closer than we ever had been.

Cami and I started to visit each other. That was so strange. We had sleepovers, mainly because we were clubbing so much that we would end up crashing somewhere. And my mother couldn't talk, I was eighteen. I actually liked being with Cami. We just spent so much time together. It was almost like we were joined at the hip. We hung out at Selorm's house, Edem's house, my house, her end, anywhere and everywhere. We were on the phone with each other, talking endlessly. I never for a minute forgot that she was one of Abena's tightest friends. But I decided I had no direct beef with Cami and she knew how to party. Knowing how to party was really important on the friendship scale. I was still extra careful though.

I now had a dual life. On some nights, it was just the clandestine four—me, Edem, Selorm and Sammi. On other nights, it was the party four—me, Edem, Selorm and Cami. It was difficult keeping a straight head. Cami or Sammi; I had to remember who knew what and who didn't.

Beyond the fun, that summer also made one thing painfully clear—I was in love with Edem.

No Longer a Game

That summer, somewhere along the line, I will admit I forgot my own golden rule: don't fall in love. It couldn't be helped. I am, after all, a woman. Even Julia Roberts kissed Richard Gere on the mouth. We can try, but we are and always will be emotional creatures.

There was now an emotional investment with Edem. On one hand, I felt loving Edem was a good thing; it meant I wasn't a complete stone-cold, heartless relationship wrecker. On the other hand, I now wanted a little bit more. For some weird reason, I didn't want a relationship. But I wanted more attention, more devotion... I just wanted more. As soon as you want more, you no longer hold all the cards. My pity and contempt for Abena turned briefly into understanding. I still thought Abena was an idiot for staying, but how different was I? I was an even bigger idiot for falling for him.

Edem and I were just spending so much time together. There was no time to pull back. He was like my best friend. I talked to him all the time. Even before anything ever became physical with us, we had a bond. We could talk, we could really talk. If I had never fallen for him, I would have been surprised. It wasn't a hard fall, not like the one for Jon, but it was still a fall.

So I let the words slip out of my stupid mouth. I told him I loved him.

We were lying on the sofa at my place. No one was home. It was just us. Selorm had been around for a while, but he'd left. We held hands and watched a movie. It felt so cozy. I half lay on him, my head on his shoulders. I placed my hand on his heart. He turned his head and kissed me. It felt different, better and maybe that was because I knew I loved him. I knew it that second.

"I love you."

I don't use those words lightly. I never ever say it until I mean it. I have said those words to only five people in my life. And I meant it each time, very strongly.

He smiled and kissed me. "Say it again."

I smacked him. He was laughing.

"I am not going to say it again. You heard me."

"I did, but I want to be sure. I could be hearing things. You never say that. Actually, you've never said it before."

I didn't want to be teased at a moment like that but he made me smile.

"I love you," I said, smiling.

"God damn it!" He jumped up, acting all shocked. He turned off the TV. "Say it again, please."

I laughed with him. He was so funny. I decided to play along.

"I love you, love you, love you."

"Better than Jon?"

Ah, he had to go ruin it, didn't he?

"I'm sorry," he said, seeing the irritated look on my face. He stopped messing around and he came to sit next to me again. We kissed. I kissed him like I loved him. We kissed for a long time. Then he started touching me, slipped his hand underneath my top. I pulled back.

I was not a prude, but sex... That was a big deal. I didn't do below the neck, never had up until that point, not even with Jon.

"Don't do that," I said, taking his hand away.

"Come on," he said, kissing my neck and slipping his hand underneath my top again. The door opened just then and I pulled away. It was Selorm. He walked in and dropped himself on the sofa next to me.

"Hey," he said, looking at me, then Edem.

Every now and then, I wondered what Selorm thought, about me, and all that I was doing. I never asked, because I would probably never get a straight answer. But I knew he couldn't think good things about me. Selorm wasn't mean and neither did he really bear a grudge. I know that night with Jon still hurt him, and he probably wasn't thrilled about Edem and me either, but he didn't let on. Sometimes, he would pass a stupid comment, but most of the time, he just didn't let on. It rattled me a little. He blew up that Saturday two years ago and that was it. I wanted him still to be mad. It would just show he cared.

"Hey," I said back, looking at him, trying to unnerve him.

He turned his attention to Edem. "What's up? You ready to roll?"

"Rabbie just said she loves me."

Selorm looked at me silently. I closed my eyes and covered my face.

"Oh my goodness, do you have to tell everyone?" I wailed. I felt embarrassed.

"After what, a year and a half since you two started talking? That's great progress," Selorm said.

I stood up; I didn't like sitting between them.

"Progress huh, when he has a girlfriend."

"You don't want to be my girlfriend," Edem countered.

"How do you know?"

Everyone was quiet. And I knew I shouldn't have said that. Mistresses shouldn't ask for more. And for once, Edem didn't have a quick comeback. I had set the tone that I didn't want to be with him; I had made it clear this was just what it was, fun. Me saying I loved him, he could deal with. Me saying I may want to be his girlfriend—ah, that was a bit much for one day.

He got up and stood right in front of me. He kissed me. We kissed in front of Selorm a lot. It was impossible not to. They were together all the time. I had stopped feeling uncomfortable about it.

"I have to go now. I'll call you later tonight."

"Where are you going now, to see Abena?"

Oh I had to throw it all in there. Ruining moments is also a girl thing. We can never leave things as they are. I had to keep it coming. I was breaking all my rules. I never usually asked where he was going, or if he was with her or what was up with them. I never cared, and I always showed I didn't care what he did after he left me. And now for the first time in a long time, I was asking questions.

"Okay, I think this is my cue. I am going downstairs to wait, Edem. See you later, Rabbie."

Selorm strolled out and Edem and I continued staring at each other.

"You know I love you. You can't doubt that. I am crazy about you," he said.

Now that I had said mine, his words felt slightly empty. I believed him back when I didn't want him. Believing he loved me fueled my intentions to hurt him and her. But now that I loved him, I found it hard to believe he really loved me. Why was he still with her? Whether or not I wanted to be with him, why didn't he just leave her?

"Hey Rabbie, look at me. You do know I love you, don't you?"

"I don't know."

He shook his head and just stared at me. "You don't know, huh?"

"No, I don't know." I stared back.

"Okay."

He picked up his stuff and then walked out. I didn't follow.

I dropped on to the sofa and buried my face in it. Oh why, oh why? Then, minutes later, I bolted after him.

He and Selorm were walking down the street. I called his name. He turned, with this "what do you want" look on his face. My ego nearly made me turn around. My heart made me continue walking.

"I love you, that's all," I said.

"Cool," he said.

Selorm continued walking while Edem and I stared at each other.

"And I believe you love me," I continued.

He didn't budge.

"Listen, I don't have time to pamper you or say sweet things to you. This is the first time in how long that I have ever sounded insecure, and if you can't understand or deal with it, then that's really your problem," I snapped.

He kissed me. My lips are like honey to the boy bees. They can't resist, can they? We kissed for over ten minutes. Selorm's figure had disappeared down the street.

"God, you drive me crazy," he whispered.

Yes!

Saying I love you has the potential to make or break any type of relationship, most especially the "on the down low" type of affairs. My perspective was changed forever. I had made myself vulnerable. The evil no-good schemes were gone. I wanted him and I needed him, and I just couldn't deal with it. Being vulnerable means I let him get away with things I ordinarily would have skinned him alive for. And the worst thing Edem could do to me, he did.

Losing "it"

To tell this part of the story, I can't mince words. I can't pretend. I can't sugar coat it. I can only tell it as it is, no more and no less.

Summer 1997, months after I turned eighteen, I lost "it." I lost my virginity, to Edem. As much as I had used those words, told him I loved him, I really didn't want that important part of my life to happen the way it did.

I was in Edem's house. There were a bunch of people there. Selorm, Cami, Nana and her boyfriend Yaw, who was also a member of the posse, Nkrumah and one or two other guys. We watched TV, movies, ate, chatted and slowly, everyone started to leave. It was just Edem and me.

We went to his bedroom. I was hardly ever there. I just wasn't comfortable with bedrooms at that point. We lay on his bed, talking, and kissing. And then Edem got really pushy. His hands were all over me.

"Calm down, I don't want to do this."

"Come on, I won't do anything. I just want to touch you a little bit."

He was so aggressive and pushy. He grabbed my hair and pulled tight. I slapped him across the face and he snatched a piece of cloth, wrapped my hands and pinned it underneath my body, as he continued to pull at my hair.

"What the heck are you doing? Edem, this isn't funny! Let me go."

He didn't. He kept trying to kiss me and when I tried to pull my head away, he pulled my head back. My head was killing me. I had on fresh braids. That's the worst thing to pull. I thought my head was going to explode. His kissing got rough, his everything got rough.

I tried to kick and knead him with my legs but he sat on them. He was so strong—how could he be so strong? He wasn't a big guy.

"Edem, listen to me, stop this now, honestly, stop it."

I don't know how many times I said no; too many to count. I don't know how long it took for me to stop trying to fight him; too early for it to matter. I lost my spirit. I lost my interest. I was done. I was so tired; my head hurt so badly and my heart hurt even worse. I had tears streaming down my face and he wouldn't stop. I said no and he wouldn't stop. I loved him—why would he do this to me? He didn't stop. He just didn't.

I have buried the rest of the details in places I can't dig up. I can't find those memories. I am not sure I really want to. For days I felt I should have fought harder. And for days I felt it was my fault. My mind was reeling, my heart was stone cold. The mind twists information till what is real and what is not is blurred. I tried so hard to excuse what he had done. I told Nana, but I really couldn't tell anyone else, because I still loved him, and for some reason my heart and my mind couldn't adjust to what had just happened.

What Edem did ended us, but not completely that summer. I refused to believe what had happened. I put it in a black box and buried it and pretended it had never happened. But you can only pretend for so long.

Tei

A few days after the Edem fiasco, I went to visit Cami. I needed to be out of my house and I wanted to be inaccessible. That's how and when one of the most important people in my history happened to me. My love number three.

Cami was dating an older guy, a much older guy. He was at least five years older, if not more, and we were only eighteen. His name was Sonny. Cami and Sonny lived only a few houses apart. She had started to spend a lot of time there. I knew about him, but I had never met him. The day I went over, Cami took me over to meet him. I wasn't that thrilled. I just wanted to lie on her bed, sleep and pretend life was not so bad.

"Cami! I was just going to call you!"

A big guy opened the gate. Sonny wasn't that huge, but he was bulky and well built. I just couldn't get it out of my head that he was older. We went in to the house and round the back. Sonny had his room separate from the main house. Older guys must need a lot of privacy, I thought.

Even as we followed him, I was tired. This was not a good idea. I didn't want to be there anymore.

We got to Sonny's door and a fair, good-looking guy stepped out just then. I am not sure what I noticed first. There was the face. He was really chiseled, with such a strong jawline. He had these eyes that just pulled mine in. And then there was the body. He was shirtless and his stomach was flat, his six pack perfectly carved. I had never seen a six pack before. I was so physically enamored with him that I froze for a second. His eyes fell on me and he smiled. That sealed the deal. He was so good looking. And so well built! Older men, such a lovely species! Boys just didn't look like this.

"Hi," he said, looking at me.

"Hi." My voice was a squeak.

"Oh Rabbie, this is Sonny's room-mate, Tei," Cami said.

I couldn't take my eyes off him. I kept looking at his chest.

"Can I touch?" I asked.

Tei and Sonny laughed, and Cami looked at me strangely. Yes, it was a strange moment. I touched his chest, his stomach, it was so hard. Goodness!

"Anything else I can help you with?"

He looked so amused. I smiled.

The next minute his chiseled arms were around me and he lifted me high off the ground. I burst into laughter. Then he set me down and kissed me hard. Darn it! Where had he been the last two years?

That was just it, the beginning of years of love, drama and heartache.

Tei and I exchanged numbers that afternoon. I liked him, he liked me. I didn't have much time left before school. But we spent most of that time together. It wasn't much. A big part of me was torn and confused. He was older. He seemed too suave and calculated, while coming across as smitten. He knew what he was doing, and I couldn't figure out what that was. Whatever it was, I really liked him. But at the time, it didn't feel like it was going to go anywhere. I just couldn't find the energy to go through something else. He was good looking, for sure, best body I had seen in ages. Jon had a great body. But he was still a boy. And this man, this twenty-three-year-old, looked so good, I was fascinated.

When we got back to school, I was different. Summers always changed me. New alliances had been formed which were going to be tested. Cami was back with Abena now, but we still saw each other in a different light. We had Sonny and Tei to talk about.

Sammi and I had Edem and Selorm to talk about. Nana and I had Yaw and Edem to talk about. My life was so hard to keep up with. And I did try to keep it all together. I don't know what reasoning I was using, but I let Edem back in my life. The letters, notes and words of love started again. We did not confront what had happened, mainly because I didn't confront it. I didn't give him what he deserved, which should have been to cut him off completely, for good. I was confused, naïve and wrought. I didn't know how to deal with what had happened, so I did the worst thing. I let it go. I remember telling him he had hurt me. But he never took me seriously, and I still stuck around.

I had walked away from Jon while he was kneeling in front of me, begging, when I loved him more than anything in the world, and yet Edem forced himself on me, and I couldn't write him off. It didn't make any sense. School and those three boys had changed me. I was needy. Horrible, but yes, I wanted to be wanted.

So I had Edem and Tei on my mind. Tei was so sweet and so thoughtful, it was unbelievable. I called him each weekend. I loved hearing his voice. And his letters! The first one was typed, but the rest all handwritten. His handwriting reeked romance. He was like me; he knew what to say and how to say it. He wrote the longest letters. They were like books, pages and pages. Edem never had the patience for long letters. Tei's letters were works of art. I started to fall in love with him just from those letters. Words are powerful. I have always known that. And his letters really proved that. Here was a guy I had barely spent any physical time with, but from his letters, I just started to care so much for him. I felt I knew him. And in a way, maybe I did, or maybe it was all just because I was needy.

Things completely changed when the love letter came.

Sometime in early October 1997, just a few months after I was back in school, Tei sent the love letter.

There was something about Tei that reminded me of Jon and Selorm. Jon said he loved me the first day we kissed. Tei and I kissed the first day we laid eyes on each other. Selorm and I had been thrown into our situation based on a random truth or dare. There was the spontaneity of those three situations. On the other hand, Edem and I had built our relationship over time. I spent more time with him than I did the others. It made me wonder if his was the real deal, if perhaps I was rushing into being with Tei.

In any case, the letter came, which changed how I felt completely.

I'm a writer; I know the power of words. I sometimes think I am immune to other people's words, but I am really not. I can write letters that can make you think, cry, hate, love and every other emotion in between. For some time in boarding school, I was writing poems and letters for other girls. A girl would come to me if she had a crush or was in love or just wanted to say something, and I would listen to her, and then write a poem or a letter. I could listen to someone, and feel what they were going through and put it in words. They were not my emotions, but I could still express them on paper. So I really should not have been floored by that letter. And yet I was.

The love letter was written on a medium-sized, three-by-four notepad, ten pages, back and front. His handwriting was cursive. He wrote like he was talking; you could almost hear the words from his mouth. He didn't start by saying he loved me, he built the story up. He started from when he met me, when we first kissed and the few kisses after that. He continued with how much he missed me, how he didn't understand it all, but he just wanted to be with me. It was a sweet flowing letter, and in the last paragraph, he said he loved me.

I think I must have shown that letter to at least a dozen girls. I guess I should be able to understand Jon showing my On Bended Knee letter to his people. For the next week or two, I slept with the letter under my pillow. I didn't say "I love you" back. Like I said, I am very selective with who gets those words. But nonetheless, I could appreciate being loved! By a chiseled older guy, no less!

A week or two after I got the love letter, I found out Abena had lost her virginity to Edem about the same week he did what he did to me. That discovery ripped through my already broken heart. That was what I needed to end all that drama. It just wasn't worth it. Sometime after that, Abena and I had a heart to heart. We didn't resolve to be best buddies, but we decided we had both not done right by each other. It was a hard conversation. I didn't admit the affair outright, but she knew. There was no doubt about it. She knew everything. I suspected she'd known for a long while.

"So I think it's time we talked, don't you?"

Abena was sitting next to me. Why did she stay in the relationship? I just never understood that. The way she clung so tightly to him didn't make sense. Abena said she wanted to be friends. I decided to give it a try. For me, I was over and done with that idiot. It was a painful realization, but any emotions I felt were out the door. I just felt pity for her. Edem just wasn't worth it. I could never be in a relationship with someone like that.

The "Nine" got slightly put back together. It didn't feel true, or sincere, or even realistic. There were still secrets, still suspicions, still little cliques within cliques. But we decided to pretend to try.

Batting for the Other Team

When I was younger, I used to think God got bored, just like everyone else. I just didn't understand some of the things that happened to me. Honestly, what was the point, what was the reasoning? What did He want me to learn, by taking people from me? A short week or two after discovering Edem was really just an ass, Tei sent another letter. This one went straight to the point. He was leaving the country. He was leaving for America, for good. Since I had been in school, he had only come to visit twice. I had been looking forward to the Christmas, looking forward to spending some more time with him. I was done with boarding school in December. I was going home! I was going to have all the time in the world, to spend with him, to build a steady relationship. I was going to have a chance to be away from girls and drama. He was supposed to be my chance at a real grown-up relationship. Did this really have to happen, now?

I cried after I read that letter. I figured this was it. Just as I was trying to break free of the group, just as I found someone breathtakingly beautiful and mature and not in my circle, I was being cursed. This was karma on some level. I really felt Tei and I had a chance to be something good, and this had to happen. Right now, to cap off everything that had happened in the last month or two. Could I ever be really happy? Were guys even meant for me?

I was in the library, feeling stressed, depressed and almost suicidal. Tei had left. I said bye to him the day before on the phone. I was really depressed. I had completely stopped talking to Edem, and trying to be friends with Abena and her crew was also tiring. Jo and Selorm were struggling. And I had my finals in less than a month. My future depended on this exam. The pressure was insane. I had to prove myself and yet I couldn't study or think. Everything was falling apart. Life couldn't be any worse.

I was sitting at the window on the second floor. My books

were spread out before me, but I had been staring out at the trees for, like, thirty minutes. My mind was all over the place. I took a deep breath and closed my eyes. I had to find my focus. I had to get back to basics. School was the most important thing in the world. I had to try to remember that. But I was an eighteen-year-old, in pain, depressed, burdened by my mistakes.

"Hey, you've been staring out forever!"

I snapped back at the sound of Nana's voice. She was trying to suppress a laugh.

I kissed my teeth and shook my head. "I can't study, seriously. I am going to fail."

"Of course you're not. What are you reading now?"

"Science," I said.

"Ah, that's enough to drive anyone insane."

I laughed a little and put my head on the table, face down. I just couldn't deal.

"Let's take a break. Let's go to your dorm. I need a nap."

"We're not supposed to be in the dorms now."

"Okay, you must be really depressed if you're concerned about that! Come on, no one ever watches your block."

I laughed. A girl in the corner glared at me and I shot a glare back, daring her to say something. I wasn't in the mood to be messed with.

We left our books at our spots and got up. I was glad she was dragging me away. Maybe the walk back to the dorm would help.

She started talking a lot about Yaw when we were walking. I preferred listening to her than digging deep and discussing anything on my mind. I was just so stressed by it all.

We got to my dorm and Nana stretched out on my bed. I lay on Afua's bed, which was right next to mine. I was deep in thought but Nana was still talking. I couldn't really hear what she was saying. Then I caught this bit.

"Have you ever kissed a girl?"

I snapped out of my reverie.

"What? No, of course not," I said, surprised.

"Not even Esi?"

"Are you serious? No, of course not," I answered, wondering where she was going with all this. I was frowning as I looked at her.

"Did you hear something about Esi and me?" I asked.

She shook her head and didn't say more.

"Come on, you can't just ask me something like that and leave it hanging."

"Maame and I kissed last week."

"*What?*" I shouted. Nana placed her finger on her lips, to shush me. I lowered my voice, and turned on my side to look at her. "Are you serious? You and Maame?"

She nodded mischievously.

My mouth dropped open. Wow. Where had I been while all this was going on? Of course, there are all kinds of rumors about things that can happen in an all-girls' boarding school, but I didn't expect to hear this from one of my closest friends. When did this happen?

"She wasn't exactly my first though, or I hers," Nana added.

I was beyond stunned right now. "I see."

I sat upright on the bed, waiting for her to divulge more. This was definitely better than studying, or thinking about Tei or Edem or whoever else.

She had a really mischievous look on her face. I knew there was more.

"Come on, tell me. Did you just kiss?"

"I am not going to kiss and tell."

"But you just did. Adding a few more details really won't make a difference."

She sat up on the bed and stretched her arms. There was this look on her face that I just couldn't figure out. She was staring at me in a way that I couldn't place. What else could there be?

She got up, walked to the window and peeked out.

"There's no one listening, just tell me." I was so curious. I just wanted her to spill it.

She came to sit beside me, that naughty look still on her face. Something was going on in her head.

"It's not something I want to say, it's something I want to do."

Oh, you gotta be kidding. I knew exactly what was on her mind!

"Uh, hey, I am not sure…"

My voice trailed off as Nana's lips landed on mine. I didn't kiss her back, at first. Then she kissed me a little harder and my lips fell apart. I am not exactly sure why I did it. I wasn't exactly curious. I didn't wake up thinking, oh, I'm going to kiss a girl today. I pulled back a little and then she stopped.

It was so awkward. I looked at her and she looked at me. She tried to smile. I tried to smile. I turned my eyes away from her, towards the floor, and then she kissed me again. I kissed her back a little more this time. What the heck, huh. One kiss or three kisses, I had still kissed a girl. Stopping now really wouldn't change the facts much.

We lay stretched out on Afua's bed together and kissed a little bit more. I was so nervous I started to shake a little. This wasn't an adventure I wanted to pursue too much. I could chalk it down in my memory that I had done what is suspected of all boarding school girls, I had kissed a girl. I was ready to end it right there.

"We should get back to the library. We left our stuff there, and people are going to head back this way soon. And we really don't want to be here. And we need to study. And I have some phone calls to make too. I am sure the queue will be insane."

Nana laughed at my ramblings. And I laughed too. I sounded ridiculous, I knew that.

"Calm down. We didn't do anything. Clothes remained on, didn't they?"

"Yeah."

I wanted to ask her questions. Who else had she done this with? How many? How far did they go? Did that mean she was officially into women now? That couldn't be. Nana loved boys. I couldn't ask any of my questions. I wasn't sure I really wanted the answers. We got up and straightened our clothes and then gave each other a quick kiss. After almost three years of boarding school, this had to happen when I had what, four weeks to go. That was it, my foray into experimentation.

Things were a little awkward and strained between Nana and me after that. You really can't kiss your best friend of the same sex and expect things to be exactly the same. My over-imaginative mind went into hyperdrive. I was worse than Sherlock Holmes. I watched each of the girls with a hawk eye. Ajua and Maame, they were so close. Had they been doing this too? Every girl Nana and Maame spoke to, or held hands with, I became suspicious of. Where were they going? What was going on? And it was worse when Nana and Maame were missing from anything we were doing. Were they at it again? How far did they take it? I tried to avoid being completely alone with Nana. It was just nerves really. We got into a few tiffs. I think most of them were really nothing. We just didn't know how to move on. I wondered how she and Maame did it.

The SSSCE exams came and went. I was a nervous wreck the entire two weeks. If I had had long hair then, I would have pulled every strand out. I prayed each day to go back in time. I had wasted so much time that could have been spent studying and learning. I hated myself that I hadn't done enough. This would have been a complete breeze, nine straight As, if I hadn't played that truth or dare in Lynn's house. That was really my downfall. Nothing had been right since. I was never one hundred per cent confident on any of those papers. Having smart genes can get you to a point, and the rest is all effort. I always try and put it in this way—studying a month ahead for an exam would guarantee me a straight A, no two ways about it. If I study a week before, or even two days before, I wouldn't fail, although if life was fair, I should fail, but instead I can get a B+, if not an A-. I knew if I had spent the last three years completely focused on school, I wouldn't fret a single minute. And I badly wanted that lost time back. All the unnecessary stuff that had happened would always be an interest-ing chapter in creating the person I am today, blah blah and plain bollocks, complete waste of time. I should have studied like a maniac.

By the time the exams were over, I needed to de-stress so badly. It was great we were given a weekend off, to spend at the beach. That was really good for me. I just let go and completely emptied my mind and soul. I was so done with thinking and analyzing and stressing. But sometimes emptying your mind and soul just creates room for more to come crawling in.

Ajua, Maame and I sat in the school church. I have no idea what we were doing there—the end of an evening service, maybe. There were other girls milling around. The beach trip had been earlier that day, and we were chatting and gossiping and talking about going home. I was hyped. We had only a few nights left in school. This boarding school crap was finally over.

"Are you guys just going to bed?" I asked them.

"We're going to listen to some music in Nana's room. I think Nkrumah has some home-cooked food. I am starved. You should come." That was Ajua.

I turned to look at Maame. She shrugged.

"Come on, it's our last Saturday. Let's hang out. If Maame won't come, Rabbie, you come."

I looked at Maame again and she reached for my hands.

"Let's go to my dorm, talk a bit and then you can go join the others later? I am just not in the mood."

"Sure."

Ajua looked irritated and she rolled her eyes.

"Alright, I'll see you guys later."

She left in a huff and Maame shook her head.

"I am really just tired. I just want a quiet night, you know," she said.

I didn't exactly want a quiet night, but Maame was in a weird mood—she probably just needed to talk.

We left the church and went to her room. She had three other room-mates but no one was there yet. We lay on her bed and she started talking. I missed half of it. Most of her talk, I remember, was centered on school. She was reflecting, thinking, talking about people, the exams, and the future. I lay there just listening and my mind started to drift. It was all over, wasn't it? Three years of Wesley Girls High School, all the bells and rules and studying and teachers, it was all over. And what did I have to look forward to? Nothing and no one.

I felt Maame pull my arms around her and I froze a little bit. Ah, you gotta be kidding me. Her bed was against the wall and I lay with my back pressed against the wall. She was in front of me, facing away, talking, when she reached behind and pulled my right arm around her. I decided to relax a little. She was in a vulnerable state. Plus any minute others would come in. She wouldn't try anything.

So I held her and we talked. She sounded pretty sad, and I had to listen. How could I not? Her back was pressed against me.

The lights-out bell rang and a few minutes later her room-mates milled in. No one said anything. Everyone in the room chatted together for a while, till the second lights-out bell sounded.

It felt strangely relaxing to be lying there with her like that. I closed my eyes for a bit and we both lay there quietly.

After half an hour or so, I felt her kissing me. And it still felt strangely normal. I sort of figured out why it felt so normal. It was her whole vulnerable sad demeanor. It was such a pull. That's why guys love vulnerable girls, isn't it? There is something about a girl who seems to need you, who seems to be completely helpless and sad. And Maame was so small, physically. Guys want to be needed, want to put their arms around someone and comfort them. And the tomboy in me was a little drawn to her "lost girl" mood. But she definitely had complete control over the situation. That's another thing about guys and vulnerable girls. Guys assume they're in control, assume the girl is completely helpless, but that's usually never the case. And it was the same here. Like most guys who think they're playing the hero, I was just an actor in a well-staged play. The lights were off, it was pitch black. She had shed a tear or two which made me hold her even tighter. The kissing had only been a natural progression. In my mind, I forgot for a minute that this wasn't her first time, that there had been Nana, but that hadn't been her first either. We kissed practically all night. Clothes didn't come off. It was just a very strange but very natural night.

I knew in my mind I wasn't going to do this ever again. I had thought Nana was the end of it, but I knew Maame was definitely the end of it. I loved boys. That was not even debatable. Even if they broke my heart and ripped it to shreds, they weren't going to get rid of me. I was prepared to try again, to find a guy and start all over. And perhaps, I could do the vulnerable thing. No need to be hardcore all the time. I was prepared to give guys another shot.

Selorm, Part Two

Okay, okay, I know what you're thinking. What is wrong with her? I really wish I could give you an answer but I can't. I honestly can't, it's not even a ploy.

Round two with Selorm was unplanned. When I finished boarding school, I had a renewed interest in guys and I was eager to meet someone new and step out of the circle. Those were my intentions. But intentions are one thing, aren't they?

Jo was applying for US undergrad schools and I was trying to help a little. She had actually started the process when we were still in school. I hadn't really thought about going abroad for school. I knew my mother couldn't afford it, so why bother? Jo's departure was almost certain. She had a school, and she was going to leave in a few months. So I started to spend some more time over at her end. Since Jo lived in the same neighborhood as Sammi and Abena, I started to see them a little more too. We all just hung out, Sammi, Cami, Abena, Jo and I. We would rent movies, go clubbing and just hang out. Nana and I started to spend a little more time together too.

Selorm, Edem and I and the rest of the group became friends again. Those were just fun times. We were always trooping in and out of someone's house. I was really having a good time. All over the place with just about everyone. I put in some extra bonding time here and there. No school, no work, nothing, just plain nothing. There was nothing like the first half of 1998, it was almost perfect.

Jo and Selorm broke up towards the end of 1997, towards the end of boarding school. There was no fighting the force that was Sammi. Sammi and Selorm never dated officially, but that bond they had just took a toll on Jo and Selorm's relationship. I think Jo decided she really couldn't deal. I felt sorry for her. She and Selorm had been a really cute couple.

Sometime early in 1998, Selorm and I started to spend more

time together. His mother had a magazine and I wanted to get into writing and publications. I joined a group of kids who wanted to start a magazine and I figured hooking up with his mother would be a good idea too. She was really sweet, beautiful and young, and pretty cool with me. So someway, somehow, I was over at his end more than I should have been and he started to come over to mine as well. The first few times he came over alone, I didn't really think much of it. We talked about writing and magazines and doing something exciting and fresh. We watched movies and we just had a cool time, till we started kissing again.

I can't justify it. I won't even try. Selorm to Jon to Edem and then back to Selorm? One group? I don't know if it was boredom, or maybe I harbored some latent feelings, or I yearned for some validation. Who knows? He would come over late, really late, and we would walk and talk and then kiss like crazy. It was all insane. I was back to having a secret and this time, I couldn't share with Sammi or anyone else. I do think Edem knew. Selorm could really never hide anything from him. It was clear from how Edem looked at us whenever we were all together. That made me feel uncomfortable and I wanted it all to end, this stupid cycle with these boys. It just had to end, now.

"How's the article going?"

I lay on Selorm's bed, and he lay beside me, kissing my neck, and trying to talk. I was a little spaced out, staring at the ceiling.

"It's going slow. I will probably have something ready for your mom on Friday though."

"She's psyched. She thinks you have potential."

I turned on my side and looked at him. He was so good looking and so sweet. Look at that face!

"She does? I hope I can be like her some day. I like your mother."

"She likes you too."

We stopped talking and focuses on kissing. I had never had any qualms about kissing Selorm.

He gently pushed me on to my back and started kissing me so gently. I liked it. Selorm was gentle and loving. He was kissing me and whispering sweet nothings in my ear. Then he slipped his hand underneath my top and touched my breasts. I was a little apprehensive when he started that. I really wasn't sure how far I wanted to go with him. But I liked the way he touched me. He didn't rush, and just like our first kiss, he seemed a little nervous, which was so endearing.

We kissed for what felt like ages, and then our clothes started to come off.

"I don't know if I want to do this," I murmured.

"We can stop, okay? Just tell me."

He looked at me with his big eyes and I melted. We kept kissing and the clothes kept coming off. Selorm had a beautiful body. He didn't have a ripped chest like Tei, but oh my goodness, he had a package down there that must have been made in heaven.

I couldn't believe this was happening. We were completely naked at this point. Was I really going to do this? Could I possibly? It was one thing to kiss a group of guy friends, but sleeping with them? Sex had never been part of my equation. What happened with Edem was not my choice, and I never had control over that. But this time, if I wanted Selorm to stop, he would. I felt him kissing my stomach, and then my breasts. But as I kept touching him, my mind started to drift. I really couldn't do this. I closed my eyes, trying to stop the tears I felt behind my eyelids. I really couldn't do this.

My eyes flew open and I pulled him up to me.

"I can't do this."

"Baby, come on."

He kissed me. It felt good to be lying there with him. But I had to be strong.

"I just can't."

"God."

He said it softly, almost like he was in pain. And he could have been. He was so hard and so ready.

"Are you really sure?"

I nodded. He closed his eyes and took a deep breath. Then he lay next to me silently.

"I am sorry," I mumbled.

"Tell me what's wrong."

"I don't know."

"Is this because of Edem, or Jon?"

Maybe it was. All I knew was that I just didn't feel it was right. It wasn't like I had made a resolution not to have sex for the rest of my life. I just did not want it to be noted that I had sex with two friends. And there was also Jo. I wasn't sure if they had had sex or not, but they had dated for close to two years. That counted for something. Once Selorm and I did it, there was no going back.

"I've made a lot of mistakes, and I don't want this to be one of them," I said.

"This wouldn't be a mistake. I like you, I really do. I wouldn't hurt you."

I took a deep breath. Be strong, be strong. I got up from the bed and started pulling my clothes on.

"Don't do this," he whispered.

"I'm sorry, I really am. But I just can't do this. It doesn't make any sense. You know that. This is messed up. We shouldn't do this. There's Edem, Jon, Sammi, Jo... come on."

"I really don't care about any of them."

"That's a lie. You care, and I care too. We just can't do this. And not just this, but I think we need to stop with the whole thing—the kissing and the late night walks, and everything."

"Were you just leading me on?"

"What? No, no, come on. This just isn't right."

"I hear you."

He got up and started to get dressed as well. He was upset. And I wished I could do something, but having sex with him wasn't going to be it. I just wasn't prepared for that.

"I'm gonna go home now," I said.

He looked at me quietly.

"Stay a bit, we can just watch TV."

He gave me a light kiss on the mouth and I didn't stop him. We sat and watched TV silently in the living room. Then his brother and mother came home. I chatted with them for a bit and then Selorm walked me to get a cab.

"I'll call you," I said.

He grinned and shook his head. "I know you won't."

"We can be friends," I tried again.

He laughed a little. He just looked so hurt. "Yeah, Rabbie, anything you want."

We stared at each other for a while and then he kissed me softly.

Jon, Part Two

I really couldn't make this stuff up even if I tried. This is what I mean by having so much baggage on my shoulders, nipping at me, dragging me down, preventing me from moving on. All this completely ridiculous and unnecessary stuff I kept getting myself into.

Selorm and I chilled on the communication front. Being around each other was not a healthy idea. I started spending a little more time at home, with my family. I just didn't want trouble. But trouble decided to come searching for me anyways.

Jon and I didn't completely stop talking after we broke up in 1995. It took a while, but we managed to keep things completely platonic, without fanfare or drama. During my time in boarding school, we sometimes ended up at the same parties and I actually didn't fall apart each time I saw him. I still cared deeply for him. A part of me knew I always would. And I left it at that, till early 1998.

A couple of weeks after Selorm and I said adieu—a slightly better one than broken beer bottles but still painful nonetheless— Jon started to come around my end. If I was a paranoid schizo-phrenic I would have thought it was all staged. How did they turn up one after the other like that? But I must say it wasn't like Jon and I never spoke. We had remained friends throughout the past two years. But we just never spent "alone" time together till that year.

It started just like regular visits, daytime visits. We'd talk, watch movies, have a laugh, go get some food and just sit in his car and talk. We never really talked about us, or about Edem or anything else that had happened. I wanted to bring all that up but it just didn't seem like the right time. We hung out with Lynn a bit, and a couple of other friends. Then we started just to hang by ourselves. It was fun, it felt right. I figured being friends could actually lead to something more. Maybe this would be it.

On some days, he'd teach me how to drive. I had a pretty good knack for it but I decided to try the witless female route, so he'd give me more lessons and hang around more. It was a week or two of slow casual hang-outs, nothing physical. It was amazing; we'd gone from being completely in love, completely obsessed with lip sucking, to now just driving around my neighborhood, with me burning out his clutch. He didn't ask questions about other people, I didn't ask questions about anyone either. He said he was single, I was single. Thinking about it, I had actually been single since we broke up. I never dated Edem, or Tei or Selorm. Jon was my one love. I could hook up with other people, but it was all really meaningless.

"Cholo died today. Simon fed him something that was poisonous."

He looked blank. "What the heck?"

I smiled. "My squirrel."

"You gave your squirrel my nickname? You're so silly."

"He was very special to me. I am really sad about it. We're having the funeral later today."

"You guys are such characters," he said, laughing.

"I'm serious, I am really sad about it."

"How many pets have you guys had, huh? There was a monkey, wasn't there? And you cried when he died. And what, the chameleon, I think you skipped school for that one."

I laughed a little; he was mocking me.

"I skipped school when the monkey died. Toffee, that was his name. He was a family member, you know. Even my mother cried."

"Like I said, you're all characters."

I smiled a little.

We were sitting in his car, parked outside the flat where I lived. I was sad about the squirrel, I wasn't kidding about that. But I decided to let him joke around. I was trying to tell him something about being sad, about losing "Cholo." He didn't quite get the angle I was coming from.

"Hey, I'll come to the funeral, okay?"

"Really? Are you serious?"

"Psyche!"

I smacked him and he just kept laughing. I smacked him across the face and he grabbed hold of my hands and pulled me to him, then he kissed me.

The earth stood still as we kissed. It had been two and a half years since we last kissed. It felt so good. We kissed long and deep and he held me tight.

Eventually we broke apart.

"I see you haven't lost your touch. That was good," I said, smiling.

He laughed. "You're really silly, you know."

"Although I think you're a little rusty. You haven't been kissing much, huh?"

He chuckled. "Oh, I've been kissing a whole lot."

"Ouch. Not the answer I was hoping for."

He kissed me again. "Come visit me tomorrow," he murmured.

I paused for only a split second. "Okay." I wasn't going to push him away this time.

"Cool. I gotta go now. Seph needs me for some errands. I'll see you tomorrow?"

I nodded. We kissed and hugged and then we said goodbye.

I watched him drive away, and my heart just kept beating so fast. Was this happening? I wasn't going to let this go. I swore it.

I got to Jon's place early afternoon. He was a little different. There was no kissing at the door. We hung out in his living room and watched TV and talked and joked. He had a few guy friends come through and we hung out. It wasn't exactly what I had been hoping for, but I toughed it out. When night started to fall, his friends left and we went to his bedroom.

"This used to be Seph's room," he said.

I looked around the large, extremely masculine room.

"Whoa, I can't imagine the stuff that's gone down here... if walls could talk."

"Ah, but you don't know what the new tenant has been doing either."

"You change the sheets at least, don't you?"

He laughed and pulled me on to the bed.

"I changed the sheets for you."

"Whatever."

"True."

"Doesn't smell like it."

"Ouch. That hurt."

He touched my face lightly and then he kissed me. I had really missed kissing him. I could have kissed him all night. But as I had come to learn through Edem and Selorm, boys didn't *just kiss* anymore.

I was so attracted to him. Our hands were all over each other. His kissing was still so awesome. His body was completely flawless. He had grown bigger, harder and even better to touch. He was down to his boxers and I was down to just my top. I was a little nervous. I wanted him to love me. And I wasn't sure if this was the right route. But I couldn't hold back. His touch wasn't as gentle as Selorm's, it was a little rough and I loved it. I loved his big hands. I loved the way he held my face, my neck, I loved the way he had control. Everything was frantic. I loved his perfectly formed ass. He was just so beautiful. I loved his arms, his chest, his flat belly and just about everything else.

"I'm a little nervous," I said.

"Your first time?" he asked.

I swallowed hard. This was not the time to bring up Edem. I prayed he wouldn't ask. I reached up and kissed him.

"We'll go slowly, okay?" he said.

I nodded. We kissed some more and he started touching me, trying to arouse me. We were both completely naked.

He pried my legs apart and slipped in. I felt a sharp pain and I cringed. Oh my God!

He kissed me. "Just try and relax, okay. It's okay. I won't hurt you."

Are you kidding? I nodded and bit my lower lip. He tried again and I closed my eyes as I felt pain again. Bloody hell! What the heck?

"Rabbie, you need to relax, okay. Look at me."

I opened my eyes. He was staring down at me.

"Relax," he whispered.

I wanted him to say more. I wanted him to say he loved me. If I heard that, if I felt the love, maybe I could relax then. We kissed, longer, deeper. He was touching me, trying to get me wet and ready. He kept whispering to me. He tried for a third time, and I knew it wasn't going to happen. I couldn't take half of him, maybe even a quarter. It hurt and I just tensed up. My body wasn't listening to me. I couldn't control it. He swore a little.

"I'm sorry," I muttered.

He lay beside me and held me.

"It's okay. It's okay. Is this your first time?"

I was silent.

"Not exactly," I said reluctantly.

I looked him in the eyes.

"You already know, don't you?" I asked.

"About Edem, sort of, but I wasn't sure."

"He forced himself on me."

"I heard that a little. But he denies it. Why would he do that though?"

I frowned. "What sort of question is that?"

"I mean, why would he do that? You guys had something, right?"

"I said no. I said no, several times. I kept saying no. He didn't have my permission," I said angrily.

Jon kept quiet. This was definitely not the conversation I wanted to have lying in bed naked with someone I was in love with. We lay there quietly for a while. I pulled a T-shirt on and he pulled his shorts on. We didn't say much.

I started to feel that Edem had emotionally and physically scarred me for life. My mind couldn't wrap itself around the idea of sleeping with Selorm and my body literally couldn't accept Jon. I was utterly shattered. I blamed Edem completely for both, especially for the Jon debacle. What Edem had done was wrong and as I lay in bed, I realized I should have done something back then. I really should have.

We just lay there for what seemed like forever. And then I fell asleep.

When my eyes opened I could hear voices. Seph was in the room. I was lying on the bed, half naked and Jon's older brother was right there. Jon was wearing just his shorts and he sat behind the computer, doing something. Seph stood behind him. I lifted myself a little.

"Hi, what's up?" Seph said.

I looked at him. Wasn't anyone slightly embarrassed? I smiled a little and said hi back then I pulled the covers up over my thighs. The two of them talked for a while and I just lay there. Eventually Seph left and then his little sister Lam walked right in. She came straight to the bed and sat next to me.

"Hey."

"Hey," I said.

"You've been asleep for, like, an hour."

I wanted to disappear into the floor then. She came in and saw me like that?

"Yeah, I was tired." I feigned a yawn.

"But you're awake now. I have a book. Do you want to read to me?"

I looked at the book. I remember, it was one of my favorites, a R.L. Stine book. Lam must have been, like, twelve. I don't know why she'd want me to read to her. I took the book all the same, and sat up next to her. She got under the covers. I read almost the entire book out loud, then I could hear her dad calling her name. Perfect—everyone was home. I hoped their dad hadn't walked in too. Lam got up from the bed and left.

"You must have been really tired," Jon said, looking at me from the desk.

"Not really."

I looked at him, hoping he'd say something sweet. But he was glued to the computer. One of his friends walked in right then. Didn't anyone knock?

"Jon, can you step out for just a sec?"

Jon pulled a T-shirt on and walked out and I just lay back. I wanted us to try again. I wanted us to try again very badly. I didn't want to leave like this. But everyone was home now, and his friends were out there too. It wasn't going to happen tonight. I got out of bed, and put the rest of my clothes on. I was disappointed. I didn't want this to go down like that. Jon was out there with his friends for a while, so eventually I stepped out. He was having some sort of argument with the guys. Temper,

temper. He looked at me, and saw I was dressed. A slight look of disappointment crossed his face, and then it was gone. Did he want me to stay?

"Hey, you ready to go? Give me a minute, okay?"

I nodded and went back into the room. Ten minutes later, he came in and pulled on jeans. He changed his T-shirt and I wondered where he was going next—to get it from somewhere else? I followed him out. Two of his friends were waiting by the car. I got into the front seat. The boys ended up talking most of the drive to my place. I didn't say much. I wasn't in the mood. It was raining really hard and I just wanted to be home. I needed to cry. I didn't feel much affection from him. At a point, he squeezed my hand briefly, and he glanced at me with a look in his eyes. But I couldn't figure him out anymore.

We got to my end and it was still pouring cats and dogs. Jon got out of the car with me and we both ran to the stairs.

"Damn it, this rain!" he cursed. He was soaked and so was I.

"Hey, I had a nice time, despite…" I said.

"Sure." He was nonchalant.

"I need you to believe me, about the Edem thing."

"Does it matter?"

I sighed. Of course it mattered.

"Don't worry about it. I have to go now, yeah."

I nodded. He touched my face and leaned forward. We kissed, short and sweet. I felt a little better. He had kissed me. That meant everything was fine, right? We kissed again, and then he was gone.

Big, Bold Gestures!

The next day, I didn't hear from Jon, and I didn't want to call. I stayed at home and just moped. Selorm called, but I didn't chat for long. I didn't answer the phone for the rest of the day. I stayed at home for days, ignoring everyone, staring long and hard at the phone, willing it to ring. For three days straight, there was nothing, no call, no visit. My heart was breaking all over again. What if we had sex? Would he have done this? Not called at all? Three days turned into four and then I called. He wasn't home. I left a message with Seph. This was absurd. I got naked for him. Didn't I deserve a phone call?

The days dragged into a week and I was ready to go insane. This could not be happening. I did not deserve this really. I called him once more, and once again, Seph picked it up. I began to feel Jon was avoiding my calls. But I didn't get it. What did I do? Just because that night hadn't worked out didn't mean it couldn't happen better another time. I felt it was insensitive on his part. I couldn't bear it.

"Hey, are you going to come eat?"

Jo, Afua and a couple of other girls were at my end, cooking. I couldn't really be bothered, but I decided to make an effort. The phone rang and I gestured to Jo to get it. I knew it wouldn't be Jon, so who cared.

"Hey Abena," Jo said. I rolled my eyes and shook my head frantically. I didn't want to talk.

"Rabbie is actually downstairs with some people. Are you guys coming here?"

Jo paused and then she looked at me with a huge question mark on her face.

"You're going to meet Jon and his girlfriend?" Jo said on the phone.

I dropped the plate I was holding and my whole world shattered with it. It felt like time stood still. I felt my heart actually stopped beating. I saw Afua rushing to clear up the mess, and she kept asking what was wrong, but I couldn't answer. I was frozen. Jo hung up and came to me. She wrapped her arms around me but I stepped away from her.

"What did she say, Jon's girlfriend? Is that what she said?" My voice was shrill.

"Yes, that's what she said. Bianca, from school."

"What? What?"

I think I was screaming at this point. Bianca had attended the same boarding school we did briefly. I became semi-friends with her. She and I had even done a performance together.

"Rabbie, you and Jon broke up years ago, right? What's going on?" That was Afua.

"Oh God, I was with him a week ago! One week. We started hanging out again, we started doing stuff again. This has to be a joke. Someone is playing with me!"

I sat down and buried my face in my hands. Shucks. The girls sat beside me, wanting details. I said the bare minimum, left out the failed sex attempt. They promptly bashed him, called him a loser. It wasn't comforting. I was so lost. I couldn't bring myself to have fun, or even try. I was so upset. I sat curled up on the sofa and the girls just ate and talked and then everyone had to split. I decided to follow Jo home. I just wanted to really let go and I didn't want anyone at home to see me.

We sat in front of Jo's house and whined wholeheartedly about guys.

"I really don't understand this. I mean obviously, he didn't just meet her within the last week. So they had been talking for a while, I'm sure. I mean, you don't just meet someone today, and then tomorrow she's your girlfriend."

"You and Jon happened like that, didn't it?"

I scowled. "I doubt this was the same."

"Whichever way, he really should have told you, said something or called you in the last week."

"That's what I don't understand! No call—I mean, why? I feel so sick, so played, so used. Was it on purpose?"

"Probably was. Guys!" Jo said.

I shook my head.

"Why would he? Like, I really want to understand this. What's the logic?"

"You need to let him go now. Hey, I'm trying to let Selorm go too."

"Huh?"

"I still care about him."

Gosh, I didn't need a guilt trip. I didn't want her to start talking about Selorm. I steered the conversation back to Jon.

"I love him so much, Jo, I love him so much. I've always loved him. I don't think I stopped. I can't deal with this."

I cried into her arms. I was so devastated.

"I need him back," I cried. "I want him back."

I cried and cried. My world was over.

The next morning, I had a thought. Big, bold gestures! I was going to show him I loved him. I didn't care who he was with. This was in no way similar to my reaction to Edem and Abena. This was Jon. I was completely in love with him and I wanted him back in my life. I really did. I had cried all night. I felt so bad. I wished the past hadn't happened. I wanted an explanation. Why didn't he want me? Why didn't he want the same thing? Why didn't he love me? How could he be over it all? Why couldn't I be over it too? But I just couldn't.

I lay on my sofa, one of my favorite places in the world, and listened to some R&B, one of my favorite pastimes. I had an idea: make a tape and say how I felt with songs. I went to get a blank cassette from my big brother's stash and then sat in front of the radio. My favorite midday show, *Slow Jams*, was on. I listened for the entire two hours, selecting songs, avoiding the commercials and talk. I put a pretty good tape together. Then I added an intro. That was the lamest part.

"I love you, Jon, I always will. I need you to believe me. No matter what I have done, or whatever happened in the past, I have always loved you, and I know I always will."

On the cassette sleeve, I wrote out the list of songs and added "For Jon." Perfect.

I didn't pause to think. I got up, grabbed some money and was out the door. Jon lived pretty far from me—in traffic, an hour or more. But it was morning, and traffic was light. I prayed he was home. I wanted to look him in the eyes, and I wanted to see if he really didn't care.

But as luck would have it, he wasn't home. No one was home, so I left the tape, sealed in an envelope with the security man. I made him promise to give it to Jon and only Jon. Then I went back home to mope.

Two days passed; nothing. I couldn't believe it. Not even a call? What was going on with him? I should have ended it there. But I was still obsessed. I think obsession is worse when you don't have answers. I just couldn't understand what had happened. Why had that night happened if he was with someone else, or talking to someone else?

I needed him to acknowledge it. So I did big bold gesture number two.

I have to say something right here. I would *never ever* advise anyone to do a big bold gesture, ever. If the person didn't love you before, a big bold gesture wouldn't make a darn difference. You watch enough movies and then you start to get absurd romantic ideas in your head. But that's what they are, absurd, nothing more. I lost my sanity and my logic. Me—smart, headstrong, independent me—reduced to a big love mess. Someone should have knocked me out cold. Why didn't they? I guess maybe because I wasn't sharing much with anyone.

So I did step two. I went and bought a lovey-dovey card, the worst type that could exist. Then I wrote a long letter, spewed my heart out and sealed it in the card. Oh, it actually gets worse. I went to Lam's school, Jon's sister, and left the card to be given to her personally. Yep, yep, I did all that, for a boy. Tragic! I can never live that one down. I don't really know if he ever got the card, but I left my name and a note for Lam, and I handed it personally to one of her teachers. Teachers were responsible people. I knew they probably gave it to her. I was pathetic. I was embarrassing. There are really no more words for it.

But I still didn't hear from him. How? It was unbelievable. All the same, I didn't know how to stop just yet. I needed to get a reaction. He couldn't be this heartless.

Edem called me at one point, and that's when his loose tongue started to roll.

"Are you okay? Honestly, are you okay?" He was being sarcastic.

"What are you talking about?"

"You made a cassette for Jon? Seriously, what was that?"

I closed my eyes. Fantastic! How could Jon tell Edem?

"That's really my business, isn't it?"

"Look, he's with Bianca. You need to let that go, man. I am saying this as a friend."

Yeah, whatever, you ruined my life.

"Are you there? Rabbie, this whole Jon thing, you have to end it. Hey, after all, your night together was a disaster. I thought that was funny. I can't believe you couldn't take him."

My whole world ended. Why would Jon do this? I hadn't breathed a word to anyone. How could he go talk about that? That was personal. I felt a headache coming on.

"I don't want to get into this now, Edem."

I could hear a couple of people talking in the background. Selorm's voice came through and then I heard Cami. Double fantastic! They all knew?

"This isn't funny, and I really don't want to be talking to you about this. And I don't think it's right that you guys are all there discussing my private life!"

Then I heard Abena's voice through the phone.

"Why's Rabbie still in love with Jon? I thought that was over?"

I could hear the sarcasm in her voice too.

I hung up. Jon was done. I was done pining. Talking about that night with Edem of all people and whoever else was wrong. I could imagine that Selorm knew too. What would he think? I rejected him and two weeks later, I was with Jon? I sat on the floor next to the phone and cried. There's a thin line between love and hate. So true, because five minutes ago I loved him, and now, I couldn't stand the thought of him. I couldn't believe he had done that. He tried to have sex with me, then he completely ignored me and, worse, he discussed our private moment with Edem, of all people? The same person I said forced me? What did they talk about? Did they make notes? Did they laugh? Bloody idiots, all of them! I hated Jon so much. He could go to hell.

Tei, Part Two

I know. I am about as tired as you with this cycle. But that's just the way it is.

Tei and I kept in touch minimally after he left. I spent the first part of the year messing with Selorm and then obsessing over Jon. I didn't have any mental or emotional room for a long-distance, doomed romance.

After Jon's unwarranted and horrible betrayal, I decided a physical liaison with anyone wouldn't work. Tei was safe. He was thousands of miles away—what was the worst that could happen?

We started communicating a lot more frequently. He was really good at that. He wrote incessantly—letters, cards, short notes—several times a week, I'd get something. We talked on the phone just as often too. I wasn't completely over what Jon had done, but it just felt good to have this distraction. And that's really how it started, a mere sweet distraction.

"Rabbie! What's up with you today?"

I liked Tei's voice. There was always some energy behind it, even when he was sweet-talking me. He never sounded down. Life was always peachy. How I envied him that.

"Just lounging, watching TV, reading, sleeping, missing you," I said.

"You have no idea how much I miss you, seriously. I can't even joke with that. I think I wake up each morning thinking about you."

It didn't matter whether he was telling the truth or not. He wasn't here. He could say what he wanted and I could say what I wanted too. But I knew, knew he had some feelings for me and I had feelings for him too. If he was right there with me, we would be together, there was no doubt about that.

"I wish you were here. Why did you have to leave?"

"I had to, Rabbie. I wish I was with you too. I miss kissing you."

I closed my eyes. Seriously, why wasn't this boy here with me? Why?

"How's Abena?" he asked.

I smiled. He called my mother Abena. It sounded cute when he said it. They'd never met, but he asked about her all the time.

"Abena is great, working too hard, as usual."

"And the rest of the crew?" he asked.

"Ah, everyone has a life except for me right now. I am the only aimless slob occupying space in this flat."

"So get a job. My girlfriend can't be slobbing about."

I paused. What did he just say?

"Your girlfriend?" I asked cautiously.

"My girlfriend, yeah, I thought you were my girlfriend."

"No, you haven't asked."

"I have to ask? I didn't know that. I just assumed, since I said I love you—although, since you haven't said the same back, I guess maybe you're right, I need to ask."

I laughed. "Ah yeah, you need to ask, so I can know if I've been cheating on you or not."

He laughed. "Wow, okay, let's make this official and formal then. Will you be my girlfriend?"

I giggled and said yes. It sounded so high schoolish and sweet. He was sweet and I cared about him, so why not?

I took my relationship with Tei very seriously. I told my family about it, and a few friends. I decided I didn't want girls in my business anymore. I wanted to put all that had happened in school behind me. I wrote him religiously and I spent all my nonexistent money on phone cards. And I was determined not to cheat on him. Here I was dating a guy I wasn't quite in love with, whom I wouldn't see for a very long time, and I was being monogamous. What was the use of kissing and sex anyways? The Bible was right; sex was just the root of all evil. It was so much better this way. My life was simpler.

Life was truly simpler for a while. Long-distance relationships are tough, no doubt about that. They take a toll on you physically, emotionally and mentally. All you want to do is be with that person. You obsess about what he or she is doing, who they're with, when you'll see them again and why they haven't called in a week. I wasn't really going through all that. I didn't quite care if he was having sex with someone else. It would be completely naïve and unrealistic of me to think he wasn't. He was a very sexual person. I also didn't care where he was or who he was with. Those were not my concerns at all. I knew he cared about me a lot. I knew he loved me. But I wasn't about to go down the path of obsessing and whining. I just wanted to take it one day at a time. Easier said than done!

After Jon, I had sort of decided I didn't want to be intimate with anyone. I swore off guys. But really, which girl doesn't do that? You get betrayed, heartbroken, mistreated and the mantra becomes "I am off boys, I swear! This is it!" Who are we kidding, really? I can't count how many times I have said that myself, or how many times I have heard close friends say that. It's the lamest, shortest declaration of war ever. I am not sure if I was falling for Tei, but I really couldn't deal with the fact that he wasn't here. I needed someone, someone to hold me, to hug me, to love me. Tei's letters weren't helping either. They were sometimes so sexual and his calls were driving me crazy. I really wanted to be good. But I was hurting. Jon had hurt me, Edem had hurt me, and I just wanted to be wanted and needed again. I wanted some sort of validation. I needed to be sure I was desirable and lovable. That's all I wanted.

I wouldn't call this next incident Selorm Part Three, because it was really nothing. But Selorm, I've realized, is a catalyst for any downward spiral. Any encounter with Selorm starts a series of events that I cannot control. He's always a prelude to something much bigger.

I haven't done Selorm much justice so far. He was a genuinely nice guy. He had, and still has, a kindness to him. He never acted in a judgmental way towards me, never snide or mean or dismissive. To be honest, it's hard to know what his thoughts are. Selorm and I are both silent people, and we carry our intentions and true thoughts close to our hearts.

He started to call every now and then. I could never discern a reason for his calls. I assumed he was just being kind. He never insinuated anything or suggested anything. He just called to talk. And we talked about very neutral stuff. He didn't ask about what had happened with Jon and he never brought up any of my embarrassing acts of love. But I knew he knew about them. One night he came over late. He was a little distraught, but he didn't say why. We went for a walk and he loosened up a little. He was just coming from Sammi's house and it hadn't gone well. I guess I sort of understood why he never judged me. He was in the same hopeless situation I was in. We were both in love with people who didn't love us back. He was a fool, just as I was.

"You know, Sammi doesn't love you. She's not going to love you."

We were sitting outside an uncompleted house in my neighborhood, perched on a large concrete block. He looked beaten but I had to say it. My words made him shake his head.

"I know. And you should know Jon doesn't love you. But he used to, he really used to. At least you have that, and no one can take that from you. He loved you before—but Sammi, on the other hand, I don't think she's ever felt that way about me."

I knew Jon didn't love me anymore. It was painfully clear. But knowing the truth doesn't necessarily mean your feelings end right there and then.

Selorm put his arms around me and we hugged. Why couldn't it be Jon right here? And perhaps he thought the same thing about Sammi.

"It's going to take a while for me to get over him. I mean, sometimes I think I am, sometimes I hate him, but who knows," I said sadly.

He kissed my cheek, and pulled me closer. Kissing Selorm that night was really nothing. We were both in pain. We both wanted to be needed, even for a brief moment. We didn't love each other, it was never like that. Our kiss that night was needy and desperate. We kissed like there was no tomorrow. We were out there for hours, just kissing. But our hearts weren't really there.

"We can't be doing this."

He nodded. I needed him to understand that. We couldn't keep doing this. I wasn't going to be with someone who I knew for sure loved someone else. And no matter what, he just wasn't going to be Jon for me. And being with him reminded me of that.

"Friends?" he asked.

I smiled. "Always, you know that, always friends."

We hugged and then we went our separate ways, for good this time.

So I Creep, Yeah, Yeah

I didn't count the night with Selorm as cheating. Three years ago I made an irreversible mistake of confessing a stupid kiss. There would be no confessions this time. I conditioned myself to understand that Tei wasn't here, and as much as I cared about him and our relationship, I wanted to be back in play. And my conscience was completely okay with that.

The girls were scattered all over the place. Ajua was working, Nana was working, Afua was out of town, Jo was focused on getting into undergrad, Maame had some beau she hadn't introduced us to and Abena and her group I really didn't give a rat's ass about. Cami, well, I can't explain it… we bonded again. She started to come around, I started to go around, it just happened. I still didn't feel like I trusted her completely, but we were friends. My family got to know her better than they got to know anyone else. We were practically joined at the hip. We did everything together. We started to roll with different people, which was the fun part. There was no core group of guys. We met new people and we hang out with anyone we wanted to hung out with. We had "adventures" all the time. Those were really fun times.

That's how Kwame entered my life. Kwame lived in my neighborhood. His sister and I were good friends; she had been in Wesley Girls as well. Kwame was also friends with my older brother Josh; Kwame, Junior and Amo, Junior's best friend, were the three musketeers. It was perfectly natural that our paths would cross. Junior and I hadn't severed ties completely. He was my brother's friend too and he came around to visit a lot. And Amo and I had been friends years ago.

When I met Kwame, I didn't think anything of him except he was joined to Amo's hip almost as bad as Cami was joined to mine.

He was a really good-looking boy, and well built. We hit it off immediately. It was pure flirtation from the start. Better yet, there were no games. We both knew what we wanted.

"What are you girls doing tonight?" Amo asked.

Cami, Amo, Kwame and I were lounging in my living room. I was half lying on Kwame, and Amo and Cami were sitting together. I am not sure if there was something going on with them, but I really didn't care.

"Rabbie and I are going to Groove FM, we're helping one of the DJs tonight," said Cami.

"We could always do that another night," I said and squeezed Kwame's hand. He chuckled and smiled at me.

"So do you want to hang with us tonight?" Kwame was looking at me as he asked.

I winked and nodded. I was just starting to feel good again. Here was a good-looking older guy who was interested in me. What Tei didn't know wouldn't hurt him.

Kwame and Amo picked Cami and I up that night from my end. We were both in a hyper mood. We'd been talking to our friend Steve at Groove FM and Steve was going to play some songs for the four of us. Steve played about three songs for us, songs we personally requested, and each time he said our names, we would just scream and shout in the car. I was texting everyone I knew to listen to the radio that night. The night started pretty good.

No one was home at Kwame's place and I figured the guys had probably set that up so they could be alone with us. I didn't care. I had no conflicting feelings about what was going to happen. We sat in the living room and talked a bit. I nestled in Kwame's arms as he and Amo drank beer and told stories of school. I wasn't really interested in the stories. It was like I was on drugs or something. I just wanted Kwame. All this talk and nonsense was a waste of time.

About half an hour after we got there, the lights went off. The country was going through random power outages at the time. It was absolute perfect timing. I couldn't have set it up any better.

"Come on, let's go look for candles."

Kwame held my hand and we walked off, leaving Amo and Cami sitting in the dark. We went into his bedroom and I sat on the bed as he rummaged through his drawers.

"You keep candles in your bedroom?"

"I know I have a few somewhere. Ah ha, here we go!"

He turned and smiled at me, holding two candles in his hands. I didn't feel like going back to the living room. I kicked off my slippers and slid further up the bed. He closed his door and then I heard the lock turn. He had a mind as depraved as mine. He lit the candles, set them on the dresser and then slowly took his shirt off.

"Are you giving me a striptease?" I asked, laughing.

"I give you one, you give me one."

I grinned. He was so sexy. He did his best full monty impersonation as he slowly took off each item of clothing. He had a really good chiseled body. When he was down to his boxers he climbed on top of me.

"You're still dressed."

"Show me how it's done," I said.

He kissed me. Kwame kissed in a different way. It was downright sensual, from the first touch of our lips to having his tongue in my mouth. He was a pro; there was no doubt about that. He just validated my thinking that older guys were just so much better in every way. They knew how to kiss, they knew how to touch and they just knew how to make a girl feel good. He took my clothes off slowly. Even though Cami and Amo were out there, we still didn't rush through anything. I figured they were probably up to no good themselves.

I had a brief panic attack as all my clothes came off. This was going to be my third try after Edem. Selorm had been an emotional block, Jon a physical block, but this one had to be perfect. I wanted this to happen, badly. He had my senses on fire.

But it wasn't perfect. As soon as Kwame entered me, I cringed, but he didn't stop. He pushed himself all the way in and I stopped breathing for a split second. What in the world was wrong? The pain was excruciating but subsided after a couple of minutes and I tried to make the most of it. But I felt so inexperienced and so out of it. I don't remember how long it took him to come but I was relieved when I felt him shudder and collapse on top of me. I wanted to go home. I was never ever going to have sex again.

"You were a virgin."

I had just lifted myself up to dress and I turned to look at him. He was staring at the bed sheet. I looked down. There was a red circle.

"Oh my God, this isn't possible. I have had sex before, once."

"You had sex but he probably didn't break your virginity, your hymen."

"What?" I was confused.

Kwame laughed. "He didn't get far enough to break it. When your hymen breaks, you bleed, although not everyone does. He didn't break yours, obviously."

"God, I am so sorry—your sheets. I'm so sorry."

I was so embarrassed, but he was just smiling.

"Hey, it's okay, honestly. The bathroom is right through there."

He got up from the bed and I disappeared into the bathroom with my clothes. I couldn't believe what had just happened. Edem hadn't broken my virginity! But that didn't really make a difference. He had still done what he did. A part of me felt relieved. This explained why it was difficult for Jon. My hymen was still there and we both didn't know. It wasn't just his size, I had been a virgin! I wasn't sure how I felt about Kwame having the prize now. He got the deed done when others had failed. Good for him, but I had mixed feelings about it all. If I had known I had a second chance, I would have planned it right and with the right person.

I cleaned up and went out to the bedroom. Kwame had changed the sheets and dressed. He picked up the candles and we went back to the living room. Amo and Cami weren't there— interesting.

"You okay?" he asked.

Kwame and I were sitting in the semi-darkness of the living room. My thoughts were all over the place. I wished Jon had tried a little harder. Then I would have lost my virginity to him instead. Kwame was sweet, he was great, but he didn't have my heart. I took a deep breath. It was done now.

"Yeah, I'm good."

He squeezed my hand and I squeezed back. Amo and Cami appeared a little later and the boys took us home. Cami came to spend the night at my end. Funnily enough, we didn't ask each other anything, not a single question. And to this day, I have no idea if anything happened with her and Amo that night.

Kwame and Amo called the next day, but I didn't feel like rolling with them. Cami and I decided to spend some time with other people. We didn't discuss it; it was like an unspoken agreement. Maybe she had a bad experience too. We rolled with a friend of mine from primary school, Afram and his friend/neighbor Sasha. We always somehow managed to find guys who rolled in pairs. Sasha had the characteristics I liked. He was mixed race, and very light skinned. He wasn't tall though, about my height or a little taller, and he wasn't necessarily good looking. But he was good company and so was Afram. Cami and I started to spend a lot of time with them, late nights and semi-sleepovers. The boys lived three houses apart and they were together all the time. It was pretty simple and convenient. I would be at Sasha's and Cami would be at Afram's and close to dawn, Afram would drive us both home. It worked for a while. But something was still missing from my life.

You Win Some...

Cami and I got over Sasha and Afram as easily as we got over Amo and Kwame. Kwame and I still talked every now and then, but I wasn't open to repeating that night. It was nothing against him. I just wanted that night put behind me. I was disappointed it had been him and not Jon, and I couldn't get past that. Unless I was in love with someone, I didn't see a need to settle. In any case, I was technically Tei's girlfriend. So Cami and I moved on.

Maame managed to take a breather from her mystery man. She resurfaced and she wanted Cami and me to meet him. His name was Samson, he was about eight or nine years older than us and he was in a serious long-term relationship with Maame's cousin. That preamble she gave us was enough to make me want to meet him and his friends. I hadn't had drama in a while and I wanted to see why Maame would risk a family scandal to have an affair with him. And even more interesting, Samson lived in my neighborhood, literally a four-minute walk away. And oh, it got even better; his house shared a wall with Kwame's house. This had all the ingredients of melodrama. I hadn't met the boy yet but I was excited. He was sleeping with his girlfriend's cousin! How radical was that?

"Okay, so is this supposed to be a secret? Like, do his friends know about you two?" I asked.

I was with Cami and Maame and we were on our way to meet Samson and a couple of his friends for lunch.

"Yeah, his friends know. It's a secret, but then again, it's not such a secret, you know. But of course my cousin doesn't know."

I knew everyone had a little evil alter ego. I always say that. Anyone is capable of anything and Maame was just proving my point.

As we walked past Kwame's house, I prayed to God he wouldn't walk out that second. That wouldn't be cool. Samson's house—or rather, his parents' house—was massive. They had a long driveway and an expansive layout. The front yard curved around the house and there was a gazebo-like thing that the drive way curved around. It was an impressive house. The living room was just as cool. It was practically the size of my living room and my mother's room combined.

Samson himself was unlike anyone I'd ever met. He was at least 6'3" if not 6'4" and huge. Maame couldn't have been more than 5'5". He hugged her heartily, almost picking her up from the floor. At first glance, he seemed like a genuinely nice guy.

Samson had a group of guys over at his end. He introduced us to the group but no one immediately caught my eye. I was disappointed. These guys were so much older! Why couldn't I like one of them at least? They were a lot of fun though. There was Abeku, who really wasn't bad looking, and a couple of other guys. None of them was my type. We hung out at Samson's house for a bit and then Samson and Abeku took us to lunch. We had a really nice time. Maame seemed genuinely smitten. And this, apparently, had been going on for a while. I wasn't about to judge her though, not me—that would be hypocritical.

During lunch, Samson called one of his friends over, Osei. Maame and Samson were trying to set Cami up with Osei. He looked okay, a little rugged and a little beaten, but okay. Cami didn't say much to him. She seemed to be more interested in Samson, frankly. But I wasn't about to be judgmental on that either. It would be great if two other friends got in a love triangle for a change. I was retiring from being the perpetual bad guy. So I spent more time talking to Osei than Cami did. I left her and Maame to obsess over Samson's every little word.

Osei wasn't my type either, but he was somewhat interesting. He wasn't fair per se, but he wasn't dark either. And he was tall, 6'1" for sure. He seemed like a fun, genuine guy. The four of them made plans to meet up later, which was fine with me. They dropped me home and I spent the rest of the afternoon on the phone with Tei.

"Hey, do you want to come out with us tonight?"

Maame called me a couple of hours later.

"I am not sure. I don't want to be a fifth wheel."

"Oh no, Osei and Cami aren't interested in each other at all. I think he likes you though. He asked if you were going to be around tonight."

I wasn't interested in him either, but they were a fun bunch of guys. "What are we going to be doing tonight?"

"Drinks, karaoke, club, whatever," she said.

"Ah, sounds like fun. What time?"

"Samson will pick you up at 8 P.M., okay?"

We hung up and I went to look for something to wear.

I heard whistling as I came down the stairs of the flat where I lived. I was wearing a really short skirt. Back then I had the legs to pull it off. My intention was not to impress any of the guys. I hadn't been out in a while and I just wanted to let loose and have some fun. The club was so much fun. Osei went to pick Jo and Cami up, and Samson got Maame and me. It was a fun group. And that night just started the trend for the following month.

Cami, Maame, Jo and I were in Samson's house all the time. Those were really good times. I loved his home entertainment systems and the scores of movies and DVDs he had. I could stay there from morning till night. He had a liquor bar, which was the attractive feature for Cami and Jo. Hanging with Samson and his crew meant a lot of drinking. Samson and Osei—all of them really—drank like horses. I didn't drink at all. The things I do and say sober, there is no way I can add alcohol to the mix. I didn't have that much control over my senses stone cold sober; how could I possibly add alcohol to that equation?

Osei was obviously interested in me but I didn't feel the same way. He was a nice person, decent enough, but there was really no excitement or drama there. He seemed safe, and I didn't want safe. I was with Tei, who was thousands of miles away. That was safe enough. If I was going to creep around on him, it should be a little exciting.

Osei called all the time; he came to visit, sometimes alone, sometimes with Samson. I didn't exactly encourage it, but I didn't completely discourage it. I liked hanging out with them. It was something to do. I had crazy fun in that house.

Osei, I give it to him, was persistent, truly persistent. He tried really hard, and I did everything humanely possible to get him to understand this wasn't going to happen. I told him I had a boyfriend and I told him I was completely in love with my boyfriend. When I meet someone I get a vibe, an instant thing, and then I know for sure how far I want to take something—that is, if I want to start at all. I didn't get any vibe from Osei, and I knew I didn't want to take this anywhere. It just wasn't going to be like that. He was a sincerely nice guy but there was something missing. Maybe it was because he was really too decent. He smoked like a darn chimney and he drank like he was swapping his blood for alcohol but that was it. He had no other obvious vices. Every other interaction I had had a little danger thing, a "no go zone," which made the person even more attractive. From Selorm, to Jon, to Edem, and even Kwame, there was just something wrong about it all. There was nothing remotely wrong about hooking up with Osei, and once there was nothing wrong, I didn't feel the need to.

I just completely underestimated the power of persistence.

Osei and I sat in his car, parked on some deserted road in my neighborhood. I wasn't sure what I was doing there. He had probably talked me into it. He talked me into a lot. When the kissing started, a part of me wanted to end it, but my will power against him was just waning. No sparks flew with the kiss, but I expected that. This wasn't going to be a heart pounding frantically against my chest type of situation. Even though we were parked God knows where close to 1 A.M., I still felt no thrill and no danger. But I went with the flow. Like I said before, Selorm had set me on a path of no return, as usual.

It was awkward and uncomfortable. I had read and heard about people having sex in cars. They make it seem so exciting and interesting and thrilling. It was absolutely nothing like that. And I think I would have felt the same way even if it was Jon in the car. My back hurt like crazy, I had no idea what to do with my arms or legs, and because of mosquitoes the windows were rolled up and I was dripping with sweat in the hot stuffy car.

I vowed never to do that again. Darn it, if a bed isn't accessible, sex isn't happening. I felt guilty, horrible and conflicted afterwards, and I hoped he'd just disappear and never call again.

Osei persistently stuck around but I was adamant that what

had happened wasn't going to happen again. He asked me out and I said no. We could only be friends. I started to see Kwame again, and a bunch of random people. I just wanted to be distracted. It worked for a while.

…You Lose Some

A few weeks after the "I'd like to forget I had sex in a car" moment, I fell horribly sick. My back hurt like it was on fire. It got so bad that I literally could not get up or walk. My doctor was clueless, everyone was clueless. He prescribed lots of pain meds that just didn't work. It dragged on for days and I really thought I was dying. Amo and Kwame came to visit. They tried to make me feel better. Lynn was around. Cami was there, as always. Jo had left for school a few weeks earlier but she called often. It was almost like I was saying bye to my friends.

"Are you feeling better today? Do you think you can make it tonight?" Kwame asked.

I was flat on my back, in excruciating pain, and I could barely talk on the phone.

"I'm sorry, I know I said I'd try, but I feel like I'm dying here."

"Is it that bad? And they still don't know what it is?"

"No. I really think I'm dying."

"Don't say that. Listen, maybe we'll come by and see you later, okay?" he said.

"Sure. Have fun."

"I'll try. Take care."

Kwame and I hung up and I lay still, trying to prepare myself for the inevitable. Something just felt wrong. I was dying. I had no doubt about it. I started to cry. Darn it, I wasn't ready to go just yet. I lasted till 10 P.M., and then I knew I wouldn't make it through the night if I didn't get help. My mother, my cousin Yaa and my brother Josh rushed me to the hospital. Lynn showed up as well. They lay me on a bench outside the ER and it took forever for a doctor to see me. I could barely breathe. I was so certain I was dying. I held my mother's hand for dear life. We were there for hours. Lynn and Josh kept disappearing and whispering to each other. I felt they knew I was dying, and were trying to be strong. They had such strange looks on their faces.

They pulled my mother aside for a minute, which sent me into panic mode. Was I done for? Could they tell?

I spent the night in the hospital. The doctors put me on a drip and pumped my body full of pain meds. And I lived.

When morning came, my family took me home but something was still wrong. Lynn and Josh sat with me all day, they wouldn't say much, but I knew they were hiding something.

"Am I dying? Did the doctor say something I don't know?"

Josh looked at Lynn, and shook his head.

"Someone has to say something right now, right now!" I said.

Josh got up and walked out of the room. I was about to cry.

"Rabbie, it's not about you, something terrible happened last night," Lynn said.

I didn't know what it was but I was already crying, crying from the pain and crying from the anxiety.

Lynn held me and waited for my tears to subside.

"Kwame, Amo, Mark and another friend of theirs were in a car accident last night. Kwame died, Rabbie."

"Oh God, oh God, oh God."

I think I started to scream then. I tried to get up but Lynn held me back. My brother came back in then but I was full-out screaming and crying. He and Lynn held me. My sobbing was putting enormous pressure on my back, which intensified the pain and ultimately intensified the crying. I refused to believe what they were saying. Kwame wasn't dead. I spoke to him the day before. Kwame wasn't dead! I wanted my mother. My brother forced a couple of pills down my throat. I don't know what they were, but they knocked me out for hours.

When I woke, Lynn was sitting beside me. My mother and Josh were in the room. They were talking about Kwame.

Kwame died at the same hospital I was at. Knowing he had been right there, so near, dying—that shook me to the core. The fears of death I had that night, it wasn't about me. It was about him. He died not more than a few feet from where I was. I couldn't handle that. I would have been in that car if I hadn't been ill. Would that have made a difference? Probably not. Amo had been driving and they were racing with some guys. Kwame wasn't wearing a seat belt and when Amo lost control and hit an embankment, Kwame flew right out of the windscreen, and cracked his skull. No one else was badly injured except for him. I was devastated. I kept playing our last conversation over and over in my head. I wished they had told me. I wished Lynn and my brother had told me, told me he was right there. But they said he died pretty quickly and my mother wouldn't let them tell me. I didn't get that logic. It wouldn't have made me any sicker. I cried and cried, and I thought of Kwame's family, his sister, his mother, his grandparents. This was so tragic; crying didn't even do it justice.

When I got better, Josh and I went to see Josh's friend, Tiny. Tiny had been one of Kwame's best friends. Kwame had died in his arms. Hearing the story of the night of the accident just tore me apart. But this really wasn't about me. I felt so sorry for his family, and his friends. Besides my grandmother, I hadn't really lost anyone close to me. Kwame was about twenty-two. He was young and he had his whole life ahead of him. I couldn't imagine it—what would I do if I lost my brother? How could this happen and why?

In life, you win some, and then you lose some…

Let's Move On, Shall We—Osei

Life was just messed up. I couldn't deal with all the nonsense that was swirling around me. I wanted to be left alone and I didn't want anything to do with anyone. Osei and I started to spend a little more time together. He was a good guy with a good heart. And of all the guys I knew, I knew Osei would never treat me badly. So fine, there was no drama. But I had had enough of drama. So there was no thrill. Where had thrill taken me to, anyways?

I didn't want excitement anymore. A stupid race had taken a boy's life. Who needed excitement? I had pulled enough stunts to last a lifetime. At that point, I was ready to throw in the towel. So I said yes to Osei. He was a good guy, I said to myself. He was dependable. I would bet my last *cedi* he wouldn't hurt me. I could see in his eyes he loved me. It was strong and it was genuine. You couldn't fake that. It was the same way I felt about Jon. I figured I deserved to be loved. I deserved some darn sincere, genuine obsessive loving. I was tired of giving. I needed this.

There was one thing I had to take care of first—Tei. I knew I could go out with Tei forever. We would both play each other like a game of roulette for as long as it took. We could drag it out for years. But what was the use? I had strong feelings for Tei but the future was bleak. I wasn't going to school abroad; my mother just couldn't afford that. So my future lay at the University of Ghana, for at least four years. And he was never coming back. That was clear. So where did that leave us? Bridge to nowhere.

So, I wrote Tei an email. Yes, I know, that was tasteless. But I couldn't do it on the phone. I couldn't hear his voice and tell him I'd met someone and I'd like to move on, especially when I still cared about him so much. The decision to leave him wasn't based on emotions—he would win that battle. It was based on practicality, and that he couldn't win that by a long shot. I think it was one of my best emails, despite the news it carried. I didn't want to completely cut him off. Who knew the future? So I was as sweet as I could possibly be, while telling him we had to end it officially. If we ever met again, and we felt we really wanted to have another go, we could.

It took him a while to respond but he appreciated what I wrote. He said he'd always love me. Sweet. I told him I loved him too. Bittersweet. And then I moved on.

Being with Osei started me on a path of simple predictable events. It was almost perfect. He was eight years older, twenty-seven to my nineteen. My mother disapproved strongly, that was a little hard. Maame was ecstatic; at least I had one person in my camp.

I settled quietly into a life of domestic stability and everything was just peachy!

The first year of my relationship with Osei was stable, uneventful and rosy. It was really my first real relationship. Jon and I had been a semi-whirlwind, and I had been in boarding school. We had our love for each other, but we didn't really have the day-to-day grind of a relationship. With Osei, it was my first serious exposure to what a relationship involved.

I got to know his family and he got to know mine. He gradually won my family over, especially my mother. He was helpful, available, generous and cool. I liked his family too. His sister Aida was awesome, and his mom and cousins were great to me too. So my days centered around Osei, my work, entrance-exam classes, my family, and to a limited extent my friends. I was with Osei all the time, every single possible weekend. We watched movies; we hung out with his friends: Samson, Agyare, Cecil, Steve, and a few others. I had an extended circle now. Saturday mornings, I'd go watch him play basketball with his friends at Legon campus. And Steve's girlfriend would cook afterwards or we'd just chill somewhere. Most of the time, we just stayed in his room and watched movies.

Jon, Edem and their constantly expanding crew were still around, but I rarely saw them or hung out with them. I rarely hung out with anyone really. Every now and then, since Cami was friends with Samson, and Maame and Samson were still having their thing, I met up with the two girls. Lynn left Ghana for the States as well, so my circle contracted even further. I got a job at a TV station, presenting and co-producing an entertainment show. It was fun and it was what I'd always wanted to do. My life now primarily revolved around Osei and work. There wasn't room for anything else.

Ato

Ato went to school with my older brother Josh. They finished a few months apart. He was a smart boy who liked to have fun, definitely in the DNA-smart category. If he took an IQ test he could possibly be proved a genius. My brother, cousin and Ato hung out a lot for a period of time, in 1998. Josh would tell me stories of their escapades and a few complicated love triangles involving Ato and my cousin. I got the impression Ato was a player. Josh said the guy probably couldn't count how many girls he had slept with. And this was 1998. When my brother was hanging out with Ato, I didn't think about him on any level. They were just stories. Josh had a lot of stories. Ato was just another character.

I started Legon in 1999, and I met Ato that first semester. I was walking with Sammi. It was evening, and we were walking across the volleyball court, through the Legon Hall night market. Ato and his friend, Kwasi, were standing near the court talking. Ato knew who I was and he called my name when he saw me. So Sammi and I stopped to talk to them. Nothing really suggestive was said that night. Both guys knew my brother and my cousins were their friends too, so they were just being friendly. We chatted really briefly and exchanged phone numbers. Ato said he'd call me later. There was something about the way he said it, the look in his eyes, the little glint that flashed behind his eyes, and I knew something had just happened. I grinned as Sammi and I walked off. I couldn't stop smiling. I knew, just knew, something was going to happen.

Ato didn't waste any time at all. He sent a text as we were walking, said he was checking if the number I gave him was correct. I chuckled and replied yeah. Then he called a half hour later, asked if he could see me later that night. I said sure. There was just something about that boy, something I couldn't quite place. I wanted to see him again. I wanted to look into his eyes again. That glint in his eyes, that look, there was just something. I knew, from my brother's stories, that he was a player. But there was something else there. I knew other players, other guys who thought they were it, who thought they had women eating out of their palms, but none of them had that look. I just had to see him again.

So we arranged to meet later that night. Close to midnight, he came to my block and I went downstairs to meet him. He was really good looking, I realized, and he still had that look. I smiled, he smiled and something just happened right there and then. This guy reminded me of myself. Everything about him, how he talked, what he said, how he looked at me, and I'm not referring to physical characteristics, it was something underlying the obvious. We walked and talked, talked about everything and nothing. We were both so direct, and so honest and so free with each other from the start. There was no trying to sass each other out. I knew exactly what type of person he was, and I knew that as he looked at me, he knew exactly what type of person I was too.

We walked for a long while and it was close to 1 A.M. when we stopped to lean against a tree, near one of the classroom blocks. And then he started kissing me. Here we go again, I thought. But there was something completely natural about what we were doing. Yes, yes, I know, I was cheating, but if you're surprised by that at this point, then you've been skipping some pages.

That was one of the best kisses I'd ever had, second probably to Jon. Ato knew how to kiss.

"Darn, you're good," he whispered in my ear.

I laughed. Yeah, I knew how to kiss too.

Kissing him was sexy, sweet, and so natural, yet so freaky and so wrong. I couldn't stop. His lips moved like mine did, his tongue was in sync with mine. It was like a frigging symphony.

"God, this is crazy. You're probably not going to believe me, but this is the best kiss I've ever had."

I laughed. I believed him, mainly because I knew I had skills.

"You're pretty good too."

"Took you a while to say that," he said.

"I have too many to compare to, takes a while to rank," I said.

Ato stepped back and started laughing.

"You're insane."

"You have no idea."

We sat on a bench and talked and kissed some more. It was so heated and so frustrating. We couldn't go to either of our rooms, because we had room-mates and slept on bunk beds. Living on campus was so limiting. After a couple of hours and some mosquito bites, we started walking back towards my block.

"Can I see you tomorrow?" he asked.

"Uh, I have to check my diary. I'll see if I can pencil you in between the boyfriend and the play I have tomorrow night. Would that work?"

He chuckled and nodded. "What can I say?"

His phone beeped then and I smiled. "Ah, looks like your 2 A.M. appointment is ready for you."

"You're so silly."

He kissed me, a different pace this time, softer. Then his phone beeped again.

"Hey, next time can you schedule her way before me or way after me?" I said, pretending to be irritated.

"I don't think I'm gonna be booking her this late again. She gets antsy at night."

I laughed. We kissed good night and then I disappeared up to my room. And that was the beginning of my end.

Ato and I did not date, nothing official, and yet it was one of the most complicated, long, difficult, messy, exciting, weird, passionate, and wrong relationships I ever had. It was a tryst that turned into a friendship of kindred spirits, a bond between two people who understood each other completely. I saw myself in him, maybe he saw himself in me. We connected on a pretty deep level. I got him, and he got me. He could be open with me, and I could be open with him. There were no pretenses, no pretenses to be people we weren't. I shared all my stories with him and he told me every single thing he did. We became best friends, lovers, partners in crime, just about everything.

On the surface, we were just close friends.

I spent years as his "wingman," his confidante, while I continued to sleep with him. It takes a very twisted mind to bear it all for years. As I think back now, I don't understand how I completely did that. How did I? How could I lie next to him in bed, and then talk about the other people we had slept with or were sleeping with? How could I look his girlfriend and other squeezes in the eye and tell them how much he cared, and then hours later, sneak out of my house to meet him? I know part of it was because I was a boys, boys type of girl. I understood boys. I couldn't stand girls half the time. I was very rarely whiny and needy and I hated weakness. I was open-minded, and liberated from the shackles of right and wrong. I was interesting to talk to, because my interests didn't center on "does he like me, does he think I am beautiful..." Who cares? This chapter of my life—Ato and I—could be a whole book, no kidding. Summarizing it here is impossible and I won't even try. It was the most insane period of my life.

You cage a lion long enough, you could probably tame it, get it to lie flat and maybe play fetch. But as soon as you take him out of the cage, and into the wild, he's going to remember instantly how life was before. The question is not which is better, caged or in the wild—each has its own issues. Being in the wild isn't exactly breezy—you're hunted, you struggle with the elements and you have to deal with competitors. In the cage, it's boring, predictable, but you're fed and you don't have to do much. Which is better really depends on what type of person you are.

Ato just reminded me so much of how I used to be, all the excitement, all the drama, before I settled into a monogamous relationship. I'd look into his eyes and I'd freak out. There was really no fighting that attraction. I was going down and honestly I wanted to go down. To be fair, I struggled with the idea of sleeping with him briefly. But who was I kidding?

Sammi and Rabbie—Partners in Crime, Again

Oh Sammi, oh Rabbie. We were such characters. Friends dating friends, story of my clandestine life. It wouldn't surprise me if Sammi and Kwasi, Ato's best friend, started the same day as Ato and I started. It wouldn't shock me a bit. It just happened. We didn't plan it. We didn't scheme. We met two friends, who liked us and we liked them back—it was that simple.

Sammi was sitting by herself on the steps in the middle of

Legon Hall on campus. She was on the phone, and I went to sit next her. It was a few days after Ato and I had first kissed, and I was just coming from his room actually.

Sammi got off the phone.

"What's happening? Where have you been, shady girl?" she said.

"Ah, with Ato," I said.

"Oh you're joking! I was just with Kwasi."

My mouth fell open. "Are you serious?"

She laughed a little.

"That is insane," I said. "Wow. I think you and I need to be lynched."

"You're the one with a boyfriend."

"Yeah, but Kwasi has a girlfriend, who is on campus. You're definitely the crazy one."

She shrugged.

"Ato's such a player, man. It's amazing," I said.

She frowned. "And you like him?"

"Frankly, I think that's the appeal, but I'm not sure. It's just something. He completely fascinates me."

"You like bad boys."

"So do you. I think you like bad boys more than I do. Remember, I settled for a good guy."

"But you're cheating on him."

"Not yet, but I will."

Sammi laughed and shook her head. Yeah, we were back at it again, the hopeless duo.

Sammi and I started exchanging our knowing looks again. It was Selorm and Edem all over again. The funny thing was Sammi and I were really secretive people. We had so many secrets it was amazing we were sane on any level. It was even more amazing that we could keep track of what we were doing at any point in time. I think one person I could never possibly judge in my life is Sammi. I can beef with a lot of girls, I can be royally pissed at a lot of girls, but Sammi, I don't recall a single moment when we had a major tiff. I don't recall a single time we weren't talking. I have had at least one misunderstanding with almost every single girlfriend I have, except for her. A part of it is Sammi just isn't confrontational. Part of it is also because of our past. I could never judge her. Still can't.

Going Crazy!

When you're doing something wrong, you need to keep a lid on it. But you also need to be able to talk about it, or you would go insane. Each secret I have ever had, at least one person knew. So perhaps I am not secretive per se. Every single person I know out there has a piece of me, a piece of my past, a piece of what makes me, me. However, there is no one person who knows everything. That's impossible for me. But trust me, it gets so hard. Deceit is a tricky thing. It's hard to keep track of who knows what.

The affair with Ato was hard to keep under wraps for a number of reasons.

First, there was the campus setting. I started university in September 1999. University was a whole different ball game from boarding school. University had boys. I don't know how or why anyone would expect me to maintain a committed relationship under such a condition. It's like giving a diabetic a job in a chocolate factory. My indiscretions were completely natural and excusable. Ah, forget it; I can't pull that argument off. Okay, so they were not excusable, but to me it was natural. I was boy crazy and for that reason alone, I should not have gone to a mixed university. For a year, being in a relationship with Osei had limited my relationship with boys. Life was all about work and him. But now, I had every excuse to be all over the place. The excuses could work with Osei but they were even tougher to pull off in front of the girls.

Abena, Cami, Ajua, Sammi and I ended up in the same school. Cami and I ended up in the same house and Ajua and Abena were actually room-mates. The girls were permanently in my life. We honestly started university as a core group. It looked like these were my friends and that was it. And I was fine with that. Let bygones be bygones.

The only catch was I still did not fully trust them and I knew we still had smaller allegiances. Cami's loyalties would forever be with Abena, there was no doubt about that.

Beginning a friendship with the girls again made my private life shrink further. Abena had a third eye or something. She either knew everything or wanted to know everything. And I think she suspected Ato and me from day one, although there was no way on earth I was going to admit anything to her.

To complicate this affair even further, Ajua developed a crush on Ato and she let all of us know it. When I realized Ajua had a crush on him, Ato and I were already sleeping together. There really wasn't much I could do about it. I could have told her, but I did not want anyone, besides Sammi, knowing about this. The girls knew I was friends with him, knew he was good friends with my brother and my cousins, and I left it at that. So I had to deal with Ajua going on and on about him.

"He's like 6'1" and he's so well built and so good looking!"

Sammi and I exchanged looks and I frowned. I turned to Ajua.

"Who are you talking about?"

"Ato, of course," she said.

"What? He's not 6'1", are you kidding? The dude is like my height or just an inch taller, come on."

We were standing in front of Sammi's hall, Sammi, Abena, Cami, Ajua and I, the posse.

"Of course he's like 6'1", if not taller."

"Oh, you gotta be kidding me right? Seriously, that's a joke. Ato is not tall, or well built."

"He's tall and he's well built," she insisted.

I was confused and a little ticked off. What the heck was she talking about?

"Sammi, you've met him, is he tall?" I turned to Sammi.

"Uh, I don't think so… I think he's even a little skinny," Sammi said.

"Thank you!" I was flabbergasted. I knew Ajua liked him, but come on, he didn't graze six feet!

"He's taller than you, Rabbie, and that makes him at least six feet, but I think he's taller."

The girl wouldn't give up. I was getting infuriated. Abena decided to jump in—she loved arguments.

"There's too much drama with that boy. Yaa has a crush on him as well. I don't know what the fuss is. You two shouldn't fight over him," she said.

That irked me even more. I hated it when people assumed all arguments to be fights. It was an argument yes, but definitely not a fight. And I was determined to win this one, on the sheer fact that I was right.

"I am 5'10", Ajua; anyone taller than me doesn't put them at six feet naturally. There's actually two whole inches between my height and six feet. I know for sure, one hundred per cent sure, that Ato is not six feet."

Ajua maintained her stance, which ticked me off further and ticked her off as well. I think later she realized he wasn't that tall, but she never openly admitted it. Abena ended the argument somehow. Ajua's attention switched to the info about the other girl with a crush on Ato. I knew about Ato and Yaa; he and I had talked about it. I couldn't be bothered. I left Ajua and Abena to yap about it. That argument was such a trivial thing, but it irked me so much. Sammi made me feel better later. We laughed about it and she wanted to know what I was going to do about Ajua crushing on Ato like that. It was a pretty big crush. I said I wasn't sure. I would think of something. I really didn't care who Ato slept with. I knew who he was sleeping with at any particular point in time. I had known him a few short weeks and I already had a list. But if Ajua got on that list, I would be pissed. We had talked about it before and he said he wouldn't. But I was still nervous.

"So, we need to lay some ground rules," Ato said.

Ato had picked me up from my block and he was driving me home. I didn't know what he was talking about. What ground rules?

"What are you talking about?"

"I was thinking about what you told me last night, about you and Selorm and Edem and Jon, and I think we need some ground rules."

I rolled my eyes. Yaa, the other girl who had a crush on him, was currently dating Selorm, a long-distance relationship. Ato told me that she liked him and I brought up my history with Selorm and his friends.

"I still don't know what you mean."

"No friends, never, ever; you can never ever do my friends," he said.

"Of course not! I don't intend to. And I won't. But I'm glad you brought that up. We need to talk about my friends—specifically Ajua."

"I already told you, I'm not going to do anything."

"Look, you know she really likes you. If you want to lay ground rules, that's fine with me, but I want this noted. You can never ever lay a finger on her specifically nor any of my friends. If we're going to make a pact, I want that noted."

"Fine." He had a mischievous look on his face.

"Ato, I'm serious. You brought this up. So let's just have an agreement now. I don't want to be worrying about this. You can do any girl you want, you can literally sleep with every girl on campus, but you cannot step into my circle."

"I said sure. Don't you trust me?"

"No."

He laughed. "That's because you don't trust yourself either. But hey I promise, no friends. Just make sure you don't do that to me either. I swear I would kill you."

"I swear I'd kill you too."

We shook hands. I hoped I wouldn't have to think about this again.

The second complication in my relationship with Ato was my older brother Josh. Josh had told me a year earlier, when he was hanging out with Ato, that Ato was a player. If Josh knew I was sleeping with him, I don't know what he'd do. It was unimaginable. But unfortunately, Ato and I became pretty close. We were talking all the time. He'd drop me at home and pick me up every now and then. A couple of times Josh saw him drop me off. At first, he didn't say anything. Then he decided to ask what was up. I said Ato and I were just friends, and he was probably being nice to me at school because of Josh, and it was really nothing. We were just good friends. Josh repeated that Ato was a player and I said I knew that and I would be stupid to do something with him. Josh warned me several times, but it didn't matter how many times he said it, I was already stupid. Now I had to be extra careful on campus, because of the girls, and I had to be extra careful at home, because of Josh.

The third complication, which really should be the first, was that I had a boyfriend. Cheating is such a hard thing to do. It really doesn't get any easier with time, it only gets more complicated. And Osei was the most possessive and controlling person I knew.

Before I started university, Osei and I had a good year together. We never argued, we never fought; it was as I initially wanted, safe and predictable. When I started school, beyond cheating with Ato from like the first month, my world also expanded. My thinking, my attitude, my whole demeanor reverted back to the pits of liberation I knew before. I tasted freedom and I wanted more.

Ato was not really Osei's downfall. He was a big part of it, yes, but he was not all of it. It was just the environment of undergrad, meeting people, making friends and going out. I wanted to live the life of a college student and I wanted to have fun. Osei sensed that and so he tried to tighten his grip. The problem, though, was I had let him be my world for a whole year and then all of a sudden, I let loose. I just didn't want to take it anymore. I am not sure if it was instant or gradual—a little bit of both, I'm sure. But whatever it was, our relationship was thrust into a whirlwind of problems.

I knew I was being bad, so I didn't want to bitch and act like I was a saint. I knew what I was doing and who I was. Any guy would be controlling around me. I was a wayward, unstable spirit.

It was two things really. A, he was naturally just controlling and obsessive and it had very little to do with me, or B, he could sense something was wrong, he didn't trust me and he was trying to save his relationship because he loved me. A, or B, didn't matter. I would say a little of both, although the latter is more likely.

So Osei's hold on me started to tighten. He wanted to see me every day. He was constantly calling, texting and dropping by.

I decided there were two ways I could play this; be a completely shitty girlfriend and not give a damn about how he felt or not fight with him because I knew I was shitty and maintain a normal relationship because I loved him. I opted for the latter; it was a no-brainer. Osei was a good guy, a really good guy and he didn't deserve my attitude or games. But note, neither of the options included a "no cheating" clause. I was going to continue my tryst with Ato for sure. I just wanted to juggle my cheating and my relationship in a respectful and manageable way! I was crazy, but we have already established that, haven't we?

Jon, Part 2.5

My first year at Legon was the best year I ever had, academically, socially and everything else in between. I was juggling Osei, Ato, friends, school, work and I still got the best grades I could possibly get. I clocked a 3.9 GPA each semester.

I made a lot more new friends, and built better relationships with some old ones. I became closer with Abena, Cami, Sammi and Ajua. We bonded, because there was really nothing else to do. We were doing just about everything together, trips to the hair salon, nails, clubs, everything.

I was enjoying my classes too. Psychology was great, Economics was rather tough but not impossible, and Sociology was just in between.

I was living on campus, which was a contributing factor to why and how my world just opened up. Living on campus was a cross between boarding school and living at home. The difference was you could walk out anytime; there was no curfew, no endless bells, restrictions or rules and no parents. It was the perfect mix. The downside was I hated my hall; it was rough being in a room with five people and sleeping on a bunk bed. And my room-mates were nothing like me. We couldn't carry on a conversation for more than five minutes. I was rarely there anyways. Besides that, everything was just great that year.

Jo came home that December, Christmas '99, and we all had fun hanging out together.

"Are you guys aware we have our first exam tomorrow? Our first exam in the university and we're going clubbing?"

All of us—Jo, Cami, Ajua, Abena, Sammi and I—were heading out Sunday night. That was Abena, trying to be the wise one. I wasn't exactly prepared for the exam the following morning but I wasn't exactly worried either. We were going to Tema to try out a new club. That was also very important, wasn't it, trying out new clubs? That club could end up as the hit club of the holidays, although Tema was way too far to have a hit anything.

"And we've been out every night since Thursday!" Abena added.

"Do you want to stay in? No one is forcing you, you know. This negativity isn't helping," I said.

Osei wasn't coming out tonight, neither was Ato. It was the perfect night to go and have some real fun. I didn't really care if either of them was coming out anyways, but it was so much easier if they didn't.

"Ah, come on, Abena, you have to come, I'm leaving in two weeks. And you guys have exams the next two weeks. I promise to stay away after tonight," Jo said.

The club was ultimate fun. It wasn't going to be a hit, but it was incredible fun. Jon was actually around that night. We had managed to be friends since the previous year. I had put him in a place in my heart where I wasn't particularly troubled when I saw him. He visited every now and then but we were completely platonic. He and Bianca hadn't lasted either, and now he was seeing someone else. I didn't know who and I didn't really care.

"So your boyfriend isn't here?"

I looked at Jon and shook my head.

"And where is your girlfriend?"

"She's home, she doesn't like to club much."

"Yeah, Osei doesn't like to club much either."

"Oh, that's his name. I keep forgetting." He said it sarcastically, with a laugh.

I laughed. "Yeah, whatever."

I didn't ask for his girlfriend's name. I didn't want to know. It wasn't important.

"You girls are really having fun, huh."

"Yep, and we have an exam tomorrow. I think mine is at 7:30 A.M. or something insane like that. I swear it might even be 6 A.M."

"You're kidding! And you're out, all of you?"

"Who cares? We have four years to catch up if we mess up this semester."

"But you know you're not going to mess up. Do you ever?"

I looked at him. I wanted to say yeah I mess up, all the time. I messed up with you, I messed up with Selorm and Edem, and I am cheating on my boyfriend with a guy who is the number one player in the world. The thought made me laugh out loud.

"What's funny?"

"Everything is funny. Trust me; I mess up a lot, maybe not academically, yet. But I am not perfect."

"I don't think you're perfect either."

I laughed. "Thank you. I feel so much better."

Jo came up to me and said the girls wanted to leave. We had been there over four hours and it was close to 4 A.M. I had to be sensible at this point. An exam was an exam.

"Hey, I have to go. The girls want to leave and that's reasonable. We all have exams this morning."

He nodded. Gosh, he looked so cute!

"Okay, I'll be leaving soon too. Maybe I'll come visit you tomorrow, if you can take a break from studying."

A little voice in my head said, "Say no, be strong, don't start this again."

"Okay, sure, call me. I don't study 24/7."

There was really no harm in a visit. I knew he was just being friendly. Jon and I would never be anything more than friends, ever again.

So the following week he came around a couple of times. We just sat in his car and talked. Déjà vu, right? But it was completely two friends hanging out. Sometimes he came with Afram, Cami's flame from our '98 days. Cami and I lived in the same hall, on the same floor. We had tried to get a room together, but that didn't happen.

"I think I'd like to head off to bed now. It's like 1 A.M. or something," Cami said.

Cami and I were with Jon and Afram. We were sitting in Jon's car, parked somewhere on campus, but close to our hall.

"Yeah I agree. I really need to study, and that means sleeping," I said.

"You guys are such babies… Come on, it's only 12:40."

"Afram, seriously, I have an exam really early in the morning. And I am tired," Cami insisted.

Jon started his car and they drove us back to our hall. We could have walked but I didn't mind. It was late and I was tired.

A group of guys standing on a balcony started whistling and shouting down at us when we got back.

"Are you guys back from an orgy? You two are out every night. Do you get paid for it?"

Cami held my hand. "Come on, and ignore them."

I looked up at the guys and stuck my middle finger up at them.

"I'm going to get you, bitch!"

I was about to shout something back when I heard Jon's door open. Now that wasn't a good sign. I knew he still carried that baseball bat.

"What did you just say?" he shouted up at the guys.

Jon knew how to get mad; he was good at it. I could see he was steaming.

"What? What are you going to do, huh? What?" the guy screamed back. Doors started to open and I saw that more people were stepping on to their balconies. I was mortified.

"Jon, forget it, it's not worth it. Come on."

"Yo, why don't you just step down here, huh? Come down and say what you want to say to my face!" Jon shouted.

If it came down to a one-on-one fight, Jon would beat the crap out of the guy in a heartbeat. The only problem was it wouldn't be just one guy. Sarbah Hall guys were a fraternity; there was no way Jon would win.

"Jon, hey, listen to me, just leave. If he comes down here, this is all over," I said.

Then something hit Jon's windshield and all four of us turned to look. It was eggs.

"You stupid idiot, I said come down here, come on. What are you afraid of? What, you think I can't come up? Watch me, just watch me."

Jon was furious. Within seconds, the boys started pelting us with eggs and water. The situation was about to get dangerously out of hand. Jon was yelling, Afram was yelling and I could hear doors and windows opening. It was a full show. Cami held my hand and she started to pull me away.

"Let's just go!"

So I started to walk away with her. I kept hissing at Jon to go. That wasn't working. So I turned to Afram.

"Afram, just get him out of here, okay? Now, seriously! You don't want these boys to come down here. If they do, and there's a fight, Cami and I could get expelled or thrown out of the hall. I can't have that happen. Jon, are you listening? You could get me thrown out!"

Jon paused briefly.

"I know your faces now, all your faces. If I ever see you anywhere, you better watch out, you hear me? You better pray I never ever see any one of you anywhere off campus," he shouted.

As he got into his car I knew he was serious. What the heck? This was my hall. This was where I lived. How was I even going to walk up the stairs and spend the night?

Jon and Afram drove off and Cami and I ran up the stairs. There were a couple of guys waiting for us on the fourth floor. We were on the fifth.

"Make sure your boyfriends never come here again!"

"Or what will you do? Huh? Do you know who I am? You lay a hand on my friends, or talk to me like that again, and I will get you thrown out. I am dead serious. You threaten me again and that will be last thing you ever do at this school!" I snapped. I glared at them and walked up to my floor. We didn't hear a sound.

Cami and I looked at each other.

"Don't let Jon come back," she said.

"He won't."

And he didn't. We spoke a few times but there were no more late night visits or sitting in a car. Being pelted with eggs and water really wasn't an aphrodisiac. He didn't need that aggravation and neither did I. I lived on campus and I was only a first-year student. The students in my hall obviously didn't like me. I didn't stay there beyond my first semester.

Close Calls

"So what's going on with you and that Nigerian?"

I rolled my eyes at Ato.

"It's Tosan, you know his name, don't even pretend."

I was lying on his bed on campus, and he was sitting behind his home entertainment stuff. I'd asked for a CD and he was putting something together for me. We'd just had sex and I was lying on the bed half naked. We talked about other people, yes, but not, like, five minutes after sex.

"Okay, fine, Tosan. What's going on with you and him?"

"Nothing. We talk."

"Really? Just that?"

"Ato, if I was sleeping with him, I'd tell you."

"Same thing Sammi says to Kwasi."

Sammi had semi-moved on from Kwasi, but he wasn't entirely aware. I didn't see Kwasi's beef though. He had a girlfriend; he couldn't possibly expect Sammi to be hanging around forever. Sammi and I had met new guys, best friends called Tosan and Ziggy, Nigerian foreign students. It's a little mind-boggling how this happens to us the way it does, but it just did. Ziggy liked Sammi, Tosan liked me. I thought Tosan was pretty good looking, and he was tall, taller than Ato and bigger. He was also very smart, a genius through and through. I really liked him but nothing was happening. There was a lot more happening with Sammi and Ziggy but she was single, she could do what she wanted.

"The four of you have been seen hanging around."

"That's all it is, Ato. We talk, we hang out, we eat lunch together sometimes, but that's all it is. When I sleep with him, I'll let you know."

"*When* you sleep with him? And not *if* you do?"

"Honestly, I don't think I am going to."

I looked at him and he looked at me. I patted the bed.

"Come here."

"You may not get tired but I do, okay?" he said.

"What, after two times?"

He shook his head and I laughed. He laughed too. My phone rang and I looked at it. Osei. Shoot, I was supposed to meet him at his place two hours ago.

"Aren't you going to pick up?"

"It's Osei, I was supposed to go over there this morning."

I got up and started pulling my clothes on.

"He's going to smell the sex, trust me."

"Shit," I swore.

I had completely forgotten about the plans Osei and I had made. It was Saturday morning, and my brain was on overdrive. What lie could I tell?

"Answer the phone," Ato said, "and tell him you just woke up, you're going to have a shower and then you'll be there. You overslept or something."

Ato was good at lying and I was learning from him. I answered the phone.

"Hey, what's up?" I tried to make my voice sound sleepy.

"Where are you?" Osei said.

"I just woke, what's up?"

"You were supposed to come to my end at 10 A.M. remember?"

"Oh, I forgot. Gosh, I was up studying."

Ato stifled a laugh and I stuck a finger up at him.

"Can you give me an hour? I am just going to shower really quickly," I added.

"I am downstairs at your place, I'll wait."

My blood froze. My brain went into hyper overdrive. My eyes opened wide and Ato frowned. He mouthed "what?" and I mouthed "at my hall." He got up to write a note but too many seconds had passed, I had to respond.

"I am not in my room. I spent the night with Abena and Ajua. Just wait for me and I'll be there in ten minutes," I said.

Abena and Ajua were in the same hall as Ato. It was the best I could do.

"I'll pick you up and you can just shower at my place. Okay?"

I wanted to faint.

"Uh, okay, so come around to the main Legon Hall entrance, okay? See you."

I hung up.

"You know he's not going to believe that shit, right," Ato said.

"He will. He has to. I have to go."

"Can he call Ajua or Abena?"

"Don't make me paranoid."

I grabbed his brush and did my hair, trying desperately to look decent. This was stressful and tiring.

"Call me later," Ato said as I rushed out.

Osei was waiting when I stepped out. I slipped into his car. I wondered if he could hear my heart beating fast. I was trying to calm my breathing. I was a pro, come on, I could handle this.

"You girls went out last night?"

"No, I was studying. We were all studying at Legon Hall and I just decided to crash with them. I didn't want to walk back alone."

My hall was on the other side of campus, so I hoped that was believable.

"You look tired," he said.

I was, tired from all the shadiness. I had spent all Friday night talking with Tosan. Nothing had happened but we had talked for hours. I slept for like five hours before Ato's text came and then I was in his room by 9 A.M. Of course I would be tired.

"What are you doing around here, anyways? I thought basketball was canceled today."

"It wasn't. I was going to call and tell you but I decided to call after the game."

Osei played basketball every Saturday on campus. This Saturday, the game was supposed to be canceled. This was such a close call. Osei was on campus playing basketball while I was in Ato's room having sex with him. That was messed up.

We got to his place and I started taking my clothes off. I needed to shower so badly. Osei got the wrong idea. He tried to kiss me.

"Hey hey, wait, I really need to shower. I am dirty."

But he wouldn't stop.

"Come on, you smell fine."

I was beginning to feel sick to my stomach. I couldn't let this happen. Since Ato and I started our thing, I tried hard not to sleep with both of them in one day. I was sure it was a forbidden thing somewhere. In any case, it was my code. I had never done that, and I wasn't about to start. The thought made me sick.

"Hey, five minutes, okay? Let me shower."

He let me go. I stayed in the bathroom for over fifteen minutes. I scrubbed and washed and cleaned but I never felt right enough.

By the time I got back to his room I saw Osei was in his boxers. How stupid of me. I had showered but I hadn't changed the day or time. It was still Saturday, just an hour after Ato. I may have showered but I could still smell him. I had a thought.

"I think I'm feeling really sick. My stomach is killing me. I was throwing up in there."

Osei looked worried. "Did you eat something bad?"

"I must have. I don't know. I need to lie down a bit, okay?"

I lay next to him and he touched my forehead.

"You have a little temperature."

I didn't have a temperature but if he believed that, even better. I lay there silently and for the next hour Osei fussed over me. My phone beeped and I snatched it. It was Ato; he wanted to know if I had survived. I deleted the text. For the first time Osei didn't grill me on who it was. I guessed being "sick" gave me some space. Osei didn't try to sleep with me that day and I managed to be very sick for the rest of the day. I swore to myself to keep my situation in check. Once again, that didn't mean the affair was going to end. I just needed to be smarter.

I lay on Tosan's bed, reading a book. He lay beside me, reading as well. We held hands. I lay on my side and looked at him. He looked up at me.

"What?" he asked.

"Nothing," I said.

"Study."

"I'm sick of studying."

"So what do you want to do?"

I grinned. And then I kissed him. It wasn't our first kiss. We first kissed the night before. And I liked it. I knew I would. He was a nerdy, goofy kind of person, but his kiss wasn't. It felt good. It wasn't earth shattering like Jon's or sexually loaded like Ato's but it was pretty good. Ato didn't like Tosan. Ato acted competitive whenever his name came up. He and Kwasi seemed really upset that Sammi and I were hanging out with Ziggy and Tosan. I knew I was going to tell Ato eventually that Tosan and I had kissed. I didn't know how, but I had to say it sometime soon.

The door opened and Ziggy entered. We broke apart.

"Hey you two, Sammi and I are going to get something to eat from the cafeteria—you wanna come?"

"Yeah, I am starving," Tosan said.

I didn't want to leave, but the decision was already made. Sammi was outside on the balcony on her phone. I stepped out and left the two boys in the room. Tosan wanted to change clothes.

"Hey," I said to her. She winked at me, which made me laugh.

"What's up with you two?" she asked.

"Nothing, trust me. He's pretty slow."

Sammi laughed and nodded. The boys stepped out then so we stopped talking. The four of us walked down the stairs together.

"Hey, Rabbie."

I swung around. A short, stocky guy stood in front of me. He looked vaguely familiar, but I couldn't place him. We were in front of the main hall entrance and Tosan had his hand on the small of my back. I felt it disappear.

"Ah, hey…" I looked lost.

"Noah, Osei's friend, from the court?" he said.

Shit.

"Hey sorry, I am so bad with faces. How are you?"

My voice was a little high.

"I'm good, good. My girlfriend lives in this hall, just stopping by."

I sincerely hoped he hadn't seen Tosan hold my back. I sincerely hoped he wasn't thinking anything was going on.

"Cool. Nice running into you. Take care, okay," I said, wanting to disappear.

He looked like he wasn't ready to end the conversation but I was done. I waved and starting walking off. Tosan, Ziggy and Sammi tried to catch up.

Tosan gave me a weird look. He was really uncomfortable with me having a boyfriend. We talked for weeks before we even kissed. He talked all the time about not wanting to mess around with other guys' girls. I couldn't even look at him. And he didn't look at me. This was just getting too hard.

The guy mentioned to Osei that he ran into me, but he didn't give details, or Osei decided not to mention the details. Osei started to get a little more difficult, checking my phone, texts, coming by unannounced all the time, asking to see me every day. I began to think Osei was suspicious. Scratch that, I *knew* he was suspicious. He didn't have the ammunition yet, but he was definitely wary. I couldn't bitch. I was a wayward girlfriend who definitely needed to be reined in.

Even as my freedom became smaller, and I was battling close call after close call, I still wasn't ready to quit my cheating ways. The idea, honestly, didn't cross my mind, once.

A Sneaky Thing Called Love

"That was my first phone sex."

Ato laughed on the other end of the line.

"Virgin, huh? I like that. I just took your phone sex virginity. Was it good for you?"

I rolled over on to my stomach and glanced at the clock. It was 2 A.M. Wow.

"I think phone sex is like eating candy when you haven't eaten in seven hours. It doesn't make a dent to your hunger," I said.

"You're still horny?"

"Mmmhmmm," I murmured.

"Do you want me to come over?"

"What? No, my brother is home."

I was home for the weekend and Ato was home too.

"I could park outside."

I didn't want to have sex in a car again. "No, I'm fine."

"You don't miss me?"

I closed my eyes. I actually really missed him. I wished he was with me, in my bed, holding me.

"I seriously miss you, you have no idea," I said.

"So I could be there in ten minutes."

I closed my eyes—so tempting. But sex in a car, I really didn't want to repeat that. Once was enough.

"You there?" he asked. "I'm getting dressed. I will be there in ten minutes, okay?"

"Ato—" I heard a click and I closed my eyes. Fantastic.

I pulled on my pajama bottoms. They were black so no one would know they were pajamas. I pulled a T-shirt on and opened my door quietly. The house was silent. I couldn't hear anything. I really hoped my brother was fast asleep and he wouldn't have a strong need to wake up and go for a walk at 2 A.M.

I snuck out of the house, and stood outside the gate. Ato came screeching around the corner in exactly ten minutes. He drove like a maniac. I got into the car. We drove off.

"Do you have any quiet places around here?" he asked.

I knew of the one where Osei and I had first had sex, which was really around the corner, but I wasn't sure I wanted to take Ato there. But I told him anyways and we drove off. We parked.

"Are you okay?" He was kissing me and his hands were under my T-shirt. I felt something at that moment though I wasn't sure what it was. But I really wanted to be with him. It wasn't as awkward as I had thought it would be. Of course it wasn't a soft comfortable bed, but it felt incredible. The kiss felt different, his touch felt different, and the feel of him in me was different. It was cold in the car, and there were mosquitoes, but we dragged it out, even spent an hour talking afterwards. By the time I got home it was almost 4 A.M. My cell phone rang as soon as I got into bed. It was Ato.

"Worth it?" he asked.

"Every minute!"

"It was crazy, huh. Shit, I think you're going to kill me sometime, honestly," he said.

I chuckled. "Gosh, I love you," I muttered sleepily.

My breath got caught in my throat. Did I mean it? We never used such words, but I said it so casually. I was confused. Why did I say it?

"We need to get some sleep." I said quickly.

"Yeah, we do. What time do you want me to get you from home tomorrow?"

"Josh is going to be home."

"I think I should come say hello. I mean he knows we're friends. He knows I see you. Josh is not stupid."

I sighed. My brother was definitely not stupid.

"Okay, come around tomorrow then."

"See you."

We hung up and I lay there. I really liked this boy. This was getting weird. I was feeling a whole bunch of emotions.

I could hear laughter, loud laughter. I was in my mother's room, talking with her. Her room overlooked our front driveway, but I hadn't heard any car come up. I stepped on to her balcony and looked over. Ato was here, and he was chatting with my brother!

They were talking and laughing like old friends, which they were anyways.

I went downstairs quickly.

"Hey, when did you get here?" I asked.

"Just now," Ato said.

Josh looked at me. I could read him like a book. He may have been laughing with the boy but he disapproved. I heard a voice behind me. It was my mother.

"Hello," she said, to no one in particular. Josh didn't do any introductions, so I stepped in.

"Ma, this is our friend Ato, he's at Legon too."

"Hello," he said politely.

My mother smiled and just stood there. This was awkward.

"So what program are you in?" my mother asked.

"BSc Admin, my concentration is finance."

"Oh, okay, Rabbie wants to get into the BSc Admin program too."

"Yeah, I know. She has a pretty good chance. She's very smart."

He smiled at me, and I looked away. It was time to end this little chat fest.

"I am going to get my stuff, okay," I mumbled and then disappeared into the house. I heard my mother behind me.

"So he's just a friend of yours?" she asked.

"Yes and don't think whatever it is I know you want to think."

"Me? I am not thinking anything," my mother said, laughing.

I looked at my mother; oh, she was definitely thinking something. She would probably grill my brother after we left. I grabbed my bag.

"See you next weekend!" she called out as I hurried away. Josh gave me one of his long stern looks as I got into the car. I knew this was a bad idea!

"That was frigging awkward, man," I said as we drove off.

"Really? Josh seems cool, man."

"I know my brother, and my mother, they'll think something is up. And they're Osei's biggest fans."

Ato was silent for a second.

"They like Osei, but you don't?" he asked.

"What? Of course I like him." His statement shocked me. I don't think I'd ever indicated I didn't like Osei.

"So what is it, you don't like him enough? That's what this is about?"

We'd never had such a direct conversation about Osei before.

"I like him, I'm just... I don't know. There's something that's just not there."

"If you're not happy, you should leave him."

"And be with whom?" I looked at him as I asked. He took his eyes off the road and looked back at me, and then he looked away.

"That's up to you, isn't it?"

I was silent for a second. And he kept talking.

"Listen, you don't have to leave him to be with someone. But honestly, if you're not happy, you should think about it. There's nothing wrong with being alone for a while."

"I am not sure I can be alone."

"You may not be," he said.

We were throwing stuff around, saying things, but I had no idea exactly what was being said. I looked at Ato long and hard. He had a nice profile, interesting eyes and an interesting face. He was skinny, a little too much, but he was still good looking. He had an undeniable style. He was suave, like he'd stepped off the cover of GQ magazine. Ato took style very seriously, the clothes he wore, his shoes; he even probably even "manscaped" his eyebrows. He was well put together, intelligent, fun, great kisser, etc. But could I date him? He hadn't even asked. He hadn't insinuated either. But it was the first time I actually thought of leaving Osei. In a year and a half, this was the first time I considered it. It was an insane thought, but once it was planted, it wouldn't leave. Ato switched the topic to something else and I followed suit. I wasn't going to leave Osei, I just couldn't.

"You're very quiet."

I looked at Sammi. I was in her room, on her bed, depressed.

"I've been thinking about Ato all day," I said.

"I think that boy isn't good for you."

"I know."

And I knew. I really did. Ato liked women, I knew that. I, of all people, knew that. But since our conversation in the car I couldn't stop thinking about him. I was missing him all the time. I hadn't crossed over the line to needy-ville, but I was hovering. Being around Osei was even more difficult. I was going crazy. I was even avoiding Tosan. I was thinking about Ato day and night.

"Osei is a good guy," Sammi said.

I was a little tired of hearing that statement. It was my own statement, my own mantra. Of course I knew he was a good guy. I created that phrase. Osei being a good guy just wasn't the point right now.

"I think I'm in love with Ato."

As the words came out of my mouth, I was as shocked as Sammi was. I couldn't believe I had just said that. And I meant it. This was like Edem all over again. Maybe I wasn't a pro after all. I definitely had feelings. It was a little comforting. This wasn't just an affair, just a roll in the hay, just fun, I had feelings. I was capable of feelings!

"You need to get over it; you need to get over it *now*."

Sammi usually didn't sound stern with me. But from day one, she had her reservations about Ato. I had the same reservations, but I was inexplicably drawn to him.

I looked at her and smiled.

"I am serious, Rabbie. You're just going to get hurt," she said.

I was done for, I was really done for.

"I'm in love with him," I repeated.

"Stop saying that."

"I've never felt like this, not since Jon."

Sammi was standing near her doorway, scanning her floor. She liked to people-watch. She closed the door and stood over me as I lay on her bed. The comparison to Jon was serious, she knew that. Comparing how I felt about any guy to how I felt about Jon was like comparing him to God. It was serious. I felt a little tear drop from my eye. I didn't want to love like that again. I loved Osei, but that was sane, controllable love. This, what I was beginning to feel, was overwhelming. I was in love with Ato. Sammi sat on the bed.

"What are you going to do?" she asked.

"Nothing… I am not going to tell him or be any different; just nothing."

She nodded. I turned away from her slightly and faced the wall. This could not be happening. I had to still my heart, slow my thinking. I had to reel it all in. I had to try and control it. I could lose everything. There were no guarantees here. This was not a love that would survive; there were no chances for it. I was already feeling heartbroken. I had a boyfriend who loved me. I had to concentrate on that.

Sammi's phone beeped.

"Abena and Cami are downstairs. They want to know if I'm in."

I shrugged. My phone beeped then. It was my younger brother.

"That's interesting, my little brother and my cousin are downstairs too. They brought invitations for my party," I said.

I was turning twenty-one in a few weeks and I wanted to make a big deal out of it. So my mother decided to throw a party for me. And I had this off-the-wall idea of doing it up in the mountains, my grandparents' home. It was a risky idea. The town was at least an hour and a half away. Would anyone want to drive that far for a party? But I still thought it was a great idea and it was something different. It was a beautiful scenic place, with a large lawn and fishing ponds and an orange garden. It was perfect for a birthday lunch.

Sammi and I went downstairs; my younger brother Xavier and my cousin were already chatting with Cami and Abena, and showing them the invitations. It looked great. The front of the invitation had a picture of my grandparents' home, shot from below the winding driveway. It showed me, slightly turned away from the house, looking at the camera. But you couldn't really see that it was me. It looked like a very artsy postcard picture.

Thinking about the party took my mind off Ato for a bit. I had so much stuff to do. I had to sort out music, decorations, food, a guest list and everything else. My family was pretty good at handling stuff. I had never seen my little brother that excited before; you'd think it was his party. He and my cousin Bernie were full-on party organizers. It was a bit of a relief but I also wanted to be busy. I didn't want too much time to think about Ato or even too much time to spend with Osei. That was just getting too hard. I was so torn and so confused and so depressed, and in love. It was the worst situation to be in. Ato didn't notice anything different. We were the same as we had been over the last eight months or so. I avoided any heavy emotional talk, which really wasn't our thing anyways. In my head I wanted to ask him how he felt about me, but I couldn't. I knew he cared about me and he liked me a lot. I was his friend, I was his good friend. I knew he appreciated how we were, how we talked, how we got along. We were so open with each other, that introducing "love" into the picture would derail all that and leave me with nothing. If Ato loved me, on a romantic level, I knew I'd know it. But thinking about it and speculating about it was beginning to drive me insane.

"Oh my God, it's 2:30 P.M. and no one is here!"

I was in full panic mode. My birthday lunch was supposed to start at 1 P.M., and so far, the only people around were family. There were a lot of us, but it was still just family. My mother told me to calm down, who cared if no one came. That was typical of my mother; she didn't live to please people. But I was a first year student, having this elaborate party up in the mountains. Everyone in school had been talking about the party. I needed people to show up. This was me!

Osei and his friends turned up half an hour later. I was grateful for that. Then, right after, cars started pulling in. I couldn't get past how many people turned up! Edem, and his whole new crew turned up, I couldn't count how many they were. Sammi, Cami, Ajua, Abena and all the girls came. My cousin Maso and all her friends came. Then Tosan and his friends actually came! My day got a whole lot better when Ato and his friends showed up. I was so glad he could make it. I think I would have crossed him off my "good people" list if he hadn't showed. He turned up with a bunch of girls, but that was fine by me. He was still here!

The party was awesome. The food was good, the music was great and everyone loved the location. Osei was there, so I had to behave, and I tried. It was the first time I had Osei and Ato in the same place. They walked past each other several times. It was weird to watch, weird to be there. A part of me wanted to walk up to Osei and say, hey guess what, I am sleeping with that boy over there, yep, the one with the black suede loafers and the YSL shirt. Tempting, but I didn't. It was a good party and I decided not to ruin it.

Osei and I were standing with his friends, talking, when Ato walked up to me to say bye. "Hey, I think I'm going to bounce now. I want to get back before it gets too dark."

I was a little surprised Ato walked right up to us. He knew who Osei was. But thinking about it, it was a party, he was just saying bye.

"Sure. Let me walk you."

I walked away with Ato. I felt there was nothing wrong with doing that. Maybe I would walk someone else to his car, just to balance it out.

"Thanks for coming," I said.

"Of course, no problem," he said.

"And thanks for bringing people."

"Oh, they wanted to come. It was a great party."

After a few minutes I slowed my steps and looked at him. Then I stopped walking completely. He stopped and frowned.

"What's up?"

I had to say something, I just had to.

"If I was single, would you go out with me?"

He looked at me, then he looked away, then he looked at his feet and then his eyes came back to mine.

"You're not single," he said.

"That doesn't answer my question."

"Rabbie, you know I like you a lot. You're my best friend."

"That still doesn't answer my question. The other time, when you picked me up from home, in the car, I thought, I thought you were trying to say something."

"I was, then. I don't know... after I met your mother, I thought about how it'd be like if we were together. I thought about it, yeah. But I don't know, you and Osei... I am not sure I get it, and I don't know if you do either. But hey, the guy really loves you and your family loves him. Look at you all."

"But what if I left him?"

"Don't. Don't do it for me. But I don't see why it has to be him or someone else. Personally, I don't think you're happy and I don't think you should be with him, but don't do it for me, or anyone else."

I felt my heart plummet a little. What was I thinking? It was a wise thing he said. It was so true. But it wasn't what I wanted to hear. I wanted to hear, "I love you, please leave him, please be with me." But I didn't get what I wanted. And as much as what he said was true, I was not going to leave Osei, unless it was for someone or something important.

"I have to go," he said softly.

I nodded. He could tell I was disappointed. He reached for my hand and squeezed it and walked away. I stood there staring at him for minutes.

"Hey."

I swung around. It was Osei.

"Hey," I said, trying to inject some enthusiasm into my voice. It didn't work; my voice was flat.

"Who was that?" he asked.

"Oh, one of my brother's friends, from Legon."

He watched Ato's back for a second and then he put his arms around my shoulders and led me away. I put my arm around his waist. This was where I was going to be for a long while.

London Bridge is Falling Down, Falling Down…

I managed to "recover" pretty quickly from loving Ato. I'm not sure if it was proper recovery, but I managed to find a small safe place in my heart for him. It was a place where we could still be friends and I wouldn't go psycho. Nothing was different after my party, absolutely nothing. We were back to the way we were before. We had sex, and we talked about people and I told him about Tosan. He was upset; he didn't believe Tosan and I hadn't done anything. I didn't care what he believed. It was the truth. Tosan and I were nothing. We were still stuck on first base.

Towards the end of the second semester, everyone was struck by some travel fever. It hit all my girls and many other friends. Ato was traveling too, so I decided what the heck, why not? It was a university thing apparently. Students traveled almost every summer, to work for a bit but mainly to shop like crazy. I decided to give it a shot. Ajua, Cami and Abena were going. I had always loved summer breaks and the idea of having twelve weeks in London, without Osei, sounded perfect! Maybe this was exactly what I needed to clear my head and find some focus, understand what I wanted and what I was going to do about my relationship.

I hadn't seen my uncle, one of my mother's brothers who lived in London, for, like, ten years. I was excited that I was going to meet him, his wife and baby son for the first time.

London was great. I loved the weather initially. It wasn't stifling hot like Ghana and it wasn't blistering cold either.

From the first day I got there, I was on the phone. There were so many people I wanted to call and touch base with. Some old friends I hadn't seen in forever, and just some of my Legon friends who'd gone to London. Sammi had started dating someone new, Leslie, who lived in London. Sammi didn't come along so she gave me Leslie's number; he apparently had a lot of friends and went out a lot, and she figured I'd get to meet some more guys. Aiding and abetting—if only Osei knew. Osei also gave me his best friend Samson's number, Maame's secret love. Samson was doing his Master's in London. Selorm was also in London and I managed to dig up his number too. So I was armed with enough sources for fun.

"So what are you up to today?" Leslie asked.

"I have to look for a job. Babysitting is sweet, but I need to work, earn some shopping money."

"Work? Can you do that? It's pretty tough, when you don't have papers and stuff."

"I have my mother's NI card, and we look alike, and it doesn't have a birth date, so I think I can pull it off."

"Yeah, once you have a number, it's easier. Anyways, I'm not doing much, if you want to hang out later. I think there is actually some gig later tonight."

"Actually I was hoping to go watch *Lord of the Rings*? That's after I go job hunting."

"Oh yeah, for sure, I want to catch that too. The party is going to be way later, so we can do the movie first. You want me to come pick you up? Like 5 P.M.?"

I paused. My uncle was a little tough and strict. He'd been on my case since I got there about the "boys" I spent all day talking to. Of course he said it in a loving way, but I used to live with him years ago, and he was the strictest toughest person I knew. If Leslie came to pick me up, I knew my uncle would grill him to the bone.

"Hey can you get here, like, 4:30? My uncle gets home at 5 P.M. I'd like to avoid you meeting him. He asks too many unnecessary questions."

Leslie laughed. "Okay, okay. 4:30. See you."

When we hung up, I really wasn't in the mood to go job hunting. I had only been around less than two weeks. All I did each day was eat, sleep, watch TV, watch movies and talk on the phone from sun up to sun down. The first week I went to meet up with Ajua and Cami for a little bit. We walked aimlessly around Oxford Street and spent money we didn't have. But by the second week, Ajua already had a job and Cami had gone off to see her sisters. I didn't feel like meeting up with Abena. So I was stuck at home, eating, sleeping and talking on the phone. My uncle kept threatening to call Osei because I was on the phone each day with a different guy, which really wasn't the case. The only people I spoke to were Ato, Leslie and Samson, and besides Ato, I wasn't doing anything with the other two. To be honest, since I got to the U.K., sex wasn't on my mind at all. I just wanted to hang out and have fun, and meet people and see places. It was my first time in the U.K.; I wanted to be a tourist and enjoy myself. I also needed a holiday job, so I really didn't have much time to think about sex or want it.

4:45 P.M., where was Leslie? I was dressed and lying on my bed when I heard the front door open. That couldn't be him. Darn it, that meant my uncle was home. I got up and went downstairs. My uncle was standing in the foyer, holding his baby son in one arm and trying to lock the door with the other hand. I reached for the baby, who was fast asleep, and took him into my arms.

"Is this normal dress, or are you going out?" he asked.

"Going out," I said.

It was best not to offer details unless you were asked for more, that was my motto with my uncle, and basically with everyone else.

"I just took him out of the car seat. If you had called me earlier, I would have taken you to the station at least."

"Oh, I'm good. I can get to the station by myself. Thanks though."

As soon as the words were out of my mouth, I heard a car honk. My heart sank into my stomach. If that was Leslie, I was going to kill him! Honk? Seriously?

My uncle opened the front door and looked out. I tried to peek but he was blocking the doorway.

"Are you expecting someone?"

"Uh, yeah, I wasn't sure if, uh, he was, uh, going to come. Uh, let me just go put Nana down and I'll leave."

"No, no. I'll go put him down and you ask your friend to come in. He shouldn't park in my driveway and blow his horn like you live here by yourself."

My mother and my uncle had this thing about visitors

honking. It irked them to their very core. My mother's room overlooked the driveway so that was understandable. But I think for both of them, it was more of a respect thing.

My uncle took the baby and I went outside. Leslie was sitting in his car.

"Dude, I can't believe you. You're, like, twenty minutes late and you get here and you blow the horn?"

"I thought you said your uncle gets home at five. Is he in? Is he upset?"

"Yes to both questions. Come on, he wants you to come in."

"You're kidding, right?"

"No, I'm not. So listen, give really simple answers, no elaboration. We're going to a movie and a party and then you're going to bring me back, by eleven."

"You're kidding, right?" he repeated.

"Dude, come on, let's get it over with."

Leslie got out of the car reluctantly. We went into the house and to the living room. My uncle was still upstairs. Leslie sat down on the sofa and I perched on the arm. I didn't want to sit beside him and give my uncle any wrong impressions. And the only seat left was his armchair. My uncle walked in a couple of minutes later.

"You're the one in front of my house blowing your horn like that?"

Leslie clasped and unclasped his hands.

"I'm sorry, I thought she was alone."

"Even if she was alone, you should be a gentleman, get out of your car and knock… unless you're not a gentleman?"

I closed my eyes briefly. I had a tactic for dealing with my uncle's interrogations. I knew he was a sweet man, and eventually the questions would stop. Plus it wasn't necessary for him to like Leslie or approve of him. He was Sammi's boyfriend, and nothing was going to happen between us. So I didn't really care if Leslie flunked the interrogation, and most likely he was going to. If it was someone I was serious about and in love with, then of course I'd help him out. But this time, I didn't say a word and focused on the clock. This wouldn't go beyond five minutes.

"I think I'm a gentleman, but I'm sorry, I wasn't really thinking," Leslie said lamely.

"Where are you guys going?"

"A movie and a party."

"Where?"

"Uh, the movie is in Brent Cross and the party is somewhere in central London."

"What time are you going to bring her back?"

"Eleven…"

My uncle raised his eyebrows and Leslie froze. He wasn't sure if eleven was too late or my uncle just didn't believe him.

"You're very sure? So you want me to sit up and wait for her to get in at eleven?"

"I'll take the keys," I said. This wasn't about helping Leslie, it was about helping myself.

"So definitely eleven? It won't be 11:15 or 11:30?" my uncle looked sternly at Leslie.

Leslie was just about done at that point. He didn't answer. He looked at me, looked at my uncle and shrugged. Blowing his horn was mistake number one, shrugging was mistake number two. I knew at that point this was going to take more than five minutes.

"No answer? You're probably thinking oh, she's what, twenty-one, so who cares what time she gets in, right? You think it doesn't matter that her mother trusts that I'll be looking out for her, so I need to make sure I know where she is?"

My uncle was definitely having some fun with this as well. Unfortunately, neither Leslie nor I could call him out on this. Leslie still couldn't speak.

"I mean I don't even know who you are, where you live, who your parents are. What if something happens tonight? What do I say? Some 6'3" boy in a white car said he'd have her home by eleven and now it's 8 A.M. and I don't know where she is. If something happens, do you want me to tell her mother that? What is your name, anyways?"

Leslie looked stricken and I laughed.

"I'll leave his name, number, address, everything, okay?"

I dug into my bag for a pen and paper. My uncle was still glaring at Leslie, who was trying to sink deeper in the chair. He finally managed to speak.

"My name is Leslie. I really don't mean any disrespect."

I handed Leslie's details to my uncle. He glanced at it and then back up at Leslie.

"11 P.M. No later."

And then he stood up and went upstairs. Leslie stood up slowly and I tried to sustain my laughter till we got into his car.

"I'm never coming back here again," Leslie said under his breath, almost as if he was afraid my uncle had hypersensitive hearing.

I burst out laughing and he smacked my shoulder.

"Cut it out. That was insane, man, seriously. I am never coming back here again."

"Awww, poor boy. He's really a sweet person. He's probably laughing about it right now."

"He knows how to laugh?"

I was almost on the floor at this point. Leslie looked so upset and so shaken.

"You know how to take the train, right? That's it from now on. And if you're ever coming to meet me, please give a different name. I feel like he's probably online right now on some database trying to find out who I am."

I laughed and shook my head. Leslie would not have been able to deal with my uncle if he had met him ten years ago. He was a tyrant then. He'd chase my older brother down the streets of our neighborhood and whip him for something naughty Josh had done. And Josh was always doing something. My younger brother Xavier and I learnt the game early. If my uncle said "bed," it was bed. He had rules, lists, curfew and all kinds of stuff. He still had a bit of that fire, but the last ten years had definitely dulled him. He wouldn't freak out if I got home past 11 P.M.

Leslie managed to get back in a good mood. The movie was really good. Watching a movie on the big screen with surround sound was another plus of being in London. We didn't have giant cinemas in Ghana. What we had were mainly houses, with converted movie rooms, that were being utilized more and more for getting laid or messing around. As a movie buff, I was in heaven. The party was a little whack though. I called Ajua to tell her about it but she couldn't make it. It was a Ghanaian party with a whole bunch of people I knew, but the music was crap and there weren't that many hot guys. And then Ato showed up.

I hadn't seen Ato since we left Ghana. We spoke on the phone a lot but he was usually all over the place. I hadn't told him I was going to be at this party and he hadn't mentioned it either. He showed up looking all suave like he was the mayor of London or something.

"Hey, I thought you were under house arrest in your uncle's little village," he said, laughing. We hugged. He smelled good.

"Hayes isn't a village."

"But it's, like, what, an hour away from civilization?"

I rolled my eyes at him. We looked at each other for a second and then he leaned in.

"When are you going to come visit me?" he whispered.

His hand was on my waist and it felt warm and good. His breath smelled of mint. I wanted to kiss him right there and then. Gosh, I was so into this boy.

"What are you doing tomorrow?" I asked.

"Whatever you need me to be doing."

I smiled. He was so naughty. "I'll come over tomorrow then."

Our lips were so close, but we were in a club and there were people all around us. As much as I really wanted to, I just couldn't kiss him.

His lips grazed my cheek and then I heard Leslie's voice.

"Hey, it's 10:45 P.M.," he said from behind me.

I laughed.

"What's happening at 10:45?" Ato asked.

"Leslie promised my uncle he'd get me home by 11 P.M."

Ato shook his head and tapped Leslie on the shoulder.

"All the way to Hayes? Good luck, man."

"First and last, trust me," Leslie said.

Leslie and Ato were friends. They had gone to the same primary school and they knew the same people. Usually Ato was suspicious of every single boy I knew or hung out with, but this time, for whatever reason, he didn't think more of it. We chatted for a bit and then I said bye. I knew my uncle wouldn't be that upset if I was late, but the party wasn't really happening, and I was going to see Ato the next day. There was no need to hang around anymore.

"Hey, can I drive?" I asked Leslie as we walked to his car.

"And if something happens? For instance, if we get pulled over by police? You have no license, I get fined and we both get thrown in jail and then you call your uncle and tell him, uh sorry, I'm going to be late tonight, I'm in jail so I'll see you in the morning. Yeah, I can picture that happening. No thanks, you can drive another time."

I laughed. Leslie was never going to be the same again.

Ato looked good all the time. Most guys had good days and bad days, days when they looked like they hadn't had a bath in forever or they'd been lying on their beds playing video games all day and their skins were deprived of vitamin D. I'd never seen Ato look like that. He probably had a shower twice a day. He had a very strong sense of self. But it wasn't obsessive, like George Clooney's character in *Oh Brother, Where Art Thou?* who greased his hair every five seconds. Ato just liked to look good, and who could hold that against him?

We met up at a train station near where he was staying. It was a windy day, a little cold, and he had on slim-fitting, dark-colored jeans—he abhorred baggy jeans—and a thick gray sweater over his white tee. London suited him. He didn't look so skinny; wearing multiple clothing gave him a little profile. We kissed as soon as we saw each other. We hadn't done that in weeks. His lips felt good, and he tasted fresh. I'd missed him like crazy.

"So what's up with you hanging out with Leslie?"

I shook my head. I thought he wasn't going to ask.

"Nothing, nothing, nothing. Come on, I am not that bad. He's Sammi's boyfriend. He's just being nice."

"He picked you up from Hayes. Leslie lives where, north-east London? That's, like, an hour away. And he did that because he's just being nice? Yeah, right," he muttered.

"There's nothing happening, and nothing is going to happen. We just talk and hang out. My mind is nowhere near there, nowhere. It hasn't even crossed my mind for a second. Give me some credit."

I didn't want to start the afternoon arguing with him. We started walking and he went on about Leslie for a little bit longer and then he shut up, because I wasn't responding. For obvious reasons, we had trust issues. We both felt the other was capable of just about anything. But this one, Sammi's boyfriend, I wasn't capable of. Ato tried to lighten the mood, stopping to kiss me after almost every five steps. I got turned on pretty quick.

"Is anyone home?" I asked.

"No, my cousin is out. He was leaving home when I left to come meet you."

I really wanted to be with him. If I hadn't come to meet him, perhaps I wouldn't think of sex, but now that I had seen him and kissed him, it was all I could think about.

I had no such luck. Ato's cousin was stretched out on a sofa, TV remote in one hand, cell phone in the other hand. He was gabbing away at the top of his voice. My heart sank and I could sense Ato was disappointed too. He gestured at a second vacant sofa and I dropped into it. This was going to be fun.

Ato's cousin got off the phone a couple of minutes later. He had a big grin on his face as he looked at both of us. I wished he would wipe it off; he'd just destroyed my afternoon.

"Hey!" he said looking at me. "Rabbie Daniels, right?"

I smiled a little and nodded.

"I know your brother," he said.

That didn't surprise me. Everyone knew my older brother. What I wanted was for him to leave!

"Yo, so I thought you were going to work?" Ato asked.

His cousin nodded. "Oh yeah, they called, like, five minutes after I stepped out. They want me to come in a little later."

My heart sank a little deeper into my stomach. I really wasn't going to have sex with Ato with his cousin around, even if there was a room available. I didn't know whom he knew, if he was a talker, and what impression that would give him. Ato looked upset too. He gave me a look, a questioning look; he wanted to know what I wanted to do. I shook my head and he nodded. It wasn't going to happen today. We both knew that. His cousin started gabbing again, Ato rolled his eyes at me and I laughed a little.

I spent a couple of hours with them, trying to mentally will his cousin to leave. He never did. After two hours, I decided to leave and go hang out with Leslie. At least I wasn't attracted to him; being around Ato and not being able to sleep with him was giving me a huge headache. It was just torture.

"You sure you want to go? I think he's going to leave in a bit."

"He changed clothes ten minutes ago, into track bottoms and a T-shirt. He's not going anywhere. I'm just going to head home," I said.

My mood had gone south. I just wanted to be out of there. We stood outside the apartment talking. Ato looked disappointed but I couldn't change that. My phone beeped and I glanced at it. It was a text from Leslie.

"Hey, I gotta go, okay?"

"Give me a second, I'll walk you."

It was a pretty solemn walk. We kissed at the station and then I was gone.

I spent the rest of the day hanging out with Leslie and his brothers and then I hopped on a train back home. Wasted day—if I was a guy, I'd have a serious case of blue balls.

Idle Hands Make Light Work

Being jobless in London can be fun, but it can be limiting if you want to shop and really have fun. I wasn't a shopper but I wanted to have fun, and it was just tiring asking my uncle for money every single time I wanted to go out. Leslie didn't work either, so it was pretty easy to be aimless with him, but that's where our similarities ended. Leslie could afford to be aimless, I couldn't.

I hung out with Samson a little bit too. But he was really busy, with school and work. I hung out at his place on the days he was gone. He had a large-screen TV, home entertainment, scores of movies and food. Perfect. I really had nothing much going on. Ajua found a job, Abena was working, day and night actually, and Cami had a job too. So I was the only one with absolutely nothing to do.

I stood at Victoria's station waiting for Ajua. Finally we were going to hang out. Samson was taking us to a movie. *Gladiator* was opening that night. I really wanted to watch that. Plus a little part of me was trying to hook Samson and Ajua up. A twisted part of me wanted them to hook up just so I wouldn't be the only bad nut in the group. Or maybe I was just bored.

"Do you really want to do a movie? I am so tired!"

"Yeah, I'm pretty tired too."

Ajua and Samson were half lying on the sofa, whining. I wasn't about to have it.

"Oh come on, people. I have been looking forward to this all week! It's just two hours."

Samson closed his eyes and pretended to be sleeping. I shot Ajua a look. I really didn't want to just stay in.

She sighed and stood up. She did look tired, but I figured she could manage one movie. Samson took more convincing but eventually we managed to drag him out of the house. We were less than halfway through the movie when I heard the snoring. Samson's head hung to one side. He was completely gone and

157

snoring loudly too. I felt so embarrassed! Then I heard a different type of snoring. I shook my head in disbelief. Ajua was gone too. Her head fell on my shoulder and that was it. There was no recovery for both of them. They slept throughout *Gladiator*, of all movies. Ajua was too tired to handle any trains and buses back home. So after the movie, we took a cab back to Samson's place to spend the night. Ajua went straight to bed. She was dead tired. Samson was knocked out on his sofa bed within seconds. I sat on the living room floor for a while, texting Ato and watching TV. Ato wanted me to meet him the next day. He insisted he was going to be home alone. I decided to take the bait. He started going on about the kind of stuff he wanted to do with me. I wanted to leave right there and then and go find him. But I decided 10 A.M. the next day was the best I could do.

When I woke up, it was past 10 A.M. Ajua was gone. She had work. Some people had a life. Samson was up in his kitchen, fixing something to eat. I realized I had forgotten to call my uncle the night before. That was definitely a no-no.

"Have you seen my phone?" I asked Samson, as I dug around his living room.

"Who's Ato?"

I froze. What did he just say? I turned around and looked at him. He was holding my phone in his left hand. I closed my eyes. This couldn't be happening.

"Ato is just a friend. Give me my phone back."

I was pissed but I was also worried. Did he read my texts? How many of them? Ato and I had been pretty explicit the night before.

"Just a friend? Just a friend?"

He flipped open the phone.

"Samson, come on. You're invading my privacy. This is none of your business."

He started reading my X-rated texts out loud. I blocked the words out.

I wanted the earth to swallow me up. I sat on the sofa and shook my head. This could not be happening. I could get really pissed and make a lot of noise about invasion of privacy and whatever else. Bottom line, he had read my texts. No matter what

I said, I could not erase that fact. And I could not think of any logical reason, any excuse, to save my ass. I covered my face with my hands.

"So back to my original question, who is Ato? What's going on? Why are you cheating on Osei? Do you love this dude?"

I couldn't respond. Samson kept talking.

"Talk to me, help me understand."

Understand what? I thought.

"Listen, you can't judge me. You're sleeping with your girlfriend's cousin, among others. So really, lay off me."

Samson shrugged. He threw the phone at me. I caught it. I usually deleted all my shady texts. But I was in London and Osei wasn't here. I had never expected this to happen. And it was really wrong for Samson to read my texts.

"You shouldn't have read my texts, honestly. You leave me here all the time. I never go through your stuff or check your email. I know you're sleeping with, what's her name again, Kokui, but you don't see me acting all judgmental and checking on you."

"I wasn't checking on you. Your phone kept ringing this morning. And I admit I got a little curious. Trust me, I'm not judging you. I wouldn't do that. I just want to understand. If you want to talk, I'm here to listen. I'm not going to tell Osei. It's your life."

I sighed. This was messed up. Samson gestured for me to come over to the dining table. He set a plate of toast and eggs on the table. I sat down and we started talking. I told him everything, every single detail. I spilled the whole deal about Ato. Samson met me halfway and spilt his own crazy indiscretions, and there were quite a number of them. I lost track of time. It was only when my phone started ringing again that I realized it was past 11 A.M.

"Is that him? I really don't think you should go. I am not telling you what you should do, but think about it. I'm a guy, I know how all this works. He doesn't love you, he doesn't care about you, and all he wants is to sleep with you. After you leave, he'll probably have someone else come in right after."

What Samson said made sense but it was hard to swallow, especially when I liked Ato so much. I glanced at my ringing phone. It *was* Ato. I had an hour to shower, and catch a train to his end. If I was going to do it, I had to leave now.

"Don't do it," Samson said.

Unfortunately, I was not that strong. I answered the phone.

"Hey, I am just getting ready to leave," I said.

"Oh, so you're still home. Listen, I'm really sorry, something came up. I have stuff I need to get done today."

I rolled my eyes. Samson had jinxed me!

"Please tell me you're just kidding," I groaned.

"Sorry, today is just messed up. My cousin got me a job, I need to go by and see what's up."

"At this rate, maybe I should think about sleeping with Leslie."

"You do that and I won't speak to you again. I have to go. Talk later, okay?"

"Okay."

I hang up and looked at Samson.

"So who is Leslie?" he asked.

I laughed. "Definitely nothing. Ato just canceled. You've jinxed me."

"It's for the best. Trust me. He's not worth it. Guys aren't worth it."

I knew he had a strong point. Ato was a player, who knew what he was really up to? Why did I bother? This was going nowhere. But I'd always known that, hadn't I? Yet, I still wanted to be with him, for the fun of it, and because I really liked him.

I left Samson's house a couple of hours later and I went to face my uncle's wrath. I didn't question for a minute whether or not Samson would tell. He said he wouldn't and I believed him. I knew a lot of his stuff too. I really didn't know a worse player than Samson. I wondered how he managed to keep track of his girls. But Samson's game was really simple. He didn't bother to keep track at all. He didn't care who knew, or who thought what. He laid his cards on the table, take it or leave it. Ato made efforts to keep things on the down low, to a degree. Samson didn't. I figured if there was one person who'd understand me, it would be Samson. He was Osei's best friend, yeah, but they were as different as night and day. My secret would be safe with him.

I spent the rest of the week cooped up at home. Then I went

to spend the weekend with my older brother's ex-girlfriend, Akua. Akua was the epitome of perfect girlfriends. When she was with my brother, I loved her to bits. She was fun, spunky, interesting and down to earth, and one of the most considerate people ever. My whole family loved her, and to this date, I don't think anyone else who's come through my family compares to her. Akua was just a different species. She was awesome, above and beyond. Unfortunately, Akua left for school in the U.K. and after that their relationship didn't stand a chance. My whole family was heartbroken when Josh ditched Akua. We just never got over her.

I hadn't seen Akua in almost two years. It was great seeing her again. She was seeing someone else now, Richard. He was a good guy and it appeared he loved her very much.

I was happy for her, happy she had got over my stupid brain-dead brother.

"You have to wear something sexy! Come on, don't you own a skirt?"

I was in Akua's room, getting ready for a party. I was wearing pants, as always, and Akua was in a short skirt and an even more revealing top. She looked really good.

"No, I don't own any skirts."

"Come on, I'm sure we can find one for you in my things."

"Hey, hey, I'm good. Come on, let's go, we're running late!"

I felt fine with what I was wearing. It wasn't over the top, and it wasn't completely boring either. It was black pants, with a black, long, silky top. I even had on short heels.

The party was really happening when we got there. It took a while to dig through the crowd outside the house to get indoors. I needed a cold drink. I was thirsty. And then I saw him.

They were nestled in a corner kissing, and caressing. I was stunned. He had his arms around her and he was kissing her lips, her neck. I stood there for a full minute and then he turned his head slightly and saw me. She looked up and saw me too. It was Ato and Lina, a girl from school I knew vaguely. We had mutual friends. She was part of the group he brought to my birthday. I knew Ato sort of liked her and that they'd been talking, but this was way beyond talking. She waved me over, a big smile on her face. If only she knew. I walked over slowly. I couldn't look at his face.

"Hey! I heard you were in town, so nice to see you! Ato told me he saw you a couple of days ago, or was it last week?"

She hugged me and I lamely hugged her back.

"Nice to see you too," I said, trying to force some enthusiasm into my voice.

She was beaming; it was too much to bear. I looked at him. He looked at me.

"I'm going to talk to Rabbie for a second, okay?" he said to her.

"Oh sure, I'm going to get a drink."

Ato and I made our way through the crowd, out into the cold.

"Wow. So what's that? What's going on?" I asked.

"Lina and I are together now. You know I like her. I really like her, actually."

I stopped breathing for a second. "What? Since when?" I asked.

"Uh, not sure. She says a couple of weeks, I say this week."

My mouth fell open.

"I thought we were friends. You couldn't tell me?"

"I was going to, of course. Come on, I tell you everything."

I couldn't believe he was now officially seeing someone. I was upset and disappointed. But I didn't want to let it show. I felt my heart breaking slightly.

"I'm happy for you," I said.

"You're not. I know you."

I smiled a little. "I'll be fine. Honest."

We stood outside for a little while and then he said he had to go back in. I didn't want to be around after that. I needed some time to think about this, to adjust and mourn. I wondered how much of our relationship was going to change. Everything felt different. There was another person in the picture now. Another girl, who thought I was just her boyfriend's close friend, his best friend. How low was I going to sink now?

Busted!

Mr. Biggs: It's two clock in the morning, where the hell you been?
Girl: Baby, didn't you get my two-way? I was with my girlfriends.

"Busted," Ron Isley and R. Kelly

My London trip ended uneventfully. I was away from Osei for almost twelve weeks and I didn't cheat. Go figure. That was the weirdest thing ever. But it definitely wasn't for lack of wanting to. Finding about Ato and Lina diminished my urges somewhat. I didn't owe any allegiance to her, but I still wasn't sure if I wanted to continue sleeping with him. There were too many dynamics now.

It was a drag being back in school. I wasn't interested in anything. I felt like I needed another escape, I needed another person. I couldn't figure out whom. Tosan was going nowhere, and frankly, I wasn't sure if I wanted to take things all the way with him. Abena and I ironically had become room-mates. There was a new state-of-the-art hostel, with everything imaginable. Fully furnished, with a TV room, computer room, huge kitchens on each floor and only two people to a room. No bunk beds. It was heaven. And Abena and I were the only ones out of the group who decided we couldn't handle the main school halls. Ajua had moved to Volta hall, Legon's elite all-girls' hall, and she was rooming with, guess who, Lina! Life was so messed up. I was beginning to feel stuff like that only happened to me. Three years ago, who would have thought I'd room with Abena, just the two of us? I wondered who was going to kill whom first.

Tosan also moved to the new hostel and his room was just doors from ours. That would have been even more interesting if I didn't have my head wrapped in this Ato thing.

My relationship was still deteriorating. Not cheating for twelve weeks had done nothing to help. I was bored senseless. I wanted something to happen.

163

It didn't take very long. Ato and I started sleeping together again, less than a month after we got back. I dealt very swiftly with my guilt and hesitation. Heck, if I could cheat on my boyfriend, what was my problem now? Lina really wasn't my friend. My only true hesitation was how she saw me. The girl trusted me. I believed I was the only person she was never suspicious of. That was her problem. Hadn't she heard of the phrase, "trust no one?"

I spent most weekends at Osei's place. Most of the time, I slept over, unless I had another agenda. And these days, with Lina in the picture, I had more time to spare. I wasn't sneaking into Ato's room as often as before. So I started spending more time with Osei.

I was in a cab, on my way to Osei's place. I was dead tired, because I had been sleeping all day. I was so lethargic, my mind started to think of excuses I could make to get out of sex. I had abused the "feeling sick" one enough. I decided to try the good ole "I am tired" one. I truly was.

Osei was lying on his bed when I walked into his room. His TV was off, and he was just staring at the ceiling. He had a strange look on his face. I dropped my bag on the floor. I was sure he'd been drinking. That gave me a perfect excuse: "I don't want to do it when you're drunk."

"Hey, you okay?" I asked. He hadn't said a word to me, and he wasn't looking at me. He didn't respond and I sat on the bed, looking at him. His face looked like he was having trouble breathing. He'd been drinking, I could smell it, but there was something else going on.

After five minutes of silence, he finally turned to look at me.

"Are you sleeping with Ato Fynn?"

It took every mental power I had to keep my face still. I didn't want to look shocked. I didn't want my face to give it away. I didn't want to close my eyes or look pained or even acknowledge what was about to happen, because something was definitely about to go down.

I stood up from the bed and I looked away from him. Dammit! Was it Samson? What the heck? Why would he do that? Why would he?

"I need an answer, Rabbie, now."

I turned to face him.

"Where is this coming from, huh?"

I tried the defense angle. But I knew that wouldn't work. Whatever he thought he knew, I made up my mind I was going to deny it till kingdom come. And then he reached for his bedside Bible.

"I want you to swear on this Bible and tell me the truth. I want you to put your hands on the Bible, look me in the eye and just give me yes or no."

I could have lied right there and then. Ato's motto was ringing in my head. Lie, lie and lie again, never admit anything. I could have done that. But it was the Bible he held. So fine, I have questionable morals and I wasn't exactly religious, but the Bible... How could I possibly lie on that? I was sure I'd be struck by lightning as soon as I did that. What was worse, Osei's anger or God's wrath? I was almost shaking.

"This isn't necessary, really. I am not going to swear on the Bible."

"So you're sleeping with him, then. You can't look me in the eye, can you? If you can't place your hands on the Bible, then I know it's true. But then we both know it's true anyways."

I looked at the Bible and then up at him. There was no way I could tell a lie on the Bible. No way.

I sat in a chair across from him and looked at him. He was a really good guy, and he deserved someone way better than me. Maybe this was how it was supposed to end.

"Yes I am."

Once the words were out of my mouth, there was no going back. I knew it was over now. And a part of me felt calm and relieved. It was all over.

"I can't believe you. I just can't believe you," he mumbled.

I didn't say anything. He lay back on his bed, his face towards the ceiling. His breathing was heavy.

"And you thought it would be a good idea to tell my friend? Huh?"

I didn't get Samson's motives. I really didn't. I didn't care if they were best friends. There had to be a motive. You just don't say that to someone. I thought he and I were friends too. I was so wrong.

"I really don't have anything to say. I can't make up excuses, and I can't justify this. I am really sorry about this, more sorry than you can possibly imagine."

I was really sorry, deeply. He was a good guy. He didn't deserve to be played like this. I picked up my bag from the floor.

"I'm just going to leave now, okay? Just give you some time and some space."

"Don't come back, don't ever come back."

I sighed. I looked at him, but he wouldn't look at me. I didn't want us to break up on a bad note, end as enemies, but I was going to accept my mistake and let him be. He deserved to be royally devastated.

"I'm really sorry."

And then I left.

I didn't have a lot of credits on my phone but I had to make one call.

"Hello?" Samson's voice sounded sleepy. I didn't give a damn.

"I thought you said you wouldn't tell Osei about Ato."

There was silence and then a deep sigh from his end.

"He put me in a tight spot. And it just slipped out."

"How does something like that just slip out? How? You've been a player all your life; you don't just let things slip out. So tell me, how did this slip out?"

"Listen, he thought it was me. He thought I was sleeping with you."

I was stunned. "What?"

"He called me like maybe two hours ago, said someone told him you and I spent a lot of time together in London, that you were in my house all the time. He was stressing me out, kept badgering me to tell him what was going on, and it just slipped out. I said I'm not the one he should direct it at, and the guy was right in Ghana."

"And you had to give a name, huh? What exactly did you say? I want details, Samson. I want a word-for-word transcript."

I was pissed off. He could have done better than spill the beans.

"He wouldn't let it go after that. I've known him for years, there is no way he'd understand why I wouldn't give him a name or explain what I was saying. So I did, I said you were seeing someone on campus, and I found a text but I didn't know how long it'd been going on or the extent of it."

I swore sharply. I was really upset with Samson. He could have handled it better. He could have. But it wasn't his responsibility, I was the cheat. That's exactly what I was, a cheat. It was a tough realization but it was the plain truth. I was just a terrible person and I had to face that. I cheated on Selorm with Jon. Then I cheated on Jon with Junior. And then I cheated on Tei with Osei. And then I cheated on Osei with Ato and Tosan. I had cheated on every single boyfriend I'd had. Who was I to be upset, with Samson or with anyone else?

I started crying in the taxi. This was so messed up. I was only twenty-one, how did I get to this point?

I was so sad about what I'd done to Osei. I knew he was probably hurting really badly right now. I got back to my hostel feeling very low and devastated. I wanted to call him but I knew it wouldn't be a good idea. I wanted to call Ato too, but I knew that definitely wouldn't be a good idea. I lay in bed and cried almost all night. I wasn't even sure why I was crying, but it was more to do with self-loathing. I felt tired, tired of this back and forth and this warped cycle I kept finding myself in. Something had to give, right now.

Moving On

Sammi and I sat on the front steps of Volta Hall. It was a pretty warm day, but not as busy as it usually was during the week. On Saturdays, most students spent the weekends at home, shacked up with boyfriends, girlfriends, other people's boyfriends or girlfriends, or just AWOL.

Sammi usually didn't go home and I was usually with Osei, except for this particular Saturday, my first Saturday in two years as a single girl. We sat there for a long while, not really saying much. I wasn't sure what or how to tell her. Sammi didn't like Ato; she didn't trust him and always felt he just wasn't worth it. I guess it was best getting busted for someone who cared about you as much as you cared about them, and even more important, someone who was available to pick up the pieces. Ato was neither. Where did that leave me? I was on my own, with nothing and no one. I decided it was probably best to just let it out.

"So Osei found out about Ato," I said.

Sammi looked up from her phone.

"What? Are you joking? What happened?"

"Uh, I don't even know where to start. So, I was at Samson's house in London, and I left my phone in the living room. Samson found it and read my texts, there were some from Ato. They were pretty explicit."

Sammi was in shock.

"Are you serious? And he told Osei?"

"Yes, he said Osei was pestering him about how Samson and I spent time together, so Samson offered Ato up as a way to get out of it."

"Wow. So what did Osei say? What did you say? Did you deny it? I mean, texts don't really mean anything, do they? And it could be Samson's word against yours."

"Come on, Samson is his boy. You think he was going to believe me if I said there was nothing, that Samson misunderstood those texts, that they were jokes, that I never said anything to Samson? That would be stretching it. I thought about it, but it just wasn't going to work."

Sammi sighed, in a way only Sammi could sigh. "I guess you have a point. So what happened?"

"I admitted it and he was upset and he asked me to leave, and I left. We haven't spoken since."

"I don't even know what to say, man. What are you going to do?"

"I don't know. A part of me is a little relieved. I mean, I am just a little tired, you know. Maybe this was supposed to happen; maybe I am supposed to be single, for life."

"So you think this is really over?"

"I slept with someone else. Trust me, it's over."

"Have you told Ato?"

I shook my head. I planned on telling him, but I wanted time to pass. I didn't want it to seem like I wanted something. I was just confused about it all. I wanted to be on my own now.

Sammi and I spoke a little bit longer and then I decided to go home. Hanging around an empty school was a little depressing. I needed to think, to put things in perspective. There really wasn't much to think about it. Osei and I were over, Ato and I were not going to get together, and so what was there to think about?

I spent the rest of the day at home lying in my mother's bed. I didn't tell anyone anything. I wanted to visualize how it would feel like, to be single, and to be back on my own. I sent Osei a text to apologize, repeated that I was sorry and I never meant to hurt him. He didn't reply and I didn't expect him to. I wasn't sure what was supposed to come next. Was I supposed just to leave it as it was? I didn't want to be enemies with him. I was still friends with Selorm, Jon and even Tei. Tei and I still talked every now and then. We had both moved on but we were still friends. I didn't want to be remembered badly by anyone. But I knew it was a little too early to expect Osei to get over it, move on and become friends. I had to give him his space. This wasn't about me. I had to realize that.

Osei called the following day.

"Where are you?" he asked.

His questioning suspicious tone usually irritated me, but I decided to let it slide this time.

"I'm at home."

"I'll be there in five minutes."

"Uh, okay, I'll be here."

After I hung up, I wasn't sure how I felt about him coming over. Was he going to be confrontational? What was this going to be about? I didn't want a scene at my place. I really didn't think there would be a scene, but who knew?

He arrived in ten minutes. I met him outside. My mother was sleeping upstairs and I wanted to make sure this was going to be civil. I couldn't read the look on his face when he stepped out of his car—calm, angry, indifferent?

I started talking straight away.

"My mom is sleeping upstairs, so I'd rather we don't do this inside."

"Fine, we can sit in the car."

I walked around and sat in the passenger seat. I was really feeling apprehensive. He didn't talk, and the silence dragged into five minutes.

"I don't know how many times I can possibly say this, but I am really sorry."

"I need to know about who he is. I need to know what this was and how long it was. I need to know everything."

Oh oh, that is the thing about victims of cheating. They are haunted by the comparison factor—a strong need to know who the other person is, to be able to compare, to see if they measure up. And what do cheaters do in that circumstance? If a cheater is ever in the situation where the existence of an affair comes out, it is more important to keep details to a minimum. Specific details around an affair are like nails in a coffin followed by cement instead of sand. Bottom line, you provide details and you just won't get out of it. There was no Bible here, so I was determined not to provide any details.

"I really don't think that's necessary, really."

"I should decide what's necessary and what's not. You cheated on me, you slept with someone else. I deserve to know who, and how long and where. I need to know how long you made me a fool."

"Can you just lower your voice? Please?"

"Just answer me now."

I took a deep breath.

"It was one time okay? Once, and it was nothing."

"Don't lie to me," he swore.

But I had to lie. No way could I count how many times I'd been with Ato. No way could I tell Osei it was over a year now.

"You asked me a question and I'm giving you an answer. That's it."

"Samson said he thinks it's been happening for a while."

I shook my head and just looked out of the window. What was wrong with that Samson boy?

"Well, Samson is wrong. That's all I can say."

"Where did this happen?"

"What? Come on, this is really not necessary, seriously."

"I want to know! Where? Here in your house, at school? Who else knows, all your friends?"

I exhaled slowly.

"I'm not going to do this with you. I really won't. I am really sorry about it. It was once and that was it."

My phone beeped loudly. I had turned the volume up when I was in the shower and I had forgotten to turn it down again. It startled me. I pulled it out of my pocket and in a split second Osei took it from my hand.

"Hey!" I snapped.

He glanced at it and laughed.

"Perfect. It's your boyfriend!"

He threw the phone back at me. I caught it in my hand. It was Ato. I cut the call off. He had to call at this second, didn't he?

"Listen, just get out. Go see your boyfriend. I'm done with this."

I figured I was done too. I wasn't trying to make excuses or not admit my fault in the whole situation, but if it was over, I just wanted it to be over. I didn't have the time or the energy to argue or fight. Without a word, I got out of the car and went inside the house. I heard Osei screech out. I just hoped my mother was still asleep.

I went up to my room and called Ato.

"When I call you, it'll be nice if you pick up your phone," he said in a mock-angry tone.

"I am really not in the mood. Everything is a mess."

"What?"

"Uh man, Osei knows about you and me."

"What? Are you kidding? What happened?"

"Samson. He saw your texts when I was in London... long story. I thought I could trust him, but he told Osei."

"And you admitted it? Come on, Rabbie, come on. Unless you're caught in bed with someone, there is always a way out." He sounded upset and frustrated, but that was not my problem. I had bigger issues.

"You're not going to understand. I couldn't get out of it. It's over, we broke up, that's it. I'm tired; I'm not in the mood."

"So he knows my name?"

"Yes."

Ato was silent. He was probably going to make this about him, go on about what if he met Osei somewhere, or what if Osei got a bunch of guys to come after him. I could care less if either happened right now.

"So what are you going to do? How do you feel?" he asked.

Those weren't typical Ato questions.

"I don't know how I feel. I mean, I feel bad about it, but I'm a little relieved too. He just didn't deserve all that, you know, so maybe it's best this way."

"You always act like he's a saint or something. I just don't get it."

"I'm not saying he's a saint. I am just saying I hurt him, I did, and that's all. Anyways, I have to go to school now."

"You want a lift?"

"No, thanks, I'll talk to you later, okay?"

I hung up and lay back on my bed. I felt so tired, physically and emotionally drained.

Two days passed and I still hadn't told anyone, except Sammi. Osei and I didn't see each other every weekday so neither Abena my room-mate nor the other girls would ask questions. I intended to wait a week, and then I'd tell everyone I was single. I just wasn't sure what reason I'd give. Oh, I cheated and he broke up with me? Nah. We decided it wasn't working and it was best to end it. We were fighting all the time anyways.

By Tuesday, I needed to take my mind off things, so I went to hang out with Tosan. He was only two doors away and I was in and out of his room as much as I was in and out of mine. Abena was completely suspicious of our friendship, although suspicion wasn't the right word. Any fool could see there was something. She didn't ask about it and I didn't venture any information.

I lay curled up in Tosan's arms. Tosan was bigger than Ato and taller; curling in his arms just felt so good. We still hadn't had sex. He kept saying he wasn't going to cross that line with someone's girlfriend. It was almost 1 A.M. and I wondered if I told him I was single whether it would make a difference. I felt his arms tighten around me. My back was to him and I could tell he was half asleep. His older brother was fast asleep in the bed across from us. I turned around and faced Tosan. I kissed his mouth and his eyes slowly opened. He kissed me sleepily and then closed his eyes again.

"Osei and I broke up last Friday."

His eyes opened again. "Hmmm?"

"We broke up."

"Yeah, okay, sorry." He obviously didn't believe me.

I nudged him. "Hey, I'm trying to talk to you."

He looked at me for a long time. "We both know you're going to be back with him by the end of the week. You're joined at the hip."

"We're not going to be back. This is it, trust me."

"Okay."

He touched my face and laughed a little. There was a touch of sarcasm behind the laugh. I decided not to say anymore. I put my face in his chest and tried to fall asleep.

Thursday afternoon, Osei called. His tone a little different, somber. We hadn't spoken in four days. I was on the verge of announcing the break-up.

"We need to talk," he said.

"I really don't want to get into an argument, and fight."

"You do owe me an explanation, you know that. I deserve that. So I think we should talk."

He was right. I was the bad person here, and if it was me, I'd want more information as well.

"Okay, tomorrow evening?"

"No, now, I'm in the neighborhood. I can be there in a minute."

Typical Osei, he was probably downstairs. He had probably been watching my hostel for some hours. It was already 11 P.M. and I wanted to go to bed, but I decided to get this over and done with.

"Okay, I'll be downstairs."

We hung up and I lay back on my bed staring at the ceiling. I looked towards Abena's bed. She looked like she was fast asleep.

I got up and went downstairs reluctantly. Osei's car pulled up as soon as I got there. I got into the car and he drove off. Neither of us said anything for a while. We drove out of my hostel, and through the main campus towards the faculty residences.

My aunt and her family used to live there, years ago. I had so many good memories of living in the faculty flats. When I was eight years old or so, my mother's youngest brother died tragically. My whole family was devastated. He was only eighteen years old. My mother, grandmother, everyone couldn't handle it. So my brothers and I were carted off to campus to live with my aunt and her family. I think we were there for weeks, at least a month, if not more. It was the beginning of the unbreakable bond between my cousins and us, most especially my cousin James and my younger brother Xavier. All six of us went to the same primary school too. David, my cousin, was my age and we were in the same class; Xavier, my brother, was the same age as James and they were in the same class. It was only my older brother Josh and my little cousin Lexxy who decided to pop out of our mothers too early or too late. They didn't understand the importance of synchronizing age.

Because Josh was older, playing red Indians and cowboys with us kids was not his idea of fun, so he sought out older people in the neighborhood. One of them was Harrison, my very first crush. That crush was the best feeling ever, especially since Harrison liked me back. It was a beautiful childish crush consisting of walks and holding hands and sweet glances. Ah, innocence. I called Harrison my boyfriend, he called me his girlfriend, but it was really nothing like that. Yeah, I definitely had some very good times at the Legon flats. I missed my cousins very much. They were some of my favorite people in the world.

"So what do we do now?"

The sound of Osei's voice brought me back to the present. I snapped out of my reverie and looked at him.

"Hmmm?"

"What do we do now?"

I didn't quite understand the question—we? What do *we* do now? Was there still a "we?"

"I'm not sure I understand."

He was silent. I could see the pain on his face. I could see he was struggling to say something.

"I really need to know how important he is to you. I need to understand what it was. Is he here on campus?"

I looked out the window. Here we go again. We weren't together anymore, so telling him Ato was on campus shouldn't make a difference. But it was still something you just don't do. If I wanted to sever ties completely and break Osei down to a pulp, I would give him what he wanted. But I was also trying to protect him. All that information would drive him crazy. His mind and imagination would be all over the place. He would second-guess everything we had and he would start digging up every time I canceled on him or wouldn't sleep with him. He didn't know it, but all that information wouldn't be good for him.

"This was nothing important, trust me; where he is, who he is, that's not important either."

"And that's the truth?"

I nodded, with my most somber look.

"I'll give you a second chance, if you're very sure this was nothing, and it was once."

I couldn't speak. What second chance? Did I ask for a second chance? I didn't. I had accepted this as over. Asking him back… that had never crossed my mind.

"I am very pissed off and very upset and I can't believe you did that. But I'm willing to work through this."

I was still speechless. I really wasn't sure how I felt about all this. For a brief moment, I was fine with being single. I looked at his face and I saw the tears in his eyes. Oh no, not that. I reached out to him and we hugged. I could feel the tears on his face. This threw me back to when Jon was pleading with me to give him a chance, when his voice sounded genuine and shaky, and I walked away. It would be cruel and unjust of me to look a broken man in the eyes and not try to make this work. What did I have? I had nothing else. Osei loved me, he loved me unconditionally. I had cheated on him and he wanted to work through it. What kind of person would I be if I didn't give him a chance? He hadn't wronged me and I had risked our relationship for a bona fide player. God would not forgive me if I walked away from this as well. One of my biggest regrets ever was leaving Jon that day in school, when I was the one who had wronged him. Maybe God was giving me a second chance. I was so conflicted, so torn and so confused.

"I don't know what to say," I mumbled.

"Say it's over with him. I don't want you to ever talk to him, see him, nothing. No calls, no texts, nothing."

I sat back in the seat and looked out the window. I was dazed. After a couple of minutes, I nodded. We were back, and I wasn't even sure how I felt about that.

Cheating Rehab

I decided Osei giving me a second chance, whether or not I wanted it, was a sign for me to change my ways. I was twenty-one and twenty-one was the perfect age to turn my life around. I made the decision to end all the drama and misguided actions. It wasn't an easy breezy decision to make. Rehab meant a lot of sacrifices—no Ato for sure, no Tosan and no flirting and pining for danger. I was going to be a faithful girlfriend, focused on school and my relationship. How hard could that be? Rehab was a darn good idea. I thought about starting Cheating Anonymous meetings. My first members, lifetime members actually, would be Ato, Sammi, Nana and Edem. I wouldn't let Samson in though, he was a lost cause. Oh, I would add Lynn as well. She was definitely a couple of steps above me on the cheating scale.

I guess for any rehab, the key step is to stay away from the toxic environment. For Ato, physical separation was not incredibly hard. He had his girlfriend and we weren't seeing each other on a regular basis anyways. What was harder was I missed him. I missed talking to him and just flirting and listening to him go on about his escapades. With Tosan, I couldn't exactly move out of my hostel or change rooms or ask him to change rooms either. I was stuck with having him down the hall. But I knew there was one thing I could do to end it for good.

"So, uh, Osei and I got back together."

"You're kidding me, right?"

I was surprised Tosan was surprised. Didn't he say he knew Osei and I would be back together?

"You said we'd be back, why are you surprised?"

"Just because I said it doesn't mean I actually thought you would. What is it that this guy has over you? I really don't understand it, seriously. You must really be in love with him."

"I'm not."

"You say you're not, but you definitely must be. You're still with him, aren't you?"

"But I'm standing here with you, now."

He chuckled and leaned over the railing. We were standing in front of his room, looking over the balcony at the courtyard. Being seen with Tosan was no big deal. I knew everyone who knew us knew something was going on. It was one of those open secrets.

"Listen, I can't do this anymore. You, me, it's not going anywhere, and I have things to think about," he said.

I expected it, I orchestrated it. I knew he'd back off once I told him I was back with Osei. But it still hurt. I really liked being with him. I wanted to kiss him so badly but I resisted.

"I understand, honestly, I do," I said.

He looked at me, shook his head disapprovingly and then walked into his room. I heard the door slam. Rehab was hard! I had just lost the only distraction I had in my hostel.

I stood there for a little while longer.

If I thought Osei was possessive before, I was completely wrong. Things took a very different turn. I decided it was best not to bitch. After all, I had handed him the right to do all that on a silver platter. I kept my phone closer to me. I wasn't cheating but I still wanted my privacy.

"So, I'm in cheating rehab."

Sammi laughed out loud and I laughed too.

"You should try it," I said.

Sammi shrugged and kept laughing. We were lying in my room and she was on Abena's bed. Abena, Ajua and Cami were just outside the door, talking across the hostel with Yaa and her friends. I could hear Abena's hyena-like laugh. I shook my head. Abena disliked Yaa to bits and yet laughed and talked with her like old buddies. That girl was just plain dangerous.

"So you haven't been with Ato?" Sammi asked.

"It's been, like, three weeks, or four?"

"Wow, four weeks, well done, that is so long," Sammi said sarcastically.

"Clear off. Rehab takes time, man. You take it one day at a time. That's what the alcoholics do. You know how they say in the movies? Three days sober, one week sober, mine is four weeks 'sober.' "

Sammi was laughing really hard now and I couldn't help laughing myself. I was ridiculous.

The door opened and the girls came in. Cami and Ajua sat on my bed and Abena lay on her bed next to Sammi.

"Did you hear who Mimi is with now?" Abena asked.

I didn't really feel like gossiping about Yaa and her friends. I actually liked Mimi. She was my friend, we studied together, we liked each other and we respected each other. But hey, maybe it was good gossip.

"She's apparently seeing one of Kobby's friends, Donald."

"Really? Oh my God, I met that boy in London. I had a crush on him. He's, like, insanely beautiful. Ajua, you remember, right? Looks like Morris Chestnut, seriously," I said.

"Of course, I remember Donald, you were dying for him. I think everyone knew you had a crush on that boy," Ajua said.

I laughed. The boy was beautiful and he was the spitting image of the actor, Morris Chestnut. Lucky Mimi and Ajua was right. I didn't remember clearly, but I was sure I had even told Donald I thought he was hot.

We met in a club, and we actually talked, a lot. He was so cute it was unbelievable. He was with a bunch of equally good-looking boys. Then we met again at another party, but he obviously didn't feel the same way about me. Such a shame, I laughed. Abena was going on about the hook-up but I was distracted. Why didn't I have that tingle, that excitement, that "crush" feeling for Osei? Was this what marriage felt like? Was it okay not to be enamored with your boyfriend? Most people believe what is most important is character. In the end, when you're both old and gray and weak, you want someone to be there for you, completely, through to the end. I believed in that too. Character is crucial. Osei had that type of character, the "I will honor and cherish you till death do us part" type. He would be faithful and loving. Yes, character was very important. But wasn't the physical important too? Of course, Osei was attractive, but I didn't feel like ripping his clothes off each time I saw him. I was comfortable with him. I liked him, he was a cool dude, but I didn't feel the urge to jump him. But how important was that? Donald was incredibly hot, sure, but what if he had liked me back? His looks didn't guarantee he was a good person. Osei was a good person and I was in cheating rehab. That was it.

We spent the rest of that day just lazing about. It was Saturday and it was one of the few weekends I wasn't with Osei. I just wanted to stay in and not do anything.

Later that night, Jon sent a text and said he was with some friends right in front of my hostel. He asked if I could come down. I wondered who he was there to see. But I didn't care. I was in cheating rehab; I didn't care what anyone was doing. I was working on my relationship now. I decided to go say hi anyways.

"Hey, it's been ages," I said.

We hugged. He looked good and he smelled good. This boy was just of a different world.

"I know. You don't look for me anymore. How are you? How's your boyfriend?"

I laughed. "You know his damn name."

He smiled, and hugged me again. "You really look good," he said. "He must be treating you right."

Jon loved to tease me about Osei. Every guy I knew liked to tease me about Osei.

"How's your girlfriend? What's her name? Ann?"

"We're kind of on the outs."

"Kind of?" I asked.

"Uh, I don't even know, man."

There was a trailer parked in the parking lot. I wondered what the heck a trailer this size was doing there at 10 P.M. as I leaned against it. Jon leaned in closer. I wanted to touch his face, but I didn't. And then it happened. I don't know how, but out of nowhere I felt his lips on mine. I didn't stand a damn chance. His lips felt so soft, so sweet. It was just like the night when we first kissed in the theatre. And just like that night in the theatre it was spontaneous, unexpected and earth shattering. I kissed him like I hadn't kissed in a year. My arms went around his neck, and his hands grasped my waist. We kissed for what felt like forever.

"Hey Jon, is that you down there?"

We both snapped apart.

"What the heck?" he cursed. He took a couple of steps back and looked up over the trailer.

"Hey, Marie, what's up?" he called up.

I couldn't believe it. Was she for real? Didn't she see us? Was she serious? What on earth was that about? How messed up was that? You see someone you know kissing and you call him?

"Eh, is that Rabbie?"

I chuckled. This bitch had some nerve. I knew who she was, but we weren't friends. And after this, we were definitely never going to be friends. I didn't bother to look up and Jon just smiled up at her.

"Jon, don't leave, I'm coming down, okay."

"You gotta be kidding me, man. Is she for real?" I asked.

Jon laughed but I didn't think it was funny.

"I'm going back to my room," I said. I was so irritated.

"Hey, calm down, she is just coming to say hello."

"Oh, she sees us kissing and she thinks this is the perfect time to come down and say hello?"

Jon pinned me against the trailer again and kissed me again. We kissed deeply. I wanted to take him up to my room and rip his clothes off. I was dying. We broke apart and I looked at him silently. I would always, always love this boy.

It was right then that I packed my bags and checked out of cheating rehab. The charade was over.

The Way It Is

Jon and I didn't have sex that night. In fact, I didn't see him again for a long while. But the moment had made one thing very clear. Sobriety was not for me, at least not right now. I wasn't ready to be faithful. I wasn't sure if I ever would be. I was a cheater-holic.

Marie, the peeping bitch, came down and I left Jon with her. He didn't call me or ask me to stay and I just went up to my room. Close to 2 A.M., I sent Ato a text. He called me.

"I thought you weren't speaking to me or something," he said.

"Uh, I was just dealing with some issues. I wanted to see if I could be faithful."

Ato laughed.

"Nice joke," he said, cracking up.

"I did try, I really did, man."

"You're like me. It's just how we are. That's the way it is."

"I'm not like you, dude. I am nothing like you," I said.

"If that's what you want to believe. If I was a girl, I'd be you and if you were a guy, you'd be me. That's it. You have to accept it. You can't hang up that jersey."

"I'm not a player," I said sternly.

"I'll pick you up in five minutes."

I smiled. I didn't even know why I was smiling. I was such a sucker.

"I'll come to you, ten minutes. I need the walk."

Ato laughed and hung up. I lay on my bed for a second. Abena had gone home earlier that night. I would have asked Ato over, but that was too risky. Lina's friends lived in the hostel and Ato over at my end at 2 A.M. would be crazy. I pulled clothes on and snuck out. I was definitely back to square one.

For some reason, life started to make sense again. It was almost like I'd been in a time capsule over the last four weeks. Doing what I was doing again seemed normal. The world was back on the right axis.

I changed Ato's name on my phone. Sammi taught me that. You give a guy a girl name and vice versa. I wasn't sure I wanted to give Ato a girl name though. Osei would want to know who this new friend was. So I just changed his name to Af—not exactly the smartest choice, but I figured the best thing to do would be to hold on really tight to my phone.

I quit my job at the TV station. Second year was much tougher and I couldn't work those hours and still go to school. Osei was pleased about that. At least I had done one thing he always wanted me to do. I got a hook-up with a friend from economics, Ransford, to write scripts for a kids' TV show his mother and brother were producing.

This was really the way things were meant to be. I met with Ransford, his mother and brother, and I was completely hooked. Ransford and I co-wrote the pilot and as soon as GTV gave the green light, we were in business.

I was involved with almost everything, from the casting to little creative details.

The money was of course peanuts, but that wasn't my focus. I was a hired writer, how cool was that?

Early 2001, my older brother got a job with a company in the U.K. I was really happy for him. Plus I wanted him out of the house. Kids who stay at home too long get to a point they think they run the house. My brother was only twenty-four at the time, but he was suffering from "I'm the oldest male" syndrome. He was acting like he was my father and not my brother, and I needed him to be the kingpin elsewhere. I was going to miss him of course, but I was next in line to the "I am the shit in this house" throne. I wanted that throne, I needed him out. I figured I could rule better.

Truth be told, I was proud of Josh. The company worked out his visa and everything. Two weeks before he was set to go, my younger brother and I decided to throw a going-away gig for him. My younger brother loved throwing parties. He wanted to throw a party for every single event. He was the Diddy of our world.

The only little problem was that Ato was Josh's friend and so naturally we invited him. And Osei of course was definitely going to be there. That was my headache but I couldn't share that with my brothers. I initially wanted to talk to Ato about it, but I decided to let it go. I would have to be really sharp that night. I was on amber alert all night.

The party was awesome. My little brother really knew how to throw one. Ato was there, but he came earlier than Osei and he left earlier. I didn't plan it, things just went my way. I was grateful for that. What didn't go my way was the next day.

My family and I were lounging at home eating *wakye* (rice and beans) from our favorite spot, Auntie Muni, and just spending time with Josh. Ato came by, he'd been to Auntie Muni as well, and he came to join us. Ato had become pretty close to everyone in my family. My cousin Albert worshiped him. My younger brother Xavier was fascinated by him and of course Josh just knew what kind of womanizer he was. My mother, and my cousins, Bernie and Winnie, were all used to him; we were just one big happy family. I don't think anyone ever suspected us, except maybe Josh. Everyone else easily and simply understood Ato was one of my best friends. He was like an adopted family member or something. If only they knew.

After a couple of hours, Ato was getting ready to leave when I heard a car outside. I peeked out the window. It was Osei. My blood literally froze. I looked at Ato and he caught my eye. He tucked his hands defensively into his pockets. And then I realized he was wearing his Arsenal jersey with Ato written across the back. You gotta be kidding! I stood up quickly and practically sprinted outside. Osei was just getting out of his car.

"Hey," he said heartily.

I was breathing so hard. This could go very badly. He hugged me and I hugged him back.

"Hey, I was just going to call you. Guess which movie is finally at the video club?"

He ignored the question and nodded in the direction of Ato's car.

"Whose car is that?"

"Oh, my brother's friend," I said in a flip tone.

At that minute, Josh, Ato and my younger brother stepped out of the house.

"Osei, what's up?" my younger brother shouted and walked towards Osei's car. I tried really hard not to look at Ato. Osei did that head-nod thing that guys usually do. He nodded at Ato and Josh, typical male greeting. Ato and Josh nodded back. Then I heard Ato talk.

"Josh, I have to go. I'll come by again before you leave, yeah? It's next Saturday, right?"

"Yeah man. Thanks for coming around, yeah."

"Oh of course, of course, I'll see you, man."

They did the handshake, chest-thump thing (did that have a name?) and then Ato walked towards his car. The others probably didn't notice, but I could tell he was deliberately avoiding turning his back towards Osei. My fingers were literally crossed. I didn't want either of my brothers to say his name at the last second. Ato just waved a little at me and Xavier and then he got in his car and drove off. I exhaled. I realized I had been holding my breath. Osei walked into the house with my brothers and I leaned against his car for a minute. My heart was racing. This was so close! I took a deep breath and I tried to calm my heart. My phone started to ring and I looked down at it. It was Ato.

"Are you insane?" I screamed. "Why are you calling me?"

"I felt if you couldn't talk, you wouldn't answer. That was close, huh. I was, like, shit, I am wearing my name on my back!" He was laughing hysterically.

"You're crazy, you know that?"

"You and me both," he said, laughing.

I hung up and smiled. Yeah, we were both insane.

Edem and Abena—A Case Study of "Are You Kidding, Four Years?"

I will state this here, because these are my reflections and I can say whatever the heck I want to say, I have never witnessed a relationship as bad and as disrespectful as Edem and Abena. I wish to God no one, friend or foe, ever has to go through that again. I don't know if any shrink could even diagnose what that was all about. Day after day I asked: why does she stay? I cannot count the instances of blatant disrespect, open indiscretions, verbal and mental abuse, and everything in between. The only thing that boy didn't do to her was hit her. He tore her apart day after day. He ripped through her self-esteem like a lawnmower plowing through ten-inch weeds. It troubled my heart and my spirit.

There were times he would compliment her friends right in front of her.

"Why can't you be as pretty as Cami, huh?"

"Why aren't you sexy?"

"What is that thing you're wearing?"

"Gosh, Abena, you are really becoming fat."

"I don't want to see you today. Don't come to my house."

Then he would flirt and touch others, even her friends, right in front of her.

"Sammi, your breasts look like they'd be good to suck on."

"Cami, come here and let me touch you a little."

"I swear, I bet sleeping with that girl over there is like heaven."

"Rabbie, can you please teach Abena how to have sex? She doesn't do anything. She just lies on her back."

Then there were the completely open indiscretions. How many times did he cheat, openly? Trying to count would be like trying to count the stars. It pained me to bits that I was at the beginning of that list! I wanted to kill him. He just didn't care. He really didn't. He never acted like he was in a relationship. He threw everything imaginable at her, and she still didn't budge. I shake my head now, thinking about it. What was it?

I remember an instance; it was his birthday, 2001. Abena bought him towels with both their names embroidered on them. And we took them over to his house. It was Abena, Cami, Sammi and I. The security man told us he wasn't in, but we decided to leave the towels inside. He tried to stop us but we managed to get to the front door when it opened. It was Edem.

"What are you guys doing here?"

"I brought you a gift!" Abena said gleefully in her screechy voice.

"Listen, I'm busy, you guys have to go now."

As soon as he said that, I knew what was going on. I stepped in front of Abena and pushed the door further in. Edem knew I didn't take shit. I heard a girl's voice coming from upstairs: "Edem, who's there?"

We all knew the voice.

"Is that Donna?" Abena's voice rose just a little bit, almost like she didn't want the girl upstairs to hear her. I shook my head. Who was the girlfriend here, huh?

"Yes, it's Donna, so what? I need you guys to leave now. You can come later, not now."

He tried to push me back.

"Don't you dare touch me. Your girlfriend brought you towels and we're bringing them in!" I said it loud, with my head tilted up. I knew the bitch upstairs had heard.

Abena touched my shoulder. "Let's go."

I span around. "What?"

Cami and Sammie weren't saying much. They shrugged. We turned around and left.

Abena and I had our differences for sure, but no matter what, how Edem treated her was inexcusable. It was troubling on so many levels. I had spoken to Edem about it before, and he said he wanted her to get the message to leave herself. He didn't do break-ups, he preferred to drop the hints. And as loud as his hints were, she just wasn't getting it. I really couldn't stand him. I wondered what I had seen in him before. He was so self-centered, so cruel, so selfish to do that to her. And she was so stupid to stay and take it all.

Abena and I, it wasn't all bad. Over the last year and a half we'd been room-mates, I had stuck by her through a lot. But no matter what you said to her, she just didn't get the message. It really broke my heart. I sincerely believed she could do way better.

Edem was still a fun guy; there was no doubt about it. He made her laugh, he made us all laugh. He was hanging out with a group of guys who were also fun to be around. There was Paa Kwesi, and his cousin Chris, and their friends Anthony, Ekow and Daren. When Edem came over, he came with most of them. And when we went out clubbing, we went with them.

I already knew Ekow and Daren. They lived up my street and Ekow was friends with my older brother. I tried to talk to Ekow, to get him to talk to Edem, get him to either leave the girl or treat her better. Ekow repeated the same thing Edem said—if Abena didn't see she had to leave, it wasn't going to be up to Edem. There was nothing anyone could do or say.

I could hear Abena crying at night sometimes. I didn't know what to say to her. How many times or different ways could you tell someone you have to ditch your stupid-ass boyfriend? I had run out of ideas. Abena, Cami and Sammi believed men would always cheat. Even Ajua openly said that once, right in front of her boyfriend. I had been completely upset then. Even if you thought it, it was stupid to let the guy be aware that's how you felt. Abena acted like it wouldn't be any better anywhere else. Maybe, maybe not, but you still don't give up on life, on chance, on being loved. I officially washed my hands of Abena, and her choices.

Some Doors Open, as Some Doors Close

Every single person has that one person who steals their heart and never really gives it back. Mine was Jon, Abena's was Edem and Maame's was Samson. Ajua eventually found hers, Kwaku. Ajua's relationship with Kwaku would take more than one chapter, more than two, close to ten perhaps. She fell so hard, she broke bones that I'm not sure are completely healed.

Just as Ajua was falling hopelessly in love, Abena was dealing with her first major gut-wrenching heartbreak. Yep, the fiasco that was Abena and Edem was finally over, summer of 2001.

Summer 2001 the girls went to London. Edem went as well, but for school. Leaving Ghana, for Edem, was the ultimate get-out-of-jail-free card. It was the beginning of a new life and new people and opportunities. Edem often said it was not his style to break up with girls and he'd leave the decision up to the girl. For four and a half years he left the decision up to Abena and she just wouldn't take the bait. But everyone has a limit, and even if Abena didn't seem to have one, Edem eventually reached his.

As the story goes, Edem told her outright he was done; he told her he had tried for years to get her to leave him but she just didn't seem to get it. And the ultimate famous break-up line was born.

"You think this is a movie huh? Let's think of it as a movie then. In my personal movie, I'm the hero and the female lead is not you. Not only are you not in my movie, I don't think you should even buy tickets to see it."

Edem said that to Abena, the guy who claimed he couldn't break up with girls. Edem was an ass, but he had been an ass from the beginning of their relationship. Abena should have left years ago, but even as he told her she was no longer in his movie, she still didn't get the message.

The worst part of the break-up story was that late one night Abena went over to Selorm's place in London, where Edem was staying. Edem was there, with another girl, in bed. He told Abena she had five minutes to present her case. And spineless Abena got on her knees and cried and begged and whined and wailed like she was losing her mother. After five minutes, he rated her presentation as poor and went back to bed with his new girl. But Abena wouldn't leave and so eventually Selorm gave her blankets and pillows to sleep on the sofa.

When I heard this story I was stunned. What was even more shocking was the effect the whole episode had on her. Abena was broken. The only somewhat positive effect was she lost a lot of weight. Everything else about that whole situation was pathetic. I couldn't understand how any girl could lose all self-respect and stoop to such depths. But Abena's self-respect was lost years ago. The trip to London was just an anchor that sank her completely.

When they returned from London, Ajua was giddy in love and Abena was an emotionally and physically drained, bitter person. The rest of us, we were just spectators. Well, not all of us.

Sammi was also in a relationship that I wasn't sure I understood head or tail of. His name was Henry and he was similar to Osei in a few ways. He was an "exter," meaning an off-campus boyfriend. He was older, close to Osei's age, and he was possessive. But his possessiveness was beyond anything I'd ever seen. As an outsider, I could have been wrong. But I kept telling myself if Osei was that bad, I wouldn't stay, ever. Like Osei, Henry was also dealing with a cheating girlfriend. Exters usually had it tougher. They didn't live on campus and they had jobs and responsibilities. That left girls like Sammi and I with too much free time. Henry, like Osei, knew his girlfriend was up to no good. What I failed to understand was, isn't it easier to break up with a cheating girl than to drive yourself crazy trying to monitor her every move? The same goes for girls with cheating boyfriends. I've never been one to riffle through my boyfriend's drawers, phone or papers looking for evidence of a cheating life. I went through Osei's old pictures once, and found a few letters, back when he was dating other people. He thought the letters made me jealous. I wasn't, not in the least. As a writer, my interest was more of curiosity and fascination.

So back to my age-old question: if you suspect your girlfriend or your boyfriend is cheating, and he or she treats you badly, why stay? Why put yourself through such agony of checking their messages and phone, making impromptu visits and even tailing them? It just didn't make sense to me. Was love that blind?

I had been a fool in love before, of course. I did a few stupid things for Jon, but that was because I was trying to let him know I loved him. And when he told Edem about our disastrous night I knew it was time to walk away.

Knowing when to walk away, that's the catch right? That is the catch that most guys and girls miss. Back then I thought I had a very clear idea about when to walk away. If I had been in Abena's situation I would have walked away after less than a year. If I had been in Ajua's situation, Kwaku would have been kicked to the curb much earlier than he actually was. Back then, my sense of what is permissible and what is not was strong. I really could not stand some crap. I thought I had it figured out. And this mentality, this inability to understand what took other girls so long, made me rather cold and insensitive. I just didn't get it, at all. Why take such disrespect?

My thoughts on Ajua and her "Jon" are varied. I felt strongly that he was given much more slack than he deserved. Ajua was in love, no doubt about it. She was so smitten it was somewhat nostalgic to watch and somewhat of a relief. I had been suspicious and wary of Ato and Ajua from day one. He claimed nothing was going on, but when she fell in love with Kwaku, it was a sign I could breathe a little easier.

Ato wasn't around anyways. He graduated May of 2001 and was in the US holidaying and preparing for the next phase of medical school. I missed him like crazy the first few months he was gone. It was unbearable almost. Up until that point, I hadn't quite realized how much I really liked him. He was such a big part of my life. I got over it after a few months though. He was gone in May and by October I was open to filling his physical spot. Emotionally, he wasn't going anywhere quite so fast, but physically, I needed a replacement.

My cheating, really, wasn't because I wasn't satisfied with what I had. Osei and I were together a lot. My cheating, and I've probably said this before, was just because I could, just because I was curious, just because I was bored and just because that's just how I was.

Ajua's love-struck life and Abena's abysmal life were dragging me down. I had a number of options for a replacement, but I decided an on-campus hook-up just wasn't the way to go. Then Anthony came along. Anthony wasn't really a major player in the events that have shaped my life. Anthony was just a catalyst to a realization that hit me as I was getting to know him.

Anthony was Edem's friend. Before the credits rolled on Edem and Abena, Edem, Anthony and a bunch of other guys used to come around all the time. Abena was my room-mate so I got to know Edem's friends pretty well. And they all became my friends. Ekow and Daren, I said earlier, lived up my road and were my older brother's friends. Over weekends, all the guys including Edem would come to my place and we'd hang out and just have fun. They would smoke pot or drink weed juice every now and then, of which I didn't approve, but I let it slide. I really wasn't interested in any of them. Ekow was the best looking of the gang but he seemed slightly aloof. He just seemed a tad bit surly, like someone who'd be too much work to tame. Ekow was also dating a girl I didn't quite like, Tara. I figured it would be too much to hook up with Ekow. He didn't seem approachable anyways.

Anthony was the next best thing, which may sound mean, but really isn't. He was good looking, fair, just about my height or so, and skinny. He was friendly and outgoing and he reminded me a little of Edem, the Edem I thought I knew before. Anthony liked me and he made it clear from the beginning. Ato was gone and Anthony's attentions filled that void.

I can't even say exactly when we started kissing. But he was a good kisser. Not earth shattering, but that wasn't his fault. Jon had just ruined the kissing scale for everyone else. I had stopped comparing.

One afternoon, Abena had gone home, which she did almost all the time now, and I was alone in the hostel. Ajua was with Kwaku, Cami was being shady somewhere and Sammi was a prisoner in her boyfriend's house, as always. I was alone and I was bored out of my mind. Alcoholics try to avoid bars and alcohol in general, and for us cheaters, boredom is the root of our evil. I called Anthony. I figured today was the day to step it up a notch.

I was downstairs waiting for Anthony when he and his friends pulled up to the hostel. I had been hoping he'd come alone. As much as his friends suspected there was something up, I didn't overtly indicate this was true. Speculation is different from getting concrete, in-your-face facts.

Anthony stepped out of the car and Ekow stepped out with him, to take his place in the front. For a brief moment, Ekow's eyes fell on mine and he looked at me, he really looked at me. There was something in that look that I couldn't quite place. I felt shivers down my spine and as warm as it was outside, I felt cold. Ekow and I were friends, I could say. We talked enough times. Every now and then he came to visit on his own and we'd chat. He wasn't the most approachable person, but he wasn't completely closed off to me. But he'd never looked at me the way he looked at me that day. I didn't know what the heck it was—disappointment, interest, lack of interest, what? And then the look was gone. He got into the car and the boys drove off.

"Hey," Anthony said.

I looked at him and forced a smile. We went upstairs to my room and he started kissing me straight away. I tried to kiss him back but I was distracted. My mind kept going back to Ekow's face, and that look I couldn't place. I felt my back on the bed, felt Anthony trying to take my clothes off. I felt him kissing my neck, felt his hands on my breasts and then I froze.

"I can't do this, I can't do this. I can't do this."

"Hmm, relax, just relax," he murmured.

I lifted his head up from my chest and looked him squarely in the eyes.

"I can't do this," I said firmly. I crawled from underneath him and buttoned up my top quickly.

He sat silently on the bed for a couple of minutes.

"What's going on?" he asked.

"I just can't do it. I don't want to take this further. I'm not ready to sleep with you."

"Can I ask why?"

Because you're Ekow's friend, and I think I have a crush on him, and I don't want to do you, because you're his friend, and that would ruin any chance of me and him—not like there will be a chance, but I have done the friends thing—Jon, Edem, Selorm—and I can't do it again, and I just can't, won't sleep with you.

I didn't say that out loud but those were my reasons. I had a major crush on Ekow. And I had no strong feelings for Anthony. It wasn't worth it.

"I just don't want to take this further. It doesn't feel right. I am really sorry."

He shook his head and picked up his phone.

"Hey, are you guys on campus? You are? Can you come back for me?"

I was glad he called the boys. They would know nothing had happened. Ekow would know nothing had happened. That was important to me.

Anthony stared at me and smiled a little.

"Friends?" I asked.

"Sure, friends," he said.

He walked out the door and I lay on Abena's bed for a moment. What was wrong with me? What was I doing? Why couldn't I focus?

I felt stressed and frustrated. I decided I wasn't going to do anything about this crush on Ekow. I considered cheating rehab again for just a second and then the thought was gone.

Things Fall Apart, the Center Cannot Hold

In Ghana, parents often do not bring up children alone. It would take a while for any child in Ghana to list all the uncles, aunts, cousins and relatives in their lives. Even if the relation is not by blood, any adult who touches your life and has an influence on your life and is close to your family is your family. Bonds are created that are hard to break, and your family becomes your best friends, no matter the distance that may separate you, or the circumstances that may challenge the bonds you build.

When I was growing up, I learnt in school and the very few times I attended church that God sent certain events our way to bring us closer to Him. Events that were so strong and so clear that you just knew there was a God. I was yet to see some of these events.

My grandparents tried to have enough faith for us all. They didn't succeed much. I definitely believed in God, I just wasn't sure what His deal was. My aunt Flossie and my uncle Kweku were another set of true believers. Each time my brothers and I visited them, we did morning devotion, went to church and talked about God. My brothers and I were surrounded by so many relatives and people of God, it was a wonder we didn't succumb to the lure of Christianity.

Christianity, I believe, is a personal experience, and we just hadn't had our personal experiences.

When my grandmother, a woman of such strong faith and beliefs, died of a horrible disease such as cancer, the battle for my soul was all but lost. There was no God, I was almost certain. Even if there was, He wasn't as kind as they claimed He was. My grandmother's death devastated me in a way I really didn't recover from. But God wasn't done with doling out pain. He really wasn't.

Late 1999, God took away someone who lived and breathed God's work. A person couldn't have a kinder soul and a more open heart. I believed strongly that if it wasn't for my grand-mother and my Afful family, I'd have no faith at all, none whatsoever. First he took my grandmother and took pieces of my faith. And then he took Uncle Kweku Afful, through another devastating disease. Here was a man who spent his days and his life for God, a man with a family who loved him. It didn't make any sense to me. I couldn't imagine what my cousins were going through, and even more, I wondered if their faith was shaken a little, just a little. How could God? If He was up there, looking down at us like chess pieces, how could He pick that piece, a piece that was working for Him? It was a heartbreaking, tragic loss. My mother was with my aunt every day and my brothers and I, and so many other cousins, tried to be there for the family. But when you don't understand God, and you don't have faith in Him, how do you offer someone else comfort and support? I just didn't believe. God had wronged a good family and He just didn't deserve to be making any decisions.

Two years later, He took away Uncle Kweku Daniels, my mother's brother, once again horribly and unexpectedly. He couldn't even give any of my loved ones a peaceful death.

Kweku Daniels was my mother's younger brother. He was a man with a kind heart and a gentle spirit. I had never heard my uncle raise his voice or cuss or look angry. He was like my grandfather's best friend. They worked together, and were inseparable. We all loved him. He and my mother were close. He was just such a good man.

My uncle had diabetes, and he got a foot infection that just didn't get better. I remember the day he died like it was just yesterday. My family and I were at the hospital. He had been there for weeks and his health was deteriorating. The night before, he had fallen into a coma. The next day, as we sat around his bed, his eyes were open but the doctors said he couldn't hear or see us. I'd read enough Michael Crichton and Stephen King books to be doubtful. My brothers and I spoke to him for hours and held his hand and encouraged him to wake up. When it was time to leave, my brother Xavier and I stood at the door and waved. And then my uncle's eyes turned to the door and he raised a hand and waved. I was hysterical. I thought it was a sign from

God. He did exist after all. We told my mother and the doctors, and the Hippocratic cynics said it was just a nerve reaction. I decided I would allow them their cynicism, they couldn't understand what had happened. This was God telling me He had heard. My uncle was going to be fine.

A few hours after we got home, the hospital called: my uncle hadn't made it. I felt my faith dissolve completely. This wasn't possible. What was God doing? In a span of five years, He had taken three good, God-fearing people away from us. These weren't heartless, cold, insensitive atheists. These were people whose lives were supposed to be testaments to His existence. And how did He repay them and their families? Disease and heartache.

My grandfather lost a bit of himself when my grandmother died. He was never the same again and we all knew that. His life was over in 1996. There was no doubt that she took away a bit of his heart and each day he pushed on, he did it for his children. And then lo and behold, God takes a second son from him. My grandparents had had eight children in total. By the time I was born, only five of their original eight lived. By the time I was eight, my dear uncle Jojo lost his battle at eighteen years old. Then God took my grandmother, and now my uncle. As my grandfather struggled to find meaning in life again, I felt there just couldn't possibly be a God. What in the world had we done to deserve all this?

I was haunted by the memory of the last time we saw my uncle, when he looked at us and raised his hand. I cried like there was no tomorrow. And I just gave up. People died, yes, but how many losses can one family take? How many losses can any one person take? And if I wanted to count Kwame, then definitely, faith had no meaning. If God was just going to take it all away, I wasn't going to care enough for it to hurt.

But then again, He just wasn't done with me, not quite yet.

One More Chance

"Hey Rabbie, what's up?"

I was half asleep when my phone started ringing at 8 A.M. It was Saturday. I hadn't gone to Osei's place the night before and I was looking forward to sleeping in.

"Agyare, what's going on?"

"Uh, Rabbie, Osei was in a terrible car accident."

My heart skipped a beat. Kwame, Kwame, all over again!

I started crying.

"Rabbie, hey, calm down, he's okay. He's injured but he's going to be fine. It happened last night, but we didn't want to call you till we were sure he was fine. We're taking him home from the hospital now. Can you meet us there?"

I still couldn't stop crying. Oh my God. My heart was beating so fast. I couldn't breathe. Abena woke when Agyare hung up and she came over to my bed. I wept so hard, my head felt like it was going to burst. She wanted to come with me but I wasn't sure what condition Osei was in and who was going to be there. So I decided to go alone.

As I sat in the cab on my way to Osei's house, I said a prayer of some kind. I told God, if He wanted there to be any chance, any chance at all, of me joining his side, this was the one person He could not afford to take from me. I said it as sternly as I could manage in the middle of my tears. This was His opportunity; if He took this away there would be no way, none at all, not even an inkling of a chance. His chances of having my support right now were slim, and He damn well knew why. If He took Osei, nothing, not even parting the Atlantic Ocean in front of my eyes, would work.

By the time I got to Osei's place, I was scared and angry. There were a number of cars parked in front of the house. Thankfully, Agyare was standing right outside. He looked slightly shaken but very calm. I hugged him.

"Hey, sorry, did I scare you? He's fine, really. Badly bruised and in pain but he's going to be fine. Come on, let's go inside."

We went round the back straight to Osei's room. Osei lay stretched out on his bed. He was a mess. His chest was bandaged and wrapped from neck to waist. His knees were bruised and cut and his right knee was wrapped but blood had seeped through. He didn't look fine. His mother was fussing over him and one of his younger cousins was there. There were a couple of other people lingering on the porch outside his room. His eyes looked tired but still alert. He smiled wanly at me. I smiled back.

"Hey you, what's all this about, huh?" I asked him.

His mother stood up from the bed.

"It was such a bad accident, Rabbie. It was such a bad accident. He could have killed himself, he could have killed himself."

I could hear the pain and worry in her voice. She looked tired. She had probably been at the hospital all night. I wondered why Agyare or someone hadn't called me earlier. Why did people always think I couldn't handle bad news? I wished I had been there with him, in the hospital. I sat on the bed and looked at him. He tried to smile but he was too tired. His eyes closed.

"He has to sleep, he has to rest. It was such a bad accident," his mother kept saying.

I stood up from the bed. His mother ushered everyone out and I sat on the porch with Agyare. Samson had shown up too. He was back from London and the two of us had gotten over his blunder. The two guys started talking. Osei had apparently gone drinking with Agyare and Samson. Minutes after he left, they weren't sure what exactly happened but he smashed head-on into a tree, probably going over seventy miles an hour. His car was totaled. Samson and Agyare sounded in awe of how Osei was still alive, considering he hadn't worn a seat belt. There was a level of sordid fascination in their voices. A cab driver found Osei, who was barely conscious. I wasn't even sure how anyone else got to know. Who called his friends, his parents? It didn't even matter. I was in shock. I couldn't believe what had just happened to him. He could have died. He could have died. I listened to the guys for a little longer and then I snuck into Osei's room. He was still sleeping. I lay on the bed, trying to make room next to him without waking him. I placed my hand on his bandaged chest, tried to hear his heart beating.

"Hey."

I looked up. His eyes were open and he was looking at me, smiling.

"Are you okay?" I asked. Stupid question.

He nodded. "Yeah, yeah I am."

He adjusted himself a little bit and I snuggled into his arms, trying not to press against his wounded chest. After a short while, we both fell asleep.

Later that day, my younger brother came to pick me up. He hung out with Osei a little bit and then we left. My brother wanted to go see Osei's car. I wasn't so keen, but I went anyways. The car was at the police yard. I wasn't quite prepared for what I saw. There was barely anything left of Osei's car, especially the front part. The front section, from the lights through the hood, was mangled right through the driver's seat. For a second, it hit me that if he had been wearing his seat belt, he would have been trapped in the driver's seat and crashed. I suspected the impact of the crash must have thrown him into the back somehow. I was overwhelmed with how close this had been, and how Kwame hadn't been that lucky. I cried some more.

Osei's accident took me back to our first year together, when I was a dutiful girlfriend. For the next two months, I was in his house every single day, without fail. On days I had class, I went straight from class to his house. And on days I didn't have class, I slept over at his place. Osei's parents didn't mind. I was his mother's nurse assistant. We bathed him, we changed his bandages, we made sure he ate and we catered to his every need. I was by his side from morning to night. Nothing else really mattered. He had come close to death and it was not the time for me to be creeping around. He couldn't work for weeks. He was restricted to his four walls, and I had to be there. I wanted to be there.

Ato came back January 2002, but I wasn't even interested in starting that up again. He was my one indiscretion and if I could avoid falling into that cycle, I'd be good. I had somewhat gotten used to his absence. He had been gone for six months. We had spoken a lot while he was gone, but six months was still a long time. I was completely determined not to fall into that mode. I was going to give my relationship one more shot.

Tei, Part Three

Another summer was creeping up. The girls and I started to talk about travel. I spoke to my aunt in America, who said she'd love to have me. A ticket from Ghana to Arizona cost an insane amount, but I wanted to see Tei. So I came up with a brilliant solution. British Airways flights always stopped over in London, no matter the destination. I could kill two countries with one stone. Even better, I was going to fly into New York, which was only a couple of hours from Tei, and then connect from New York to Arizona. My aunt said she would cover the connection. Perfect. Once the idea took root in my head, there was no getting it out. I was going to America. I was going to see Tei after five years. Five years! Within weeks, my idea sounded appealing to the girls too. Ajua's heart-throb Kwaku was in grad school in Atlanta at the time, so all of them decided to hitch a ride on my US bandwagon. We came up with a plan. It would be a thirteen-week summer vacation. We would stay in London for eight weeks and work and then spend four weeks in America. The girls wanted to work in London a little bit longer but I had two stops to make in the US and I needed enough time to spend with Tei. So they extended their stay in London but I stuck to my eight-week schedule. We all bought BA tickets, with the same departure from Ghana and same return date back from New York. I was pretty excited by it all. And the girls all planned on coming to Phila-delphia, where Tei lived. Tei was pretty excited about the trip too. He said there'd be a place for everyone to stay.

As excited as I was, the universe just kept throwing obstacles and distractions my way from the moment the idea was born.

Osei and Ato

"So, where are you going to be in America?" Osei asked.

"My aunt's, in Arizona," I said.

"The entire trip?" he asked.

"Yeah, the entire trip, I think. I may go to New York, but I haven't quite decided. Ajua and the rest of the girls are coming too, and we're planning on perhaps meeting up in New York."

"Who's in New York?"

"Cami's uncle." That wasn't a lie. Cami did have an uncle in New York.

"So, are you going to see Tei?" he asked directly.

I wasn't sure how to answer. I had thought about it a million times. And each lie just didn't sound plausible.

"I don't know. I haven't seen him in five years. Even if I do decide to see him, nothing is going to happen, seriously. I've moved on, he's moved on. He has a daughter and he lives with someone."

Osei sighed and shook his head. We were in his room, lying on his bed. I could have lied, but I wanted to test his reaction. Keeping my planned three weeks in Philly from him was going to be hard.

"Just because he has a daughter doesn't mean anything. I don't want you to see him. You can't see him. I'm serious. I'm really serious about this."

I nodded.

"Don't just nod. I know you still talk to him. I know you do."

I knew he did. One of Osei's close friends, George, was also one of Tei's close friends.

There had been an interesting, semi-uncomfortable incident once, after Osei and I had been together a few months. Osei and George came by my house. I didn't know who George was then, didn't know Tei knew him and Osei didn't know Tei knew George either. Osei introduced me to George as Rabbie. I remember the look on George's face, a look of recognition as he studied my face.

"Oh yeah, yeah, Rabbie, you're Tei's girlfriend right? Tei is one of my best friends. I just got back from America last week. He's got your pictures. Wow, it's incredible to finally meet you. I was telling Tei he needs to come back for you, marry you soon."

I had already emailed Tei breaking up with him, but he hadn't sent that information down the wire to his crew, obviously. Osei didn't say anything there and then. But he explained to George later that there had been a little change of batons. I never really liked or trusted George after that. I had sincerely hoped he would fall off the radar for one of them. But he remained both Osei and Tei's close friend. If Osei knew Tei and I still talked, I wasn't surprised.

If I went to Philly, there was a very strong possibility Osei would find out. It was all so risky.

"I really can't say I wouldn't see him."

Osei looked stunned. "I can't believe you. I swear, you're unbelievable!"

"Listen, listen to me, honestly, even if I do see him, I will not let anything happen. I am telling you. It's just that I am going to America, and I haven't seen him in five years and I am just trying to be honest. There's a difference between wanting to see him and sleeping with him. I wouldn't sleep with him, ever."

Osei got up from his bed and hit the door. He cracked it. My breath got caught in my throat. Okay, so testing his reaction was not a good idea. Honesty was not going to work. I would have to go to Plan B.

"I'm not going to see him. I am not going to see him," I said softly.

"If you see him, we're through. You hear me?"

"If you see him, we're through, you hear me?"

I looked at Ato like he was high on drugs. What was his case?

"Are you kidding me? This is Tei. This is someone I haven't seen in five years. Someone I never got to sleep with! You must be joking, right?"

Ato got up from his sofa. We were in his house and we'd just had sex. Yeah, I had slipped right back into my familiar routine. And I had just told him about Osei's reaction to my trip and the possibility of seeing Tei. And Ato, without reason, was flipping as well.

"I don't like him."

I laughed. "You don't even know him! What's this about?"

"I don't get what it is, why you're still so hung up on him. You're on the phone with him for hours, talking like you guys are getting back together. What the heck is all that?"

"Unfinished business, that's all. He left too early. That's all it is."

"And he's with someone, and it doesn't bother you?"

"Ato, you're with someone too."

"I don't have a child."

I laughed and looked at him quietly. What really was his beef?

"I'm just going to sleep with him. I am telling you, honestly, there is no way I am going to see him and not sleep with him. Know that now."

"If you do, I am honestly telling you, this is over—me, you, it's over."

I smiled but he looked dead serious. I didn't care. He was a joker.

When it was time to leave Ghana, I was still feeling exhilarated, despite Ato and Osei's threats and warnings. I knew what was going to happen was going to happen. There was no way I could stop it, unless something drastic happened in London over the next eight weeks that was going to change my mind.

On the night the girls and I were leaving, Ekow came by my end to say goodbye, and he came alone. It wasn't unusual for him to show up at my end alone. He was friends with everyone in my house. We went for a walk around the block. I had only a couple of hours and Osei was coming by too. I didn't have enough time. We walked quietly for a while and then we started talking.

"I think I'm going to miss you," he said, with a little smile.

I couldn't believe what he had just said. Ekow was never sweet in any way. We were friends, yeah, but we didn't have that kind of relationship. We weren't sweet on each other.

"Really, you will? I think I'm going to miss you too. I'll miss your stone cold 'I don't give a shit about anyone' attitude."

He laughed. "Well, I give a shit about you."

"Aww, my goodness, you have a heart!"

He shook his head, still laughing. I was touched though. He had a tough-guy attitude, and a stone-cold look almost all the time. But he was acting really soft that night.

"Will you call me?" he asked.

I had a very strong urge to kiss him then. We had walked

around and we were back in front of my house. I saw that his cousin Daren and a few of his friends were already waiting for him outside the gate.

"I'll call you, I'll text you, you'll get sick of it," I said.

"I don't think I'll get sick of it. Call me soon as you get in."

I wondered where all this sweetness was coming from. My writer's paranoid mind was wondering if this was just another distraction sent by some bored higher being to prevent me from thinking about Tei.

We hugged for a long time and my mind was helter-skelter. I really liked him. But now was not the time. This was Tei's time.

London was uneventful the second time. My old friend Fiori who was living there now asked me to stay with her. I could have stayed with my uncle again, but he really lived too far and he was too strict for me to handle for two whole months. Fiori was my age. I figured it'd be fun.

Fiori lived with her aunt and cousin and it honestly wasn't the greatest living situation. Looking for a job once again took forever. I had too much free time. Thankfully, Ajua also didn't have it swift and easy getting a job so we hung out on most days. Abena for some reason always managed to find work within days, and Cami had a well-to-do London guy she was rolling with. She definitely wasn't pounding the pavement for work.

When my departure date for New York rolled up, I had had enough of London. I wished I hadn't even stopped there to begin with. I should have spent all thirteen weeks in America. Tei and I had spoken so much that I could barely breathe. Both Ato and Osei had reiterated their warnings over phone, but neither of them stood a chance. It was impossible. I needed to see Tei. I just needed to.

My US trip started off disastrously. I felt like I was really jinxed. Someone was trying to mess up my mind and my resolve. My suitcase, with all my clothes, and the shopping I had done over two months in London, got lost somewhere between New York and Arizona. I was devastated. I had bought clothes meant for my reunion with Tei, and now they were all gone. I had nothing but the clothes on my back and my purse with my passport and ticket. I was certain Osei, or even Ato, had placed a curse on me. I hadn't even been in the US for twenty-four hours and everything was going wrong. But I was determined not to be deterred. This was the trip I had waited years for. With, or without clothes I was going to see Tei.

I hadn't seen my aunt in close to fifteen years and I was really happy to see her. She, my uncle and my cousins were wonderful. I spent my days sightseeing, sleeping, watching TV, taking walks, talking to Tei and relaxing. This was what a holiday was, not running around London looking for a job, standing on the Selfridges shop floor watching parents spend £500 on a jacket a child wouldn't wear in a year. My aunt bought me a new suitcase and we slowly filled it up. By the time I left Arizona, I had a suitcase full of stuff. But that wasn't even crucial. I would have gone to New York with just the clothes on my back if that's what it came down to. But I was glad I didn't have to!

Lights Out…

The day I was leaving for New York I couldn't think straight. I was nervous all of a sudden. The excitement was tempered with the thought, what if Tei didn't like me? We hadn't seen each other in five years. I looked different, older and bigger. What if he wasn't attracted to me? Expectations were so high. I needed to see him so bad and I didn't want him to be disappointed. When I stepped out from the airport, I didn't see him straight away. My nerves were all over the place.

"Rabbie Daniels!" a voice said from behind me.

I smiled, spun around, and there he was. He looked so beautiful—bigger and older as well, just perfect. Before I could say a word, he kissed me. I wanted to melt right there. His lips were so soft and incredible. His kissing touched my core. It reminded me of how kissing Jon had felt. We kissed for so long. My hands were on his face, holding him to me. I loved the feel of his arms around me, my chest against his, his hands on my back.

"We should go before I get a ticket," he mumbled, laughing.

I nodded.

"I'm so happy to see you, Rabbie," he said, kissing me again.

We kissed, like, every five minutes on the way to Philly. And then we parked somewhere and kissed some more. It was so crazy. I had waited so long for this moment. The second time we parked, I thought we'd never get to Philly.

"I need to call my friend, where we'll be staying; I just want to make sure he's home."

Since Tei lived with his baby mama, I was going to be staying with his best friend, who lived in the same apartment complex as Tei. Potential for drama, but I really didn't care.

"George, what's up? We're on our way, where are you? For real, we're on the same highway, exit 27. Okay, okay, see you in a few."

He hung up and looked at me. "So funny, George was also in New York, I had no clue. But anyways, he's on the highway, a few exits behind us. We'll just wait for him here."

"Where is Cami? She's already here, right?"

"Yes, she came a few days ago. I had Jonah pick her up. She's staying at his end."

Tei had it all figured out. Ajua and I were going to stay at George's (a different George from the Ghana one) and Cami and Abena were going to stay at Jonah's. It worked out, since Ajua and I got on better than either one of us with Cami or Abena.

We sat in the car kissing and talking, waiting for George. He turned up fifteen minutes later. George was a tall guy, incredibly tall. We had spoken on the phone a few times and he was a really nice guy.

"Hey! I finally get to meet the myth, Rabbie Daniels!"

We hugged heartily.

"Dude, you are so frigging tall, man. I think I'm going to hook you up with my friend Abena."

"Uh, I've heard about that one, we'll see. What are you guys doing in the car? You can't wait to get home, huh?"

He threw his keys at Tei.

"I'm going to be out all night. So you guys should have fun! Just don't break any stuff!"

Home alone, my first night with Tei... that sounded awesome. Tei walked George to his car and I sat back in the car. The boys talked for a bit and then Tei came back. George sped off and Tei followed suit. They were both driving so fast. As we approached the tolls, George did the craziest thing. He swung his car left and cut across six lanes, doing probably a hundred miles an hour, and then he disappeared in the opposite direction.

"That looks like a good idea," Tei said.

"What?"

Before I could say anything else, Tei followed suit. He accelerated, cutting across the lanes of oncoming traffic. I was panicky. What had they spent the day doing, watching Ronin, or James Bond? Tei had nearly cleared all the lanes when I saw her. She was in a black Ford SUV gunning towards us and the toll booth at full speed. My breath got caught in my throat.

"Tei!"

I screamed his name but he just wasn't fast enough. The Ford smashed into us with such force I felt my body jerk painfully against the door. My head hit the edge of the door and then it was lights out.

"Rabbie, Rabbie, come on, wake up, look at me."

I could hear Tei talking and I opened my eyes and looked at him. The front of the Ford was buried in his side. He was reaching over me, trying to open my door. His left arm was cut and bleeding.

"We have to get out, that car could explode any second," he said.

I looked at the Ford; the hood was gone and there was steam and smoke coming from underneath, right in front of us. The driver was slumped over the steering wheel and I couldn't even tell if she was alright.

"Rabbie, come on."

I tugged at my seat belt, but it wasn't coming out.

"I can't get my seat belt out. I can't get my seat belt!" I was screaming.

Tei reached out and yanked at the belt. It came off and we crawled out. The Ford had smashed into his side and yet he was strong and lucid enough to get me out of there. We stumbled across the highway and then within seconds chaos broke out. There were police cars and ambulances coming out of nowhere. Tei held me as red and blue lights completely surrounded us. I couldn't think or focus. I heard and felt EMTs talking to us, asking if we could walk, if we were okay. Tei was talking and I just wanted to cry. My back hurt, my neck hurt and my shoulder hurt. I heard George's voice as well. He had heard the accident and stopped on the other side of the highway.

"Rabbie, you okay?"

I looked at Tei's face and nodded. He kissed me and hugged me and then the EMTs bundled us into an ambulance. They strapped Tei down and I realized he was badly injured. He could barely stand straight and when they lifted his T-shirt his whole left side was cut and bloody. I had no idea where his focus and resolve was coming from. We held hands throughout as they prodded us and injected us with God knows what. I lost consciousness again and the next time I came to, we were both being wheeled on stretchers into a hospital. George had followed the ambulance and he was right behind us. There was a lot of activity in the ER, a lot of people talking. They propped us in a room and then there was a swarm of doctors and nurses. Tei was incredibly strong and awake and even cracking jokes. I heard him tell one doctor he was getting a BJ when his ex-girlfriend decided to ruin the moment with her Ford. It made me think of the other driver. I wondered how she was.

We spent the rest of the night at the hospital, undergoing test after test, and scan after scan. I was completely cleared and given some drugs for my pain. My shoulder and hip were bruised but that's all it was, soreness. Tei was going to need physical therapy. He was wrapped up tightly and for a selfish moment, I wondered if he could have sex.

George took us home sometime the next afternoon. We'd been in the hospital close to twelve hours and I just wanted to get out.

George had a two-bedroom flat, and Tei had already set up the second room for us. We lay on the bed and George fussed over us. He and Tei started talking about how crazy the accident was. Boys just have a very weird fascination with death and destruction. I remembered Samson and Agyare's awe with Osei's accident.

I had to call my aunt in Arizona, and let her know I had landed safely. I wasn't sure I wanted to mention the accident. The police from last night had taken my passport briefly and asked for a name and address. I gave them my aunt's but I wasn't sure if they'd call her. But I knew I had to call her and my mother anyways.

Falling in Love

True to form, my aunt and my mother completely went berserk. Even after both spoke to Tei and George, they weren't completely calm. I told my mother we wouldn't have been discharged if I wasn't okay. I didn't want to call Osei. I was paranoid enough to think he had jinxed me. All this trouble, losing my luggage, the car accident, what was all that about?

"Are you sleeping?"

I turned at the sound of Tei's voice. The room was really dark and we lay cuddled up on the bed. I smiled at him and he kissed me. I loved kissing him so much. He made my heart beat so fast. When I felt his hands underneath my T-shirt, I stopped him for a minute.

"Are you sure?" I whispered.

"I've waited for this for five years. I am not going to let a speed-crazy woman in a Ford stop me."

I chuckled and kissed him back. It was a little awkward at first. I wasn't sure how to touch him. We started off really slow. Slow kissing and gentle touching. I was on a high. He was so sweet and gentle. He kissed and touched me like I was the fragile one. And he kissed and touched me everywhere. With every single touch, I fell in love with him. There was really nowhere else I wanted to be. And he was right; no Ford SUV or lost luggage, or even Osei and Ato, could have prevented this moment. We made love like we were the only two people in the world. Nothing else was important. I didn't want it to end. He felt so perfect. Everything felt so perfect.

We lay there for hours and then I heard girls talking and then George's voice. The door opened and the light switch was flicked. I blinked and stared at Abena and Cami. Tei and I were half-naked, lying in each other's arms as the girls came in and sat on the bed.

I knew keeping my affair with Osei a secret would be tough

with the girls in Philly. I had a boyfriend back home, someone they all knew. I would have preferred secrecy but I had decided that would be impossible. Tei's arms tightened around me.

"Oh my God, are you guys alright? What happened? I heard the car is a complete wreck!"

I looked at Abena and nodded. She was usually dramatic but I could hear genuine worry in her voice.

George came in then and we all sat or lay there talking for ages. After a while, I decided it was time to call Osei, and maybe Ato. I went into George's room to use his phone.

"Hey, how are you?"

"Ah, she finally calls."

Despite Ato's sarcasm I had missed his voice.

"So where are you?" he asked.

"I'm in Philly."

"You are so unbelievable. Incredible! Let me guess, you've slept with him, huh?"

I lay on George's bed, closed my eyes and stretched out.

"I was in a serious accident last night. We both were. We were in a hospital, ER, all night, and all morning."

"Rabbie, I really don't care. I just want an answer to my question."

"Yes, yes, I've slept with him, but I told you it would happen. I don't know why you thought I wouldn't, seriously."

"I don't want you to call me again. I don't want to talk to you again."

"Are you kidding? Come on, what the heck?"

I heard a click on the phone and my eyes flew open. He had hung up on me. Abena and Cami stood in the doorway.

"Was that Osei? Did he hang up on you? I'm sure you can fix it when you get back home," Abena said.

I decided to let them believe it was Osei. I was upset Ato had just done that. He didn't even care I had been in an accident. His damn ego could only think about the fact that I had slept with someone else. That wasn't even the entire reason. Ato knew we both had our own lives, but he liked to believe he had some ownership of my heart. I knew the whole problem was because I actually cared about Tei. Ato finally had competition over my feelings when he thought he had it completely covered. I decided I wasn't prepared to call Osei after that call.

Ajua joined us from Atlanta the next day. But the party mood had changed drastically. We spent the first few days at home. Abena and Cami and Jonah, and another of Tei's friends, Brian, were around at George's with us, day and night. We ate pizza, watched movies, hung out and just talked. Tei hadn't been home to his own apartment in over four days and I didn't ask questions. We were all over each other all the time. We just didn't care. We were kissing all the time, openly, in front of the girls and his friends. I was so crazy about him, and he seemed so crazy about me.

I managed to call Osei twice during the first week, but I said I was in Arizona. It was a big risky lie, but there was no way I could say where I really was. I tried to talk to Ato too, but he hung up on me one more time and I decided he wasn't worth the aggravation. I was happy, I really cared about Tei, I had missed him and Ato wasn't going to bring me down.

The boys eventually had Tei's car towed home and it was shocking.

"Oh my God," I exclaimed as George took the tarp off the car. Tei was holding me in his arms. Cami, Ajua and Abena looked stunned as we all stared at the wrecked BMW. George and Jonah took their cameras and started taking pictures. The driver's side was bashed in and mangled with the rest of the left side. It reminded me of Osei's accident. But Tei had been wearing his seat belt, so it was even more shocking. He didn't even remember how he managed to get out of his seat. There was nothing left of his seat. I hugged him and kissed him as we looked at the car. Then to make light of the moment, we all started taking pictures around the car. That's when I finally saw her, Tei's ex-girlfriend and his baby mama. The laughter and talking ceased and the boys all turned to look in one direction. The girls and I turned and I saw her. She was standing a few meters off, staring at us with her arms folded across her chest. She looked pissed off. Tei kissed me on the cheek and said he'd be right back. I felt her glare pierce through me and I turned away. Darn, that was intense. The rest of us left the parking lot and the whole conversation upstairs centered on the drama that was Tei's life.

Tei, his girlfriend and his daughter had tried to make a life together. According to Tei's boys, the relationship had ended soon after the baby was born. They still lived together, for the baby, but apparently Tei's girl was rather extreme and hard to live with. There were tales of her hitting him, screaming matches, cops at their door. I knew a lot of parents, some married, some not, who lived together for the sake of their children. Most often these living conditions were just as toxic and negative on a child as a divorce, if not worse. Tei and his baby mama were seeing other people while still living in the same apartment. It was just insane, and apparently she knew about me, knew that Tei was staying at George's because of me. It all felt so weird. It got much stranger that day when Tei came back to George's with his daughter.

I have never been gaga about children, never. Before, I thought it was a genetic defect on my part—what girl doesn't love babies and children? But I just wasn't like that. All my friends go completely bonkers over babies, making funny noises and funny faces, but I get so bored with kids within minutes. I could appreciate a cute child, but I really didn't like kids or babies that much. Seeing Tei's daughter completely threw me off. He held her lovingly, looking so proud and completely comfortable. She was a little over two years and she was adorable. Ajua, Abena and Cami reached for her immediately. Abena made a stupid comment, told her I was her stepmother. Everyone laughed but I didn't. Eventually Tei set her in my arms and I was nervous. I didn't know if it was a test or something. I had no clue what to do with her. She sat on my lap for a short while. I didn't make funny noises. I didn't try and chat, we both just sat there quietly observing the talk and noise around us. After an hour or maybe a little more, her mother called and I was relieved. She was an adorable, good child but I just wasn't a baby person and I wasn't completely comfortable. Tei took her home and the show-and-tell was thankfully over. Abena kept taking jabs at my mothering skills but I wasn't moved.

The two or three weeks in Philly went by a little too fast. Tei and the boys took us out clubbing a few times. My alcoholic girlfriends were introduced to apple martinis and they were hooked. We all went shopping together, had breakfast at IHOP and did just about everything else. Abena and Cami went to New York for a couple of days, which was a relief. But Ajua was staying with us, and I didn't get much privacy. We still managed to have sex as often as we could. Tei's chest was better, and even if it wasn't, he wasn't about to let it slow him down completely.

As each day went past, I realized how completely enamored I was. I didn't want to go back home. I wanted to stay with him forever, even if that meant being a stepmother.

"I love you," I heard him whisper in my ear. It was my last night and we were lying wrapped up in each other's arms. I had been depressed and moody all day.

"I love you too," I whispered back. I hadn't felt so strongly about anyone like this since Jon. I had felt something deep, with Ato, but he had killed it pretty fast. And even with Ato, I had said those words in a casual, jokey way. This was totally raw and real and I felt vulnerable. I was so in love with Tei, it was insane.

"I don't want you to go. I want you to stay with me forever. Leave that kid behind in Ghana."

Tei and I hadn't really spoken about Osei. It was a sore subject for him, which was understandable. I left him for Osei. And many years on, I was still with Osei. I tried not to talk about my relationship with him.

I didn't say anything and I buried my face in his arms. He kissed me long and hard. I loved kissing him. We heard George and the rest of the crew outside. Abena and Cami were spending the night at George's, to make it easier for all of us to get to the airport. I could hear their voices but I didn't really feel like going out there. We lay there for the rest of the night, talking, kissing and loving each other.

By the time it was morning, I was in such a foul mood. Tei was a little solemn himself. Ajua was also cranky because she was leaving her love in the US of A. Ghana wasn't appealing at all for either of us. For me, I had a bigger headache. How was I going to deal with Osei?

The airport goodbye was much harder than I had thought it would be. It was the wrench that ripped my heart from my chest.

"Remember what I said to you last night." Tei kissed me softly.

I shook my head and looked at him, my eyebrows arched.

"Remember I said I loved you?" he said.

I nodded, still looking a little confused.

"I lied," he whispered.

I froze, and stepped back. What? He looked so serious.

He pulled me closer and kissed me on the lips.

"I lied. I don't love you. I'm in love with you. I'm so in love with you."

I started to cry. He had this intensity, in his eyes, in his voice and his kiss. I felt it down to my bones. I quivered. I wrapped my arms around him. His eyes were teary too. The girls were standing near the entrance of the terminal, waiting for me with our bags, but I couldn't let go.

"I need you to remember, and believe me, always. I'm in love with you. I'm really in love with you," he said.

My breath got caught in my throat as we kissed.

"I'm in love with you too."

We hugged for what felt like forever and then eventually we let go. I turned my back and walked into the terminal. I had tears in my eyes. Abena tried to comfort me. I wasn't sure if it was genuine or if my misery was appealing. I turned around and looked back. He still stood there waving. I wanted to drop my bags and just walk away with him. Damn Ghana, damn school and damn everything else. But I couldn't. I think I cried right there. I didn't care about the girls or anything else. I was broken. I was a miserable wreck and I felt there was just no way I would recover. No way.

Busted, Remix

Girl: Frank, please hear me out, I can explain everything.
Mr. Biggs: Ain't nothing to talk about. Right now, I want you out this house.

"Busted," Ron Isley and R. Kelly

I knew keeping the Philly trip under tight wraps was going to be impossible. There were too many witnesses and too many loose ends for me to control. From the moment I got back, I braced myself, ready for whatever was going to happen. Because I knew there was no way Osei wouldn't find out. The question was how and when. And the how completely threw me off.

My mother and I sat outside on our lawn, or should I say our wannabe lawn. She had put a couple of deck chairs out there and we were just lounging. My eyes were closed and I could feel the burning sun on my face.

"Osei's here," my mother said.

I hadn't even heard any car. I lifted myself up slightly as his car came up the driveway.

"He's not even wearing a seat belt," my mother said, a hint of annoyance in her voice. Osei parked, got out and walked towards us. Before he could say hello, my mother launched her seat belt attack.

"Why aren't you wearing a seat belt? It's very dangerous, Osei. And when you had your accident, you weren't wearing a seat belt then, right?"

"Uh, I think it was because I wasn't wearing a seat belt that I'm still alive," he mumbled.

"That was lucky," my mother went on sternly. "Seat belts save lives, Osei. You shouldn't play with yours like that. If Rabbie and Tei hadn't been wearing seat belts when they had their accident, they definitely wouldn't be alive. I'd say it's best to wear one than not to."

If I was white, my face would be completely red. I hadn't told Osei about the accident. In fact, Osei had absolutely no clue I even saw Tei. And even though I figured he'd find out one day, I never expected my mother to be the one to let it out. But I couldn't blame her. I had woven a tangled web of lies that I just couldn't control. My mother had no idea there was an issue. I had told her Osei knew I was going to see Tei. She never thought for a second there was a problem. Osei glanced at me and I avoided his eyes. I looked at my mother and then the smart woman figured it out. I could see it in her eyes. They had both caught me in a lie. I had lied to her and I had lied to Osei.

"I'm going inside now. Osei, please remember to wear a seat belt always, okay?"

She got up and left and then I took a deep breath. Here goes.

"I don't even know what to say. Each time I think we're going to be fine, that everything's going to be fine, I realize I'm such a fool," he said, shaking his head.

He sat down where my mother had been sitting and glared at me. I made up my mind right there and then I wasn't going to confess to sex. That was never going to come out of my mouth. My head was spinning as I tried to think of a story. It would never be good enough, but I wanted it to make some sense at least.

"I went to New York, all of us did, the girls and I. I really wanted to go see New York. Tei picked us up, picked me up, to take me to where Ajua was staying, and we had an accident, a bad accident. We were taken to a hospital, stayed there overnight and then his friend came to pick us up, dropped me at where Ajua was, and that was it. I didn't have much contact with him after that."

Truth mixed with big lies—I could have sworn my nose grew an extra centimeter.

"So you lied to me, you lied to me for three weeks. All that time you called and said you were with your aunt. Why? What do you want? I don't understand you. How do I know nothing happened? You've been lying to me, so how can I know what is true and what isn't? You want me to believe you saw him, once, and then that was it? He knew where you were staying, and yet you never saw him again?"

I put my face in my hands. Dammit. This was so hard.

"I tried not to lie, I told you before I left, that it would be impossible for me not to see him. I tried to be completely honest, and you were throwing ultimatums at me that weren't fair."

"What ultimatums? What? You think because I took you away from him I should understand?"

I hadn't said that—I had thought it, but I hadn't said it. And once he said it, I knew that was the part that troubled him. Karma was a bitch. The first time I slept with Osei, I was technically Tei's girlfriend. He knew that. That was the part that troubled him. What if the boy had never left? he was probably thinking. If it was straight up between him and Tei in Ghana, who would win?

"So what happened? Did you sleep with him?" he asked.

"I saw him, a few times, but nothing happened. Ajua, Abena, Cami, everyone was there, nothing was going to happen."

"Nothing was going to happen because you didn't have the opportunity or because of me?"

Hard question, deep question and the truth was not the right answer.

"Because of you," I mumbled.

He stood up. "You're such a liar. You're just such a liar. I just can't trust you."

He started to walk away and I let him. There was no fighting this. If my deck of cards was going to fall, there was nothing I could do to stop it. And a part of me, a very strong part of me, wanted all the cards to fall. I didn't want to be in the relationship anymore, but I wasn't going to be the one to make the call. Thinking that way reminded me of Edem and his declaration he'd never be the one to leave someone. What was the difference between him and me? I was a cheat just as he was. Our partners had done nothing to wrong us and yet we just couldn't be straight. And like him, I didn't want to be the bad one. The writing was on the wall. I wanted Osei to figure it out. I wanted the decision to be his. I was not going to influence it. I was in love with someone else. Osei was a good person, which made it so hard. He had done nothing wrong. All he had ever done was to love me, and for that, he deserved so much more.

I didn't hear from him for a couple of days. The girls figured something was up and they assumed it was over. He hadn't said those words outright so I wasn't sure what to think. And then he called.

"Are you near an internet café?" were his first words.

"Uh, no," I said.

"Find one. I sent you email; call me when you've checked it."

And then he hung up. My curiosity was piqued and I was on campus anyways, so it was pretty easy to find a café. I sat behind a computer and logged on. He had sent a bunch of pictures and my heart was beating as I downloaded them. For five minutes I was stunned as I looked at each one. They were pictures of the day we posed around Tei's car. There were a number of pictures of Tei holding me, and one of him kissing my cheek. I looked content. We looked in love. I felt my heart sinking, not because I had been caught, but because I could not imagine how Osei must have felt, looking at these. I closed my eyes and rubbed my forehead. I just needed to let this boy go. I hoped this was it. I really hoped this was it. I didn't call him straight away. I went back to my room to brood a little. Tei called just as I lay on my bed.

"Hey baby."

Hearing his voice calmed me for a brief moment. But the pictures were still weighing on my mind. I decided to tell him about them.

"Osei just emailed me some pictures, of you and me, the day we were looking at your car."

"George, George, George. Brian emailed him the pictures, I'm sure. I don't know anyone else who would. But George is my friend and I've known him longer than Osei. That's just not cool, really."

"Yeah well, it's happened. I knew it would."

"So it's over? Are you free, my love?"

I couldn't say yes, or no. I really wasn't sure. But after seeing pictures like those, Osei wouldn't want anything to do with me, would he?

"I think it is over."

"You think?'

"It is over. It is," I said, trying to step up the conviction in my voice. It *was* over.

"I love you, I always will. And I'm here for you," he said.

"I love you too, always."

We hung up a little later and I lay on my bed solemnly. Was I single? I believed I was. I didn't even know how I really felt. I was sad about what I had done to a good guy and I was apprehensive about being alone. Ato was acting like a complete dick and Tei was not here. He had no plans of living in Ghana and I had no idea when I'd ever go back to America.

By the time Osei called again, Abena, Cami and Sammi were in the room, so I left to find a quiet spot in our common room. I curled up in an armchair.

"So, I'm going to ask you, only once: did you sleep with him?"

"Yes, I did."

There was a long silence and I felt a surprising tear on my face. I was really sad and disappointed in myself. Why couldn't I love this man, why couldn't I be faithful?

"I don't understand what's wrong with you. I don't understand why you'd do that."

His voice was shaky and then I started to cry. I hadn't cried when he found out about Ato. But the pain in his voice was so real and so deep, it completely broke my heart. I was such a horrible person.

"I'm sorry, I'm so sorry," I said in between sobs. But as sudden as the tears came, I quickly pulled myself together. This was over. I couldn't do this to him or myself anymore.

"I can't talk right now. I have to go," he said softly.

He hung up and I curled up even deeper in the armchair, crying. I felt so alone. I wished Tei was with me. This was so hard. I took deep breaths and tried to calm down. I couldn't. It was past 10 P.M. which meant early A.M. in Philly, but I needed to talk to Tei. I wanted reassurance.

He sounded pretty awake when he answered.

"Tell me you love me," I said as the tears started again.

"Of course I do. Come on, what's wrong? Baby, talk to me, what's wrong?"

"I just feel so alone. I just don't want to be alone. I can't stand this. I have no idea when I'm going to see you again."

"Hey, hey, calm down. Don't cry, baby. You're not alone. I love you. Don't cry. I'm here for you, you know that."

My tears stopped for a moment. I missed him so much, it was painful. We spoke for half an hour and then I went to bed.

The next day I spoke to my mother a little about the break-up. I didn't give her all the details, but just enough. She wanted me to do what was best for me, but she added that Osei was a good guy and he obviously cared and I should give him a chance. I spoke to my aunt Flossie as well. She was also a fan of Osei. Everyone in my family could see how much he loved me and there was really no one who'd say leaving him was the right idea. We'd been together over four years. My aunt said finding someone who loved me as much as Osei did was rare. But what about how I felt? I did a mini focus group with the girls. Once again, I left key details out. But the girls had the same mentality, that "good guys are rare" mentality. But it was not just about good guys for them anyways. They would stay on in any relationship for as long as it took, even if the guy was a clear dickhead. Men in general, good and bad, were rare. Girls didn't want to be alone, no matter how bad the situation they were in was. I wasn't in a bad situation per se, but it wasn't healthy either. I used to regard Abena with scorn, disgust that she couldn't leave Edem. But how different was I?

A couple of days later, Osei called. I was sitting on the verandah outside the common room at my hostel, staring at cars and brooding. I was so confused and so lost. I stared at the phone for a while before I answered.

"Hello?"

"Hey," he said.

"What's up?" I asked quietly.

"I can't get over what you've done, but I can't let you go either. I love you so much."

I couldn't believe what he was saying. I tried to interrupt, tried to stop his flow, but I couldn't find the strength.

"I don't know what it is, I really don't. I wish I did. But I want to try again. I love you and this feels right to me and there is nowhere else I want to be," he said.

I didn't feel the same way. I honestly didn't. I cared about him, but I was in love with someone else. My heart didn't ache for him the way it ached for Tei or used to ache for Jon.

Osei was talking and I had half tuned out. I kept willing myself to stop him, stop this cycle I had created. The words were on my lips, but I couldn't say them. What in the world had he ever done? I had done him wrong so many times and he still wanted to try and make this work. How could I walk away? Women didn't get this type of love often. This was a guy who worshiped the ground I walked on, who loved and adored me and was forgiving my cheating ass for the second time. What was wrong with me? If I left him, I felt like I'd regret it for life, just as I regretted the Jon situation. What was love, anyways? Like my aunt and everyone else said, the other person has to love you more, right?

"Are you there?" I heard him ask.

"Yes."

"Did you hear me?"

"I did. I don't know what to say. I didn't expect you to say all that."

"But you really can't do this to me again, really. I understand that maybe you needed to get him out of your system, but I hope it's over. I hope there is nothing lingering with you and him."

There is, Osei, there is. I love Tei so much. But he's not here, and you are, and I don't know how to tell you that you need to move on. I don't know how.

"I'm done. I'm here," I said.

"I love you, I really love you."

I couldn't respond. My boyfriend was forgiving me for cheating and all I wanted him to do was to walk away. I hung up and sat on the balcony and cried.

"You must really, really love him, no matter what you say. Because I don't understand this, it's only if you love someone this much that you can't leave him. How many years has it been? You could leave me for him, but you can't leave him for me?" Tei raised his voice and I cringed.

A week had gone past and I couldn't put it off any longer. I had to tell Tei I was back with Osei.

"I love you, I love you so much, you have no idea," I said.

"Then be with me, me. Why is that so hard? You left me, you left me for him. You cheated on me, with him, and I am sure you weren't this wrecked when that happened."

"You don't live here. I don't think I can do long distance, I don't think you can do it either. Especially when I have no clue what the future is. You've sworn not to move back to Ghana and this is my home."

"The future is the future, and right now, I love you, and I want to be with you. We deal with the future when or if it ever becomes a problem."

"I just don't know."

"Then I'll tell you what I know. All that happened with us, it was just a fling for you, huh. It'd been five years, you came, had fun and that was it. You're back where you want to be," he said angrily.

"Don't say that, you know it's not true. I love you too."

"But it's not enough, huh. What does this Osei character have, huh? I don't get it. I seriously don't. I don't believe you. I don't believe anything you've ever told me. It doesn't make sense. This is simple. How can you say you love me, you don't love him, but you're going to stay with him? What fucked-up logic is that?" he snapped.

The conversation just went downhill from there. I couldn't get a word in. Everything he said made sense. I just kept repeating that he wasn't here, but what exactly did that mean? If I loved him, why should that matter? I did love him. I loved him more than my heart could handle. But I was overburdened by guilt— guilt for the things I had done to Osei, over and over again. From Ato, to Tosan, to Anthony and the random numerous people I had kissed in between. The ultimate betrayal was having an open affair with Tei and falling in love. If Osei still wanted to be with me, and he was right here in Ghana, what could I do? Tei lived thousands of miles away, with his daughter and whatever situation he was in. How would I fit in?

But it was done. I could hear it in his voice. Tei didn't understand, didn't get how I could say I loved him but not be able to walk away from Osei. With each word he uttered I could hear his heart close to me and I knew it was done. I had made a choice. My heart knew it was the wrong choice, but my head had taken over, trying to rationalize something that wasn't meant to be rationalized. I had stopped being a romantic after Jon and I ended. I wasn't like the characters in the movies who shouted "screw you" to the world and went after their true loves with everything. I didn't have my head in the clouds. I couldn't see a future with Tei and once I couldn't see a future, I couldn't make that ultimate leap of faith.

By the time we hung up, I was a wreck. I had been a wreck for over two weeks. I knew my life was changed. I was never going to be the same. This was one of those regrets, like the kiss with Junior that altered the direction my life could have taken. This was a big one. This was an irreversible one, and it would haunt me for a long time.

Ekow

I was lying on my bed at home, trying to sleep, but I just couldn't. I kept tossing and turning. It was 11 P.M. on a Friday night and I was home for the weekend. I was in a bad mood. Osei and I were fighting even worse than before. Ato was really acting weird and he was still pissed about the Philly trip. Tei and I were barely speaking now and I just didn't have the energy to deal with Ato on top of all that. I missed Tei, but I knew I had messed up and it was best to let all that go.

My phone beeped and I glanced at it. It was a text from Ekow. While I was in London, Ekow and I kept in touch every now and then. It was all really casual and platonic. He sent a particularly interesting text to me in London: "I miss you like whoa." That text had me thinking all kinds of things, but I still wasn't sure if he was just being friendly. I didn't want to jump to any conclusions. I read the text and smiled a little. He wanted to know if I was asleep. I replied, "No, can't seem to sleep. What are you doing?" A minute later he replied, "Watching TV, bored."

I grinned. Gosh, what was I doing? Did I want something to happen? After everything that had happened in the last few weeks? But I liked Ekow. I was fascinated by him. He was mysterious, complex and darn sexy. I replied, "Let's walk, talk, whatever." He replied, "I'll meet you in front of your gate in five minutes." I replied, "Sure."

I got out of bed and pulled some clothes on. I felt a little excited. I was so tired of the fighting with Osei, Ato's tantrum and Tei's disappointment in me that I needed something else.

I went to the gate and stood there waiting. Ekow turned up a short while later. He looked good and I was really excited to see him. I broke into a wide smile. We hugged tightly.

"Hey," I said, grinning.

He smiled and put his arms around me. "What's up?" he said.

"I'm just tired, and stressed. Let's walk a little."

We started walking and talking, about everything and nothing in particular. We walked for ages, down my street and other unexplored streets. We walked along a main street and then branched off on to dark paths and then towards Junior's old neighborhood. We held hands and just walked. It was so sweet and so cozy. After thirty or maybe forty minutes, we stopped on a dark tiny road and I leaned against a tree.

"Your text—'I miss you like whoa'—I thought that was interesting," I said, smiling coyly at him. He looked a little embarrassed.

"Did you really miss me?" I asked.

"Like whoa," he said.

I laughed and reached for his hand and squeezed it. He squeezed back.

"Did you miss me?" he asked.

"Yeah, I actually did. I thought about you more after the 'whoa' text. That was a good one, honestly."

He was so close to me that I wanted to kiss him. We had walked for over thirty minutes and no one had made any move. I wasn't sure I wanted to be the one to make the first move. I wanted him to kiss me. We stood around the tree for a while, holding hands and talking. There was so much tension and electricity. I wondered how long it'd take him to kiss me!

"What are you doing tomorrow?" he asked.

"Staying home, sleeping, whatever."

His face was so close to mine. I wondered if he was teasing me. I wondered how long I could last. This was unbearable.

I could feel his breath on my cheek. We were that close. And then I felt it. His lips touched mine, slowly, gently, as if he wasn't sure. Then I took control. I pried his mouth open and kissed him. His big arms went around me and he pressed me against the tree. We kissed for ages. There was just no end to it. He started off as an uncertain kisser, but he got into it gradually. We kissed for so long. He felt so good, so different. I loved being with him, out there on the street, in the dark. It was exhilarating. Our kiss fest stretched close to an hour, if not more. His body felt good against mine. He was tall and muscular and sexy, and I rubbed my hands over his stomach. I was so turned on it was driving me crazy.

"What time is it?" I asked when I managed to pry my lips away.

"Wow, it's, like, half one," he said, glancing at his phone.

I laughed. "Wow. We should get back, huh?"

His lips touched mine again. I felt my heart beating so fast. This boy felt so good pressed against me. I forgot about Osei, Ato, Tei; everyone just faded. Nothing else existed. If the setting wasn't so inappropriate I would have taken his clothes off. I pulled away.

"We should go," I whispered.

He nodded and stepped back. I held his hand and we made our way back home. We paused to kiss every now and then as we walked back. When we got to the corner of our street, we stopped. We lived only a minute's walk apart.

"This is so weird! I can't believe you and I are doing this," I said. I was genuinely thrown by all that was happening.

He touched my hair and I reached out and hugged him tightly.

"I love kissing you," he said.

"You're pretty good," I said, smiling.

"Nah, I'm learning from you. I can't do squat."

I laughed. "I'll talk to you in the morning, yeah," I said.

"Text me when you get into bed, okay?" he said.

We kissed again, softly. Each time his lips touched mine, something just happened to me. I deepened the kiss a little more and then I stepped back reluctantly.

We said bye and I walked home light-headed.

I was on a high when I got into bed. I just didn't understand the meaning of fidelity, did I? We spent another half an hour texting. From that moment on, he snuck permanently into my life and my heart.

Ekow and I toured our neighborhood like a million times. We walked almost every night that I was home, and kissed like kissing was sex itself. It was so intense. He didn't really say much. He listened to me and held me and kissed me and I just loved it. I told Ajua about it and Sammi, but that was as far as I took it. His cousin Daren knew, but I wasn't sure who else from his group knew. We were texting all the time and trying to see each other as often as we could. He was still with Tara and I was with Osei and for some reason, he didn't want to take what we had up a notch. I wanted to sleep with him, badly, but he kept me at arm's length.

"I can sneak you into my room," I whispered in his ear.

We were standing outside my gate, kissing.

"Hmmm, sounds appealing," he murmured.

"Well?"

"I don't want to rush it."

I stepped back a little. "Huh?"

"I like this, I like you. I don't want sex to change all this," he said.

"It won't. I really want to be with you."

I kissed his lower lip and slipped my hands underneath his T-shirt.

"I don't want…" He paused. "I don't want this to be just… I don't know, sex? You have a boyfriend, I have someone. I just… I just think we should take it slow."

I was a little disappointed, but I decided not to press it. He had a point. I wanted to sleep with him, but did I want more than that? I wasn't sure. I was just so sexually attracted to him. It was all I could think about. Just kissing him was pure torture.

"You're driving me crazy," I said.

"Oh, you have no idea what you do to me," he said.

He kissed me hard and I ran my fingers over his nipples. I felt his breath quicken.

"Okay, let's stop now," he said. He stood back and exhaled deeply.

"Okay, it's your call," I said.

He chuckled. "Let's see how long I last, huh?"

I tried to keep my thing with Ekow under wraps but it wasn't the easiest. Ekow and his group were around my hostel every now and then. We tried to keep our hands off each other. We tried but we failed.

"I seriously want to take you into my room."

Ekow and I were leaning against a wall in my hostel. There was a party going in one of the common rooms and we had snuck away. The hostel was still pretty busy and it was a huge risk we were taking.

I felt him harden against me as we kissed. He pressed against me harder and I wrapped my arms around his waist, pulling him closer. We came apart for air and I closed my eyes. Was it possible to want someone this much? I turned my head away from him and then I saw Cami at the corner of the floor. She had been looking at us. She glanced away and then continued walking down the floor.

Ekow's eyes had followed mine.

"Was that Cami?" he asked.

I nodded. I realized I didn't care so much. I really didn't care. It was shocking, but I realized I could care less if everyone knew, or if Osei found out. There was no hope for my relationship. There had never been any hope to begin with. My heart wasn't in it and my body wasn't in it. I could get busted several times, but it just wouldn't make a difference. Surprisingly, Ekow didn't seem deterred either. We just kept kissing. We didn't discuss our relationships much. Tara was in school in Canada. She'd been in Canada since the beginning of their relationship.

"Yo, Ekow, the boys want to head out."

We broke apart at the sound of Anthony's voice. I buried my face in Ekow's shoulder and shook my head. Anthony didn't seem surprised to see us, which was weird. I felt a little bad. Just a year ago, he was the one I was sneaking around kissing. It was the old clique all over again. Friends! When would it all ever end?

Ekow nodded at Anthony and then turned to me.

"I'll call you later," he said.

I nodded. He kissed me softly and then followed Anthony.

I took my phone out of my pocket and dialed.

"What?" Ato snapped.

"Clear off with your attitude, man. Where are you?"

"I'm actually just leaving campus, heading home."

"Pick me up," I said.

"Buy a plane ticket to Philly," he said.

"Okay, now listen; you're going to have to get over that crap. Pick me up and stop being such a dickhead, seriously!"

"Be at the corner of your road and Sarbah in ten minutes. I won't wait."

I hung up. Ekow had left me physically needy. I needed to be with someone. I needed to have sex or I'd go crazy. I needed something I hadn't had in a while. It had to be Ato.

I packed an overnight bag and told the girls I was going home. I met Ato at the corner and we drove off. I had actually missed him. I think he had missed me too, although he tried to act like he didn't care. But it was obvious from the way he kissed and touched me. It was like he was trying to brand me, or remind me of how good it was before, remind me of what we had before Tei. We parked in my neighborhood and had really good sex. He really didn't have to do much work. Ekow had worked up my senses and my appetite. When he dropped me off at home, I knew we were going to be at this all over again.

I was now juggling three guys: Osei, Ato and Ekow. This was going to be delicate!

When I Look into My Future, I Don't See You in It

"I think Kwaku is cheating on me."

Ajua and I were sitting in front of Volta Hall, when she said that. I wanted to say, so what's new?

"What's up?" I said instead.

"I heard he's seeing someone else at Tech. Apparently, he's been dating her for about as long as he's been dating me."

I laughed, then I looked at her serious face and I choked on my laughter.

"No, sorry, I'm not laughing at you. I am just waiting for you to say it's not true."

"I don't know if it's true or not. I suspect it's true but I really don't know. One of the girl's friends is here, on campus. And she said her friend—I think her name is Yaa Akyaa—is dating Kwaku."

"Wow. You have to ask him, you have to call him."

She buried her face in her hands. "I don't know if I can, if I want to."

"It's either he's just sleeping with her, messing with her and he's with you, officially. Or vice versa, you're the other woman or, even worse, neither of you is really is his girlfriend. I mean, can he be dating both of you? As in you're both his girlfriends? That's messed up."

I didn't mean to dissect the possibilities but I was fascinated. I had never really trusted him, but this?

"There's more. Apparently, he and his girlfriend in London are still together."

I was impressed. This guy was smooth.

"Wow. I mean, I never really believed him about that London girl. What the heck does separation mean? That's what he said, right? That they were separated?"

"He said his family didn't approve and so it wasn't going any-where. Anyways, I'm not sure they ever broke up."

I was silent. That was some serious BS. She had to ask him.

"Call him. You know how I feel about stuff like this. I don't believe in speculation and this person said this, or that person said that. Ask the guy. Girls spend too much time chasing their tails trying to bring other girls down. Tell him you need the truth and if he lies to you, he's through. You have to be firm."

"Does that even work? He could still lie."

I knew that was also possible. But the thing about confrontation is that at least you've thrown it out there. At least the other person will know you're on to them. It forces a person to re-evaluate sometimes. I had been busted twice, so I wasn't really the one to give advice. When it came to my girlfriends, my preferred advice was very simple: "Break up with the idiot." Cheating was a habit, it just wouldn't end. I felt it wasn't worth it. A cheating spouse or partner never really leaves the relationship either. It's always up to the victim, and once you decided to stay and deal with the shit, you were stuck. Case in point, Osei; he busts me, not once but twice, and he stayed. He could say it was because of love, and it probably was, but at a point, love just isn't enough. That's how girls lose their self-respect and dignity. "I love him, I love him," and they suffer in silence as a trifling boyfriend hops around... sickening.

"I am afraid to call him, afraid to hear what he'll say."

It took Ajua a while, a whole week, but eventually she mustered the courage to call. Volta Hall had a bank of phone booths that was usually very crowded and busy, and waiting in line to make a call was tedious. But since Kwaku was in Atlanta, it was really the best way to call him. Calling direct from cell phones was just not reasonable. I waited in line with her and then she stood up and walked to the phone booth. Ajua looked so scared. That to me meant there was a very strong possibility he was seeing other people and she had known about it or at least suspected. Kwaku was too suave, a lot like Ato. Yeah, that was it; he was a *lot* like Ato. They had that stupid charm over women. They were good for sex but once you gave them your heart, you were doomed. I wish they walked around with a sign around their necks, warning all women off. Wouldn't that be sweet? The thought made me smile.

Ajua was on the phone for a while and I looked around at the girls, wondering who they were sleeping with and who was sleeping with whose boyfriend, or worse, whose father. That thought made me laugh as well. And then I saw Lina, Ato's girlfriend, with her posse. They walked directly towards me.

"Hey, Rabbie, what's up? I hardly see you around," she said.

"Yeah, trying to study, man, you know, final year."

"Ato says you're always trying to compete with him."

I laughed and shrugged.

"That Ato, he's annoying me right now," she added.

"Oh come on, you know he loves you, seriously."

"If you say so, then I'll believe you," she said whimsically.

"Ato worships the ground you walk on," I said firmly.

She smiled. I wondered why she didn't see me as a threat, didn't suspect me. Wasn't I hot enough to be a threat? But I preferred it this way anyways. Very few girlfriends allowed their boyfriends to have close female friends, so I wasn't going to complain. Lina actually always sent me a birthday card, signing it "from Ato and Lina." I was such a horrible person. But like I said before, trust no one.

"Anyways, I'll see you around, yeah."

"Yeah sure, take care. Tell Ato I said what's up," I said.

She smiled, nodded and walked off.

A few minutes later, Ajua was done. She looked terrible, like she wanted to break down. She had tears in her eyes. I reached for her and hugged her. We walked out to the courtyard and sat down.

"Do you know what he just said to me? Do you know what he said?"

I waited for her to go on. I wasn't up to guessing. And in any case, there is no way I could have ever guessed.

"He said, he said that yes, he's seeing Akyaa and the London chick. And do you know what the last thing he said was? He said, when he looks into his future, he doesn't see me in it."

I was shocked into silence. What the heck? What the heck? I was stunned! "What? What? What does that mean?"

"I am not in his future. He said yeah he's seeing Akyaa and what do I want to do about it? Gosh, I can't believe that boy. I can't believe this."

I didn't know what to say. I was upset for her, but I'd always thought he was a tad bit shady. Game recognizes game, I guess.

Kwaku's statement, "When I look into my future I don't see you in it," got me thinking though. It was a profound statement, completely heartless and cold, but still deep. When I look into my future I don't see you in it. Maybe I could try that. I started thinking, trying to picture my future. Did I see Osei in my future? Did I see us married, with kids? The answer was no. I tried with Tei; did I see him in my future, long-term future? The answer was a surprising no there as well. I really couldn't see it. I wasn't sure if it was because of the distance between us. Was that blurring my vision? I tried to picture Ato in my future as well. I could see faint images of him. I could picture something but I wasn't sure what. And then I tried with Jon, reluctantly. He wasn't in my future either. So all of them, Osei, Tei, Ato and Jon, I couldn't see as husbands—boyfriends, yeah, but nothing more. So Kwaku had a good point. If you really couldn't picture being with someone long-term, then what was the use? If you couldn't picture yourself married to someone, having kids, living together, raising a family, then why bother?

There are people that we sometimes meet, and we're passionately attracted to them, but when we force ourselves to be honest and picture what we really want out of life, we just don't see that person fitting in. Long-term means commitment, partnership, mutual respect and understanding, similar goals, drive, and I strongly believed in that. But I knew I hadn't found that yet. So the question was, if you haven't found the person you want to spend forever with, was it wrong to be with someone else in the interim? My answer at that moment was no.

Ajua was understandably heartbroken. And as girls we reacted like typical females; we bashed Kwaku day and night, just to help her feel better. But I know that never works. Getting over someone, it's a personal thing. No matter what people say, no matter what you hear or what you see, you have to come to that realization that it needs to be over on your own. It can't be forced or pushed or argued through. I still cared about Jon—heck, maybe I still loved him. No matter the evidence, no matter the facts, the signs, no matter what, you can't will love like that away. It's sad, but that's what it is.

But that doesn't mean you can't help a friend along anyways. There is really no harm in trying. So we tried our best to paint Kwaku as completely undeserving of Ajua, just as we had tried with Edem for Abena. Would it work? Who knew?

When I look into my future, I don't see you in it. Ditto. Cold and cruel, but well said.

Tei, Part Four

I managed to get to the end of my university career without any further dramatic bust-ups. From the moment we first kissed, Ekow and I had this incredible never-ending kissing affair. It was insane. We were hooking up all the time and kissing all the time. And no sex! That was the insane part. I had tried, but he didn't want to take it there and so I gave up trying. I wasn't hooking up with Ato consistently anymore. There was really no definite reason for that. We had become such close friends that sex wasn't the only reason we hung out or talked. I wanted to use that on Ekow and say, "Hey we can have sex and still like each other and still be friends, Ato and I do it pretty well." But I decided that wouldn't quite work. So anyways, Ato and I had reached a comfortable lull. We were now best friends, who happened to have sex every now and then, and not the other way around.

Because of all the student strikes that caused university close-downs across the country, our university system was out of whack. There was a year and a half waiting period between graduating from secondary school and getting into university; and then a six-month wait period between graduating from university and the obligatory start of national service and official graduation ceremony. Most university students used that long break to travel abroad and work. Some came back, most didn't. Ajua, Cami, Abena and I had gotten U.K. work visas the previous summer, and we had one year left on our visas, so we decided to go work in London for the six months. Sammi was also coming along to London, so it was going to be the whole crew. Six months was a very long time and I wasn't even sure how I felt about that. Osei wasn't thrilled either. And what was worse, I decided I'd go to the US at the end of my six months, just before coming back home. I didn't tell him about the US trip before I left though, because my final destination was not Tei anyways. I was going to fly into Maryland from London, stay with my cousin Akua, then fly to

238

Michigan to see my cousins, James, David and Lexxy and then back to Maryland and back home. There was no New York or Philadelphia in the plans. Tei was still upset with me and I wasn't sure he'd even want to see me, especially if I came over as Osei's girlfriend.

London was once again uneventful and a few months before I left for America, I decided I wanted to see Tei after all. I loved that boy, I really did. I couldn't deny it anymore. I was in love with him and I wanted to see him. My heart ached for him and if I couldn't see him, and tell him how much I loved him, I'd die.

I called him a couple of times before I left. He was just non-chalant, didn't sound overenthusiastic, but didn't tell me not to come either. So I had a new plan: D.C., Michigan, D.C., Philly, D.C. I couldn't wait!

Washington, D.C.

The first time I got to D.C., I knew I'd love it. The first day, jet-lagged and tired, my cousin took me to a club at Adams Morgan with her room-mate and some friends. I could barely stand and it was freezing, but it was one of the best nights ever. We went clubbing again the next day. I'm really not sure what was keeping me going. I literally hadn't slept in over seventy-two hours. Ato's best friends, Kwasi (the one who hooked up with Sammi) and Kofi lived in the D.C. area. I called them up and they came by to take my cousin and me out. I tried to set up Kwasi with my cousin. I do that a lot, matchmaking, it's a really fun thing to do and watch the connection evolve. I think they liked each other; and Sammi was over him, so cool beans. I'd met Kofi a few times. He used to live in my neighborhood and he was good friends with my brother Josh. Everyone was good friends with Josh. But when I saw Kofi this time he looked different—attractive, something. I was instantly drawn to him. He was tall and skinny but not light-skinned. He was crazy funny, and fun and nice to be around. I knew Ato and I had this "no friends" clause and up until then, neither of us had broken it—at least, not that I was aware of.

"I think I have a crush on Kofi."

"Huh?"

"Kofi, your friend, Kofi," I repeated.

"I know who the heck he is. Did you fall and hit your head or something?"

I laughed. There were moments, such as these, that I really missed talking to Ato.

"Yeah, I have a concussion," I said.

'I thought so. Anyways, none of my friends would ever do anything with you."

"Why not?" I asked.

"Because they're my boys; they would never do that to me. Not Kofi, not Kwasi, not any close boy of mine."

"You sound very sure."

"That's because I am. They just wouldn't. That's just the bottom line."

I didn't like Kofi that much to want to prove Ato wrong. So I couldn't be bothered. I sort of believed him anyways. Boys had a much stronger code than girls. So I put Kofi on a back burner... another day, another time, perhaps.

Michigan

January 2004 was just the worst time ever to visit Michigan. It was the worst winter to hit America in over ten years and I just happened to visit at that exact time. It was the first time I saw snow and in the beginning, I was so excited, till the temperature dropped below freezing and the snow was practically up to my knees. Despite the shitty weather, it was one of the best holidays of all time.

I stayed with my cousin Lexxy, in a dorm-like apartment with four to five other girls. My days centered on shopping, sleeping, TV, chatting, shopping again, sleeping and just doing nothing. Lexxy's brothers James and David lived close by and David would come hang out with us a couple of times. James apparently was a bona fide party boy, and his days were spent sleeping, working or clubbing. I really had no clue how or when that kid changed. David was practically as I remembered him: quiet, intense, serious and mature. Lexxy was perhaps more outgoing. She lived to shop and she was just the life of any place, anytime. Before Michigan, I had figured James was just like my brother Xavier. They'd been like peas in a pod for years, best friends. Xavier was a pretty quiet kid. He never went out, didn't club and wasn't a social butterfly. I had thought James was the same. But he definitely wasn't. I'd been gone from home for seven months now and I wondered if by the time I got back to Ghana, Xavier would have morphed into a party boy too. God forbid. If Xavier clubbed like James, my mother have a fit. I think I would too. Xavier was the quiet baby of our family and I wished he would stay just like that.

James did manage to join us once or twice to watch a movie. He hung out with us and Lexxy's friends a couple of times as well. I think all the girls worshiped the very ground he walked on, but he seemed a tad oblivious to that. Lexxy had some cool, pretty friends, but who knew what boys wanted? Not their sisters' friends I guess—unless of course you're Josh Daniels, then anything goes.

Lynn, my estranged former best friend, lived in Ohio, four hours from Lexxy. When Lynn left Ghana in 1998 for school, we'd grown apart. Long distance is hard on relationships and friendships. We still kept in touch every now and then, but we weren't as close. She invited Lexxy and me up for the weekend and we figured, why not. Lexxy liked to travel and have fun anyways.

Ohio was fun. It was good to see Lynn again. She had grown into herself. Lynn had been a little stifled at home. And now, she could do exactly what she wanted to do. We hang out the first night, cooked, watched movies, old friends came to visit and we had a pretty lazy night. The next day, we shopped and then went clubbing. I figured there was just something about America and clubbing, everyone I visited just seemed to love clubbing.

I really enjoyed Ohio. I was having fun everywhere. But Tei was going to pick me up from D.C. in just a few days and Osei had been calling and reminding me over and over again that we would be through if I did anything with Tei again. For the first time, I was confused. I didn't want to hurt Osei, I really didn't.

"Rabbie, I really don't think you should go to Philly," Lexxy said.

My cousin Lexxy is three years younger than me, and was twenty-two at the time. I wasn't sure if she'd ever had a boyfriend, or been in love, I'd like to believe the answer was no. But I'd shared my Tei/Osei dilemma with her and her room-mates, and a debate was raging on in the living room as we watched *America's Next Top Model*. Camp Tei had very few supporters—just one that I remember actually, Nana Yaa. Camp Osei was Lexxy, Cathy, Nena and Esi. Tough team. Nana Yaa and I really didn't have much of an argument so we decided to base it on love; shouldn't you be with someone you love, no matter what?

"Okay, okay, so if Rabbie has decided that she loves Tei, then why can't she go see him? Honestly, nothing is achieved by her staying away, it won't change how she feels," Nana Yaa said passionately. I loved her passion, but I wouldn't tell her to switch from medical school for law school though. We hadn't made a dent in Lexxy's argument.

"My point is Osei is her boyfriend. He loves her, I know him, he's a good guy," Lexxy countered.

"This is not about good guy, bad guy; this is about who she loves!"

Nana Yaa was really passionate!

"If she doesn't love Osei, then why is she with him? Why not be with Tei then?" Nena asked.

After almost forty minutes of back and forth, Nena finally asked the question I had been expecting someone to bring up from the beginning. The question I had no answer for. Why in the world was I with Osei? All eyes turned to me. Drat.

"Girls, I really don't know. Honestly. I do love Osei, in a way, you know. Lexxy is right, he's a really good guy with a good heart. You know how they say you should be with someone who loves you more?"

"That's just BS!" Nana Yaa interjected.

Her comment just ignited another passionate back-and-forth.

"No, no, that's the truth. It's important to be with someone who loves you more! Listen, when you're old, and you can't even walk, you want someone who's going to be by your side!" Cathy shouted.

"Of course he'll be by your side, because he wouldn't be able to walk himself!"

Nana Yaa's comment cracked me up. That was a good point.

"Rabbie, listen, you said yourself you don't think there is a future with you and Tei, so why jeopardize your relationship with Osei?" That was another wise one from Nena. These girls were pretty young but pretty smart. I doubted I sounded that wise at twenty-two.

"There you go," Lexxy added.

James walked in right then—perfect timing. I knew almost all of the girls were in love with him and I wondered if I could use that as an argument somehow. Cathy was hot for him, and she had a boyfriend, but if she knew James liked her back, wouldn't she want to be with him? Wouldn't she be a little confused, like I was?

David joined us as well and we put the Osei/Tei debate on hold for a little bit. I wasn't feeling that well either. My back and tummy had been hurting for days. I was physically and mentally distressed. But I knew I was going to see Tei again. It was unavoidable.

"Hey, how are you?"

Tei reached for me and hugged me tightly. I had missed him so much! I didn't want to let him go. Unfortunately he stepped back much earlier than I wanted and he didn't kiss me. I started to worry.

The three-hour drive from D.C. to Philly was a little strained. We chatted about nothing much. The last time I saw him, his favorite song was Boyz II Men, "Color of Love." This time it was Isley Brothers, featuring R. Kelly, "Take a Ride." I started to read a little too much into the song. The lyrics centered on a guy asking a girl to take a ride with him, leave everything behind; he'll take her on a road that leads to love. I wanted to scream, "Yes, yes, take me with you, please!" As I sat in the car staring at Tei, I realized I really loved him, deeply did. I really didn't know why. I couldn't put my finger on it. This boy just had me under a spell and I couldn't break free.

We got to his apartment safely, despite the icy roads and falling snow, and lingering memories of a Ford. I was grateful for that. I showered and we lay on the floor in his living room and ordered in. Over five hours had gone by since he picked me up, and he still hadn't kissed me. At that point, I wasn't sure if he expected me to make the move. He wasn't being romantic or emotional. Frankly, he wasn't being anything. It felt like I was just another house guest, not someone he'd been looking forward to being with.

His baby mama had moved out so he was living alone, in the same apartment, right across from George's place, where I had stayed before. George came by later that night, and we chatted and just hung. By the time it was time for bed, I still hadn't had a kiss. My heart was in the pit of my stomach. This was vastly different from the last trip. And worse of all, Tei brought up Osei constantly.

"Won't you call your boyfriend and let him know you're safe?"

"Shouldn't you call Osei?"

"So how's Osei doing? When is the wedding?"

The sarcastic questions wouldn't end. I couldn't even make the first move to kiss him. He was a different person. He didn't love me anymore. He was over it. It was stunning and painful. What did I expect? How stupid was I? I left him hanging a year and a half ago, for the second time, and that second time was just his last. Why in the world did I expect he'd still be in love with me? I needed to rectify this.

"We should talk, shouldn't we?"

"About?"

"I love you," I muttered.

"No, you don't."

We lay in his bed and my heart was just breaking. I didn't want to go to bed without a kiss, some acknowledgment. I touched his face. The last time, he told me he loved it when I touched his face. I stroked his face and his eyes closed briefly and then I kissed him. He kissed me back, slowly at first and then a little deeper. After a short while, he pulled away.

"You should get some sleep. You must be tired," he muttered.

He turned his back to me and switched the lights off. I lay in the dark, on the verge of tears. I turned away and tried to sleep. This really couldn't be happening.

When I woke the next morning, he was already up and dressed. He was lying stretched on his sofa watching boxing. So it wasn't a bad dream after all. I hadn't imagined the previous day. Tei was over me. I had a shower and lay in the bedroom for a while, thinking, crying softly.

My back was to the door when I felt his arms around me. He kissed my neck and I melted. I turned to face him and we kissed hard. His hands were all over me and my hands were pulling his clothes off. It wasn't as sweet as before. The closeness I had felt with him before was gone. But I wanted him badly. I wanted some validation. I didn't feel any love pour from within him. It was just physical on his part, and as emotionally painful as that was, I needed him. I really needed him.

We didn't cuddle afterwards. He got up and went to the bathroom, and I knew nothing had changed.

The rest of the week was just as bizarre. There were fleeting moments when I felt he loved me, when I could see it in his eyes, heard it in his sarcasm, felt it in his touch. Then there were the intensely cold moments, when he zoned out and treated me like I meant nothing. The era of Rabbie Daniels was up, he seemed to say. And those moments were more frequent and more painful. I was hurting more than anything. On some nights, I sat in his living room and cried. Other days, I tried to talk to him, ask him what was wrong. I begged, nagged, whatever it took. He said nothing was wrong, and then he'd bring up Osei and make more sarcastic remarks.

We didn't make love often. It was like a carrot he dangled and then yanked. He could tell I wanted him, and not just physically, but he was done with my bullshit.

It was the worst week in a very long time. No declarations of love moved him; nothing worked.

The strangest thing happened at that exact moment Tei withdrew from me. I realized I had to let Osei go. It was as clear as day. It took Tei to stop loving me for me to see this. It was so strange to me. When Tei told me he loved me, declared he was in love with me, that hadn't motivated me to leave Osei. But now that Tei was gone, lost to me, it just hit me that this was my fault.

What logic had I been using? Why stay with someone because he loved you more and adored your very being? How selfish was that? How cruel was that?

I loved Osei, he'd always be a special part of my life, but he wasn't my future. He didn't have my heart. I needed to let him go, so he could find someone who'd love him back. It was time.

The Break-up

Who thought this day would come? Not Osei, not Tei, not me, not anyone. But it was here. Osei and I had been together for five and a half years. It was a very long time. He had bonded with my family and I had bonded with his. But this was a relationship that shouldn't have gone beyond a year or two. From the moment I cheated on him with Ato, it should have ended. He didn't deserve the last four years. It was four years in which he could have found someone who would have loved him better, the way a person like him deserved to be loved. I hadn't thought through how I was going to do it, but the idea felt liberating. I wasn't leaving him for someone else. I was really leaving him for *him*, so he could be free of me, so he could be like Tei, done and over with my bullshit. This was really for Osei's sake. I could drag this out forever, and Osei would let me, no matter what I did, but I just couldn't in good conscience let that happen anymore.

Osei was excited to have me back after almost eight months away. But I knew it was best to drop the bombshell as soon as possible. I wanted us to still be friends, and dragging the break-up out could jeopardize that. Once my mind was made up, and I knew it was the right thing to do, it was a done deal.

We sat out in the wannabe lawn at my house, lounging in the same chairs I had been in when I got busted about Tei. We had had a fight the night before. I wasn't sure what it was about. Fighting was part of our thing. It was another reason this break-up was necessary. Osei and I were constantly fighting. Everything was drama with us. We argued like cats and dogs, and most times, I couldn't even remember what we were fighting about.

"I don't think we should do this anymore," I said quietly.

"Do what anymore?"

"Us, you, me, all this fighting, and all the issues we have. I don't think it's good for you, or good for me."

"I don't understand what you're saying."

I wondered if he was being naïve on purpose.

"I think we should break up, Osei. This isn't working. You and I both know that. We've known that for a long time."

"It's because you don't want it to work. I mean, you're the one who slept with Ato, and Tei and God knows who else."

"That's the point, Osei, God knows who else. So why would you still want to be with me?"

"Because I am the one who loves you and cares about you, and I see good in you, and I just want to give you a chance."

"Stop giving me a chance! Why do we keep doing this? Now we're arguing about breaking up!"

"What is this? Is this about Tei? Did you see him again?"

"I saw him, yes, but it's not about him. It's about you and me. I really don't think this is healthy for you, for *you*. I am thinking of you. You deserve someone to love you, Osei, better than I can."

"But I love you, and I'm fine with that, unless you don't love me at all."

"I do love you. I just think you need better than I can give you. Can't you see that?"

"Shouldn't I be the one to decide what I need? You say this is about me, but you're making my choices for me? Telling me what is best for me? I need you."

I sighed. Where had I gone wrong? This is what happened the last time, when we broke up over Tei and he forgave me. This complete declaration of love, that's what always got me. It was the toughest thing ever, to look a man who wholeheartedly loved you in the eye and say it was over.

I stood up. "Let's not do this again, okay, please?"

I was tired, really tired. He looked angry and disappointed and frustrated. We bickered for a while longer and then he left. After he was gone, it still didn't feel like I had closure. I felt he hadn't quite heard me, that he thought this was another argument. But I decided to accept it was the end. This was it. I was not going back. I was not going to succumb to the easiness of having him love me.

January/February 2004 was break-up season. Ato and Lina broke up, a couple of weeks earlier than my break-up. It was a complete coincidence. What got even stranger was that Ekow and Tara also broke up, within a couple of weeks of my break-up. At the time I thought it was the strangest turn of events ever. Was this a sign from somewhere?

Ato was a mess after Lina called it quits. He went through different phases of loss similar to Elizabeth Kubler Ross' stages of mourning—denial, anger and eventually acceptance. I was an ear for him to bitch, vent and rail against Lina and her bad judgment. Ato would never have ended that relationship. This came out of nowhere for him. He loved her, in his own way, and this was the person he thought he'd be with for a long time. But time changes people, and different experiences can mess with your mind. My personal opinion was Lina lost sight of what and whom she really wanted. Just like me, she went away for six to seven months after we graduated. She met new people, and her world just opened up a bit more. New people can be distracting. They can make you feel you can have it better. It's only an illusion. I was never deluded to think I could have it better elsewhere. My break-up was solely based on the fact that I didn't love Osei enough. Lina... I can never say for sure, but my guess would be she thought she was in love with someone else, and she probably was. But Ato will always be Lina's Jon, that one person she'll never forget. The break-up would be the one choice she'd always regret. There was no doubt in my mind about that. As trifling as Ato was, he loved her, and he didn't love easy.

"Sometimes it crosses my mind, how it would be if you and I were together."

Ato and I were sitting on the front steps of my house, staring out into the dark, joking about our completely wayward lives. I didn't take his comment seriously. I knew him well enough to know he flirted with such ideas every now and then. But he never really meant them. I'm sure he had thought about it, about the remote possibility of us dating, but it was more of what it could possibly look like. We both possessed traits the other liked and respected. I thought he was smart, interesting, focused, driven, good looking. He thought I was smart, interesting, ambitious, focused, mature, with a good head on my shoulders. We acknowledged that about each other. But that was it.

"We wouldn't trust each other. I know too much of your shit, your games, your tricks. It would drive me insane. I'd be a paranoid wreck!" I said.

He laughed. "I know, right. It would be crazy though."

"Suicidal."

He laughed again.

"You think it's really over with you and Lina?" I asked.

"It's done, man. It's done," he said whimsically. He looked me in the eye and asked, "You think it's over, you and Osei?"

"End of an era, baby, end of an era."

We sat in silence for a while.

"Lina's going to regret it," he said finally.

"Yeah, I think she will."

He shook his head and closed his eyes, his face turned upward. I looked at him, felt a little sorry for him. But it made me realize I was taking monumental steps. Osei and I were over, but I wasn't thinking of dating anyone else, not even Ato. I just wanted to be me for a while. That's all.

"So you and the man, really over?"

I laughed at Ekow's question. Why was everyone asking me this? Was it so hard to believe?

Ato had left just thirty minutes earlier and Ekow and I were curled up on the sofa in my younger brother's living room.

I looked up at his cute face and kissed him.

"It's done, my dear. I'm done, for good. And you and Tara, no possibility of a comeback?"

He shook his head. "It's been dying for a while," he said.

I didn't feel like talking much. I had missed him the last eight months. I had missed kissing him, touching him, and having him drive me into a frenzy. I wrapped my legs around his waist and urged him on top of me. We were in a semi-open area of the house. My brother's living room faced out to the driveway and there were huge windows on two sides of the room. The room also had two doors, currently unlocked. One door led to the lower level of the house, where Xavier's room was, and the kitchen and another bedroom. The other door led to the outside of the house and the driveway. Ekow and I had never blatantly hooked up in my house before. We always went walking or something. This was the first time we were kissing and touching in my house.

And I had no idea it was about to get steamier. His hands were all over me and we were kissing long and hard. I felt his hands slip under my nightdress and open up my bra. I knew something was about to go down because Ekow never took it below the neck. For a year and a half, we'd just kissed and kissed and kissed. When he started unbuckling his jeans I could have died right there. This was crazy. Anyone could have walked in. My mother's room was directly above the room we were in. It was close to midnight, and I hoped she was fast asleep. That first time with Ekow was exciting, crazy and awkward. I had wanted this moment for so long, but the location was hindering my complete enjoyment. But I still didn't want to tell him to hold on, and try another day, a better place. No way. If Ekow was ready to do this, after all this while, then so was I.

I realized it meant he wasn't lying before, when he insisted he didn't want us to have sex because we were both in relationships. The minute we both became single, this was happening.

For that week, and weeks and months and years later, Ekow and I were like horny bunny rabbits. We spontaneously and systematically christened every room in my house, no kidding. The next day we took it upstairs to the other living area, and the following day, the third living area. We did it in my room, the guest room, my brother's room, both kitchens, the front yard and my mother's room, I am shamed to say. And no one saw us once. We also christened his house extensively. We did it in and around the empty pool, the upper deck, the lower deck, the garden— gosh, we were just insane. I had never had that much sex before. Ekow got into my very core, very fast. We were hooking up so often and the sex was so intense and so crazy, I couldn't think of anything else.

Ato royally flipped when I told him. His beef, he claimed, was Ekow was not good enough for me. I told him Ekow and I were just having sex. We were both free as birds and it had been building. There wasn't talk of a relationship. This was crazy good sex and Ato was not going to take that away from me. Part of

Ato's disappointment, I knew, was he really didn't want to think about guys I was sleeping with. He had a possessive nature which was strange and slightly misplaced. It wasn't about love; it was about being IT in a girl's life—he wanted to be the one she was hooked on and couldn't let go of. He wasn't my IT, and when that realization was clear, our physical intimacy dwindled. We never officially said no more sex, we just reduced how often. We didn't completely stop sleeping together; it just wasn't as often as the first few years. In some ways, we became better friends. He was over at my end all the time. He really bonded with my family and it was just comfortable. Ekow had me wrapped up in his element so tight, I couldn't see anything or anyone else. Ekow and I didn't put labels on each other either. We were having a good time. I hung out with him and his friends at his end and they visited me as well. I was sure his friends knew, but I didn't care. I wasn't cheating. Darn it, for the first time in a very long time, I wasn't cheating!

The Day My World Stood Still

February 2004 was my undergrad graduation. I graduated with a first class, which was one of the best moments ever. I had been apprehensive and worried about not graduating with a first class. I think I would have been a depressed, broken, suicidal person if I hadn't. Ato graduated with a first class, and that definitely formed a part of my ambition. He didn't show up for my graduation. I deducted a couple of points on his friendship scale. I was really disappointed he wasn't there. Osei showed up, of course. My ever-loving Osei. I was touched he came, but a part of me knew he would. That was just Osei. He had a good heart and a good soul. I really wished I could love him more, give him what he truly deserved, but I couldn't. Ajua was in London and she missed graduation, but Cami was there.

Cami and I started to bond fast and thick that February. It was like an overnight phenomenon. We were completely inseparable. It was like back when we graduated from secondary school. I decided to go with the flow. We spent almost every waking moment together. She became like a permanent fixture in my home. Ajua had temporarily been replaced in absentia.

The back pains that took me to the hospital the night Kwame died had plagued my life since that night. Several times a year, I'd end up incapacitated and at the mercy of excruciating pain. The pain was unpredictable, random and uncontrollable. I had done so many blood tests and taken so many painkillers—still nothing. It happened when I was in Michigan and D.C. and it happened after one particular high-octane session with Ekow. This had to end.

Wednesday

"So we're going to do another blood test. We haven't tried this one before, so let's give it a shot, okay?"

I sat in the doctor's office with my mother, and I was nonchalant about it all. Yes, yes, another blood test. It had been a struggle getting to the clinic and I just wanted to be lying on my back.

"I'll put a rush on this one; we should get the results by Friday."

I went through the routine I had gone through a thousand times before. My mother and I went to the lab, they drew my blood, gave us a time and date to check back with the doctor, and we left. I went through the usual lying on my bed, waiting for the pain to abate. It usually lasted a week. By Friday, the day I was supposed to go back to the clinic, I was feeling better. I could walk and I didn't feel listening to the same old gibberish the doctor had to say: "I don't know what's wrong. The blood tests were negative."

Ekow and I had another session over the weekend. I couldn't stop living because of those pains. It seemed like they just weren't going anywhere. The doctor, my mother, me… no one had a clue what it was and I couldn't put my life on hold.

Monday

On Monday, a day like any other day, my doctor called. I didn't even know he had my number.

"Can you come see me today?"

I sighed. "Uh, today is a pretty bad day. I'm really busy. It's going to be hard. Can we do Wednesday or Thursday?"

"It's very important, okay? And you need to come with your mother."

I felt the first chill down my spine. I had known this man all my life. He was my pediatrician. He'd been taking care of me since I was in diapers. He'd taken care of my mother, her siblings, my grandmother and practically every single member of my family. And for the first time, he sounded panicky. I let the silence drag and then he spoke.

"It's very important, Rabbie. Is your mother with you?"

"My mother's traveling," I mumbled.

"Can you come, please?"

"I'll be there in ten minutes."

The clinic was about five minutes from where we lived. There was a small crowd of children in the waiting area but a nurse ushered me into the doctor's office. I put on my bravest face and sat down. He took out an envelope.

"I got your blood tests back. And I'd like to refer you to a specialist, a good friend of mine."

"Huh? What? Why?"

"There're signs of very high infection in your blood, signs of a problem somewhere. Normal blood infection levels are usually twelve to thirteen—yours is currently eighty-three."

I choked and for a second I thought I couldn't breathe. I felt him tilt my head, examine my eyes, check my throat. I was gasping, struggling for air. After five minutes, the gripping fear I felt subsided.

He was still talking. I heard bits of it, something about an appointment, the next day, with his friend. And it was important to take my mother. He handed me the blood test results.

I don't remember how I got home. I was in a daze for a bit and then I calmed down. So there was something wrong, but he didn't know what. It could be nothing. No diagnosis had been made. I got calmer when my mother came home and I gave her the tests and told her what happened. She was my rock, my strength. She said everything was probably fine, and not to worry. I believed her completely. She'd been with me every single time I went to the doctor; she'd taken care of me throughout each pain. I trusted her.

Tuesday A.M.

The doctor I was referred to was also only five minutes from where we lived. The appointment was 9 A.M. We were there by half eight. We sat in the waiting room for over fifteen minutes and then the doctor finally called us in. His office was small and dark and foreboding. I was uncomfortable already.

"Can I see the test results?" he asked as soon as we sat down. I assumed my pediatrician had given him the heads-up.

My mother handed them to him. He looked at them and a strange look crossed his face. He stared for so long, I wondered if there was some other invisible information there. He looked up and stared at me and I felt the second chill down my spine. My hands were shaking. He asked me to lie on his examination table and I had my first truly uncomfortable gynecological examination. Afterwards he asked to talk to my mother privately.

The thing about Ghanaian doctors, which is truly annoying, is doctors don't tell patients squat. I was a grown woman, and he was asking me to leave to talk to my mother. Who the heck was the patient?

I sat outside for ten minutes and then I lost my composure. I knocked on the door and entered. My mother had a little tear in her eye.

"So what is the problem? Is everything okay?" I asked.

"Oh yes, don't worry. I just want you to have some more tests, okay?"

Bullshit. Second annoying thing about Ghanaian doctors, beyond not telling you shit, they usually sugarcoat the situation or lie when they decide to talk.

My mother gathered up the test requests he had written. He told us to do the requests that morning and be back in his office by 3 P.M.

10 A.M.

My brother Xavier and I sat in the waiting room at the lab. I was a nervous wreck but I tried not to show it. My mother had dashed off to the office to finish up some stuff. When my name was called, I was so ready to be done with it all.

I lay on the table, and the lab tech lady rubbed gel on my tummy. Then she started the examination.

"Jesus Christ!"

Her curse caught me off guard. I strained to see the monitor.

"What? What is it?"

"I don't know, I don't know. I need to do this again. I need you to drink more water, lots of water."

For the next hour, my brother held my hand as I consumed gallons and gallons of water. She did three examinations in total. By the third, I wasn't sure who was worse off, her or me.

"You need to take your sister back to the doctor now."

I was irritated with her. Why was she talking to my brother, handing him the results? What was this? I was the patient!

"What is it? I need someone to tell me now."

"I'm not the doctor. I'm not allowed to give you an interpretation of the results. But you need to go back to your doctor now. I'm going to send someone with a wheelchair for you, and we can also call an ambulance if you don't know how to get back."

I went berserk. I got up from the chair and she reached for me but I ducked and strode out. I heard her panicky voice talking to my brother, telling him not to let me walk. So I decided to run.

I raced down the stairs and rushed home. The lab was a few minutes' walk from our house. My brother caught up to me just as my mother was just driving in.

"We need to go back to the doctor now," I said.

My brother gave my mother the lab results and I climbed into the car stoically. I was darn tired of the vagueness and I wanted answers.

Noon

As soon as we got back to the doctor, I didn't spend a second in the waiting room. I entered his office straight away and I could hear my mother mumble something to the receptionist.

"Okay, so I am not going to stay in the waiting room this time. I just want to know what is going on," I said to the doctor and sat down. My mother came in and sat next to me. She quietly handed him the results. He took them out, looked at them for what seemed like eons and then looked at me and my mother. I opened my mouth, poised to say something, when he started his monologue.

"You have an ovarian cyst on one of your ovaries. It appears to be the size of a softball hanging on a twisted thread-like cord. You've most likely been carrying this cyst in you for six years, if not more. As it's grown larger, and moved around, the cord has grown thinner and more twisted. The twist is what has been causing the pain. The cord is very delicate right now, and it contains toxic fluids, which is what caused the eighty-three points on your blood test. I suspect there may be a leak. I am going to be direct with you, because you look like you can take it. If this cord breaks, and the fluids get into your blood, you will die. The cyst has grown too large and is weighing the cord down dangerously and each time you move, it twists. That cord is going to break, any minute. You need to have surgery, within the next twenty-four hours, or you will not live past Friday. There is no way that cord can carry that cyst any longer. You need the surgery or you die. That's my professional opinion."

My heart plummeted to the pit of my stomach and the world stood still.

Nothing, Absolutely Nothing, Matters More Than Life

The rest of the conversation went in one ear and out the other. I caught bits of it. My mother wanted details—how much would the surgery cost, where would it be done, by whom, how serious was this, could it wait a day or two, it was a lot of money to come up with in twenty-four hours. I remember the doctor insisting that the situation was dire, and the cord would not hold for more than a day at best. Even moving now was endangering my life. My mother made arrangements for the surgery for the next day, first thing in the morning and then he gave her strict instructions to keep me immobile for the rest of the day, no activity or moving till the morning of the surgery.

I started crying before we even got home. I wailed and wailed and bawled and screamed. My mother got me into bed, and tried to comfort me and reassure me, but I couldn't stop crying.

"The doctor said you shouldn't move. When you cry like that, you're going to make it worse. Stop crying. It's going to be okay, just lie still."

Xavier kept telling me to stop crying. He looked scared and worried and my crying was making him worse. Within hours, Ato was over. Xavier called him and he came by. His office was only a few minutes from where I lived. Everything was only a few minutes from where I lived.

Ato tried to make light of the situation. He tried to make me stop crying. He didn't quite get it, I thought. Either he didn't understand the seriousness of my condition or he just didn't want to show it. He tried to joke with Xavier and me. I couldn't find it in me to laugh at anything. My life was flashing before my eyes. I could die in the next minute, the next second. This thing, in me, could drop any minute. The very thought of it had me shaking. Ato went back to work after a while, and then Osei turned up right after. Close call, but I couldn't be bothered. They could meet and duke it out for all I cared.

There was nothing, nothing, more important than my life.

I lay there, stretched out on my mother's bed, for hours. My crying eventually subsided after some hours and I contemplated writing a will. But I didn't have property. I didn't have anything to my name. If I died in the next twenty-four hours, what substantive thing would I be leaving behind?

You know how people say when the fear of death is at your door, eventually you accept it, embrace it and just prepare for it? I never did. I did not want to die. That was the bottom line. I wasn't ready for it and I didn't want to. People were in and out of my mother's room: my aunt Flossie, my brother Xavier, Ato, Osei, Ajua who'd arrived from London a few days earlier, Cami, Ekow, his friends, more family and more friends. Xavier was my rock through it all. It was the first time I saw him really afraid. Xavier usually struggles with being a softie and being hardcore. But that day, he was neither. Each time I moved, he'd panic and race to my side. He led me to the bathroom a couple of times, holding me steady. I couldn't lift my head from the bed without Xavier asking what I wanted. The "no moving" instruction was what scared me the most. The past couple of weeks I had had some insane sex and used my body in ways I didn't think possible. And all that time, this time bomb was right inside me, jostling up and down and twisting and getting ready to send me to hell. I thought if perhaps I hadn't had as much sex as I had in my life, the cord wouldn't be that twisted and fragile. Perhaps if I hadn't clubbed and danced so much; if I hadn't been so active and all over the place, I wouldn't be lying stretched out like a mummy. Six years or more of carrying this humongous thing every single day, up and down; and now it was about to end me or I was going to end it.

Neither my mother nor I slept that night. Xavier was in and out of the room that night too. Probably to make sure I was still alive. Thankfully I made it through the night, with my eyes wide open and my body motionless.

Slice Me Open, But Let Me Live

I think the morning of the surgery was far worse than the night before. Ovarian cysts are typically not life-threatening. But the word "typical" is the catch. There is always that anomaly. I knew if I'd been a grown woman and stopped seeing my pediatrician, another doctor could have found this straight away. I'd been going to the same children's doctor since I was two years old and at the time I was twenty-five years old. What did I expect? He had examined my back, chest, head, whatever, and never thought to refer me to an appropriate doctor. What did I expect?

There were quite a number of people with me that morning. My aunt Flossie, who looked like she hadn't slept either, Cami, my ever-present sidekick, Xavier, my cousin, Winnie, my granddad, my mother, and more aunts and uncles. I wanted to say something to my mother when the nurse started prepping me for the surgery. There were words in my throat but I didn't know how to say them. So I started crying a little. She told me she was going to see me in a few hours and I needed to be brave. But I couldn't be. The gyny doctor popped in a few minutes before I was due to be taken in. The doctor, who now couldn't stop being stupidly direct and honest, said it was going to be a delicate surgery, separating the cord from the cyst and removing both without any spillage. He gave me a fifty–fifty chance and it was right then I reached out to God after how many years.

"This isn't for me, dear God. This is for my mother, and Xavier and Josh. My mother can't take it. And even if, dear God, you think the time is now, I'm asking you to reconsider. She can't take it. Don't do it for me. Do it for her. Do it only for her. She needs to see me again, with my eyes open and alive. She needs to see me again, today."

I prayed that prayer over and over again as they rolled me into the surgery and I watched my mother's eyes disappear as the distance widened. I prayed the prayer over and over as they laid me gently on the table and the anesthesiologist asked me to count back from ten. It was only then that I paused my prayer and started counting. And then everything went black.

"Rabbie? Rabbie?"

My first thought was that it was my grandmother calling my name. God actually killed me. I was in heaven. I knew that voice, it was my grandmother! Darn it!

"Rabbie? Wake up."

My eyes flickered open and fell on my mother's face. Before I could smile, a searing pain tore through my body and I screamed.

Anesthesiologists need to include a very important clause or statement to patients. They need to say something like, "oh by the way, I'm not taking your pain away. I'm just delaying it for a couple of hours, but once you wake up, you're going to feel the blade cutting you all over again. We just don't want you thrashing on the operating table." Something like that would help instead of the crap count-back from ten!

It was honestly like someone was slashing a knife right across my belly and I couldn't stop screaming. I couldn't move my arms or legs and I felt so powerless. The nurse came rushing in, injected me, and then I was gone.

When I came to again, there were a dozen faces around me. I couldn't really see. Everything was blurry. I was thirsty but I wasn't allowed water. I was hungry but I wasn't allowed food. I wasn't allowed to speak either. Nothing, not even air, was supposed to enter my throat or body. At unpredictable intervals, pain tore through me like a shard of glass across the throat. It was unbearable. I vaguely remember Cami by my side, holding my hand. I vaguely remember Osei and Ekow. But the rest of the night was an excruciating blur. It was too much of an effort to stay lucid.

The next few days in the hospital went by slowly. I wasn't allowed to eat for days. I couldn't walk or talk, or drink or do anything. I was in and out of consciousness, battling the pain. It took Ato a couple of days to visit, and I permanently knocked off ten points on his scale. As much as I was half delirious with pain, he could have been there, that first day even. Osei was there every day. Ekow was there and Ajua and Cami, but no Ato. He showed up once, I think, two or three days later. I was a little more awake then. He helped my mother feed me and he hung out for a while. But the points were gone for good. He should have been there, earlier, and he wasn't. What if I hadn't made it that first night? Why wait three days? Osei was in and out of the hospital. He was there, when the doctor brought my tumor to me, in a jar. It was twice as large as Osei's curled fist. We were both stunned. It was a miracle I had been carrying that huge mass in me for years. I briefly thought about keeping it, but the doctor said it had to be examined, and it was being sent to South Africa. It was such a huge thing, which made it crystal clear to me how serious the situation had been. This was a miracle, my miracle.

Asare

My close brush with death did slow me down; don't let the title of this chapter fool you. Yes, yes, I met someone new, but that doesn't mean I wasn't a little more appreciative of life and love. Osei was gradually accepting we were through. And I was still certain I wasn't going to go back to him. That wasn't an easy realization to come to. Throughout my recovery he was constantly by my side, but that was just his nature. I knew how things would be if I ever went back. I'd just cheat on him. That was guaranteed.

My recovery from the surgery was slow and really painful. I wasn't completely mobile but I was really eager to get back on my feet. Ajua and Cami were around a lot, especially Cami. Ajua's sister was in town so Ajua was a little busy. Kwaku, her old flame, was also sort of in her life. So Ajua and her sis were hanging out with Kwaku and his crew most of the time that I was tucked in bed. Cami had a new man too. I'd met him briefly at the hospital but we hadn't really hung out.

The doctor told me no sex for four to six months. Of course, I thought he was insane. But I was willing to give it a shot. I'd come close to death, I wasn't about to disobey a doctor because of five minutes of mindless gratification.

After a couple of weeks, sometime in early April, I could walk and move, and I was allowed to hang out in the neighborhood for a few hours. I was grateful to finally be free of the pain. It wasn't completely gone but I felt almost back to normal. It was just hard not to think of sex as I started to get better. It was darn hard.

I met Asare through Ajua. Asare was Kwaku's best friend, one of his boys. I had met a few of Kwaku's boys earlier in university but not Asare. The first time I met him, Ajua, Cami and I were at JE's, a little sandwich place a couple of minutes from my house. Asare was in the neighborhood when he called Ajua and she asked him to come over. As soon as I laid eyes on him I felt my breath catch in my throat. Asare was drop-dead hot, seriously. He was tall, at least six foot two. He was lean, with beautiful chocolate skin and a gorgeous face and a killer smile. I melted like butter. He was so smooth and suave. He was a taller, better-looking version of Ato. He was just a darn sexy boy. He came with his friend, another one of Kwaku's boys called Terry. The guys joined us and we sat and chatted and ate and just hung out for a bit. Ato called me and I told him where I was, and he came over on his bike. Ato knew Asare and Terry so he hung with us for a bit.

I really couldn't stop staring at Asare. He was so good looking. After a couple of hours, I had to head back home. It'd only been a month since my surgery and my mother was a little paranoid about where I was and what I was doing.

"I think I have a crush on Asare," I whispered to Ajua as we got up to leave.

She laughed. "Really? He had a thing with my sister when she was down a couple of weeks ago."

"Are you kidding? Shoot, let's forget it then."

"No, no. It was just a thing. She doesn't like him like that, trust me. I'll hook you up."

"Uh, let's not, it's just going to be weird. No biggie, okay."

But Ajua wouldn't let it go. After Asare dropped us off at my house, she sent him a text telling him I had a crush on him. I was mortified! But he replied and asked for my number and that was it. Asare and I started.

A few days later, we set up a semi-date. I managed to convince my mother I was healthy enough to go out for a drink. What I didn't add was we were going clubbing. I really wasn't sure clubbing was a good idea a little over a month after surgery, but hey, I wanted to be with Asare.

We set the date for Friday. When he came to pick me up, I really couldn't get over how seriously good looking he was.

"You're sure you're okay? We can always do this another time," he said.

I flashed a bright smile at Asare. "Oh yeah, I'm good. Trust me, I wouldn't jeopardize my health. I'm straight, yeah."

He smiled and opened his car door for me to get in. He

looked so good it was criminal. He was wearing all black, like I was, and he had such a lean lithe body. He had a sexy, slightly mischievous smile and I was completely hooked. I didn't dance that night. I knew my limits. I had a scar across my belly that was barely healed. If the doctor said no sex for months, I bet somewhere in his mind, he meant no dancing too.

I had a really good time with Asare that night. He was attentive, sweet, interesting, funny, engaging, just about everything. Cami was around too, and it was a pretty good night.

When Asare dropped me off, I was really disappointed the night was over. We walked hand in hand from my gate up to my front door. Then he followed me in.

"I had a nice time," I said.

"Yeah, me too. You feel okay? No pain somewhere?"

I laughed. Everyone felt I was fragile. "I'm good."

He nodded and I stood there quietly. And then the next minute, his lips were on mine. It was a soft kiss. His lips felt really good and I melted into him as the kiss deepened. We kissed for a long while and then we slowly broke apart.

"I'll call you in the morning," he said softly.

I nodded and then he was gone.

"You *what*?"

"Dude, when am I ever going to tell you something and have you go, 'Really, how nice, that's sweet. I hope it works out.' "

Ato shook his head at me. "It's because you have such bad taste in guys. Do you have any idea who Asare is? Any idea?"

I rolled my eyes and sank deeper into my sofa. Here we go.

"He's just like me, just like me. No difference, except though, I think my game is better," he continued.

My heart sank just a little. I knew there was something about Asare that reminded me of Ato but I figured it was his sense of style and poise.

"He has a reputation. Everyone knows it. He's a player, plain and simple. This is not going to go anywhere. Rabbie, come on, look at his circle—Kwaku, Terry, all of them. It's like a circle of... I don't know."

I sighed. "Remember I told you my brother told me the same thing about you?" I said.

"Your brother was right."

"I know. And if I'd listened, we wouldn't be friends now. And I really don't regret us hooking up."

Ato shook his head. "I know you, Rabbie. You'll fall for this guy. I know you. And I really don't want to see you get hurt."

It was one of the sweetest things Ato had ever said to me. I reached out and kissed him. "I'm just going to see where it goes. If it goes nowhere, fine. But I want to see where it goes."

The thing with Asare was very slow and very gradual. We were never alone much. It was usually him and his friends with me and my friends. Ato hung out with us sometimes, and Ato hung out with Asare and his boys without us girls a lot too. We watched movies, and chilled at my place, and went clubbing. And I didn't notice any shadiness until my twenty-fifth birthday.

Xavier decided I needed to make a fuss for my twenty-fifth "silver anniversary." He dubbed it the thanksgiving/birthday party. He said it was important to celebrate the fact that l managed to get to twenty-five, when six weeks earlier, getting past twenty-four hours was a challenge. I couldn't agree more. So my mother put up the cash, I came up with some guests and Xavier organized the party.

It was a really good party. As I've said, Xavier knew how to throw good parties. Osei came by earlier in the night, and Ekow and his crew sometime later and then Ato, Asare and their crew rounded off the night. It was fun hanging out with them.

"Where are you guys off to? Are you going clubbing?"

I was sitting on Asare's lap outside my gate and Cami and Ato were standing side by side. Lance, Asare's friend, was sitting in the chair next to Asare and me. Cami wanted to go clubbing after the party, but I wasn't sure.

"I think I'm done, I'm going home," Asare said.

"Yeah, me too," Lance said.

Ato shrugged. "I may pass through the clubs, see what's up."

"I want to go out! Come on, Lance, Asare," Cami whined.

I laughed. I didn't mind stepping out for a bit but Asare seemed like he didn't want to go.

"I am really tired, sweetie," he said to Cami.

His phone rang then and I got up from his lap. He walked

away to talk. Cami came to sit on my lap. I hoped her weight on me wasn't straining my still-healing scar.

"Rabbie, come on, let's go out. Let's go with Ato. Or you can drive, right?" she said.

"My mother doesn't want me driving for a while. But if you really want to, I guess we can."

"Hey, you guys can call me if you want to do something. Just let me know and I'll come get you," Ato said.

He said his byes and then disappeared. A few minutes later, Asare got off the phone and said he had to go. Cami was still whining but Asare said he was really tired and he just wanted to sleep. Lance was riding with Asare so he was going home too.

"I'll call you in the morning, yeah? You should go to bed. You look tired," Asare said to me.

I nodded. "I am. It's bedtime."

We kissed and they drove off.

"Go get dressed, we're going clubbing."

I turned to look at Cami. "What?"

"Asare had a black shirt laid out in the back of his car! I swear those boys are going out!"

"Come on, it could have been a shirt he picked up from the dry cleaners. He said he is tired and I am tired."

Cami wouldn't let it go.

"Rabbie, I am so serious. I can feel it in my bones. Those boys are going out. This is it. We're going to nail them. Don't let this chance slip by."

I paused. Asare had just said he was tired and he was going home. Would he lie so blatantly?

"Okay, Cami, let's go clubbing."

Just before Cami and I left home, I sent a text to Asare, asked him if he was home. And he responded and said almost there. I had given him one more opportunity to come clean. I sincerely hoped he was almost home. There were two possible clubs Asare would go to. When we got to the first one, he wasn't there. I needed to catch him in a lie, or my reasons for sneaking out with the car when I wasn't supposed to be driving would be stupid. Cami's instincts paid off at the second club.

Asare and Lance were the first people we saw when we

entered the club. Asare was leaning against the bar, whispering something in a girl's ear. I recognized her straight away and alarm bells went off. When his phone rang back at my end, I glanced at it and I saw the name, Ama. The girl he was talking to right now at the club was also called Ama. She and I had mutual friends and apparently Asare was one of those mutual friends. Cami didn't waste any time. She walked right up to them.

"Hey you," she said and nudged Asare.

He smiled slowly, like he wasn't sure if smiling was appropriate. His eyes fell on me and he walked past Cami to me.

"Hey, what are you doing here?" he asked.

"I could ask you the same thing, Mr. I'm Almost Home."

"I was, and then Lance just kept bugging me to drop him off here. And then I saw a couple of friends downstairs and I came up for a drink. I'm not going to be here for long."

He sounded like Ato, but Ato definitely had better game.

"You decided to change shirts just to drop Lance off?"

He froze and looked at his shirt and then he took a deep breath.

"I'll talk to you later, okay," I said.

I didn't want to hear any excuses. I motioned to Cami and we walked off. Asare didn't follow. I really felt like going home then but I noticed Ekow and his crew in the corner, and Cami and I went to join them. Ekow stayed by my side the whole night while Asare and I kept exchanging weird glances. It was like we were pretending we weren't watching each other when we were. After a couple of hours, he walked over to me. Ekow was standing right behind me, his hands on my waist, when Asare walked up to us. He barely glanced at Ekow.

"Can I talk to you for a minute?" he asked.

"I'm listening," I said.

"This is not what you think, honestly. She's just my friend. I didn't come with her. She was already here."

"You changed clothes, Asare."

"Look, I know how that makes it look bad, but it's really not."

"Did she call you, at my house?"

He sighed and fell silent. And then he tried again.

"This wasn't planned. Honest."

I shrugged. We weren't dating, we weren't a couple. He could do whatever he wanted. He shook his head.

"Can I just talk to you downstairs, please? I'm leaving."

I didn't want to talk to him, but his big eyes were just staring at me mournfully. I told Ekow I'd be right back and I followed him out.

"Listen, this is seriously not what you think."

We stood beside his car.

"You really expect me to believe it? You left my house going on about how tired you are and thirty minutes later, you're all dressed up in a club."

"I was tired. I was, and Lance just convinced me to come here."

"Asare, it doesn't matter, yeah. I know what I believe and that's just it."

"And who was the guy grinding up against you all night? You didn't even talk to anyone else."

"You don't want to go there, trust me."

"Did you even see me even dance with her? I was with my boys. I wasn't up against a wall with some girl."

"Do not try and turn this on me. Don't. It won't work."

I heard Cami singing and laughing behind me. I turned around. She and Lance were walking towards us.

"Busted!" she said and jammed her finger against Asare's chest.

He looked irritated. He motioned to Lance. "I'm going home. Are you coming with me?"

"Nah man, it's happening in there."

"Cool. I'll catch up with you guys tomorrow."

He looked at me and I looked back.

"I'll call you," he said.

I shrugged and he drove off.

I turned to Cami. "I think I'm gonna go home."

"Ah, come on!"

But I was done for the night. I sent Ekow a text that I was going home and I'd see him later. I left Cami with Lance. They both looked like they were having fun. Asare called half an hour later, wanting to know if I was still out. I said I was in bed. He didn't say much else and we hung up.

The incident with Asare opened my eyes a little better to the dilemma girls face. He had obviously lied and deceived me and gone to meet another girl. But despite that, I still liked him. And I wanted him to like me even more. I couldn't withdraw from him.

Ajua was still in love with her ex, Kwaku, and before I couldn't understand, but now I did. Those boys just had something.

After that night, Asare just got a little better with his playing. He controlled the situation. He came by when he wanted, sometimes unannounced, and he'd leave and I had no idea what he did after. There were a few frenzied kissing moments, at my house, at his house, but nothing further. For one, my six months of no sex wasn't up and on his part, he never pushed me to have sex. He never brought it up. When I first met him I told him I couldn't have sex for a while. We didn't talk about it again.

Ekow started to notice Asare's car at my end. There were a few times Asare and his friends turned up when Ekow and his friends were leaving or vice versa. Ekow asked who he was, and I said a friend. Asare asked who Ekow was and I said a neighbor. I wasn't dating either one of them. Yes, I was physical with both of them, but neither one of them needed to know that.

I couldn't stop thinking about Asare, wanting to be with him, talk to him and everything else. Ato, every now and then, tried to shake me out of my delirium, but it didn't quite work.

"Have you seen Asare lately?"

Ato and I were on my sofa. He came by a lot after work. We just talked. I mostly talked about Asare.

"Yeah, I saw him yesterday, on campus," Ato said.

"He was on campus?" I asked.

"Yep, I went to see Gigi and he was there to see Gigi's roommate."

"He said he was working late."

"Do you actually think you're the only one he's hanging out with?" Ato asked.

"No... I don't know. I just don't know what this is, he and I."

"It's nothing. Rabbie, he has other girls. He's not going to settle down anytime soon, neither of those guys are."

"I really like him," I said wistfully.

"Get over it. I'm not even sure if you're his type."

I frowned. "What does that mean?"

"The girls I usually see him with are skinny; you're not."

"Are you being cruel on purpose?"

"No, I'm being honest. Anyways, Cami is kinda looking hot these days, huh?"

"Dude, she's my friend, she's part of the no-go area."

"I'm just saying she looks good. Can't I just call her?"

"I know you, you don't just call people."

He laughed. "I'm not going to do anything. I did call her, earlier today. I told her I'd pass by after work."

I buried my face in my hands.

"Ato! I know you, I know you! Do not do anything!"

He kept laughing. "I'm not. I'm just going to pass by and say hello. I'll talk to you later, okay."

By the time Ato left, I hated him and all boys like him, including Asare. I was ready to be done with the whole bunch.

The First Betrayal

"What are you guys wearing to Asare's birthday party?"

It was sometime in June and Cami and I lay stretched out on my bed. Ajua was sitting on the other bed. Neither Cami nor I responded to Ajua's question. My mind was on Asare and his increasingly distant behavior. I don't know where Cami's mind was. Ajua tried again.

"Are you guys going naked or something?"

"What?" I said, trying to figure out if she was joking.

"I asked what you were wearing. No one answered."

"Oh. I don't know. Jeans, top, clothes," I muttered.

Cami laughed. She turned to me.

"We should go do long weaves. You know, like insanely long ones, jet black, straight. It would look so cool."

"Yeah, I like that. The party is Saturday right, we should get it done on Thursday or even Friday, so it'll be fresh looking, you know," I said.

"Yep, yep," Cami said.

We discussed clothes and boys and hair a little longer. I was a bit apprehensive about the party. There were going to be girls around; what if Asare ignored me? I was nervous. I wanted him to like me so bad.

The day of the party came. I don't even remember what I wore. Cami and I did get our long jet-black weaves. I think we looked good. Ato offered to drive Cami and me to the party; Ajua was getting there by herself.

The party was at 4 P.M. I waited for Ato for almost an hour and then he called.

"Hey, can you take a cab to my end, since I'm closer to Asare's place? It just doesn't make any sense for me to drive your way and then back this way."

"Oh yeah, sure, definitely, I'll be there in a bit. I just gotta call Cami and go pick her up."

"Cami is already here."

I froze. What did he say? "Huh?"

"Cami is at my house. I'll see you in a bit."

"Hey, don't rush off the phone like that. What's Cami doing at your house?"

"Rabbie, I can't get into it now. Talk later, okay?"

By the time I got to Ato's end, I wasn't sure whom to be pissed with or what to think. Cami didn't know Ato and I had anything. She, and almost everyone else, assumed we were just close friends. But all the same, to keep her movements from me, she must suspect something, suspect I wouldn't like it. But ultimately, Ato was the shady one. What was he doing? Had something happened? When did this start? They both looked fairly guilty when I got there. I sat in the back of his car in silence.

The party was pretty uneventful. Asare didn't ignore me, but neither did he pay me any special attention. He was the perfect host. I tried to have some fun, taking pictures with Cami and Ajua and the rest of the guys there. My mind was still on Cami and Ato, but I tried not to let it show. Later that night, Ato dropped Cami off at home and he and I sat in his car in front of my house.

"What's going on? Just be honest with me," I said.

"Come on, you know what's going on. I told you I think she's pretty hot. And we've been talking. I told you that too."

"Ato, you told me you'd gone by to say hello, like, a couple of times. As far as I know, besides that, you only see her here, at my end; you flirt, which I assumed was harmless, and that's it."

"And that's how it started, here, in your house," he said mischievously.

"Huh? What?"

"We had sex, here, in your house, in your bed."

I was stunned. What did he just say? Was he kidding? He didn't look serious. And he didn't look guilty either.

He continued rambling on, about how they'd done it in my house, twice, and his house once. He sounded like he was just telling me about one of his escapades, as always, no big deal.

"Ato, Ato, why would you do that? This is one of my closest friends!" I was practically screaming.

"Oh come on, Rabbie, this is no big deal. You told me you had a crush on Kofi."

274

"Crush, Ato, nothing happened, and nothing would have happened. It was just a thought. You went from flirting and insinuating she's hot to actually having sex with her! Here, in my house, my bed—Ato, come on. That's an abuse of trust."

Ato and Cami were in my house so often, the idea wasn't completely implausible. More than once I'd left them both there. They weren't strangers to my family. It wouldn't be unusual for them to be there without me. For some reason, I didn't want details or specifics or dates or times. He didn't seem to understand what he'd done. To him, he'd just slept with another girl. I couldn't understand Cami either. She had a boyfriend. And she knew Ato's reputation. And even if she thought Ato and I were just friends and nothing more, why wouldn't she tell me? Shouldn't that enable her to tell me, if she really thought he was just my friend?

I couldn't get Ato to understand what he'd done was wrong which damaged my feelings and perception of our friendship. How could he not see it? We'd been sleeping together for five years. How could he then sleep with one of my closest friends, right under my nose, in my bed!

I didn't ask Cami about it. And Ato said it wasn't going to happen again. Her boyfriend was back in town. The fact that she cheated on him, with someone like Ato, surprised me. I knew my friends were just as shady as I was. Although Sammi and I were the ones in the group everyone naturally assumed to be shady, I knew each and every one of them was capable of worse. Cami sleeping with Ato just didn't make sense to me. This was the same boy she knew Ajua had this everlasting crush on, the same boy Abena and Sammi never hesitated to diss because he was such a player. I couldn't wrap my head around it.

Asare's attentions were dwindling slowly, Ato and Cami had hooked up and I still couldn't have sex... I needed a break. I needed to be away from them all.

Jon, Last Act

A couple of weeks after Ato's betrayal, I took a trip to America to see my aunt, and stopped over in London for about a month. There was no Philly planned. Tei and I were basically over. I wasn't going to put myself through that hot/cold experience again. Xavier was also coming on the trip, just a couple of weeks after me. Ajua had also returned to London soon after Asare's birthday party. I just needed to be away from Ato, and Cami, and Asare and even Ekow. I wanted to see my brother Josh. He'd been scared during my surgery and recovery, and he needed to see me. My aunt also wanted to make sure I was okay. It was the perfect time to go away.

Jon had left Ghana some years ago for school in Germany. And then in 2004, just a few months before my trip to London, he'd moved to the U.K. to work. I hadn't particularly planned on seeing him, but I figured, why not. I sent him an email with my details and he called a couple of days later.

"What are you doing the rest of the day?" Ajua asked.

She and I were hanging out with a couple of Asare and Kwaku's friends in London. Ajua was strongly tied to that crew.

"I'm meeting Jon and Selassie for a movie," I said.

"Jon? Wow. Ahh, someone's hoping to get some, huh?"

"What? No, no. It'll be nice to see him again, but I'm not expecting anything to happen. But I wouldn't mind if it does!"

My phone started to ring. It was Jon. I said bye to Ajua and the boys and left. I was pretty excited to see Jon again. I hadn't seen him in three years or so. I wondered if he looked better. I wondered if he was single. I wondered if he'd find me attractive. I wondered if sparks could possibly fly again. I was wondering way too much.

Selassie and Jon picked me from the train station. Selassie acted a little happier to see me than Jon did. But it was still a fun night. We went to watch *King Arthur*. Jon sat next to me and Selassie was on the other side of Jon. There were a couple of moments that I felt there was a little electricity, and I wanted to reach out and kiss him. I really wanted to. But I didn't want to be too forward, and I definitely didn't want to be rejected. What if he didn't kiss me back? When they drove me back home, Selassie kept teasing us, insinuating that Jon and I were going to spend the night together, and I was sort of hoping the same. I was staying in a friend's apartment in East London and I had the whole place to myself. But Jon said he needed to go home. I was disappointed but not quite ready to give up on the whole Jon hook-up. We had unfinished business. I wanted to sleep with him. I wanted to be with him. I wanted to know if he liked me, a little bit.

A few days later, we spoke again. And I went by to visit him at his place. I was hoping that would be the moment, the moment Jon and Rabbie started again. He was staying with a couple of guys but none of them was home. He met me at the train station and we talked as we walked back to his end. They didn't have much furniture in the living room so we sat and half lay on the floor as we talked and talked. And that was practically it. We just talked and talked and talked. I didn't want to make the first move, and he didn't make any moves. I couldn't figure out what he was thinking. If he wanted something to happen, he'd do something, wouldn't he? Or did he want me to make a move? Was he not sure what I wanted? But a part of me knew he knew what I wanted. The ball was in his court. I couldn't do much more. So that ended another uneventful meeting between Jon and me.

I went to my brother's end for the weekend. And I tried to take my mind off Jon and the obvious lack of interest on his part. Josh and his wife were expecting a baby, and his wife Jay was close to six months' pregnant. I couldn't believe Josh was finally settling down. One player was off the playing field, jersey hung up in the closet, ready to roll up his sleeves and play daddy. There was still hope for us women if Josh could fall hard and give up the game. But I think he had started to give up the game a while ago. Jay was such a beautiful girl, so in the end, he nailed the big catch and figured what else was there? What more could a guy want? What did guys want anyways, the next beautiful girl? Josh had been there, done that, and he knew one girl today was just like the next girl you'd meet. I realized it was the same with what I was doing with my life. There was no "the next good guy." There were just more Atos and more Asares. They were all the same.

Jon called one afternoon while I was at Josh's. We had arranged to meet up; either he'd come to Josh's end at Birmingham or I'd take a train to meet him in London. I was hoping he'd come to Josh's. That would be an effort on his part that would surely signal some interest.

"Hey, how's it going over there?" he asked.

"It's fun, man. My cousin Albert is here as well. We've been sightseeing, went to museums, the city center, watched a movie in this completely high-end luxury room, shopped; I'm just having a ball."

"Sounds like it."

"You should come," I said.

"Yeah, about that, I don't think I can. Selassie and I have a couple of things we need to get done today. And then I have to work tomorrow and the next couple of days."

My heart sank. What had I really expected?

"That's cool. I understand. Tell Selassie I said what's up."

I could hear Selassie's voice in the background.

"Yeah, I will. I'm really sorry. I'll call you later, yeah."

"Sure. Bye."

"Bye."

I closed my eyes. Damn! I looked at my phone, planning on calling Ajua, when I realized I could hear Jon's voice. Was he still talking to me?

"Hello? Jon?"

It took a second, but I realized he was talking to Selassie. He hadn't hung up the phone!

I said hello a few more times but he couldn't hear. He had no clue I was still on. I could hear them distinctly and after a minute I realized they were talking about me!

"I really thought you guys were gonna hook up or something," Selassie said.

"Uh, I don't know. I briefly thought so. I mean, I know that's what she wants, but… I mean, that's just complicated stuff. I really don't want to get back to all that."

"Why not? What if it's just a hook-up and not a relationship? If the girl wants to sleep with you, do it, and I'm sure you both can be adults about it."

"Seriously, I just don't want to. There's that whole baggage with Selorm and Junior and Edem. I can't get that shit out of my mind," Jon said.

"Are you kidding? That's how long ago? It's not like she slept with them."

"She slept with Edem—sex, rape, whatever it is she claims."

"That was what? Once? Hey, we all did stupid stuff back then."

"It's just drama," Jon said.

"Hey, it's your call. I just thought, the girl wants you, you guys have history, you can handle it."

"Plus there is her surgery. I don't think she's supposed to be having sex anyways."

"Ah yeah, that must have been some scary shit for her, huh? Cami was telling me about it. She almost died, right?"

"I don't want to hit it and then whoa, stitches come off or something, blood all over the place," Jon said, laughing.

"That would be some crazy shit. So you're definitely not touching that?"

"Nope, done deal; I don't think it's worth the drama, or the whole surgery thing, or all the little bits and pieces. Not sure how to tell her. But it's not gonna happen."

I took the phone from my ear and hung up. Then I sent Jon a text: "Next time make sure you've hung up the phone before you start talking about me."

My phone rang a couple of minutes later but I didn't answer. Both Selassie and Jon kept calling me back and forth but I just let my phone ring.

I went up to my room, lay there and cried. My chest felt tight. I could barely breathe. He sent a text, said he was so sorry, really sorry, and we should talk. I didn't reply. I didn't want to speak to him. I didn't want to hear his voice. I didn't want to talk to him. I was so embarrassed and disappointed and shamed. I felt like a fool. And it was painful. This hang-up on Jon had to end, it had to end now. I'd been making a fool of myself for years. I cried and cried and couldn't eat for the rest of the day. This was Jon, the last act. I purged all latent feelings I felt for him. It was so clear and so plain. It had taken ten long years, ten years of carrying him always in my heart, on my mind, pining for him consciously and unconsciously, but now I was done.

I started to think back… Would Jon and I still be together today if we had never broken up? I doubt it. To think that it's a possibility that we would have made it would be immature and unrealistic on my part. We were like two different people. He would have frustrated me and I would have frustrated him. He had a free spirit that I wouldn't have been able to tame. I had a free spirit too, and he wouldn't have been able to control mine either. Sometimes people need to grow on their own, explore on their own, be who they need to be on their own. We would have stifled each other and we would have hated each other. The memories I have are fine. We loved each other very strongly, when we were young and impressionable. I would always remember him. He would probably always remember me. But to think or want more would be futile and unnecessary. I knew I was a different person, and he was not the same either. This was over. This was truly over. It felt right and it felt appropriate. Ten years later, almost to the day, and I felt at peace. I felt light-headed for a minute. It felt like I weighed much less. I rolled my head back and pulled my knees up to my chin and shook my head. God, God, God.

I needed to overhear that conversation to be able to let go, didn't I? Sometimes it's only through pain that you can see the truth. Well thank you, you took your time, God, it would have been great if you helped me let go years ago, but thank you, better late than never, right? I let the curtain down and prayed I was permanently closing the chapter on Jon. I truly believed I was. I could never picture having feelings for him again.

There Will Always Be Someone

When I got back to Ghana, I had made some key resolutions. The thing with Asare was not going anywhere and I was not going to hang around and hope he'd pick me to settle with. I really liked him and liked spending time with him. He was truly one of the best-looking guys I'd ever met, but all that was not worth it.

The day after I got back, he came by the house, being all sweet and lovey, saying he'd missed me. It was so strange, how his words went in one ear and out the other. As I stared at him, everything was so clear to me. I was done.

"Hey, so, I know this isn't going anywhere. I like you. I think you're a pretty fun guy and I've had a good time hanging out with you. But I think we should just be friends. Let's not pretend this is anything else. I can't do that anymore."

We were leaning against his car and I didn't waste any time. He wasn't like Osei or anyone like that. He wouldn't be hurt or devastated. I knew a part of him would be relieved. We weren't going to be in a relationship. It was never going to be more than just friends. He looked solemn for a minute.

"If that's what you want, what can I say?"

Just as I had expected he didn't ask questions, drill me or pretend he was devastated. I respected him for that.

He tried to kiss me then, but I stepped back.

"Let's just be friends. I think that's what you want too, and that's what I want. And we're not going to do kissy stuff."

He laughed.

"Kissy stuff… okay. But we can hang?"

"Oh yeah, of course," I said distractedly.

We hugged and then that was it.

I didn't get over Asare immediately, I have to admit. But it wasn't difficult or long-drawn-out either. We fell pretty easily into friendship mode. He still called and I still called. And he passed by my end every now and then. There wasn't any awkwardness. A few times I fantasized about being with him, but I knew it wasn't going to happen and I was tired of deluding myself when it came to guys.

The other helpful thing was I had Ekow. Ekow and I still had our thing and it had become a very comfortable semi-relationship. We were seriously having way too much sex. It was still mainly on the down low. My friends knew about it and his friends knew about it, and some of our family members, but we were never openly together. Whatever it was we were doing, it worked perfectly for both of us. We had this incredibly physical relationship and he was also someone I liked being with. For now, it was good as it was.

When I got back from my trip, I got a job as a copywriter with a media organization. It was a challenging yet fun job on a small team and I was pretty excited about it. And since I didn't want to lose my media experience, I got a part-time gig with the same company as a presenter/reporter. It was just a couple of hours a week and everything was just about perfect. I was prepared to focus on work and myself and not get caught up in any drama. I had a great job, great constant sex, Cami and I were great, I had new friends from work and everything was just peachy for a while. Ato was on a semi-back burner. I was really disappointed with what he'd done but I decided not to bring it up again. Unfortunately, and I'm ashamed to say this, we didn't exactly stop sleeping together. It was very rare but it still happened, even after he'd desecrated my bed with Cami. I have no idea what I was thinking then. I just wasn't ready to write him off. He was my best friend. He knew me, and I knew him. I couldn't talk to anyone else the same way I talked to him. So he stayed in my life.

A couple of months later, someone else slipped unexpectedly into my life.

"Hey Rabbie, can you run this down to marketing? We need them to sign off on this contract."

I scowled inwardly at my boss but smiled outwardly. I hated running errands within the building. The news desk sat on the sixth floor and marketing was all the way down on the first floor. And the elevator was out, as usual. I took the document quietly and walked out, running a speech in my head to spew to my boss later. I was tired of being used as an assistant. I was barely involved in any decent work.

I hated marketing. It was loud and busy and full of obnoxious people. As a media company, marketing was a very important function and they knew that. So they acted like they were the heart and soul of the company; they were just a bunch of arrogant people.

I went straight to the office assistant's desk.

"Hey Martha, we need this contract signed. I think it's urgent, so can you sort it out?"

Martha smiled. She was a pretty nice woman, just a bit grouchy on some days.

"Can you please just go drop it in the CMO's office?"

I frowned. "CMO?"

"The company hired a new Chief Marketing Officer. If you leave it with me, it could take a while for me to get it signed. I have a lot to do. But he's not busy now, just take it in there."

She gestured towards an office at the back of the floor. I sighed and nodded.

The CMO's office was open but his back was to the door and he was on the phone. Just as I was about to knock, he spun around and I froze. Whoa, hello handsome.

"Hey I have to run now. I have a visitor. I'll call you back later."

He hung up and stood up from his chair. Whoa, hello Mr. Tall.

He smiled as he walked towards me and I just kept melting.

"Hi… I'm Jesse."

"Hi, I'm Rabbie. I work here and I have a document for you to sign," I said quickly.

"I know who you are. You're on one of our networks. You present the late news show, on Fridays. I never miss it," he said with a grin.

Gosh, I was dying.

"Come in, have a seat. It's nice to finally meet you," he said.

I sat opposite him and we stared at each other for a while. He never stopped smiling. He was a tall guy, at least six two, with a great body, handsome face and a killer smile. I was a nervous wreck. I could barely find any words.

"So when did you join and from where?" I managed to throw in.

"I've been here a week or two. But I moved to Ghana from South Africa, like, three months ago. And before then, I was in America for a while. It's good to be home though."

I nodded, not sure what else to say.

"I think you're very good at what you do. I couldn't believe it when I was told you're also a copywriter. Don't you want to do the presenting thing full-time?"

"Oh yeah, it's great and fun, so maybe later."

"You're really good at it."

I smiled. Yeah, I know I am.

"Thanks. So Bill needs this signed. I think it's urgent. But if you want to look over it first, that's fine. I can pick it up later."

"Yeah, I'll look over it and I'll call you when I'm done."

I stood up and he stood up as well. His eyes were just boring into me!

"Nice meeting you, Rabbie."

I nodded and then bolted.

Each time my office phone rang for the next couple of hours I hoped it was Jesse. I couldn't stop thinking about him. And then it was him.

"Hi, Rabbie Daniels here," I said distractedly as I answered the phone.

"Hi, it's Jesse, from marketing."

He had the perfect phone voice. This guy was scoring pretty high marks.

"Hey, I've been waiting for your call," I said lamely.

"Yeah, sorry about that, I got caught up in a lot of meetings, so I eventually signed it and had Martha bring it up to Bill. I'm calling because I said I would. I don't want to be rude."

"Oh sure, no problem, that's fine. It's good you signed it."

I hit myself on the head as the words came out of my mouth. How stupid was I? "It's good you signed it?"

"Are you leaving work soon?" he asked.

"Yeah, in a bit," I mumbled.

"Are you driving?"

"No, I was just gonna take a cab."

I wondered where this line of questioning was going.

"If you don't mind waiting for, like, an hour, I can drop you off."

Yes!

"Sure, thanks. That'll be nice," I said, grinning from ear to ear.

"I'll call you when I'm done, then."

When we hung up, I leaned back in my chair and just grinned. I could definitely find something to do for an hour. I couldn't believe he'd just offered to drop me home. We had just met! I was excited and I couldn't sit still. Did he like me? Did I like him?

An hour and a half later, he called, apologized profusely for keeping me waiting and said he was ready to leave. A thought struck me as I packed my bag to leave. Inter-office relationships weren't forbidden—there were married couples who worked together—but office gossip was seriously rife. I didn't want to be fodder for the water cooler. But it was pretty late and most people had left already. It wouldn't hurt to have him drop me home.

When I saw him again, I really couldn't believe how good looking he was. He was handsome in a very manly way. He looked grown, mature and downright sexy. He was thirty-six to my almost twenty-six. Even though Osei was eight years older than me, he didn't look his age. Osei was very boyish, in behavior and looks. Jesse was, like, the complete opposite. There was no way he could be mistaken for a boy. He exuded authority.

We had a really nice talk in the car. He was smart, interesting, charming and sexy. We sat in his car for a little bit and talked. He said bye and then he left.

The next few weeks Jesse and I just talked on the phone, during lunch, after work and over the weekends. I was falling hard for him fast. He met my mother a couple of times and she seemed to like him. I was ecstatic and a little over myself. Here was a guy who was so mature, so good looking, with a great job, damn smart and driven, and he liked me.

We did our best to keep our developing relationship on the down low. He was a senior executive and I had to be cautious. But I really liked him.

"Hey, what's up?" Jesse said as he hugged me.

I had stopped by his office some weeks after our first meeting. I wondered if any of the marketing people suspected anything. It wasn't my first time down there. There were so many people in and out of the marketing department all the time—I hoped they didn't suspect. Jesse's office was tucked discreetly at the back but the side facing the rest of the floor had a huge glass window. I didn't like that bit.

"Nothing much, I just came to say hello," I said as I hugged him back.

We stepped apart and looked at each other. He had a naughty smile on his face.

"What is it?" I asked, laughing.

He shrugged and then the next minute his lips were on mine. I was taken off guard. We were standing in the doorway of his office, in the middle of the day and he chose that moment for our first kiss. I wasn't sure which would be worse, kissing him back or stepping back. His arm went around my waist and then I didn't have a choice. I kissed him back. We stood there, in front of his office and tongue kissed for like a minute. It was crazy. We heard a small cough and we jumped back. Martha was standing right there!

"Sorry to interrupt, but Jesse, you're needed upstairs."

Then she walked away.

I buried my face in my hands. "Oh my goodness," I wailed.

He chuckled and touched my face. "Looks like I have to run to a meeting. Talk to you later?"

I nodded. He kissed me again, quickly, and then I ran off. I kept my head down and avoided eye contact with everyone.

After our first kiss, Jesse was a little more open with our relationship. I wasn't sure what it was we had exactly. We snuck in a few more kisses in his office. I couldn't get over all that was happening.

"So, Ansah is like my best friend. We've known each other for like twenty-five years or something."

I laughed. "That's my age."

He smiled. "Yeah, you're such a baby, huh."

We were on our way to a birthday party for Ansah. It was our first public outing. I suspected there would be work people there, but I didn't care. He had asked me to come with him and I was glad to do so. If he was ready for us to make an appearance together, then so was I.

Although I suspected there'd be a number of work people, I really didn't expect that many. There was a good handful of co-workers. And in addition, there was Ekow and his whole crew. I felt instantly conscious. It was a huge full-blown party and I wasn't sure we'd made the right move. We held hands awkwardly, more on my part anyways. He introduced me to his friends as his girl. I didn't expect that. I wasn't sure if "girl" was the same as "girlfriend" though. I've always thought "girl" was a not-serious version of girlfriend. You call a person that when you're not ready or sure of the girl. Ansah, the best friend he'd known as long as I'd lived, hugged me enthusiastically and said he was glad to finally meet me. I liked the attention I got from his friends. It meant something, right? If his friends had heard about me, especially Ansah, I must be important and special to him, I thought. I broke apart from Jesse's group for a moment to go talk to Ekow.

Ekow and I, it was just such a simple yet weird relationship. As much as we had independent lives, we never really flaunted it. He'd seen Asare at my end a couple of times and asked about it, but he didn't react. And here I was with Jesse, holding hands like a couple. What made it weird was Ekow and I were still sleeping together. Matter of fact, the last time was just four days earlier. If it had been Ato at the party, I wouldn't have cared, but there was something about this thing with Ekow that I couldn't explain. As much as we both understood what it was, I really liked him and I didn't want him to get the impression I was all over the place.

"Hey you," I said and poked him in the tummy, his rock hard tummy.

"So who's that?" he asked immediately, nodding his head in Jesse's direction.

I looked back in the direction of his nod, even though I knew who he was referring to.

"Oh, that's a friend of mine, from work," I said.

I really didn't know what to call Jesse. We hadn't defined what it was. We'd only been kissing less than a week.

"Friend, huh? Interesting."

I smiled at him. Ekow was so good looking. His body was rock solid and he had such height and frame. He smiled back. I felt a hand around my waist and I turned. Jesse was right behind me.

"Hi," he said to Ekow. Ekow said hi back. Jesse kissed the side of my head, just above my ear and whispered, "Do you want a drink?"

"No, thanks, I'm good." I wanted to chat with Ekow a little bit longer. This closeness with Jesse was making me feel slightly nervous and uncomfortable. Ekow's friends were there, the same guys who knew I was sleeping with him. I didn't want Jesse touching and kissing me right in front of them. After an awkward moment of silence, I told Ekow I'd talk to him later and I walked away with Jesse.

We found a quiet spot somewhere in Ansah's garden without much lighting and cuddled up. When he kissed me, I couldn't resist or fight it. He was the boss, and if he was comfortable enough, then fine with me. It was just a couple of kisses and then we mingled a little bit. I hung out with a couple of people from work and then some of Ekow's friends who tried to tease me about Jesse, but I killed that pretty fast. After a long while, I was ready to call it a night.

"Can you spend the night at my place?" Jesse whispered in my ear. He had his arms around my waist as we walked towards his car. I was caught off guard by the question. Things were escalating pretty fast. We'd started so slow and then all of a sudden he was kissing me in his office, inviting me to a party thrown by his best friend and now he wanted me to spend the night.

I hesitated for a moment and then I decided to go for it.

"Sure," I said slowly. He smiled.

My mother had traveled so I could do it. My brother wasn't a tattletale anymore. I could definitely do this.

He didn't rush things when we got to his place. We curled up on the sofa and watched a movie and talked and kissed. I was so nervous it was almost like my first time.

But Jesse was incredibly gentle and there was no pressure. When we were ready to go to bed, we lay there for ages, still talking, cuddling. When we eventually got down to it, he was gentle and sweet and loving. We fell asleep close to 5 A.M.

The next day, we woke up late and he made me breakfast. He was really notching up the high marks. Then we cuddled up some more. In the afternoon, we went for lunch at his friend's place. I wore his T-shirt over my pants and tried to look like I was coming from my own home. It was a much smaller gathering, no more than ten people, all coupled up. I felt good showing up with him. I felt this was it, really.

No One Is Any Different

The first month or so after our weekend together was pretty low key. We didn't overtly do anything at the office. We were more careful than before. I spent a couple more weekends with him, but that was still low key. After that first month, I started to pick up a weird vibe. I didn't talk about Jesse at work, but some of the girls in the news center started to talk about him. One or two had crushes on him and one of my closest friends at the news center, Indira, thought he was too smooth.

It was Indira who worried me the most. She took jabs at him too often and my instincts made me feel she was hiding something. I didn't tell her about Jesse and me but I felt she knew. I was almost certain she did.

There was one instance that jarred me. Jesse asked me to another one of Ansah's gigs but I wasn't feeling well. So Jesse said he was going alone. He came by my house first, looking all dapper and handsome. I couldn't shake off that funny feeling. Right after Jesse left, I called Indira, who said she was going to the same party with some friends. The tingly feeling got worse. I had a bad fever so there wasn't much I could do. I couldn't get up and go to the party and I didn't like to be paranoid. That wasn't me.

But the next morning, I called Indira, and she coyly said she was curled up with a man. Indira had a lot of men, a lot. There was a new person every day. If she wanted something, she went for it, which was why she was the first person who raised my paranoia. No matter how she tried to diss him, there was always something in her voice. I asked her who she was with and she said just some guy. I knew it would be weird to call him right after. So I waited a couple of hours and then I called him. He didn't pick up. I waited till afternoon and then called, still no answer. I tried hard not to go crazy.

I didn't call again that day. I wasn't going to be the stalker girlfriend type.

The next day, Jesse called.

"Hey, I'm sorry about missing your calls yesterday. I kinda got crazy, with the drinking. It was so bad; I was so hung-over on Saturday."

He was smart enough to come up with a good excuse. What he said could be true or he could have been in bed with Indira. I had no way of knowing. Until I knew, I couldn't bitch.

We chatted a bit and then I said I had to go. I really wasn't well. For the next week, I still couldn't shake off the feeling! Something was just off!

So I did the unthinkable. Without any evidence, I decided to go with my instincts.

"Is everything okay? Your text sounded serious."

I tried to smile at Indira. I had sent her a text earlier in the day and told her to meet me in one of the conference rooms after work. I added that it was urgent.

She sat across from me, looking curious and worried. I decided to go for it.

"This may sound off, like it's coming out of nowhere. But is there something with you and Jesse?"

The most important thing was to read her face, her reaction. Her lower lip quivered a little, and her eyes rolled sideways, like she was trying to think of an answer. The pause was too long. I had my answer, but I needed her to say it. And in order to get her to say it, I had to go out on a limb first.

"I've been seeing him for like two months now, maybe a little more," I said.

"What? Are you joking?"

I shook my head. She laughed a little.

"Oh that's fantastic. Hmm, he and I started a little while ago."

I closed my eyes briefly. Damn it. I hated to be right. Why was I right? Why? Why and how had this happened? I stood up from the chair and leaned against the wall, devastated. I had thought, I had really thought I had a good thing. I wanted to bang my head against the wall. My mind was going haywire and I needed to reel it in.

I sat down again and she showed me a text she'd gotten that day. It was the same text I'd gotten just that morning. It said, "I'm missing you baby." I was stunned—same words. He didn't even change it up a little. I was so pissed. How could he? She was my friend. He knew that. She was my closest friend at work. I spoke about her all the time. What the heck? What was wrong with him? My anger just started to build. Right there and then, he called. It was freaky. I put him on speaker.

"Hey baby," he said in his smooth phone voice.

"Hi," I said quietly.

"I've been thinking about you all day."

I wanted to gag. Idiot.

"Really?"

"Yeah, I really miss you. Can you come over tonight? I have wine, movies and myself," he said laughing.

I rolled my eyes.

"I can't. I'm still at work. I have a lot to do. I'm going to be here for a while and then I just want to go to bed."

"Aww, I really miss you. Anyways, don't work too hard. I'll call you in the morning, okay?"

"Sure," I said.

As soon as I hung up it hit me right there and then.

"We need to get back at him," I said coolly.

"How?" she asked.

I smiled. I had it. I had the perfect plan. It was ingenious. The thought made me giddy. I sat down and looked at her, grinning.

"You're going to call him now. Say sweet stuff and tell him you want to see him. Add that you're working and you'll come by late, like midnight. And then I'll call him back, in a little bit. And tell him I'm heading there now. He's gonna try and call you to reschedule, but guess what? Your phone is gonna be off! But I'll tell him I can only stay for an hour, so he'll figure he can still get away with it. Me in now, 8 or 9 P.M. and you at midnight, but instead of leaving at ten or so, I'll stay till midnight. He can't throw me out. And your phone is still gonna be off. Just show up at midnight and then put your phone on!"

The idea was just falling into place in my head and I was getting excited. Indira looked skeptical.

"It sounds complicated," she mumbled.

"No, it's not. It's so perfect. You just have to do exactly as I say. Trust me. This is going to be beautiful."

She frowned and I grinned. It was so good! I had outdone myself.

"Call him now," I said.

She dialed and put him on speaker.

"Hey you," he said.

My blood curled. Idiot.

"Hey," Indira said, looking at me with a questioning look.

"What are you up to?" he asked.

"I'm at work," she said. She sounded too uncertain. I thought she was going to ruin my plan.

"Can you come by afterwards?" he asked.

I rolled my eyes. Predictable! I gestured at her to agree and I mouthed midnight.

"Yeah, sure, but I'm working late. So more like midnight and then I'll spend the night."

"Great, perfect. I'll see you later then."

When they hung up, I felt pain, pain at what he'd done, but I also felt exhilarated. I was going to get him back.

"Indira, you have to listen to me, okay? This is going to work. Keep your phone on, till I get there, and then I'll text you. As soon as you get my text, turn your phone off. That's all. Just keep your phone off till you get to his place. I'll still be there. Text me as soon as you get there, and we'll put on a show."

She nodded. I repeated the instructions and then left. This was going to work.

"Where are you going?" my mother asked when I reached for her car keys.

"Jesse is cheating on me, with Indira. And I just came up with the perfect plan to bust him."

My mother raised an eyebrow. "What?"

"Yep, yep, I've devised a plan, really brilliant plan. I'll let you know how it goes."

"Ah Rabbie, it's not necessary. Don't do this. Just write him off."

"Oh I'll write him off, but first, this."

My mother tried to talk me out of it but my mind was completely made up. I took her car keys and left. When I was ten minutes away from Jesse's place, I called him.

"Hey, are you still at work?" he asked.

"No. I'm actually in your neighborhood. I came to drop some papers off for my mother, just round the corner from you. You home?"

"Yeah, yeah, come by."

"Cool, but I can't stay for long, okay? Just like an hour. I'm really tired and I need to get some sleep."

"Sure, I just want to see you. I've really missed you," he said.

Such a liar.

When I got to his place I sent Indira a text and told her I was there. I hoped she'd turn her phone off right after. As part of the plan I kept telling him I couldn't stay for long. We sat in the living room and he popped in a movie. My part of the plot was more challenging I thought. How was I going to stay there for three hours and prevent him from touching or kissing me? I didn't want him to suspect something was wrong. And worse, he was so smooth and sweet. Carrying on a conversation was also hard. Each time I looked at him, I wanted to smack him. I couldn't stand all the fake stuff he was saying. He was being so sweet; it was almost as if he could read my mind. And then for the first time ever, he said it.

"I love you."

I hated him even more when he uttered those words. But something else also happened. I felt weaker. The anger and pain ebbed and all I wanted to do was believe him. He'd never said that before. I so badly wanted to believe he sincerely liked me, or loved me. When I felt his lips on mine, I didn't resist. I tried to tell myself this was for the last time. I tried to tell myself I didn't believe him. But I wanted to so badly. I didn't stop him, didn't stop anything from happening. I had hours to kill before the opening curtain, so why not? I didn't say the words back; that I couldn't do. I didn't love him but I wanted to be loved by him. I wanted something to work. I couldn't deal with all the failure, from Osei, to Tei, and Ato and Asare and this weird thing with Ekow. I needed something of my own and for weeks I had thought Jesse was it. The realization that he wasn't the one was hard to bear.

As we lay in bed together, he kept making phone calls. I knew he was trying to call Indira, to cancel their midnight rendezvous. He cursed a little and I guessed she'd done the right thing, and turned her phone off. It just reminded me of what he'd done, how mean, shady and wicked he was. How could he tell me all that stuff, when he'd been seeing her all this while?

I wanted to leave but I was so determined to nail him to the wall. I wished I hadn't let things go as far as they had, but three hours was a pretty long time just to sit and talk with someone you're supposed to be dating.

A little after eleven, Jesse started to get antsy but I wasn't going to leave. I was too close to the finish line. He just couldn't get off the phone.

And he still couldn't ask me what time I planned on leaving. His agitation was so obvious. Indira played her part perfectly. At ten minutes to midnight she sent me a text and said she was outside Jesse's gate. At that exact moment I told him I needed to go home. And then his phone beeped. I knew it was Indira texting him that she was outside the gate.

His face contorted and he looked stressed as I picked up my bag and started to walk out without him.

"Do you need to leave now?" he asked.

I was already out the door, walking towards the car.

"Yeah, I gotta go now. Can you get the gate for me?"

He sighed and nodded and started walking towards the gate. I got in the car, started it and drove slowly behind him. When he opened the gate, I saw him step out and he was acting strange, like he was shielding someone. I stopped the car, stepped out and the show began.

"Who's there? Is someone there?" I asked.

And then I heard Indira's voice on cue. "Who's that? Why are you trying to hide me?"

She stepped through the gate and into the light.

"Indira? What are you doing here? What's going on here?" I was good.

"What are you doing here?" She was good too.

We both turned to him and started bitching. He looked like he wanted to disappear through the concrete pavement. Indira's voice got louder and mine followed.

"Ladies, ladies, please, please, calm down. It's late and I have neighbors," he said, looking really stressed.

"I don't give a damn about your neighbors," Indira snapped. I was losing my energy though. I didn't want to scream and fight. I was disappointed in him but I was too tired and let down to scream. He dragged us back into his house by our arms. Indira was bitching and I was sullen. I was really pained.

"Why don't you try and explain this? What is Rabbie doing here?"

"Indira, don't even start, don't even start. You and I both know what this was. I'd appreciate it if you'd just shut up right now," he snapped.

He tried to pull me aside from Indira.

"Rabbie, Rabbie, listen to me please. I am sorry. I am really sorry. I love you. Please. Are you listening?"

I had a stone-cold expression on my face. Indira started shouting again. I thought she was getting too loud. My head was hurting.

"I'm going home now, and I'm taking her with me," I said quietly.

He swore under his breath.

"Rabbie, I know you're angry. But please listen to me," he said, reaching for my arm.

"Don't touch me," I hissed. I turned to Indira. Game over. We had busted him but I wasn't about to leave her there.

"Let's go. I'll drop you home."

"She lives like forty minutes from you, Rabbie. She can take a cab. It's too late for you to be driving at this time."

I glared at him. He probably didn't want us chatting in the car.

"She's coming home with me," I said and walked out of the house. Indira followed and so did Jesse. He reached for me.

"Rabbie, listen to me, please."

I shrugged him off and got into the car. Indira got in next to me. We drove off.

I was silent in the car. Indira was going on about how brilliant the plan was. Yes, it was a perfect plan in terms of we achieved our objectives, but flawed because he told me he loved me and I slept with him. I couldn't speak. I needed to take a shower and sleep. There was no way I was going to work the next day.

Jesse called all night and eventually I turned my phone off. The next day I skipped work and lay in bed all day. He didn't stop calling. I was getting sick of it. Eventually I answered.

"Rabbie, you have to give me a chance to explain everything to you."

"So give it your best shot."

"Not on the phone, please. Can I come by tomorrow?"

I sighed. This was so hard. I thought I was so tough before. I was always telling girls to cut losers quickly, no hesitation. I'd never tell a girl to give a cheater a chance. Why had I done what I'd done last night? Why listen to him? But I decided to listen anyways. He said he'd come by the next day. Later that night, Indira came by. I told her Jesse wanted to talk and he was coming by the next day. And she came up with her own plan.

"You should tape him, with your phone. And I'll tape him with my phone whenever I talk to him. And then we'll play it back to him. He's just a liar and a cheat."

She'd gone along with my plan so I decided to go along with hers.

"My phone can't record though," I said.

"Use mine. He's coming tomorrow morning, right? So you record first and then I'll see you later tomorrow."

Indira's plan was almost good but she didn't think things through. She took her sim card out and gave me her phone and I put my card in. As I did it, I knew I had the perfect opportunity to find something out once and for all.

The thing Indira forgot was that text messages remain on phones no matter the sim card. All her text messages were still on the phone. Late that night, I lay in bed and scrolled through her texts, going back three months. Everything I read didn't really shock me. The texts showed Indira was the one who approached Jesse. There were texts back and forth about her wanting to see him and him putting her off. There were more where he told her he was seeing someone. Her responses were she didn't care. The killer text was where he said he was involved with me, and she said that was not her problem. The night before, when we played out our drama, I had a faint suspicion something was off. He was outwardly angry at her but pleading with me. I thought it was odd then. And now I knew why, why he kept begging me and not her. She knew. She'd known all along about me but she'd slept with him all the same. I lay in bed staring at the ceiling, feeling like I'd been stabbed twice. Eventually he'd succumbed to her. Indira was good. She was a sexpot. She always got what she wanted. I wondered why she went through with the charade yesterday. Why didn't she just lie, say she had nothing to do with him? Why admit a relationship? I figured she must have been upset with him for something. Maybe she wanted more and he didn't want to give it.

By the time I'd read everything I was confused. He was still a cheat. But he cared about me. He told her about me. I tossed and turned, debating how to treat him when he came. A part of me, a very strong part of me, wanted to be back with him. It was madness. I now knew what all those girls felt, Ajua, and Cami and all those girls whose boyfriends cheated and they still stayed. For the first time, I felt the same. I wanted to stay with the bastard. I wanted to love him. I hated myself for feeling so weak. I wasn't in love with him, not yet, but I was almost there. And I hated him for taking that away from me. I had really thought this was it. I really thought he was it!

"You have to believe me, it was nothing with her."

We sat in my living room and I looked at his beautiful face. I wanted to kiss him, hold him. I wanted to cry. I was such a mess. Why did he do what he did?

"You still did it. You were sleeping with her, my friend, my co-worker, for weeks."

"It wasn't more than two weeks and I am sorry. I really am. It's not what you think. I told her, but she didn't care."

"And you? You should have cared enough. You should have respected me enough. You slept with my friend! And she didn't rape you!"

He fell silent and exhaled.

"I am sorry. I have no excuse. But I love you."

I wanted him to stop saying that. I buried my face in my hands. I felt his hand on my back, stroking my shoulders. I had this urge to be with him. It was so strong. But someway, somehow, I managed to dig the old me from within the depths of my pain. He wasn't it. He did a foul thing. And God knows how long it could have gone on. I shook my head. This was not me. He was not going to get another chance.

"I'm sorry too, Jesse. But I can't do this. I don't want to see you anymore. I just can't trust you and I'm pissed off. You messed up. And I'm not the type of person to take that shit."

He didn't say anymore. He could tell I was serious. A couple of minutes later he left and I lay on my bed and cried. Why was this happening? Why couldn't I love and be loved back? I was angry and pissed at him and the world.

I gave Indira's phone back to her. I never recorded anything. I told her I didn't know how to figure it out. I also told her I was through and done with Jesse. I didn't want to play anymore games. I didn't confront her about anything. It was not worth it. I didn't trust her. I didn't trust anyone.

The following weeks dragged. I started looking for other jobs. I wanted to be far away from him as possible. And then Osei turned up. And he brought conflicting news.

"So you started dating and you didn't tell me?"

I had a blank look on my face. What was he talking about?

"Your boyfriend, Jesse," he said. I was a little surprised. How did he know?

"He's not my boyfriend," I said.

"Yeah, I heard. You guys broke up."

"He was never my boyfriend," I said firmly.

"Really? I was at a bar, last night and he was there. He's actually an old friend of mine. We went to the same school, you know. We have mutual friends."

I shrugged. I could care less.

"He was talking with his friends. They were on his case, about how he messed up with you. They insisted he should get back with you," Osei continued.

"He wasn't my boyfriend. There was something, but he wasn't my boyfriend," I repeated.

"Really? It didn't sound like that to me. He sounded serious. He said he loved you but you wouldn't give him a chance."

I choked a little. He didn't love me. I had to remind myself of that. I didn't care what Osei had overheard.

"He really wasn't my boyfriend. We were getting to know each other and then he slept with a friend of mine. That's it."

"I see. Did you love him?"

I shook my head.

"But you really liked him, right? Don't say no. I can see it on your face. I could tell last night. The way they were talking. This was serious enough."

I shrugged and sighed. "It's done. Whatever label you want to call it, it's done. And I really don't want to talk about it."

I was surprised Jesse was even talking about it with his friends. He confused me. Did he for a minute think what we had was a relationship? But I was really done with him. A part of me was glad he was pained, glad his friends were giving him crap about it. But I also knew he'd be over it in a minute. I didn't want a future with him. I really didn't.

The Hits Just Keep Coming

A short while after Jesse, I got a job with another news station. Office romances really are a bad thing. I didn't want to be near him and I didn't want to deal with rumors or anything of the sort. Getting over Jesse wasn't easy at all, when it really should have been. He cheated, with one of my closest friends, my co-worker—it was so disrespectful. But despite his wicked ways, I kept thinking about him, wanting to be with him, wanting him to grovel and beg. But after his initial "I am sorry"s there were no more. He got over it pretty easy, I thought, and I just couldn't work in the same building with him. His office assistant Martha called me after I quit the company. She told me she'd had a long conversation with him, and he did care about me, but he was confused. She felt he didn't know what he wanted. And then she did what most women do. She told me men would always cheat, and I had to learn to deal with it. She actually told me to accept him as he was, if I really liked him, and turn a blind eye to what he'd done. I hated it when women did that, that "men will always cheat" thing. Let them cheat, but I just didn't want to be the victim. I was never going to be the victim.

I still kept my Friday night news gig, which meant I had to deal with Indira. Funnily enough, our friendship didn't really suffer a hit. Indira was who she was. Cutting her off just wouldn't make a difference, and Jesse was not that important. The thing with Jesse was a bad moment that I wanted to forget. He was the one person I had actually thought would make a great boyfriend and potential husband. It was painful to realize how wrong I'd been. Ato, Asare, Tei… I could sense their womanizing traits from the get-go. I could tell there really wasn't a future with them.

I'd been single for less than a year and I was already making bad choices. Being single was hard. It was so much easier to have a boyfriend and just cheat!

I decided I didn't want any new complications in my life. If I needed to get laid, there was always Ekow, and if I needed someone to talk to, there were Ato and Cami. I was fine, for a while.

"So, what's up with Ato and Winnie?"

I looked up from the book I was reading and looked at my brother Xavier and my cousin Albert.

"Huh? Winnie, our cousin Winnie?" I asked.

"Yeah, Albert and I went to campus yesterday, to see some friends. And we saw Ato's car parked by the side of this road. It was really late so we stopped, walked over and it was him and Winnie, all cozy."

My heart stopped for a second. I wondered how much more betrayal I could possibly take. Ato and Winnie? Winnie was my cousin and she'd been living with us for over ten years. She was much younger than I was and I didn't hang out with her that much. She was more with Xavier's crew because they were the same age. But Winnie knew Ato because he was in the house all the time. Everyone in my family knew Ato. They didn't know what it was between Ato and me and after a while, they just assumed it was friendship, couldn't be more. I couldn't wrap my head around it. What was Ato doing with her at that time? He'd crossed the line with Cami; he couldn't possibly do it again, not with my cousin!

"They both looked so guilty," Albert said.

"Doesn't Winnie have a boyfriend?" I asked.

"Yeah she does, but these days, what does that mean? A friend of ours who was with us said Ato's been coming around to see Winnie a lot."

I nodded slowly. "Interesting. I'll ask him and see. Did you guys ask her?"

"Yep. She said it's nothing. He's just visiting," Xavier said.

I chuckled. "Yeah right."

"Ato is Mr. Smooth! That guy is my hero," Albert said.

I shook my head. I was going to kill Ato.

"Dude, is there a problem? Really, seriously, is there a problem?"

Ato looked lost. We were standing next to his car in front of my house. I was so upset I could barely stand still.

"What the heck are you going on about?" he asked.

"Don't act like that with me. You know what this is about. You know what you did."

"You're gonna have to explain it to me, because I am lost."

"Winnie," I said simply.

He smiled a little, and then he did a slow shrug, like he didn't quite get the fuss.

"What the heck is wrong with you, Ato? Seriously? What is the problem? That's my cousin!"

"I haven't slept with her."

"Oh, don't expect me to buy that bullshit."

"Oh, honestly," he said, laughing a little.

I glared at him. "I think it's best if you tell me the truth now."

"Look, I've been to see her a couple of times, yeah. And maybe some stuff happened, but I haven't slept with her."

I shook my head, disappointed. What was I going to do with him? Why did he do these things?

"There are some lines you just don't cross, Ato."

"Oh come on, Rabbie, it's no big deal," he said in a nonchalant way.

"We said no friends, or family or close circle, Ato. We said that," I said, raising my voice. I didn't care who heard. I doubted anyone was home anyways.

"How we were back then is not how we are now, is it?"

I looked away from him. Why did I keep going through this? How disrespectful was he? I could never sleep with his cousin, or Ekow's cousin or Asare's or anyone else! Why didn't he get it?

"You can't sleep with me, and then sleep with my best friend and then my cousin. It's not right. It's disrespectful. And it's not like you and I had sex once. We've been sleeping together for a long time now. You don't do some things. You need to draw a line somewhere. What the heck? Huh? I mean, come on."

He started to say something and then he stopped.

"I'm sorry. Nothing really happened. It's no big deal."

I leaned against the car and shook my head. I thought I had issues, I thought I was twisted, but Ato was a lost cause. I was so hurt and so disappointed and pissed off. What he'd done was wrong. Nothing would convince me otherwise. I decided maybe it was time to write him off. The era of Ato had to end sometime.

My relationship with Ato was strained after that. And I was upset with Winnie too. I knew I was a fool but I thought others had better judgment than I did. Obviously, I was wrong. Everyone had their demons. Both Cami and Winnie had messed around with Ato when they had boyfriends. They were no different than me. No one was any different. Everyone was twisted, with questionable intentions and morals.

Sometime in February 2005, Ato went away for a bit to London. I was glad he was gone. I wanted to purge my system of him. I didn't know why he got to me like this. I wasn't in love with him. I'd gotten emotionally over him years ago, but he was still supposed to be my best friend. I still expected a level of respect from him. He didn't even know how to be a friend. By the time he came back, I thought I had it figured out. He was a lousy guy, but he was still my friend. But I was about to learn Ato was a whole lot worse than I gave him credit for.

"So, aren't you coming to Ghana anytime soon?"

I was on the phone with Ajua. She'd been in London since the year before, working a dead-end job, and I didn't know why she still stayed.

"I'd like to, but I don't know what I'd do back home," she said.

"It's not your fault. You must be having fun. Having sex every night I'm sure," I said teasingly.

"Ah nah, it's more the opposite. I haven't had any in a long while. Oh wait, actually, that's a lie."

"Ah, shady girl, spill the beans!"

"Hmmm, it's Ato. We had sex when he was over here last week."

That moment is imbedded so deep in my mind that I can't lose it even if I wanted to. I was lying on my mother's bed, facing the ceiling. There was no one at home and only one small light was on. I had actually seen Ato earlier that night, no more than thirty minutes earlier. He'd stopped by after work. I was trying to be friends with him again.

And now this!

"You slept with Ato," I said. It wasn't a question; it wasn't even quite a statement. I was saying it out loud, to myself. I just couldn't believe it. Ato slept with Ajua. How many times had I told him that was the one person I never ever wanted him to cross the line with? How many times?

"Yes, oh, it was just one time. My moment of weakness," Ajua said with a little laugh. She had no clue what she'd just done to me. She was oblivious to the pain that was searing through my heart. How much more of this could I possibly take? In the space of a year, he'd slept with Cami, Winnie I was sure, and now Ajua. What insensitive madness was that?

"I have to go now, Ajua," I said quietly.

"What? Are you upset?" She sounded shocked. I didn't want to buy completely into her naivety. As much as I hadn't discussed Ato with her, or Cami or Winnie, they should have known there was something. They should have!

"Yes, I'm upset. I'll talk to you later."

I hang up before she could say another word. I dialed Ato's number.

"Hey Rabbie, I was just going to call you this second. You won't believe what just happened," he said in his usual, annoying, cheerful voice. I was so pissed.

"You slept with Ajua," I said.

There was silence. He said nothing for a long while. And then he recovered. "Who said that?"

"I just got off the phone with her. She told me she slept with you while you were in London."

Silence. He just didn't have an excuse or comeback for this one. He couldn't even try. We had had so many conversations about Ajua, so many. I had emphasized over and over again how she was completely off limits. She was the one person I had gone on and on about. He really had nothing to say.

"Rabbie, listen, it wasn't anything."

"You're just an asshole. Seriously, that's all you are. I can't believe you'd do that. I just can't. Cami, Winnie, Ajua; what is wrong with you? What is wrong with you?"

I didn't realize I was crying till I felt the tear drop on my chin. I tried to hold it back. I didn't want to cry on the phone.

"Rabbie—" he started to say.

"I don't want to talk to you right now," I muttered.

I hung up and lay on my mother's bed and cried. I was so tired of this, so tired of all these losers. It just made me another loser. I cried till I couldn't cry anymore and then I called Sammi. She was also in London; she had been there since we graduated almost two years ago.

"Hey, what's wrong? Do you have a cold?' she asked.

"No, I was crying," I said.

"What's going on? Is it Ato?"

Sammi had a keen sense of the disastrous situation I was in with Ato. I had told her about Cami and Winnie and she'd told me to stop being friends with him. She kept saying it wasn't worth it. He was never going to see the error of his ways.

"He's just unbelievable, seriously. I just spoke to Ajua, and I was teasing her that she must be having a lot of sex. And then she says not really, but the last time she had sex was when Ato was in London, last week."

"Are you joking?"

"I wish I was. I really wish I was. I mean, he just completely wiped out every bit of little respect I had for him. What does that make me? You get what I mean? As much as we weren't in a relationship, I still thought I was somewhat special to him. I still thought I meant something to him. But if he can sleep with Cami, and Winnie and Ajua, then I mean nothing to him. Then I'm just another girl he's slept with and happens to be friends with. I mean nothing to him. He doesn't respect me."

That was the bottom line. No matter what stuff I did, who I slept with, Ekow, Jesse, whoever, I still regarded Ato as a special part of my life. But he obviously didn't feel the same way.

"That boy doesn't care about you, Rabbie. He doesn't. He knows how you and Ajua are. Why would he do that? He's just thinking about himself. He's just selfish, inconsiderate, a player, a cheat, everything. He's not worth it. He's not worth you crying."

I was still crying. I felt so betrayed.

"Did Ajua know about you two?" Sammi asked.

"No."

"I think you should tell her."

"I think I should too."

Sammi listened to me cry and vent for a little bit longer and then I hung up. I made up my mind to tell Ajua. But I didn't feel like talking to Ajua and Ato so I decided to write them emails. I did better with writing. This way I got my entire message across; no interruptions, no lost words, no hanging up the phone. It was my way to say everything I wanted to say. I told Ato what he'd done was wrong. There was no way to justify it. There are codes for everything. You cannot sleep with one person and then systematically sleep with her close friends and family. What was that? I let him have it. And then I wrote Ajua, told her everything about Ato and I, about when it started and how I'd insisted he could never sleep with her, and how he had broken my trust. I was very upset. It was one of the worst moments I'd ever experienced. And this happened, so soon after Jesse. Why did things like this keep happening to me? What was wrong with me? Was it me? Was I the problem? I needed to grow some balls and cut these people all off, especially Ato.

Ato tried to get defensive after the email. Ajua got on his case for what he'd done, and I was pissed, so he was getting it from both sides. And I was upset with Ajua as well. I knew she had this everlasting crush on him but I figured since she'd become so tight with his ex girl, she'd never take it there. Everyone really had no morals, did they?

"Are you home? Can I come by?"

Ato usually didn't call to say he was coming by, he just showed up. But with what he'd done and the resulting tension, things were a little different.

I was still irritated with him but I hadn't seen him since I found out about him and Ajua and I wanted to look him in the eye and tell him he was a terrible person.

"Yeah, I'm home," I said.

"I'll be there in five minutes," he said.

I hung up and paced my room. I was really going to tell him off. I was so upset, I couldn't even focus. The Ajua factor was so important to me. Ajua was my best friend—how could he?

When his car pulled up I was waiting on my front steps.

I was surprised to see how somber and devastated he looked. I was thinking he'd be all defensive like he'd been the last few days.

"Hey," he said softly.

I stared at him, not saying a word. I wanted to hear what he had to say.

"Listen, I'm sorry. I'm really sorry. I didn't think it would affect you this way. I know it's something you didn't want me to do, but... I don't even know what to say. I am really sorry I hurt you."

I was stunned. I didn't expect that at all. My defensive posture slackened a little.

"You really shouldn't have. Cami, Winnie, and then this? Ajua? You really shouldn't have. It's very disrespectful to me,' I said, choking a little.

And then I saw a little tear in his eye. Damn it! I was hoping this would be a fight, so that I could scream at him and tell him off, and tell him never ever to speak to me again. He reached for me and hugged me and all my defenses just crumpled. He held me tight and kept repeating that he was sorry. I forced the tears back. I was not going to give him the satisfaction of my tears. He held me a little bit longer and then we sat on my front steps and talked.

I'm Ready to Love You Forever

After Ato's continual betrayals, Jesse's thoughtless tryst with Indira, Asare's lack of interest and Jon's insensitive statements to Selassie, I realized being single was not a joy in the least. In one year, I had experienced more pain and anguish than my entire five-plus years with Osei. I missed him, missed his kindness and generosity and open heart. Most importantly, I missed being loved by him. Osei loved me unconditionally and these other idiots had no clue how to do that. But I still knew it would be selfish and cruel for me to go crawling back to Osei. I just didn't love him like that.

I was moody and mopey for weeks. I tried to concentrate on graduate school plans. Ato had gotten admission into Harvard Medical School and he was leaving that fall. Ato had worked pretty hard on graduate school, which got me motivated to start thinking about graduate school. For as long as I'd known Ato, I'd always respected his academic and professional decisions. He was smart and driven, and I liked that about him. When Ato got a first class for undergrad, I had to get a first class. And now that he'd gotten admission into Harvard, I needed to be focused as well. I wasn't particularly interested in Harvard. Their creative writing program was fifteenth in the US, pretty wack in my opinion. I wanted to get into the number one creative writing program, which was New York University. Graduate school applications and work became my primary goals.

The thing (it's terrible to call it a thing but I'm not sure what else to call it) Ekow and I had was coasting along pretty okay. We'd had one or two difficult moments, and a few times I'd sworn to quit but we just kept at it. There seemed to be no end in sight. On some days, I didn't mind the undefined nature of it, but increasingly I began to question what it was we were doing. I really liked Ekow. There was no doubt about that. The sex we had was just so incredible, that pulling away from him was too much of a challenge. It went beyond sex, I felt. There was just something about him I liked and couldn't get enough of.

Ekow was pretty aloof, bordering on rude in some ways. But we had good chemistry and we could talk. I just didn't know what was happening and what I wanted, and most importantly, what he wanted. And then something happened that changed all that.

"Whoa, what date is it?"

Cami looked up from the magazine she was browsing.

"I think it's the fifteenth or sixteenth. I could be wrong. But one or the other," she said.

I froze. What? It was already the middle of the month? Oh my goodness! I felt my heart race a little faster. I hadn't had my period in over six weeks. And it was so timely you could plan a year-long calendar of events around it.

"What's up?" Cami asked.

"Uh, nothing, I forgot to mail in a report," I lied.

I was hoping I had messed up my mental calculations somehow. I leaned back and tried to calm down. I waited for Cami to leave later that night and then I dashed to my room and flipped anxiously through my diary. The cold truth hit me hard. I was late. I was late! I lay on my bed and swore loudly. I screamed obscenities at the ceiling and punched my pillow. Ekow was the only person I'd been with in three months. And he and I were pretty serious about protection. I had no memories of any accidents, unless there was one he hadn't shared, but I would know anyways. So how could this happen? My diary indicated I was over three weeks late. That was insane. That was completely insane. I had been so busy with work and studying for the GREs, I had completely forgotten there was something called a period. Maybe it was stress? Maybe it was exam anxieties? I was pretty stressed. But I had been stressed thousands of times before but my little girl was always damn punctual. Was I sick? I refused to draw any other conclusions for a while. I would give it another week and then check.

"So, we may have a problem."

Ekow was walking me home from his place. It was Friday night and I had gone over for the usual food and drinks he and his friends had at his place every Friday.

He waited for me to continue.

"Uh, I'm late, by almost four weeks."

He stopped walking.

"But we haven't had any accidents," he said.

"I know, but like they say on the packages, contraceptives aren't one hundred per cent," I said quietly.

He took a deep breath and exhaled. He looked pretty calm but I was sure he was fretting inside.

"What are you going to do? Have you taken a test?"

I shook my head. "I haven't. I was just hoping it would show up. But at this point I'm going to have to test."

"Do you need me to come with you? Or are you going to do one of those home tests?"

I laughed. "Oh definitely home test. I'm not going to walk into a clinic for a pregnancy test!"

He smiled a little and then the smile disappeared.

"Wow, four weeks is a little scary. And you're pretty consistent, right."

I nodded.

"If you are... Have you thought about it? I mean, I know you have work and you want to go to grad school and you have plans..." His voice trailed off.

I shrugged. "I haven't thought about it fully. One step at a time."

He nodded. We stared at each other for a while.

"Anyways, I gotta go. I'll take the test tomorrow and let you know, okay?"

He nodded. We kissed and hugged and then I walked the rest of the short distance back to my end.

I lay in bed for a long while that night, thinking about Ekow and how I felt about him. I'd had conflicting feelings for him for a long while. And after the fiascos of the last year, I didn't want to fall for another person. But the more time you spend with someone and the longer you're intimate, the more complicated things become. Here I was lying in bed and I could be carrying Ekow's baby. Four weeks late was scary. I had to seriously consider the option that I was pregnant. As difficult and scary as the thought was, I realized I could deal with it. Ekow was smart.

He was sexy. Our families were friends. Our parents knew each other. My mother adored him. She called him her adopted son. And to be honest, I was kind of crazy about him. But could I live with him and have his child? Could I put everything on hold to raise a family with him? I wasn't sure. I did have my plans. I wanted to go to graduate school. I wanted to experience new things. But I was also prepared for anything. After a long while I managed to fall asleep.

The next day I called Cami. Cami was a habitual pregnancy tester. She took pregnancy tests at least once or twice a month. She abhorred condoms and too often she avoided them. Surprisingly, she'd never been knocked up. I think she'd just gotten hooked on pregnancy testing even when there was no danger or possibility. I knew she'd know which brand I could get. I needed a fast but reliable answer.

"Wow. I thought you guys used condoms all the time. I thought you were a walking billboard for condoms," Cami said when I told her my dilemma.

"I am. We didn't have an accident, but I'm still late, seriously late, man."

"That's serious."

"So, I need to get tested, today, now. Your pharmacy, are they open on weekends?"

We were sitting in her living room. I was not going to do this at home.

"Oh yeah, let's go."

Just around the corner from Cami's house was a little pharmacy store. The proximity of the pharmacy was probably another reason why she was so addicted to those tests. It was a short walk, but it felt like forever to me. This was it. I was so nervous. We bought Cami's favorite brand, the most reliable, she said. And then we hurried back to her house. She said it was best to do it early morning but it was already past noon. I still wanted to try so I bought two; one for now and one for the morning, just to be sure.

As I sat on Cami's bed, waiting, I couldn't stop thinking about Ekow. I could do this. I could really do this. Why not him? He was a great guy. He acted like he really cared about me. He was there for me. He'd never done anything to me; so really, why not? I was crazy enough about him. My hands were shaking a little as I held the tube.

"Are you okay?" Cami kept asking.

"Yeah, it's not a big deal, even if it's positive. I think I'd actually prefer it."

"Really, are you serious?"

"Hey, it's gonna happen sometime. I can deal with it now."

"Wow."

After a minute or two, Cami announced it was time. Despite my brave statements I was still a little nervous. I pushed the stick towards her. I couldn't look. She glanced down and raised an eyebrow.

"Oh, stop being dramatic, what is it?" I squealed.

"Negative."

"Really?" I shouted.

I grabbed the stick back. It was negative!

"Good for you. But you definitely have to try again in the morning."

I sat back. I felt a little disappointed. This could have been it, a child to end my drama. Of course, a baby would be drama in itself but it would be Ekow, me and a child, and whatever other issues. My brother had a son. If he could do that, at twenty-seven, I could do it at twenty-six. A part of me hoped the test was wrong. I decided to wait till morning to try again.

"So, did you try again? What was it?"

It was after 8 A.M. and I'd been up for an hour, thinking and pondering my fate. I sent Cami a text that I was going to try again. She called, eager for results.

"Not yet, just trying to psyche myself up."

"The first test was negative. Why are you still worried?"

"I'm not worried. I'm hoping to change the results."

"You're crazy."

"I'm going to be a mommy!" I said laughing.

"You're very crazy."

"Okay, I'll call you back."

I hung up and went into my bathroom. When I was done, I lay on my bed and stared at the ceiling, waiting for five minutes. When the time was up, I was pretty calm, especially since I was completely comfortable with the results either way.

I glanced at the stick. Negative. Damn it! I wrapped the stick up, threw it in the trash and lay back on my bed, cussing. I was really disappointed. The image of Ekow and me with a family was deeply ingrained in my mind. I sighed and sent Cami a text that it was negative. I didn't want to tell Ekow over the phone, so I sent him a text that I wanted to see him later that day.

He came by that night and we sat in my living room. My mom and Xavier were out and Winnie was in school, so we had the place to ourselves.

"I called you a couple of times yesterday," he said.

I looked at him and smiled a little. He was so sexy.

"Yeah, I decided to disappear a little. I was at Cami's place. She took me to get a test. So I'm not even going to stretch it out. The test was negative. I did it twice."

He looked relieved. I didn't blame him.

"Phew. I was worried for a second. I mean, I kept thinking, four weeks? It's just so long to be late. What could have happened?"

"I guess I've been really stressed with the exams, and grad school."

"I kept thinking about that too, about your plans and the stuff you want to do."

I squeezed his hand.

"I wouldn't have minded," I said.

"What?"

I shrugged. "I wouldn't have minded, honestly. I like you."

"I like you too, but a baby? That's serious."

"I love you," I said.

As soon as the words came out of my mouth, I wanted to take them back. I hadn't used those words in almost two years. The last person I said that to was Tei. I hadn't said or felt it with Asare or Jesse. I was stunned but I realized it was true. Gosh, I loved him. I loved him!

"Rabbie..." he said, looking at me.

My heart fell. He didn't feel the same way.

"I like you. I like being with you, but…"

I took a deep breath… Okay, that's tough.

"It's okay, it's okay. You don't have to say anything. I just wanted you to know."

My heart was breaking. He didn't love me. I couldn't quite let it go.

"Why can't we be together? We like each other, we're good together, and we get along. We've been doing this for a while now. What's missing?"

He sighed.

"Is it because of Tara?"

I had always felt that Ekow still had some feelings for his ex. They hadn't seen each other in such a long time. It was close to four years. I wondered if he was still holding out for her, waiting for her to come back. He always denied that but there had to be something.

"It's not about Tara. I keep telling you I'm over that. I'm just not ready. I'm really not ready. I can't settle down now. I don't have the time. I just started school and there is so much stuff I need to do. It wouldn't be fair to any girl. I know myself. It would stress me out and it would stress her out."

That was the most Ekow had ever said in one breath. It made sense, to a degree. I could understand the whole "not ready" bit but I wondered if he'd ever be ready.

"I understand that. I respect that. I really do like you. I don't know if I can keep doing this though," I said.

He kissed my cheek. I closed my eyes. This was so painful.

"Why not? You said what we have is good. I'm addicted to you," he whispered, turning my face towards his. I smiled and kissed him fully on the mouth. His hands went around my waist, pulling my body towards his. After a minute or so of kissing, I pulled away and held his face in my hands.

"I can't keep at this, Ekow. I have feelings for you; you don't feel the same. It's going to be hard for me to keep doing this. Because I am ready; I am ready to love you now."

"I can't," he said simply.

I wanted to cry but I just nodded. I stood up from the sofa. He stood up too. I walked him to the gate and we hugged goodbye. I went up to my mother's room, lay on her bed and cried. I called Ekow's cousin Daren and cried, asking him why Ekow didn't love me. He said he felt Ekow cared about me, but Ekow was complicated and he wasn't ready. He just wasn't.

I wondered if it was best to keep things as they were, to keep sleeping with him and hope that somewhere along the line he'd be ready. I wasn't sure that was wise. But maybe what I needed was dedication. Maybe I needed to be patient, and give him time, time to come around. If he did care about me, eventually, when he felt ready, I'd be the one.

But I wasn't sure I could do that. Maybe it was time to really let it all go.

Heartbreak Isn't Limited to Geography—the Very Last Acts

The most unexpected and uncontrollable love that hit me was Ekow. But it wasn't reciprocated. Ekow wasn't ready, he said. And I realized I needed to be the priority in my life. I needed to let it all go, once and for all. Everything and everyone in my life had to go. I had to start from scratch. So in January 2006 I made a resolution to retire from the game, to hang up the jersey and not look back.

Retirement was not the easiest thing, but honestly it wasn't as hard as you'd think. I just reached a point where life and love didn't make sense to me anymore. I'd been single for two years and it'd been a difficult two years. Quitting Ekow completely was much harder than I expected. It drove me crazy. But by February 2006 I couldn't deal with the situation anymore, so I stuck to my guns and stopped sleeping with him. After February, that resolution was the best resolution I ever made and kept. I completely ended all involvement with everyone, whether physical, emotional or otherwise. Getting into graduate school became my focus. Nothing else was more important. I wanted a fresh start, a new beginning. I wanted to be away from all the drama that had plagued me.

Late April, most likely early May, I received an admission letter from New York University. It was one of the best moments of my life. NYU was a top-notch school with an excellent creative writing program. I was finally getting the opportunity to leave my woes behind and pursue my dreams. I felt life was finally getting better, finally heading in the direction I needed it to head in. There was hope.

September 2006, I said a teary goodbye to family and friends and left for NYU. I had a lot of expectations for this new journey. I expected everything would be better now. But it really wasn't.

Tei

When I got to New York I called Tei. He lived only a couple of hours away and it would be rude not to call. In any case, he had moved on. He was seriously involved with someone now. I had even spoken to her on the phone a couple of times and she seemed nice. I was happy for him. I still had some latent feelings for him, but it was nothing earth shattering. I'd been retired and celibate for close to eight months now and it felt good. I was not interested in sex or love.

Tei asked me to come see him a couple of months after I'd been in school. I never managed to find the right time till sometime early October, when Ato went to Philly for the weekend. Since I hadn't see Ato in over a year since he left for school, I decided it was probably perfect timing.

Ato wasn't amused I was coming to Philly to see Tei as well, but I wasn't about to explain or defend myself. Nothing was going to happen. I just hadn't seen Tei in close to three years. I just wanted to see him, nothing else. He was with someone now.

I took a bus from New York and went to Philly. Ato had a friend's apartment to himself for the weekend. The night I got there, I called Tei and he came by a couple of hours later. Tei knew Ato a little bit, from a couple of mutual friends in Philly. But the two of them weren't exactly friends. Ato still didn't like him. And Tei had no clue I had any history with Ato. I didn't think it was necessary to tell him. There was nothing going on between me and either one of them.

"Hey, you look good," Tei said as we hugged.

I smiled. He was looking good too. He'd grown more muscular and built. And there was something calm and fresh about him. We walked side by side up the road where he said there was a little Chinese joint. We didn't say much at first. It had been a while since we last saw each other. We talked about random stuff and I didn't bring up the last visit when he'd been hot and cold. The past was in the past. Eventually the conversation became personal. He told me about his girlfriend and a couple of other things. The subject of Osei came up, as always, and I tried but failed, as always, to convince him that I had really loved him and not Osei. He was fixated on the notion that he didn't mean anything to me and he wouldn't let it go. I didn't know what else to say to him to convince him otherwise. It was like beating a dead horse. He wouldn't budge. Someway, somehow, the topic veered off to Cami.

"So Cami called me just a couple of days ago. She said she's coming over and she's gonna come stay with me. Usually I don't mind, but I'm traveling that same weekend and I was wondering if you could take her. Plus she's flying into New York anyways."

I was stunned into silence. Huh? Cami was my best friend, and she was coming to the States and I had no idea she was coming or when. She hadn't called me, or shared her plans with me, or asked if she could come over or even bothered to include me at all. I found that very strange. After Tei left Ghana, Cami had lost all ties with him. She had no clue where he was or what he was up to. But Tei and I kept in touch and it was only through me and the 2002 summer trip to Philly that Cami had reconnected with Tei. I knew after that summer they kept in touch. And twice she'd come to America and stayed with Tei. I didn't exactly have a problem with that. I met Tei through Cami. They were friends. Cami knew what Tei meant to me. I didn't think or suspect anything each time she stayed with him. But now, I was in America and I was her best friend. Why wouldn't she call me? Why wouldn't she make plans with me? Why talk to Tei first? Her excuse each time she stayed with him was she didn't really know anyone else. So now that I was here, didn't that change? And the bit that was nagging at me was that Tei had been teasing me on and off for years that he'd slept with Cami before. I usually took it as his way of tormenting me. But now, she cut me out of her plans and called Tei, it just set off alarm bells in my head.

I didn't directly respond to Tei's question. I didn't give a damn where she stayed. If she couldn't call me or ask, then why should I care? As far as I knew, she hadn't said anything to me about a trip to America.

Tei and I talked a little bit longer and then he left. I was tormented. My mind was helter-skelter. I became suspicious and paranoid.

Ato didn't make any advances and I wasn't interested in sex anyways, so it was best. I could tell he was upset about me seeing

Tei and he went on a little bit about that. But I knew this was just a visit and I didn't see why I needed to explain that. We lay side by side in bed in silence. My mind was on Cami and Tei. Could it be remotely possible? That was just outrageous.

When I got back to New York, I held court with my new friend from school, Marie. Marie had a pretty clear head. She was the one who'd encouraged me to go see Tei that weekend. She loved stuff like that. She was like a foreign version of me. I told her everything about Tei and the nagging suspicions about Cami; from her staying with him multiple times, from Tei repeatedly saying he'd slept with her in the last few years, to little incidents I had shoved in the abyss of my memories. There were quite a number of troubling suspicious incidents. When Ato started Harvard, Cami had traveled to America and stayed with Tei. Ato had offered to get her a ticket to see him in Boston but she said the "guy" she was staying with would be pissed. When Ato told me, I was surprised. Why would Tei be pissed if Cami went to visit other people? And I'd never put anything past Tei. He was like an older version of Ato.

Everything was rolling and crushing around in my head. I had been pretty mute about my little suspicion about Tei and Cami but Marie felt it was wrong. She said I needed to ask Cami or I'd never feel right. And so I did.

Cami and I were chatting online and I brought up the subject. I was pretty careful not to accuse her of anything.

"So I hear you're coming to America and you haven't told me?" I typed.

"Oh I would have told you of course. It's just not definite."

"Not definite, but you could tell Tei and not tell me? He said you asked to stay with him but he's not going to be around and so he was wondering if I could take you. I mean since I'm here now, why wouldn't you let me know, even if it's not definite."

"You know I would have come to yours eventually."

"Come to me eventually? Cami, America is a huge place, it's not like going to London, where you can easily fit seeing all your friends in a trip. Honestly, it's weird that I'm here now, and you don't even share your travel or accommodation plans with me."

"How can I come and not come see you?"

After that note, she went offline and my messages started to bounce back, so I called her.

"Okay, you should be able to see my point. You come here all the time and you stay with him. You always say it's because you don't know anyone else. So if I'm here, shouldn't that make a difference?" I asked.

"I would have come or called you, you know that."

"Listen, I've been pretty laid back and quiet about a lot of stuff. It doesn't matter if I met him through you, but this is my ex-boyfriend, someone I had feelings for, for a very long time. Anyone else would have been completely upset and angry about you staying there as much as you do. But I haven't said anything, even when he's been going on that he's been sleeping with you."

"So now you believe him?"

"I didn't say that. But you should be able to understand where I am coming from. I have never taken any of that stuff seriously. But if I'm here now and you're coming here, how can you not share your plans with me? Can't you see that? It's like I'm going to London and I don't tell Ajua, I don't share any of my plans with her and I discuss it with someone else, someone she's had feelings for. It doesn't matter how well I know him, she's supposed to be my best friend. She's supposed to come first."

"My line is breaking up," Cami said, and then she hung up.

I swore a little. Conversations such as these were difficult for me and I expected a little openness. I tried to call her back several times but she kept cutting the call. Eventually I quit and threw my phone on the bed and went into the kitchen.

When I came back, I'd missed a call, from Tei. A feeling of dread came over me and I picked up the phone to check my voicemail. What I heard was shocking and unexpected.

"Why won't you pick up your phone? I have Cami on the phone here. What's all this, huh? Why do you have to call her and harass her? What is wrong with you? Don't call my friend and harass them. If you know what's best for you, you'll pick up your phone!"

I was stunned. What? I'd never heard Tei like that. What was up with the screaming and shouting, and what was wrong with Cami? What harassment?

I called Tei back immediately.

"What the heck is wrong with you? Why are you calling Cami to harass her? This has to end right now. This is really ridiculous. I am tired of this bullshit. My business is my business. You and I are not together anymore, so who I sleep with or who I have slept with is none of your goddamn business!" he shouted as soon as he answered.

"Are you insane? Is there something wrong with you? Cami is my friend. I called to talk to my friend. I didn't accuse her of anything, so don't even start."

I was pissed and stunned and shocked. Was he high?

"You gotta deal with your goddamn insecurities and stop harassing and questioning people!" he screamed.

"You gotta be joking. You're the one who's been telling me for years you've slept with Cami and you kissed Ajua and you wanna tell me I'm being insecure? Are you for real?"

"I have Cami on the phone now, ask her what you wanna ask her now. Ask her. Let me hear it."

It was surreal. Tei kept on screaming and cussing at me. And Cami didn't say a word. I was shocked. I only called to ask why she didn't involve me in her plans. What did I say to her? I was her friend! Why did she call him to call me? What did she need to say that she couldn't say to me?

I began to shut down. Tears were streaming uncontrollably down my face. I was gasping. I dropped on to my bed and pulled my knees up to my chin.

"You can't say anything now, huh? You can't talk now? You know what? Lose my number, bitch! Don't call me again!"

When the line cut, I thought I was going to die. I kept trying to call him back but he kept cutting the calls. I tried for ages, over and over again like a maniac. Then I called Cami. I couldn't stop the crying at that point.

"What is wrong with you? What did I say to you? All I asked was why I wasn't aware you were coming here. And you call him and let him do that to me?"

"Why are you crying, huh? What's that about? I can't pick sides. He's my friend. I've known him for a long time."

I choked. What? What?!

"You've known him for a long time? I'm supposed to be your best friend! And you let a boy curse me and shout at me and treat me like that? What did you call him for? What, you and I can't have a conversation anymore? You had to call him and let him do that to me?"

"What do you want me to say? I don't know what you expect me to do."

I'd never heard Cami sound that cold-hearted before. This was me. I couldn't believe it. I was crying and bawling like a baby, and this was what she could say to me?

I hung up and lay on my bed and cried. My whole world was crashing down around me.

I had very strong principles about what friendship meant. Friendship first and foremost means standing up for each other no matter what. I was such a firm believer in that. Even as Edem abused Abena, I always stood up for her. I always told him off. And Edem was someone I'd known since we were both in diapers. He was someone I'd been involved with and I still stood up to him. Each time any girlfriend of mine had a problem, I was always, always on their side, not matter who the guy was or how well I knew him. If my brother ever spoke to his wife the way Tei had spoken to me, I'd kill him, and that was someone who was my blood. What Cami said, that she couldn't take sides, was bullshit, complete utter cold-hearted bullshit.

I was disappointed and shocked at her. What a lousy person. How could she? How could she? What she'd just done transcended all incidents and suspicions. This wasn't a fight over a boy. What she'd done was lousy. Tei insulted me, cussed me to high heaven and as my supposed best friend she should have stood up for me, told him to stop, told him off, and said something! There was no doubt in my mind about that. And that was the biggest crime of all. She didn't have my back. I didn't care if she'd never slept with him, that wasn't the point. It's about honor among women. No matter what, I believed strongly that girlfriends were supposed to stand up for each other.

I cried all day and all night. I didn't eat for days. And I completely flunked an exam I had that week, my first and last flunk. What Tei and Cami did killed me, gutted me. I couldn't function. I played the voicemail over and over. I made Marie, Lynn and a bunch of other people listen. Everyone agreed he was an ass to do that, and worse, she was an even bigger ass to let it happen.

After a week of barely eating and barely living, I completely wrote them off. This was about a code and principle I held dear. If you couldn't stand up for me, be by my side, understand my pain and communicate with me, then I couldn't trust you to be there for me always. And if I couldn't trust you, then there was no use faking a friendship.

Tei, I was done with him too. He was a psychotic jerk and I didn't want to know him or even hear his name again. This was the end.

Ato

Ato was my solid rock when I told him what happened. He'd always hated Tei anyway. But he was so understanding and empathetic—I really hadn't expected that. He told me never to speak to Cami again. He said I didn't need friends like that around. He listened to me cry and vent and he was just there for me. I really appreciated it. Marie, Katzi and Amma, my friends from school, were very understanding too. Lynn was also my rock. Lynn had moved from Ohio to Boston and a couple of weeks after the incident, she suggested we go on a trip to Virginia. I was a mess. I needed the break. My cousin James had also moved from Michigan to Virginia, so I was all for the trip. And Ato was also going to be in Maryland.

I was grateful for Lynn's support.

By the time Lynn and I left on the trip I was feeling much better. And I really wanted to see Ato too.

"So who is this Ato person you keep going on about?" Lynn asked as we drove down.

I shrugged. I wasn't sure if I wanted to give Lynn details just yet. And then a thought went off in my head. I'd been keeping Ato a secret for way too long. Ajua, Cami and Winnie… their whole excuse bordered on the fact that they had no clue about Ato and me. I didn't think Lynn would hook up with Ato, but I'd suffered enough pain and hurt in the last two years and more to know that anything was possible. People were just evil and mean and selfish.

So I told her the whole story. I told Lynn every single thing possible. I told her about how and when it started, how I felt about him and how it had gone downhill, first with Cami and then, worst of all, Ajua. I confided in her about every single pain and disrespect I'd felt. I told her how I was sure I was over Ato but there was still something. I told her how I couldn't completely let it go. She was on my side; she understood how I felt and why it was such a struggle. We talked about boys and the perpetual quest for love and fulfillment. As Lynn and I talked, I sent Ato a text and told him that I was coming to M.D. with a friend, who was off limits. I really didn't want any excuses this time. I told him I had a limit and if he did anything with her that would be it.

The weekend went great. I saw James and we all went clubbing at some whack African joint at Adams Morgan in D.C. Ato was there, with Kofi. And Winnie's boyfriend, the same guy she was seeing during her slip and fall with Ato, was there, along with a couple of his best friends. Lynn brought along a friend as well. All in all, it was a great night.

Ato and Lynn exchanged numbers, which was a little worrying for me, but I tried not to think about it. They lived in the same city. Plus I had warned them both. I had done my part.

Life is just a funny thing. It's like you can see something happening, but you just don't know how to stop it or you don't have the power to stop it. Ato would call every now and then and say he took Lynn to dinner or they went to watch a movie or he went to visit. Lynn, on the other hand, never mentioned any meetings. She was completely silent on the Ato front. My instincts were, however, in overdrive and I told Ato this would really be the last straw if he did anything. A part of me felt Lynn just wouldn't, though. I knew she was higher than me on the shady scale but she said she'd retired as well. And I believed her. After everything I'd said to her about Ato and me, I really felt she just wouldn't.

"So some bitch is spreading rumors about me on facebook. She's created a page that's, like, dedicated to bashing and dissing me," Ato said.

I was on a three-way call with him and his friend Kwasi. Ato wanted to know if I had any ideas who would do that to him. The correct answer was everyone. But I decided to listen to him go on about the different possibilities.

"I mean, this person actually sent an email to Sara going on about me and the stuff I've been up to. I really can't imagine who it could be."

Sara was his immediate ex. He dated her for a year during his first year at Harvard.

"Are you sure you have no clue, Ato? After all you've done?"

"Oh Rabbie, come on. I'm still friends with everyone. This person claims I slept with her, broke her heart, all kinds of garbage and she's emailing it around."

"I'm sure it's someone you've recently been involved with," Kwasi said.

"That's why my first suspect is Lynn."

Alarm bells went off in my head. What did he just say?

"Lynn? You suspect Lynn? Why would you suspect her? If this is someone who claims you've slept with her, and…" My voice trailed off. "Oh damn it, Ato. Have you slept with her?"

"Rabbie, this is not the time to talk about this. I need to figure out who this is."

"And I need to know if you've slept with Lynn!"

"I didn't sleep with her. We messed around, did some stuff, but we didn't have sex," he said flatly, like he was checking off a list.

"Oh, the same way two years ago you said you didn't sleep with Winnie, but just a few months later you admitted you did have sex with her, multiple times. Is it the same thing? Huh?"

"Rabbie, I didn't sleep with Lynn and this is not about that."

"Fine, I'll talk to you guys later."

I hung up and started screaming. What was wrong with him? What was wrong with him? And how could she? After everything I told her. I had poured my heart out to her about Ato. How could she still hook up with him? What was wrong with people? I started yanking my clothes out of my closet and throwing stuff in my room about. I was so angry and so pissed off. I could barely breathe.

I called a few friends and screamed and cursed. Their advice was simple. Ato had to go. This was unnecessary and unhealthy.

I was leaving to see my brother Josh in the U.K. for a few weeks so I decided to put skinning Lynn and Ato alive on hold. I'd deal with my back-stabbing so-called friends later. I couldn't believe this was happening so soon after Tei and Cami's letdown.

Ato's latest betrayal put a damper on my holiday. I poured my heart out to Jay, my brother's wife, about the losers I kept letting into my life. Her advice was nothing I hadn't heard before. Bottom line, Ato just wasn't good for me. He had no sense of right and wrong. Anyone and everyone was fair game. I was a complete mess. His behavior was mind-boggling to me. I tried my best to enjoy my nephews. And Sammi and I spent some time together. I needed to be distracted. I didn't want to sit at home and think. So I visited Abena as well. She was now married and had a family. I was glad she'd managed to move on. I remembered how I used to think of her as pathetic when she was with Edem. And now she appeared to be happily married while I was in an unhealthy situation with Ato. I was now the pathetic one.

Sammi came to visit me at Josh's end in Birmingham and I told her all about Ato's latest indiscretion. Even Sammi, who expected the worst of Ato, was a little surprised he could do it again. There was just something really wrong with Ato. I thought perhaps he was missing a genetic strand, something tied to morality or something of the sort. I also knew I was partly to blame. I had to find the strength to cut him off.

When I got back to New York, I confronted them both.

I called Lynn first.

"So when were you planning on telling me about you and Ato?"

"What?" Lynn said.

"You and Ato, Lynn, let's not play games. It's best if you tell me now."

"There is nothing going on."

"Okay, don't play semantics or grammar or whatever with me. Let me rephrase, yeah. Has anything ever happened between you and Ato, whether it's in the past, or now or whatever? Just answer the question."

"Where is this coming from?"

I rolled my eyes. "Please give me a little bit of respect and don't play games with me. Please," I snapped.

I heard her sigh and take a deep breath.

"I didn't sleep with him. Stuff happened but I didn't sleep with him."

"How could you do anything with him? After everything I told you, how could you still do anything with him? I told you how the Ajua thing really hurt me." I was shaking with disappointment.

"I thought you were over him. Why are you so upset? Is there something still between you two?"

I slapped my forehead, exasperated. Was she for real?

"Are you kidding me, Lynn? Seriously, are you kidding me? So you think it's okay that you messed around with a guy that I'd had something to do with for years, and who has slept with my cousin and two of my best friends. You think that's okay? You think there is nothing wrong with that? Are you kidding me?"

I was so pissed and angry.

"It's not like you haven't done that to me before."

"What?"

"Forget it, just forget it," she said.

"Lynn, you're not even apologizing for anything. You're just making excuses and trying to justify what you did. Just answer me, straight, and no long-winded answer. Do you think you did absolutely nothing wrong by messing around with a guy I have or had been involved with and who slept with my cousin and two best friends?"

There was a long silence at the other end of the line.

"I'm not saying that. I am sorry. It shouldn't have happened."

"I have to go," I said, and hung up.

I felt like I had just dragged the apology out of her, and it made me wonder if she really believed it. I was tired, tired of having people like that in my life. It was so clear to me. The relationships you form with friends and family most often determine the type of romantic relationships you have with others. From my entire teenage to adult life, I'd been in weak, strained and doubtful relationships with friends. Who was truly my friend anyways? Cami's loyalties had always been to Abena. I questioned now whether we had ever truly been friends. Abena and I had the worst back-and-forth relationship. The past was like a ton of bricks dragging both of us around. No matter how hard we tried or pretended, Abena and I would never trust each other. And now Lynn! Lynn was my oldest friend, but the length of knowing someone does not necessarily determine the quality of the relationship. I was too much like Lynn and she was too much like me. We'd both done stuff to each other and I doubted we both ever truly trusted each other. When she left for school, the distance had made it a little easier to hide what was wrong with us. But within months of being in the same country, this had to happen. What did that say?

I was alone, really alone. I had spent too much time and too much energy on things and people that weren't good for me, and I wasn't good for me either. My thinking had changed along with my retirement. I had expectations of what friendship meant, and I didn't think that was a bad thing. I wanted—no, I *needed* people who would truly be there for me, love me unconditionally and have my back. No matter how lonely or lost I felt, I just could not compromise on those basic tenets of friendship. I just couldn't.

When I called Ato, in a very flip and nonchalant way, he said he didn't want to talk about Lynn. I realized at that moment he was truly an ass. When I hung up, it was hard but it felt right. I was done.

Ekow

With an end to all matters Ato and Tei, I was depressed for months. My self-esteem was at a record low. I desperately needed validation. I was an emotional wreck. And the culmination of all the heartbreak Tei, Cami, Ato and Lynn had done to me led me to break my vow of celibacy and retirement. In a span of six months, I had lost four "friends." Ato and I hadn't spoken in four months. Lynn and I weren't talking either. Tei and Cami, I hadn't spoken to since the call.

By the time I went to Ghana for Christmas December 2007, I just needed to feel good about myself. I was struggling with what had happened over the last year and nothing made sense. So, against my better judgment, I slept with Ekow.

"I missed you," I said, as l lay next to him, stroking his chest.

"I missed you too," he said softly.

"So, when are you moving back?" he asked.

"I'm done by May. I really don't know what my plans are after that."

"Is coming back an option?"

I raised myself on my elbow and looked down at him.

"Do you want me to come back?" I asked, smiling.

"Why not? I mean, if it's something you want, or if it's part of your plans."

"It's definitely something I'm seriously thinking about."

"So think about it..." he said.

"I will. I heard Tara was in town," I said quietly. I'd been nursing that little info for a while. I wasn't sure whether to bring it up before or after sex. This was as good a moment as any.

He looked at me and laughed. "I'm sure you've been dying to ask for a while," he said, nudging me.

"Well? So?"

"Yeah, she's in town. I saw her a couple of days ago," he said.

"Did you sleep with her?"

He chuckled.

"Yes, I did. It was just once."

"Are you guys getting back together?" I asked hesitantly. I wasn't sure I wanted to know the answer.

"No. That is done. We're not getting back. It was just something that happened."

I was satisfied with the answer. Ekow was a direct and open person. He said whatever he wanted to say. I felt good about the conversation we'd had. I started to think about the possibility of moving back home after graduation. I wondered if Ekow and I could have a chance if I was right there with him. I knew he really cared about me. And a part of me wanted to be there when he was finally "ready." Ekow had been single for as long as I had been single. None of us had moved on and made other commitments. I started to fantasize again about a future with Ekow.

We lay together for a while and then it was time for me to head home.

"I want a picture of you," I said as we were heading out.

"Oh, you know I don't do pictures," he said, laughing. I took my camera out and managed to get a snap. Ekow had such a big thing about pictures. I had never seen a single picture of him, not even with friends.

A week later was Ekow's birthday. I called him the night before, asked if he wanted to do something. He said he was going on a day trip out of town with his cousin and a couple of friends. I didn't want to invite myself so I wished him a happy birthday. Ekow was a pretty private person. I didn't want to be all up in his life.

A few days later, I fell pretty ill and I was bedridden for the rest of my holiday. My days revolved around forcing tons of pills down my throat, injections and all the joys of flu and chest infection. There was no room for sex. The hook-up with Ekow was my first in over a year and my last for a very long time.

When I got back to New York, we kept in touch. We'd always kept in touch from when I first left anyways.

Unfortunately, just like his predecessors, the era of Ekow had to come to an end as well.

One night in early February 2008, I started browsing facebook. Joining facebook was my cousin James' idea. He was the regular social butterfly. It wasn't really my thing. Keeping in touch with friends was a hassle anyways, and to add an online networking tool was a little too much effort. But I joined anyways. It was the same online tool that someone had used earlier in 2007 to set up a "Women against Ato" page. I'd been on facebook for over a year and I rarely checked my page, perhaps every two months. I was having a little bout of insomnia when I decided to browse and that's when I came across Tara's page.

Tara's page had a plethora of things that sent my world crashing down, again. First was her status—"Tara is currently in a relationship with Ekow." Second, there were multiple albums of Ekow and Tara on a beach resort in Ghana. In almost all the pictures, Ekow was either holding her, tight no less, or Tara was holding him. Third, underneath almost every picture were comments referring to Ekow as her beau.

On their own these three things would mean nothing. But in context, it was a bitter pill to swallow. First, Ekow had told me he was single, as recent as just a week ago. So Tara's relationship status on her page was a shocker. Second, Ekow abhorred pictures! He wouldn't even let me take a picture of him. And these pictures with Tara were taken a week after I'd been with him, on his birthday, when he said he was going away with friends. I couldn't believe it. How could he shy away from letting me take a picture and then pose with Tara? And they weren't candid camera pictures; they were posed pictures! He was smiling and holding her all over the place.

It was past midnight New York time so it was too late to call him. But I couldn't sit still and I couldn't sleep. I dialed his number several times, hoping I'd wake him up from some deep, peaceful slumber. After the third try, I lay back in bed and called Katzi, one of my NYU friends, and sobbed like crazy.

The pictures devastated me the most for some reason. I had tried to take pictures of him and he'd been ducking! And now this stuff, all over facebook! If he was back with her, why would he lie about it? Tara was his ex-girlfriend. I'd always suspected he was hung up on her, so why not just tell me? From her page, it was obvious they were back together, and had been for the last three months! I was cursing and screaming and I fully expected a neighbor would knock on my door and tell me to shut it. Looking at the pictures and knowing that they were taken just a few days after the night he and I were together was hard. And how he looked in the pictures... they looked like two people who really cared about each other.

I sat up all night, waiting for it to be some reasonable hour to call Ghana. One of Ekow's friends, Anthony, came online and I decided to ask him about Ekow and Tara. Anthony said Ekow didn't know about the pictures and he'd probably be pissed if he knew. He added that Tara wanted Ekow back, but Ekow was not ready for that. Ekow just wasn't ready to change his lifestyle, not even for Tara. Anthony said Tara also vented about Ekow, that she wasn't making any headway. But still, even if her status was not entirely true, he'd posed for the pictures! He looked like he was with his girlfriend. He was holding her tight. I called Ekow again a couple of hours later. He finally answered.

"I just happened to check Tara's page last night. And her status says she's in a relationship with you. There're pictures of you and her, cozy lovey-dovey pictures from your birthday. So, what's up? Are you back together?"

I hadn't slept in over twenty-four hours. I didn't have the energy to beat about the bush.

"Gosh, those pictures! Everyone is going on about those pictures. I haven't even seen them. Listen, we're not back together. Yeah, we hooked up when she was here, but we're not back together. It's just a misrepresentation."

"You posed for those pictures, Ekow. You were holding her. I tried to take one picture of you and you were ducking. Ducking! I am so disappointed. Do you have any idea how that makes me feel? It makes me feel like I'm an insignificant nobody, just a sex buddy or something less, even."

"Oh come on, come on. You know that's not it."

"Are you sure you're not back together?"

"I am positive. I am sorry about those pictures. I really am. I am sorry if it hurt you. Don't think it means I think less of you."

But it did. No matter what he said, those pictures were the sign I needed to realize I was a fool and I'd been a fool for over four years. What was I thinking? Did I ever think? I couldn't talk anymore. Everything was painfully clear. The writing was right there on the wall. I started crying and I couldn't stop it.

"Don't cry, please don't cry," I heard him mumble.

"I have to go," I said, "I'll talk to you later."

I lay back on my bed and shook my head. I was a grown woman and I was still making the same mistakes, over and over again. It just never ended with me. I didn't know what to do with myself. How can a person make the same mistake consistently for years? Was I suffering from some "learn from your experiences" deficiency?

It was so clear, I wondered how I'd missed it. What had Ekow done wrong? So he didn't want to take pictures with me; that was his prerogative. What was my excuse for still pining for someone who didn't even want me to have his image? I was the one who'd told him I loved him. I was the one who'd carried him in my heart for years.

He'd never been deceitful. Throughout all these years, he'd never made me think this was more than it actually was. He'd been pretty careful about what he said and did. He'd never said it in words, but I knew he cared about me and that was just about it.

It'd never been more than that, and I'd always known that.

I could never resent him for that. This was my fault. He didn't play me, or hurt me or break my heart. He never said directly to me, "I love you, or I want to be with you, or you're the only one for me" etc. I thought being patient and waiting for him to be "ready" would do the trick. But if someone doesn't feel a certain way about you, time won't necessarily change that. It had been a delusion on my part. I tell all my girlfriends that instinctively you know when a guy truly likes you or not—it's not a matter of his words or texts, you just *know* it.

And honestly, I'd known it, known the feelings weren't mutual. Sometimes, we believe what we want to believe, but in the end, the reality doesn't change. What is, is what is. Love can't be forced or willed at all.

This was like Osei in reverse. Osei loved me and I didn't love him the same. Five years hadn't made a difference to my feelings.

Towards the end of that Sunday, after I had slapped my forehead a hundred times, I sent Ekow an email. I told him I knew he'd done nothing wrong and he'd never deceived me. I'd always known what it was. I added that this was really it for me. This was my last and final goodbye. There would be no future hook-ups or anything remotely close.

I really cared about him and I missed him. But damn it, I was tired! I really, honestly, truly, definitely couldn't do any of this anymore. I closed the chapter on Ekow.

Epilogue—Present Day

I opened my eyes and sighed. I am back in his room, the room I wished to God I wasn't back in. I wasn't sure how long I'd dozed off, thinking about the past and the actions and choices that had brought me to this point, to this bed.

I got up slowly from the bed and went downstairs. I looked around and noticed Ato sitting at his dining table, working. That's where I was, Ato's house. He was the one I drove six hours in the middle of the night to have sex with.

I sincerely thought his betrayal with Lynn would be the end of our relationship. And I did try to make it the end. I stopped speaking to him for several months after I confronted him about Lynn. And at that time, his flip attitude towards the whole thing had put me off. I was so sure that was the end. He crossed the line. I just could not see us ever speaking again. And now, a little over a year since he slept with Lynn, I was in his house, in his bed, in his life.

Someway, somehow, we'd started talking again. It had taken a few months, and I didn't even remember how we started talking again. That was just the way we were. Nothing made sense with me and him.

I stared at him for a minute from the stairway. He was engrossed in his work and he didn't look up. He was such a good-looking guy. The years had been good to him. He was more muscular, with a better build. He looked older, more mature, but that was just an appearance. To me, he hadn't changed much in the last nine years, and honestly, neither had I.

I just should not have come. I had taken the situation with Ato and me to be "the way it was;" he'd mess around, he was a dickhead most of the time, but he was my friend, one of my closest friends. So I tried so hard to justify it all. That was why I was here. But thinking back, looking back at the last fifteen years and my entire relationship with him, made it so clear that this was so wrong. Standing in the stairway looking at him, my mind was flooded with images of Lynn, Cami, Ajua and Winnie. I remembered so vividly the pain I had felt each time.

I shouldn't have been there. I had made a mistake that was so clear to me now. This thing with Ato was nine years old, and it shouldn't even have hit two years. I felt gross and stupid. But thinking back had helped. I should have done this earlier, instead of breezing through life without a clear idea of what I needed and what I deserved. I had made the most stupid mistakes imaginable. I was like a dog chasing her tail. Each time I thought it was over, I let someone back in. It just didn't make sense. This was so unhealthy for me.

I felt like I'd been in a mentally and emotionally abusive relationship. This thing with Ato, it was about time I ended it. This friendship, or whatever it was, had taken a toll on my perspective, my emotions, my mental well-being. I was done.

I had deluded myself for years. On some days, I justified it all. We weren't dating and had never dated, so he owed me nothing. But that was wrong, for two really strong reasons. First, we were supposed to be friends, supposed to be good friends. And you don't treat people who are your good friends with this level of disrespect. Ato didn't understand the concept of friendship—at least, not our friendship. Had he really ever been there for me in the last nine years? Not really. I could cite so many important instances when he hadn't measured up; like my graduation, my surgery, my hospitalizations, when I tried to talk to him about personal issues, all those times when a true friend was supposed to be there. So on the true friendship front, he had failed miserably. On the physical front, I didn't care whether or not we'd dated. We had slept together, for a long time, and he had consistently slept with my best friends and my family, people I cared about. And the worst part was that he had absolutely no remorse. That was wrong. Why would I still care about a person like that? Why would I still want to be friends with someone like that? It wasn't good for me. It had never been good for me.

Nine years on and I was done on both fronts: friendship and the physical. It had taken a very long time, too long. He was an interesting, charming person, the kind of person whom everyone wanted to be around, but I had tried it, and I couldn't hack it. What made all this worse was after nine years he still didn't see my point of view. He still didn't see that he had done anything wrong.

But the bar had been raised now. There were actually decent people out there, who were interesting and charming and just wouldn't do what Ato had done to their friends. My cousin James wouldn't do that to someone, whether he ever dated them or not. My brother Xavier wouldn't do that. Even my older brother Josh, a retired player, would never have done that in his heyday.

I had to be the leading lady of my life. I had to take back control. Such behavior was unacceptable and I didn't need or want someone like Ato in my life.

I moved towards him and he looked up from his work; his eyes met mine. I felt a pang of regret, of pain. I hesitated for a minute. Why was it so difficult with this boy? Why was this particular love so difficult to let go of? It should be so simple, because there was nothing in his eyes that remotely resembled affection for me. And maybe there had never been. As much as I had said it several times before, I knew this time I meant it. This was the end for me.

"Are you okay?" he asked, staring at me quizzically.

I was standing a few feet away from him, staring at him. I probably looked weird. I smiled and nodded.

"Yeah, I'm okay. I'm just... just thinking."

Our argument earlier in the day was fresh on my mind, the argument that started my journey to the past. His inability to recognize the error of his ways, that was the main catch. If only Ato felt remotely remorseful, if only he did. But he just didn't.

"Are you sure you're okay?" he asked again.

I was still staring at him. For some reason, I wanted to tell him that I loved him and that I always would, but he kept hurting me and disrespecting me too much, and I couldn't deal with it anymore, so I was ending the friendship and everything else. I loved him more than he could ever possibly imagine. It had always been about him. I wanted to say all that to him, right there and then. But I had used enough words and he would have thought I was melodramatic anyways. He felt I got too emotional and analytical. I preferred communicating with words, but with Ato, I needed to put words aside and show him what was in my head and my heart. To make him understand my pain and what he'd done, I had to cut him off. There was no point doing anything else.

So I said nothing and turned around and went back up to his room. I packed my bag and went to Kwasi's room to say goodbye to him.

"You're leaving?" he asked. Kwasi, Sammi's flame from university, lived with Ato now. Sammi also had some sort of back-and-forth with Kwasi, but they hadn't seen each other in five to six years, so it was really nothing. I felt he was a nice guy, and he'd be good for Sammi, but he had his life in America, and she had hers in London. In any case, I wasn't sure if Kwasi was really any different from Ato. I used to think he was, but after they started living together, I realized they were like two peas in a pod.

I sat on his bed and looked at him. I was so sad. And Kwasi could tell.

"What's up, Rabbie? Talk to me."

I sighed. "It's the same old thing. Your friend... it's just torture for me."

"Come on, we were just talking about you guys doing something for your tenth anniversary yesterday. What happened today?"

I shrugged. "It's not like something happened today. It's been happening. I know he's your best friend, but I just can't deal with being around him anymore. It's not good for me and I'm just tired. I'm literally tired, just drained."

Kwasi was quiet for a minute.

"You should talk to him."

I shook my head. "I've talked and talked and I'm done talking. Gosh, this is not even a relationship! It's just really stupid of me, to feel like this, and be like this, over what?"

"So what do you plan on doing?"

I stared at my hands. What did I plan on doing?

"I'm going to cut him off. Maybe one day, someday way into the future, he and I can be friends again. But not now."

Kwasi smiled. He didn't believe I meant it. I didn't blame him.

"You and him, I don't know. He's always going to be your boy, and you're always going to be his girl. You're always going to love each other."

I smiled back at him and I chuckled.

"He's not my boy, and I'm not his girl. I can understand your skepticism, though. But I know I've just reached my limit."

I stood up from Kwasi's bed and he stood up too.

"Come here," he said and hugged me.

It took a lot for me not to cry then. I hadn't said it to him, but I didn't plan on being friends with him either. My blackout on Ato would have to be like an EMP device—wipe out everything within 800 miles.

I left Kwasi's room and went downstairs with my bag.

Ato looked up, stared at my bag and then at me. He knew I was a little upset because of the argument earlier, but he wasn't going to ask.

"I have to leave now. I have work in the morning," I said quietly.

"It's early yet, you can stay a little longer," Kwasi said. He was right behind me.

I shook my head. I couldn't stay. Ato stood up from the table and walked over to me. And then we walked out of his house together.

"So, drive safe and call me when you get back," he said.

I nodded. There was too much going on in my head for me to say much. We didn't hug, we didn't kiss. Knowing it was the last time I planned on seeing him, I wanted to hug him at least, but I didn't. I got into the car and sat there quietly as he walked back into his house. When the door closed behind him, I let out a long breath. God give me strength.

As I drove away, I started to feel calmer. The chaos that had licked my heels for the last fifteen years was beginning to subside. My hands tightened on the steering wheel.

What had happened in the last fifteen years? What had happened since that moment with Selorm, that truth or dare? What was I looking for, love? I have loved, for sure. I have felt very strongly for a number of people. But either I loved them and they didn't love me back the same, or they loved me, and I didn't love them back the same. It's that vicious cycle. It's so hard. To love someone, and have them love you back. I have never felt that complete balance. I have never looked in a guy's eyes since that first night with Jon and thought, this guy loves me as much as I love him.

Was that what I had made all these mistakes in search for? I wasn't even sure. I knew there were good guys out there, men who would really love me and respect me and treat me like I deserved. I just had to stop, take a deep breath and start all over again. And I had to mean it this time. Within me, something strong had stirred. I felt fatigued. The journey down memory lane had woken me up. Who I had been for the last fifteen years wasn't who I was meant to be. I knew that, I felt that, and I believed it.

There was no way I could do it anymore. And this wasn't an empty resolution. All other resolutions hadn't been based on an assessment of the past, an assessment of the vicious cycle I had engaged in over the last half of my life. Thinking of everything I had done shamed me deeply. I was more shamed because it was the same thing over and over again, and that was a sign of weakness and stupidity. I had trapped myself in a time warp, and it was time to step out.

And the most important first step was final closure on Ato. Ato was not the beginning of my downfall but he was going to be the end of this disastrous cycle.

As I cruised down the highway, I felt I was driving towards a new future. I had survived some pretty tough times. I had lost people dear to me. I had survived two surgeries, one pretty harrowing and life-threatening. I had also survived a few near-death crashes. But I was still here. Damn it, I was still here! I had completed my graduate degree in a great school and I had an awesome job with CNN. There was a higher purpose to my life. I felt it, deep within me. And that higher purpose did not involve chasing my tail like a dumb dog. This boy stuff had been crippling me for years, keeping me from my true potential. It just had to end.

I felt exhilarated and light. It was about time! I laughed a little. Then I started laughing harder. I felt good and prepared. I had no regrets, because I was moving on, and I was not going to dwell on anything that had happened in the past. I had dug deep and thought about the past, and now it was time to get over it.

I realize I am a work in progress. No one is perfect. But more importantly, I had taken a hard long look at my life. I had faced my past demons for the first time. And I was still standing. As I sped further away from Ato, every pain, self-loathing and regret I had ever felt disappeared with the receding miles. I hadn't felt this certain, this sure, this confident of the future in all my life. No matter what happened, no matter what life threw at me, I was ready for it. I was actually looking forward to it. I really couldn't stop smiling. I glanced at the rear-view mirror and caught my reflection. I grinned at it.

"We can do this, Rabbie. It's over. We can do this," I whispered softly in the silence of the car. And I completely, wholly believed it. I could do this.

I stepped on the gas and disappeared down the highway, back home, to the future that awaited. I could do this... hopefully.

www.ingramcontent.com/pod-product-compliance
Lightning Source LLC
Chambersburg PA
CBHW020903200626
46814CB00001BA/153